JOE FABER AND THE OPTIMISTS

Gill Oliver

ahBut
Books

Published by Ah But Books 2020
3 Twines Close, Sparkford,
Somerset
www.gilloliverauthor.com

ISBN 978-0-9935976-4-0

Cover design by theoryunit.com

For Terry, who suffered for my art.

Foreword

This book is a novel about an imaginary craftsman called Joe Faber and his family. At the heart of the fiction, however, one thing is real: my stroke. In April 2013 I suffered a severe brain haemorrhage. I was told by the consultant how lucky I was: apparently, only around 15% of patients survive such an event.

Every stroke is different. The only common factor is that it can be life changing for the patient and family and people around them. In terms of its effects and the process of recovery, Joe Faber's stroke is modelled on mine.

Shortly after the stroke, Gill decreed that we would face the bad times together, look for every situation that was amusing or inspiring and laugh whenever we could. I couldn't disagree because at that stage I could barely speak.

My wife is a writer and perhaps it was inevitable that she'd turn to fiction to share our experience of it all. Seven years on, our need to reach out to other survivors, families and carers is just as strong. Before the stroke, I never expected her to write about anything that had happened to me. I wish she'd had no reason to. I'm very proud she did. Although I'd like to point out that, fiction or no fiction, Joe Faber stole some of my best one-liners.

Terry Oliver, Somerset, April 2020

PART ONE

Ruin

'I don't know what she sees in him. And neither does she.'

'Well there you are, then. That proves it's serious.'

Joe looked up from the workbench and grinned at his wife, who shrugged.

Fran was just being provocative. He was more concerned right now with his current commission, the model of ancient Athens, which had reached a critical stage. He took a sable brush to the flat of the acropolis, where flakes of polystyrene snow had become electrically bonded to the bedrock.

'Seriously…What've Matt and Jess got in common?'

'They trust each other,' said Joe.

Fran snorted. 'How can you trust a man who turns up for a week in the mountains with a pair of white trainers and a phone?'

'Proves he's open to new experiences.'

'You sound just like him,' she said.

Bit by bit, the polystyrene was deposited onto a microfibre cloth, where it stuck. Joe folded the cloth loosely and turned to place it out of harm's way. Then he pushed the stool on its castors back, stood up and uncurled his spine.

This was his most ambitious piece to date. Waiting on the side table, his Parthenon wasn't much bigger than a shoe-box, the sculptures tiny, Poseidon – the god of the sea – a mere shrimp; but between Joe and his wife, and filling the big project bench, the flat hill of the acropolis rose like a magnificent cake stand waiting for its luscious load. He'd only just stuck the marbles on the Parthenon when Fran had appeared unexpectedly early, back from the lab. He'd worked all morning in strict silence. A more routine day would have meant music. You couldn't sit still to Bob Marley, though, and the last thing you needed, when your gods and your giants were less than an inch tall, was a tremolo effect on the hands that were cementing them to the wall. No foot tapping, no elbow jives, not even the faint scrapings from a fiddle lesson next door: Jess was at the Tea Room today. So although it was nice to have his wife's company, right now he was itching to slip his model of the Parthenon onto the flat of the hill, just to see how it looked.

But Fran was troubled, so he conceded: 'Matt's in a funny line of business, all right.'

She snorted again. 'You're a fine one to talk. Most people stop making models when they reach puberty.'

He followed her gaze around the workshop. Shelves, pots, boxes, bins. A tidy mess. Half a lifetime chasing commissions, lean times, good times, everything from futuristic cityscapes to doll's houses. Years of happenstance had gone into his array of tools and gadgets. That thin sheet of aluminium on which his Parthenon temporarily sat was a back plate he'd picked up at a boot sale. His dad's uncompromising steel rule: a full yard marked only in imperial. Rule Britannia. A really swanky architectural scale he'd bought in Berlin, a stone's throw from the Bauhaus. Its friend, Mack the knife. Pipettes which you couldn't call droppers because they'd come from a real laboratory, thanks to Fran. Tools that felt good in your hand.

He'd acquired some impressively spiky dentistry equipment, too, which he'd used on the plaster sculptures; clever, sharp, probing implements. Although chiselling away at Athena and Poseidon without an anaesthetic might be thought unethical.

'Scoff if you like,' he said, 'but at least I'm producing something tangible. You ask Matthew what he does for a living, and he tells you he's a trainer, and you say, what do you train people to do, and he says, oh, anything, what do you want them to be able to do?'

'It's called soft skills. And the less you know, the quicker it is.'

She thought for a moment, then added, 'I just hope this wedding isn't a terrible mistake.'

'I bet your mother said the same thing.'

'True.' Then her eyes fell on the little side table where his Parthenon stood waiting.

She gasped, 'Oh! You've put the lid on! And the marbles, and everything. You've finished it!'

At last she'd noticed. 'I believe the architectural term is *roof*.'

She walked around the workbench and up to the side table so as to admire it.

'Don't touch,' he said, although he knew she wouldn't.

'Is she really inside? Your Athena? Only I never said goodbye!'

His statue of Athena was a detail, and an internal detail at that. A lesser craftsman wouldn't have bothered. She was a tiny thing, a fancy; not only painted gold and ivory like the original, but with full make-up.

'Oh, yes, she has to be there. She was the main attraction. Ten metres tall. Imagine the impact when you stepped inside the temple and saw that! Anyway, one thing I don't need, at

3

this point in my career, is for some ten-year-old to slap her phone to the Perspex, and say ooh look, the Parthenon's empty. First she'll tell her mates, then she'll tell her parents, and they'll complain to the museum, next thing you know it'll be half way round the world and I'll never work again. But this way, if you squint between the columns at the open west door, you will just get a glimpse of two tiny golden feet inside.' He took a theatrical breath and whispered, 'And you will marvel.'

'No ten-year old will get that close,' said Fran.

She might have a point, but he shook it right out of his head. 'This is designed to be future-proof.'

Fran stooped to inspect the delicately painted temple – in its original colours, so different from the bleached and craggy ruin the whole world recognised as beautiful – and bent her head to one side, to see through the entrance.

'I can't tell from here. Did you ever wipe the smile off her face?'

Fate and a dodgy elbow had transmitted a nano-wobble to the hand and brush, and made Athena's mouth rather crooked.

'No. And anyway, if Athena's the goddess of Wisdom, that makes her the goddess of better-luck-next-time. A smug expression is quite appropriate.'

Fran stood up. 'I can't see her at all from that angle. It's too low.'

This was all the invitation he needed.

'OK. Stand back. I'm going to try it in place. Then we can check the full effect.'

He moved across to the side table and ran a clean finger down one of the finely fluted columns. Lovely. Then he lifted the miniature temple on its lightweight tray, ready to slip it onto the flat of the acropolis.

4

But as it turned out, it was Joe that slipped onto the flat of the acropolis and slammed smack into the limestone escarpment.

It started with the feeling that level wasn't level any more, then the swooping certainty he was going to faint; and if he was going to fall over, he had to decide how best to do it. Something inside him was draining rapidly away. He must be dying. If his face hit the metal cabinet to his left, or the edge of the table, Fran would face not just a corpse but a disfigured one, and you couldn't un-remember a sight like that; so he tried to steady himself, which meant dropping the model and folding himself onto the polystyrene hill in the middle of the workbench.

Then a white fog absorbed everything.

It would be over a week before he remembered what had happened: how later, half-conscious and lying on the floor, he'd heard Fran's voice asking him things; then being carried out on a stretcher; then being in A and E with a piece of plastic in his arm and electrodes on his chest.

News

It had been a busy morning, with the Cherry Tree Tea Room full of people in for the farmers' market, and the hours had flown by. Waiting on tables was a form of dancing; you had to set the right pace, find the right poise, and turn nimbly between the tables, watching where you put your feet, because a waxed jacket draped over the back of a chair might well conceal a bag, an umbrella, a walking stick, even a dog.

5

Jess was late taking her break. Matt had been waiting, smiling to himself and nodding towards her whenever she went past, while the froth crawled down his latte. People had turned their heads when he'd walked in: that one-in-a million combination of childishly fair hair with chestnut eyes and skin which tanned easily, plus a huge white smile. This was what had first drawn her to him and made her think, now he's something out of the ordinary.

She apologised with an easy kiss. So how had his morning been?

'My morning? Good, thanks. Nice people. I think I helped them.'

He smiled a steady, contented smile and his huge eyes gazed into hers as he sighed, 'You know, self-reflection is surprisingly hard on your own.'

Was it?

'So, it was a worthwhile meeting, then?'

'Oh yes. I told them how, if you've got loads of strengths, your weaknesses are irrelevant, sort of thing.'

She'd never said anything like that to any of her violin pupils. Maybe she should. Matt was always doing this, coming out with important things you didn't realise you knew.

'It's an empowering thought,' he went on. 'When you think about it. Oh, and my mother rang to say could I share the photo of the ring. I think she wants to post it.' He shook his head in amusement, and his brown eyes shone. 'Oh Jessie, she's so excited for us! Everybody is. It's just like, wow.'

'Oh, your family... I'm still kind of... relieved?'

Prior to their engagement a couple of weeks ago, on the few occasions Jess had met them, his mum Janet had seemed cool towards her, but Matt said that was just her way. His father Derek was one of those old blokes with a post-box face – he

6

never gave his feelings away – so Jess had been amazed, on the night of the big announcement, when he'd actually come to the phone and congratulated her personally. 'Congratulations,' was what he'd said. It must have taken a lot. Matt's sister Zanna had been wildly enthusiastic and you could hear her shrieking in the background long after she'd handed the phone back to her mum. 'A wedding, a wedding! My big brother's getting married!' A couple of minutes later she'd returned to the phone, interrupting their conversation – in fact it sounded as though she'd snatched the handset – to ask, 'So does this mean I'm going to be a bridesmaid?' 'Well, I suppose so,' Jess had stammered back, realising she hadn't thought about the wedding at all.

'Anyway,' said Matt, 'I can see how your morning's been.'

'Yeah. It's fine.'

She checked her watch.

'I'm good for another quarter of an hour. So, what's the rest of the world been doing while I've been dancing round the tea room?'

She set her phone on the table. No texts. She ate her sandwich with one hand whilst the other scrolled down a dozen notifications. A series of missed calls from a mobile she didn't recognise. Five emails since this morning. Quick look. Selling, selling, selling, selling... Four selling, but here was one telling. And when she saw what it told, she dropped the sandwich right into her lap. It was a gig. A potential booking. Not just any booking, either. The Shetland Fiddle Frenzy. Someone had dropped out, two months before the date. They were asking, would she be available? Would she come and play? For money this time.

'Would I?' she shouted. 'Would I?' She sat upright.

'What would you?' Matt's face was all excitement.

7

'It's incredible. I'm going to play alongside Archie McNuckert! *The* Archie McNuckert!'

Matt's eyebrows lifted higher and hovered, inviting explanation.

'He's a total legend. The fiddler's fiddler.'

He screwed up his face.

'No, really, he's huge in the folk world.'

'Oh, *that* Archie McNuckert.' He dropped his head to one side in a way that left her in no doubt that he'd never heard of the man. 'One of your rumpitty-tumpitty lot. A straw-sucker.' Then he flashed that lovely white smile and reached for her hand. 'Congratulations! Is this your big break then?'

Maybe it was. She tingled all over.

'I don't know. I mean, I've been going to the Frenzy for years now. They all know me up there. But even so...'

'The Frenzy?'

She was sure she'd already told Matt all about the Shetland Fiddle Frenzy, but he couldn't have taken it in. She re-capped: a summer school devoted to a very particular style of fiddle playing, with a full week of workshops and concerts. He was listening now, his eyes trained on her, his lips shaping 'oh...oh' as she filled him in on the detail. He didn't seem to be picking it up, so she had another go.

'People come from all over the planet.'

'Wow! Isn't Shetland in the Arctic circle? Although it can't exactly be Disney World, Jessie, or I'd have heard of it.'

'It's much, much better than that.'

'Course it is. My brilliant Jessie!' and he gripped both her hands and glowed at her.

Now she saw the perfect conjunction in her stars: not only might it be the real start of a professional playing career, but Matt, the man she was going to marry, was ideally placed to support her. He understood all that businessy stuff she'd need to get her head round, now that her student days were over and the Frenzy gig had just dropped into her lap.

She took a huge breath. She couldn't take in her luck. Work would be exciting, but she'd always have a calm place to come home to, because life with Matt was soothing. No nerves, no drama. He got on with everyone and everyone got on with him. And it had been a breath of fresh air, to go to a gig with someone who didn't nit-pick at every detail of a performance. Matt loved everything she did, unquestioningly. He'd help her stay grounded.

'You better ring your parents, they're going to be so thrilled for you!'

'Yeah… My dad's just gonna explode when he hears this.'

She sat down and called him, then her mum's mobile, then the land line, and her dad's mobile again.

Nobody was answering.

Pieces

Joe is floating in a strange world where the only time is now.

Nothing hurts. Everything's… switched off…

Fran's there.

Can you drink this? says a voice.

He's alive.

Wet. There's water somewhere.

Bright like the workshop, not the workshop.

Nurse.

Ooh what's this? she says and she's rolling him towards her, why's she doing that?

It often happens immediately after the stroke, she says. She's telling him or she's telling Fran.

More things she's telling him, or she's telling Fran. Life will be very different now. Stroke, is what it is.

Thought so.

*

A man is talking to his wife, nice voice, he's crouched down to talk to her, black shiny hair on the back of his head, sleek and very short...

Haemorrhage... conservative treatment... Would you like to see the scan?

They'll let Fran see it. Now they're out of sight. Fran comes back: It's OK, love, you've got a brain. They found it.

He's making a noise. Chuckling.

What month is it Joe?

His mouth is... missing... that's funny... January... he's just said January, that's funny, why did he say that, he knows it isn't, he laughs, they all laugh.

*

Can you drink this?

Didn't know he was so thirsty. Gulps it down.

See how that swallow has improved already?

We'll get him up to the ward soon... Waiting for a bed.

Did you see that?

She's showing Fran something.

A little movement, there. He doesn't know where.

She's telling Fran what Fran's job is going to be now. She has to notice the little things and keep remembering how it was, because Joe won't always see the improvement.

But Fran has a job already.

His reflexes are normal.

You're not really paralysed, Joe. Your brain has lost the connection, that's all. It can re-wire. Your job is to keep trying.

What month is it, Joe?

January… no, it won't be said, he's being silly… they all laugh…

No, it isn't, you know it isn't. Let's try this. Is it January, June, or October? June, he's said out loud, and they're cheering and smiling. Of course it's June, what a silly question.

*

It's chilly in here.

Is it? He doesn't know. Nurse says they keep it cool in rhesus. Re-suss? Rhesus? What's that? Something to do with blood. No.

What did you do, Joe? What line of work were you in?

She said did and were, but he's alive, isn't he? His mouth isn't doing what it should, it snags on ma, ma for maquette, mo for models, may for make… Make things. Fran can tell her. Fran's telling her he makes models for a living. Fran says makes not made. Good.

Well Joe, your body says you need a rest, you mustn't think about working for at least eight weeks.

Fran, did you hear that? She says I can't work.

She's talking about a bed. To get him on the ward. Which ward?

*

Won't be long now, she says. She'll go up to the ward with us. The nurse asks is there anything else that Fran would like to know? Is there anything he'd like? Of course there is, he wants to see it... He's making a noise and nodding, trying to explain. So hard.

Fran knows. Fran says, He wants to see the scan.

Yes, yes, yes, that's what he means.

We can fix that. Fran's telling them, he loves to see the way things work. He always has to look at the insides of things. Her voice is warming up, she sounds pleased. Delighted, even. They wheel him round and tilt him up, and there's a little desk with a computer, and someone clicks on the keyboard and up it comes on the monitor: a grey knobbly egg shape folded down the middle, symmetrical, except for the white oval on one side which is the bleed. The doctor says this part of him is dead. The rest of him is not.

Technically, they say, he's not paralysed. He just can't move.

Still

At 6 o'clock, the vast hospital canteen was empty, but a smell of pastry lingered, and there was food on the hotplate. Somebody emerged from the kitchen to serve Fran a plate of macaroni cheese which she carried to a table in the very middle of the room. She took her time choosing a seat, and picked one as far from any wall as it could be, with a view of a handsome red camellia which was in its last flower in the shady basement garden. A strip of rectangular windows went half way round two walls. The sun was lower now, but still wide awake. Hundreds of people must have passed through this room today, and left not a mark, because every surface was smooth and made for cleaning. Now they had all gone home. It was strangely soothing, this silence, after so many words and actions and questions and all the new places she had been in one afternoon.

The debacle in the workshop. Joe lying on the floor with his curly head close to the skirting board and his long, thin legs poking out under the other side of the workbench, barely able to articulate, just mewling *he'p me, he'p me.* His wire-rimmed glasses slightly awry. Something had taken a trowel to the putty of his face and smeared it flat, so that the only part of it which had any power of expression was the top of his forehead. But it had arched when he recognised her. His gaze, steady and heavy with the weight of words he couldn't utter. The blunt, lipless way he confirmed he had no pain. Her fumbling about for the telephone. Kneeling by his side, waiting for the ambulance, the gentle grip of his left hand which could still squeeze hers.

It wouldn't have helped to be afraid, or let him guess how dreadful he looked. *Joe, have you got a smile for me?* It had been frightful, weak and lop-sided, but it was unmistakably there. She'd told him he was doing fine, knowing that might not turn out to be true, maybe they'd arrive too late, maybe he was dying.

While they waited, he'd tried to say something which she couldn't understand. *Pih, bih, bih.* He'd raised his left arm and pointed: was it the open door? The bottom shelf?

'Bin?' That was it. Balanced on top of the big grey bin which stood beside the door, and glistening white against the black plastic liner, there it was: his Parthenon, still intact, marbles and all, but at the 45-degree angle at which it had

13

fallen. It must have slid off the table and flown through the air. She'd picked it up, showed it to Joe and scrutinised his newly unfamiliar face for some sign that this was what he'd meant. He'd made a low noise on a heavy out-breath and his eyes remained trained on her. His forehead was definitely waking up, though, and the muscles around the eyes were starting to shape something, even if they looked as if they were working against an invisible film of glue. In so far as a starched brow could express anything, Joe had looked pleased. She knew she might be wrong, but that was how she chose to read it.

The hill was smashed to bits. There was a great dent across it and the displaced material had pushed sideways, sweeping everything away in a landslide. She'd set the Parthenon carefully on the remaining end of the stony plateau. Which, she now realised, was exactly the sort of radical re-planning Joe's brain was going to have to undertake.

She'd tried to enter the ambulance at the driver's door, how silly. Then the awful separation of the waiting room, which mightn't have been more than half an hour but seemed like ages; and how many hours in a cold place called resuscitation? At least, after all this, she'd left him somewhere safe and friendly; three other male patients, one fully dressed and sitting in his armchair, had greeted them cheerily on their arrival at the ward.

So she sat in the middle of everything and of nothing, puzzling at what she'd been told – *both your lives are going to be different now* – and eating slowly, waiting for Jess to come and join her. She'd delayed calling her daughter until she knew for sure what it was she had to say: and yes, it was sensible to avoid creating an emotional cliff-hanger with your communications; but if she was honest, she had yet to take it all in herself; and telling somebody else, saying those words, *your father's had a stroke*, had been like diving from a height. She'd had to breathe and calm herself first. And now she was guiltily relieved to have some time alone to let things settle in her head. Jessie had answered so brightly, *Mum, did you see my text, I've been trying to ring you, it's such good news...* Fran had been careful to lay things out in the right order: *Your father's going to be all right, but he's in hospital, he's had a stroke. That's where I am now.* Jessie was quick to weep. Fran was far from that.

Fran was learning, today, and new things always fired her up. She'd been watching and listening as never before, because the content mattered more than any demonstration back in her official student days, more than any Biochemistry lecture. Linda knew so much. Linda was the stroke nurse who'd been in and out of the resuscitation room all afternoon while they waited for the bed, keeping an eye on them both, explaining things, noticing things, making calls to chase the deep cleaners, and helping push the gurney up to the ward herself, for lack of a porter.

Oh, but Fran had been rude! About signing Joe up for the clinical trial. Not only had she felt a deep indignation at being bothered by this request, but she'd managed to express it, tapping into an annoyance which wasn't part of her normal way of talking to people. Had she really said, 'You'll have to tell me, I can't read it, I can't take this in'? She had. She'd said, 'I can't think about this now,' in full awareness that she was choosing to be a little bit childish. If the same papers had turned up in her in-tray at work, she'd have skim-read them in seconds. She hadn't liked being on the wrong side of the clipboard, had she? They needed to start the double-blind trial within twenty-four hours; it had to be a prompt decision. No drugs were involved, only the intensity and timing of physiotherapy. Making a decision whose implications she didn't understand seemed utterly impossible to Fran. It was a glimpse of what it must be like to be asked for organ donation in that first pang of bereavement.

Here am I, she thought, in this huge canteen, eating food cooked by a stranger, and how many of the visitors who have eaten here today have had much less to hope for? He's alive. He could have died. How could I have been so lacking in grace? It was only when Linda had told her, yes, she could change her mind tomorrow, that she'd signed. And now – already – that seemed the obvious response. Of course Joe would want something good to come out of this. Funny, though, how logic had been a handrail she'd fumbled for in her distress.

When Linda had gone off to ask the computer which group to assign Joe to, physio normal or physio extra, Fran had been confident of one thing. 'I can tell you now, whichever group you put him in, he'll overdo it. That's just the way he is.' And here was the thing: his face was changed, his mouth was crooked and downturned at one side, his speech was slurred and he couldn't find his words, but by a miracle he still seemed to be, recognisably, Joe. That bit of his brain that made him Joe – no, those bits of his brain, because they were many – those bits were still alive. It was pitiful to see him like this, and she would have understood if he'd been tearful or anxious. But Joe seemed to be, oddly, patient. Rolling with it. Perhaps it was because he had no energy and no real sense of what was going on. But look at what had happened with the January question, when he'd made a fool of himself and known it. Instead of panicking, he'd laughed. It wasn't even a decision, to laugh like that. With him, it was an instinct. And at that moment, Fran had recognised her husband and knew that he'd come through.

Racing

All the way from the empty house to the hospital, Jess was racing – heart, feet, mind. Only a week ago her dad had been full of life and keeping them all entertained in the holiday cottage whilst the rain poured down outside. On the last day of their week in Wales it had stopped raining and he'd lent Matt his boots to do the climb up Cadair Idris, her favourite walk... What if her dad was never going to need his walking boots again? Or never act the clown, because he'd been so funny that week with his terrible tales... Matt had lapped it up. Especially the old one about how her parents had spent their honeymoon in a converted pigsty with three crowns from the Welsh Tourist Board; how they were woken in the night by a grunting and banging, and he'd gone down stark naked to the door, armed with an empty thermos flask, and felt something warm rushing against his legs. *Mr Pig. Come to trash the place. And you had to sympathise with him, after all that nasty business with the eviction order.* Of course, she'd never believed it. Her dad worked in miniature, but the way he told a story always made things bigger than they really were.

What if it all dried up, the puns and the corny jokes that made them groan, and his crazy little speeches, laced with long words which nobody understood, his made-up expressions and spoonerisms, his skits, his rhymes...? And now the unfamiliarity of everything in her path became unbearable. The car park was impossibly tight. You needed the right change. You had to find a floor plan or wait at reception to be told where the canteen was. You had to pick the right set of lifts to get to the basement. It was a horribly staccato journey, and the more she hurried, the more abruptly she was forced to stop. She'd followed directions and found herself standing under a sign that said *Mortuary*. This was as bad as it could be. Left should have been right. The whole world was set awry.

A scrape echoed round the empty refectory as her mum pushed the metal framed chair back and got to her feet. She looked so little; and why had she picked that table, right in the centre of the room? They stood for a moment hugging each other, and Jess promised herself not to blurt out all her questions at once. There was a certain voice, a sensible, explaining voice, which she recognised immediately in her mother's insistence they sit down for a minute. It was a voice designed to keep the whole truth from a child.

'I don't want you to rush in and then get a shock when you see your father, because that would only upset you both.'

The soothing notes were at odds with the actual words, which made Jess's heart race all the faster. How could she be more shocked than she already was? What horror was she going to see? She scrutinised her mother's face. She hadn't been crying, but she looked flushed and tired, and there was a tension about her eyes, from trying not to frown.

'He's OK, Jess. He's out of danger.'

She sounded honest. Jess listened. Her heart was a quivering meter that measured every statement, good news, bad news, with panic at one end of the scale and hope at the other. He'd lost the use of the whole of his right side. Right arm, right leg, right side of his face. His mouth had drawn down, so he looked all wrong. And they couldn't give him one of these clot-busting drugs because that could have killed him. It wasn't that sort of stroke.

'It's a question of waiting to see how he recovers.'

'Can't they do anything?'

'Only physiotherapy.'

'Can he talk?'

'He couldn't at first, but it's coming back already. Quite quickly, in fact.'

Jess let out a huge breath. That was so good.

'You say he can't walk or anything. Will he always be like that?'

'They don't know. They're sounding positive. But they can't tell what sort of a recovery he'll make, or how long it will take. The consultant says – well, they all say – every stroke is different. They just won't predict. Linda says – oh, there's this brilliant person called Linda, she sat with us in A and E, she told me so much – she says that if you work at it, you can still be making progress years down the line. Because the brain learns to re-wire. A bit of his brain has died, but other parts can learn to take over.'

Years down the line? Jess shook her head; the tears were coming again.

'Honestly love, he's much better already. It's been an incredible thing to watch… almost beautiful, really.'

That was a strange thing to say, particularly when *beautiful* wasn't a word her mother used lightly. It made no sense. And she was far too patient about the wait. Nearly four hours before her father had got a bed! That was outrageous. The needle on the meter swung way back: what kind of place was this, and was he going to get the care he needed? But you could never predict her mum's take on things.

'D'you know what?' she said. 'I'm glad we waited all afternoon. Because I saw how things changed by the hour. To start with, he had almost no expression, then it was as if a line moved down,' – she held her hand in front of her face, to mask it, then drew it slowly downwards at an oblique angle to demonstrate – 'and above the line, the expression came back.'

She looked almost excited. She really meant all this.

'Oh Mum, it must have been awful for you.'

'No... no, it wasn't awful at all. Because he was improving in front of my eyes.' Jess could tell from the raised brows and the sudden grin that her mum was realising something as she spoke. 'If they'd whisked him up to the ward straight away, I never would have seen all that. They'd have tucked him in bed and I'd have had to say goodbye and go home thinking God knows what. And if we hadn't spent so long in A and E, he wouldn't have got to see the picture of his beautiful brain, because there wouldn't have been time.' Then her mother told her about the scan, and the perfectly straight line down the centre fold of his brain which meant there was no pressure and he wouldn't need surgery.

It was as if, in talking about it, she was energised; she was looking almost happy. Which made Jess smile. 'Mum, you are weird.'

'It was the change in him. In his face. It was like... watching a frozen turkey slowly thawing out.'

Now Jess had to laugh. 'He's going to love hearing that.'

Her mother's eyes lit up and something electric arced between them: the realisation there was mischief to be made.

'Come on then, let's tell him.'

As they stepped into the lift, her mother remembered: 'Oh, but what about you? You said you'd had good news. When you answered the phone, it was the first thing you said. And I never asked you.'

The shine had worn off now. 'Ah. I've got a gig at this year's Frenzy. If I want it. Someone else dropped out.'

'Oh Jess, that's great news.'

'With Archie McNuckert.'

Her mum gasped. 'That's wonderful. And your father will be so proud.'

'But look, Mum, I'm not sure about it. It all seems too much. Specially if you and Dad can't be there. It's only a couple of months away.' The tears welled up, just thinking about it.

'You haven't turned them down?'

'No... But I haven't accepted either.'

'Auntie Nell will be there, and the cousins.' Unexpectedly, she raised her voice a couple of notches for a telling-off: 'And for heaven's sake, Jess, you don't need your parents to make it real. In fact, I can't believe what you just said there.' Just as quickly, her voice softened again. It had been a flicker of annoyance. 'Sleep on it. And whatever you decide, you must tell him, it'll really buck him up. It doesn't have to be today. There are other things to say today.'

In the mirror walls of the lift, Jess could see a series of thoughts passing rapidly before her mother's eyes. She was quietly whirring away like a little computer.

'They'd have sent him to Bristol if he'd needed surgery. Imagine doing that journey every day for visiting. We're so lucky.'

Are we? thought Jess. Perhaps we are.

The doors opened onto the ninth floor.

Weight

Wide screen. Wide canvas. No, it's a window.
Hospital. In the sky.

The grey had changed, it was tipping into blue now.

When did that cloud change shape? Didn't see it happen. Too slow to notice. It was too slow. He was too slow.

What had the cloud looked like in the first place? He didn't remember. His thoughts seemed to gather and vanish.

He tried to follow the lengthening of the white lines… which were called contra something… Contrails. Contrails of jets. Bright white on blue. Cuts in the sky. They looked close but they were far away. The picture looked 2-D, but it wasn't flat at all. Because there was perspective. A thing he used to know about.

The lines moved so gradually, but that was allusion. Delusion. Illusion. An illusion. Jets covered hundreds of kilometres an hour. Whereas he was going nowhere. Worse than going nowhere, he'd gone backwards. Because yesterday, he could place tiny statues on tiny plinths. With tweezers.

Now his hand was permanently clenched in a fist, and he couldn't do the simplest thing.

At least he was good at looking. Always had been. When you couldn't move, looking was what you did most.

Birds crossed the window. They flew without effort. He was a heavy lump. Stuck to this bed.

If those birds had noses, they'd be thumbing their noses at him as they flew past. And hands. If birds had hands and noses. They wouldn't be birds.

Nothing could be less like a bird than he was. He was more like a helicopter. Just listen to that one now, grinding away noisily, clack, clack of the engine. Like a pulse. But an ugly pulse. The helicopters had to work so hard to stay aloft, you could hear the weight of them in the sky.

If you want to keep flying, don't look down.

Who'd said that? Matthew. Matthew was Jessica's boyfriend. He knew that. Matthew said it to Jessica. Why? When? Joe couldn't remember. It was the sort of thing Matthew said.

Jess's Notebook

From upstairs, Matt heard the heavy front door shut. There was a draught on the back of his neck so he closed the sash window, which turned out to be stiff. Jessie was such a fresh air freak, and these windows were out of the stone age. Inefficient. Maybe none of the upstairs frames on this side of the building had been replaced. He wondered why for a moment. He'd never been alone in this house before and he didn't really like the quiet; it made him feel like an intruder; so he put on some music and got down to the task in hand.

Jess's notebook was something else.

It looked smart from the outside. It had a proper hard cover of an intense blue, with a grey ribbon for a bookmark and blue elastic to hold it shut; another piece of elastic gripped a pencil at its side. A very neat job, and if you *had* to do pen and paper, very professional. But when you opened it, you discovered a complete mess. On some pages there would be a name, a phone number, maybe an address, and a whole load of spidery notes in pencil. Sometimes it was as if she'd tried to keep a log of what was going on in lessons, because there were multiple brief entries and numbers that might be dates in varying ink. Some pages were just a list of names or telephone numbers. Or email addresses. A number, or a date, or a venue, or any combination, with a list of tunes. Doodles. A cartoon man with a huge moustache. There was no single organising principle at work here. It apparently had to be read in conjunction with a huge calendar plucked from her bedroom wall which served as an appointments diary: again, a beautiful, stylish thing, featuring high quality matt photo prints of Shetland with acres of arty white margin around; then, in illegible fine fibre tip – yellow, I mean *yellow* – times and pupils' names. Usually it was just one name, and it wasn't always clear whether this was surname or forename.

He'd asked Jess, *how can I help? Just say. Anything.* He had absolutely no idea what tangible steps he could take to help her deal with her father's sudden illness, or what he should be offering to do, but he trusted her to tell him, and had spent the last twenty-four hours on standby, awaiting orders. Of course, his shoulder was there for her to cry on, and she'd cried plenty. She was very close to her dad. Matt hated to see her so distraught. And distracted. She couldn't seem to concentrate on anything; she was off cooking, off music, off TV, off sex. Then, when he'd repeated his offer - *just say, anything* - she'd asked him to cancel her Monday lessons for her, because she didn't trust herself to hold it together. *Best thing is to text them*, he'd said, *that way it's quick and they have a record.* That wouldn't do for Jess. *Oh no you can't do that*, she'd told him, *it's too impersonal.* The numbers were in the blue book, which she thrust into his hands. She had them all on her phone but she needed that with her. She didn't know what words to use. So would Matt mind ringing them for her? Just to say she'd be in touch to re-schedule.

I can do that, he'd said, thinking, piece of cake, I'm great on the phone. He'd been a big success in his call centre days. But he hadn't bargained on the GCHQ recruitment test of matching names to contact details. And now she'd gone off to spend Saturday night at the hospital with her mum, so he'd have to figure it out for himself. She ought to have this lot on a spreadsheet really. When things were calmer, he'd tackle her about that.

Matt was relieved not to be going back to the hospital with them. He knew, from all the work he'd done on personal strengths and weaknesses, that he wasn't good round sickness. For sure, he was a people person, but a *healthy* people person. He was still shaken by their lunchtime visit. He liked Joe and couldn't believe someone who bounced around so much had been cut down. Barely mobile, and his face distorted, making sucking movements when he tried to speak... he looked completely out of it. Still, if Joe didn't really know what was going on, it wouldn't be so bad for him, would it? It was hard on Jess's mum, though. She'd seemed fine in the hospital, quite calm really, but acted a bit weird round the house just now. She'd gone completely hyper, like she was on something, and also, she was showing a scary side he'd never seen before, really snappy. Understandable though. Classic state of shock. And Jess was crying a lot. Well, it was his job to stand by her and if she felt incapable of phoning her Monday pupils, he'd do that for her. Right now.

There was one booked in mid-morning and two school kids for late afternoon. Hardly worth it really, and wouldn't it have been better to group the three together? You couldn't manage your time effectively like that. He found numbers for the afternoon pupils where she'd said, on the back page, and decided to start with them. Planning the script was easy. He'd open with 'So sorry to interrupt your evening, I'm calling about Tammy's lesson,' just in case he had the wrong parent, because people hate to be called by the wrong name. They'd hate that more than if he attributed the wrong child to them. Client serenity was important.

Sure enough he charmed the pants off the first parent, who was in the middle of baking a cake. 'I do appreciate it's very short notice but Miss Faber has to cancel Monday's lessons because of a family emergency. She'll be in touch to re-schedule.' The second one was a bit sniffy at first because little Emily had her grade exam coming up in a month's time and she couldn't afford to miss a lesson. 'Oh yes, totally, Miss Faber's conscious of that,' he said. 'In fact, she asked me to make a suggestion. She says perhaps Emily could devote the time she would normally have spent coming in for her lesson to having a really good practice. With you, at home.' This was of course a lie, but such a creative one, and really if Jessie had had time to think it through, it was what she *would* have said. The parent said, 'Oh God,' like a bad thing was going to happen. Matt added: 'And specially to work on her scales, because they're the key to everything at this level. As I'm sure you know.' The bit about scales was something he'd heard Jessie say more than once, but the *at this level* was all his own. A great coaching phrase. It implied context.

Fran's Manifesto

Sunday, and no alarm. No phone call overnight, so the chances were that Joe was still alive. He might be sleeping now. Alone in bed, Fran propped herself up on pillows as if she were the one who was sick, and wondered how she felt about all this.

She was ready to admit that she was tired. Yesterday had started early and run late, with chores squashed between afternoon and evening visiting times, circular discussions with Jess, and after bedtime, another long report back to her sister in Shetland over the phone. It was strange to be waking up alone, but good to lie in bed. Being busy sapped your energy, but this was more than physical tiredness. This was the silent, deep exhaustion which came with facing the truth. A terrible thing had happened, a thing that wouldn't be put right by wishing, or by any arrangement she could make, or anything she could do. It was time to cry.

It sickened her to imagine the horror Joe must be feeling.

Yesterday, he'd answered their questions about hospital food, and one side of him smiled back when they smiled at him; but her Joe, who always talked so very much, had listened without connecting. Perhaps they'd lost that Joe forever, the Joe whose spark set conversations alight. The nursing staff stubbornly refused prognosis, and so had her sister Nell, who ought to know, with her nurse training and years of experience with the elderly. Oh blimey, was Joe the elderly now? Promoted to their ranks at fifty-six?

Three days ago, when Fran had first told her, the tone of Nell's voice was worse than anything she'd said; 'Oh, no,' delivered as if the bottom had fallen out of something. And still last night her sister was quiet, taking deep breaths on the other end of the phone. Nell did that when she was making

27

any sort of judgement: sticky toffee / lemon drizzle, suits you / doesn't suit you, good thing / bad thing. Die / recover.

Now Fran ransacked the jumble of all that she'd seen and heard yesterday in search of encouragement, the way she'd rummage through a waste bin looking for a lost piece of jewellery. His eyes had softened since the previous day. But he wore a kind of clown face, which puckered in unexpected places; and he was so tired that he'd seemed almost indifferent when they said goodbye. A press of the hand was all that he could summon. It had been firm, though, and that was something.

He wasn't much better.

But he wasn't getting worse, either.

Whereas Jess was on a downward slope. Oh, Jess. No sooner off the ward than in tears again. It was a complete funk, worse than the worst audition nerves; brooding one minute, full of childish questions the next. Will he be better tomorrow? When will he be coming home? She'd collapsed into a teenage self, hugging cushions, shuffling between loud music and the fridge.

The girl was terrified. She didn't have to name her fears: they were Fran's own. She was going to have to tame them, though.

As the day warmed, so did Fran's resolve to tackle this head-on. She lay in bed trying to figure out why she'd been taking everything at a run, why she was so reluctant to voice her fears. Simple. You could either run away and cry, or make your stand. That first reaction was instinctive, visceral, maybe biologically determined. But this was all going to play out over a long time. *Your life will be different now.*

If this was a new world order, she would have to meet it. She'd need to draw up her manifesto. And suddenly her head

28

was alive with ideas. On the floor not far from her side of the bed there was an old spiral-bound lab book which she used for the allotment. It contained lists and sketches of her planting schemes, proposed and actual, with dates. It opened flat: *9 April Planted first salad leaves. Garlic. Prep seed bed for fennel. Sow peas.* She flipped it upside down, went to the back of the book, and opened the first clean double page to write.

> *1. In this new world no-one can predict the outcome. We all know that. Joe knows that. That knowledge puts a responsibility on those who love him not to talk up the negatives.*
> *2. Worry is inevitable, but it saps the energy we need to deal with what's in front of us. So controlling our own worry is now a necessary skill. We need to know the negatives, but we need to find a way of putting them in cold store.*
> *3. We have a choice between optimism and pessimism. Our attitude affects our expectations. Our expectations affect outcomes. Therefore, we must back optimism.*
> *4. We have to lend our optimism to Joe, as necessary.*
> *5. We have to turn that optimism into action. It's got to be a chemical reaction, a change in us, otherwise it's no better than buying a lottery ticket. Because it's not just a matter of what I say to him, or what feelings I might betray. It's what I say to myself.*

The sun was getting higher. She jumped out of bed to lower the top sash window an inch, and a green scent rushed in. Down below, in her own and her neighbours' gardens, the walls and the fences were disappearing under a mass of foliage. Climbers were flowering, shrubs and trees were spreading out, everything was growing more lush by the minute.

She'd made her choice, and decided to act like an optimist. If she was wrong, who would get hurt? Fran didn't care if it was her. She'd take the risk of being disappointed, if it helped Joe feel better about himself along the way. Although this was just the start. She was going to have to find out what acting like an optimist entailed.

She went back to her manifesto and added:

6. We're not going to tell him lies. No fortune telling, either. We must just latch on to the good stuff in front of us. We must look out for little things that are better today than they were yesterday, and talk about those things. And we won't just tell him, we'll tell everyone. We'll tell anyone who'll listen.

She heard Jess padding downstairs in search of breakfast. Before they got to afternoon visiting, she'd need to recruit her to this cause.

Her chance came soon enough. As visiting time drew nearer, an uneasy line spread across Jess's brow and her eyes grew sad. There wasn't time for lunch. Jess sat down at the kitchen table with a packet of crisps, ripped it open and heaved a great sigh.

'I want to see Dad. I really do. But at the same time, I really, really don't.'

'He'll be better for seeing you, though.'

'Yeah…' Her eyes had watered over. 'And anyway, I know I've got to go because…'

Jess was sobbing and her head had dropped low.

'Because you think you might not see him again.' When she nodded Fran saw only the golden crown with its ripples of hair.

'I'm scared of what might happen. And I'm scared of what I'll see.' She gave a long sniff as she drew herself up and looked across the table. 'And the worst thing is, I feel so useless.'

'Look, Jess, the way I see it, we have a choice here. We can worry ourselves sick. That's always an option. There's no lack of fuel to drive down that road.' Fran held back from pointing out that even if Joe survived, this might only be the start. The medical risks – never mind all the other things like money and the house – were enough to scare her witless. 'If I really work at it, Jess, I could end up paralysed myself. Unable to decide or do the least thing to help any of us.'

She reached out for her daughter's hand, and met the little bump of her engagement ring.

'Believe me, if I wanted to list all the things he's lost right now, all the things he could do three days ago and can't today, not just all the functions he's lost, but all the pleasures he's lost, the things he does for other people, all the little things, believe me, I could be here all day, and I could get very sorry for myself, because I've got the inventory up here, you know?' She tapped her head. 'There are so many lovely private little things about your dad that we can't access right now. They're not gone, but they're locked away. And you know what he'd be telling us, don't you? If he saw the pair of us snivelling over the kitchen table like this?'

She turned to grab the kitchen roll. They were both crying now.

'What?'

'He'd accuse us of running around like headless chickens waving our hands in the air.'

Jess burst into sobbing laughter. 'Oh God, yes, that's exactly what he'd say.'

Joe mixed metaphors the way he mixed paints, with huge relish and satisfaction, and colourful ones like this were passed round the family.

'So that's not an option, right?'

Jess settled, listening.

Fran said, 'I've been thinking about this. I've written something down.'

She ran upstairs to fetch her manifesto. When she got back and Jess recognised the lab book, she teased, 'Oh God, Mum, you're not planning crop rotations at a time like this?'

'Read it.' And she opened it, back to front and upside down, at the page. 'It's a sort of manifesto.'

Jess seemed to read it through a couple of times.

'I do know not to cry in hospital. Because that's not good for him, is it? Only it's so hard to hold it together.'

'Listen. What does it help to think: that he'll get worse, or that he'll get better?'

'That he'll get better... of course...'

'So, fix yourself to that.'

'But it might be wrong.'

'I'm not suggesting for one moment that we spin your dad some yarn about how he's going to jump back into action any minute. Just stick to the good things, the improvements. And please... please try.... Don't let him catch you looking scared.'

Jess wrinkled her nose. 'Sounds like you're putting on an act. A performance.'

Fran quickened.

'You bet. All the time I'm with your father now, I've got one question on my mind. What does he need right now? In this precise moment, what does he need to hear? What does he need to see? And he doesn't need to see us doubt his ability to pull through. He just doesn't need it. So yes, maybe this is a performance. Remember that masterclass, when you were, what, fourteen? You had terrible nerves about playing in public then. Your bowing arm used to wibble-wobble about, and you just couldn't get any tone. Remember what happened? Remember what Nicola said? Everyone gets nervous before playing and that's just fine. But once you're on that platform, you owe it to the music not to think about yourself. Don't think about how you look or what might go wrong or whether you're doing it right. Just think about the music. Just think about your dad, Jessie.'

She watched the fine lines about her daughter's face flicker, then settle into recognition.

Lingering

Better a bare wall and sunlight than a nasty mural, in Joe's book. Above the height of the curtain rails that marked off each bed space, there was a long strip of cream which might veer to yellow or to grey, and where shadows marked the progress of the day, unimpeded. You had to snatch at every scrap of beauty in hospital, where nowadays even flowers were banished.

Joe was starting to notice things, and to think about his place in all this. He watched the nurses and the care assistants with a special warmth; he viewed his fellow patients with interest too, them and their visitors. He vaguely knew he shouldn't stare at people, and especially not the patients trotting to and from the loo. Lucky sods.

Fran looked nice. That was lipstick and maybe she had combed her hair. As for Jess... there was something different going on there too... a bit puffy, a bit pink in the cheek... she looked as though she'd been crying. Her edges were never well defined at the best of times, and she was a bit of a blur today in a shapeless jumper and skirt that might be a dress, trousers that might be tights, a scarf thing that might be a jumper, all mixed up in a smoky, uncertain blend of blues and greys; her hair was a soft, dulled straw colour that looked like pastel marks smudged deliberately by a thumb. Or maybe it was these mucky glasses.

The mad-haired blonde and the tidy brunette sat at his bedside and nobody would have taken them for mother and daughter, although kinship wasn't all about the way things look, and their behaviour today was very much in step. They were playing that game of counting their blessings, which marked them both a real pair of Pollyannas. How great it was he'd had his teeth fixed the week before: how much harder to eat and speak if he'd been in between dental appointments, waiting for a bridge. And he'd just had a haircut. Very important for your public, they teased him, gesturing at the ward full of yesterday's strangers. Hm, he said, you mean I might have looked even worse. And another thing, Fran said: he'd picked a Thursday so she'd only had to take one day off work.

Jess was encouraging. 'So... Imagine a nice old-fashioned set of cast iron scales, like the ones your granny had in her kitchen, you know, the noisy ones that went *kerchunk*. Imagine every one of those good things is like a big fat round metal weight. So, teeth – that's 250 grammes; hair, 250 grammes; weekend, 250 grammes at least. And Mum took her half day on Thursday instead of Tuesday, so she was there to call the ambulance. That's got to be worth a whole kilo.'

'Two pounds,' he said, 'my grammy… my granny's scales worked in pounds.'

'Whatever. Come on, Dad, drag yourself into the twenty-first century. Let's say it was mum's snazzy scales at the lab, all gleaming and shiny, with a digital display, if you like. It doesn't matter, the thing is, to visualise something. All those little good things, that add up.'

'Also,' said Fran, 'You're in no pain at all, are you?'

This was true: he hadn't had so much as a headache.

'That's worth a pound or two.'

'*Kerchunk!*' cried Jess.

He tried to tell them it was much less in modern money, but his lips stuck. He screwed his face up and paused to start again. Different, simpler words came out.

'Yes, *but.* I'm barrellised. Paralysed.'

It seemed to Joe that they didn't even make a weight as heavy as that. He couldn't explain this to them, now that his thoughts ran so far ahead of his tongue. Wherever feeling had gone, a dead weight had replaced it. It took two people heaving up the slip sheet to help him sit up in bed. Since the bed was too short for him, he would gradually slide down it, until his feet got mangled in the bars. He had woken at night to find a long squidgy thing in the bed next to him, which turned out to be his right arm. He kept rolling on to it in his sleep and waking up with a lump in his back. The ward sister had been sympathetic, and warned him how important it was to reclaim the affected side: look at your right arm, she said, and touch it, rub it with the other hand; look at your right leg, touch it with the other foot, help your brain to re-establish that it's part of you. According to her, some people actually banished the affected limbs completely from their consciousness. He'd adopted a more aggressive stance: look at it? He stared at it. Stroke it? He pummelled it. Talk to it? Silently, he took it on. *'What are you doing there? Creeping up on me like that?'*

Joe's patient notes, in what looked like a big blue school register, were marked confidential, and kept conveniently above the bed in case anybody wanted to read them. Fran scanned them; there had been very regular checks, she said, and already a knitting pattern was building up. There was nothing his wife loved better than hard data.

'You're not paralysed. Look. There's a key here. P for paralysed. You haven't got any Ps in that column.'

He didn't believe her and had to see the chart for himself.

'P would mean, there really can't be movement. But they told us right at the start, your reflexes are normal. Your brain just isn't telling you to move.'

'So what you're saying is, I'm lingering... *Ma*-lingering.' He grinned at his own invention. Lingering was a fair description. 'I'm a lingerer. A loiterer. They'll run me in for loitering with a tent.'

'It's your sense of humour that's lame, Dad. But then, it was before.'

Joe recognised the verbal equivalent of a found object. Take, for example, Duchamps' urinal, or the Surrealists' famous bottle rack: you knew what it was, you just didn't know what it was doing in an art gallery. Similarly, his tongue was bumping into words which already had a perfect sense and function, but had no real business being in his mouth at the time. Pure Dada. License to talk tosh. He might as well enjoy it.

Wonder White Weddings

It seemed to Jess that now Matt was on her case too, because throughout Sunday, he'd messaged almost by the hour, encouraging her to tell her dad about the Frenzy gig, because good news was the best tonic, and besides, he deserved to know, which was just what her mum had said; and as she got over her first wild panic, she could see they were right. He'd promised to pick her up so they could visit together in the evening. But when he rang at lunchtime to firm up arrangements, things didn't sound to be going well. Matt had been busy all weekend preparing a management workshop for Monday morning. He was having a lot of difficulty, he'd said, working out where things should sit on the Decision Matrix.

('What's a Decision Matrix?' she'd said. 'It's a tool that helps you to decide things.' She'd never heard of it. 'Ah well,' he said, 'that might be because you've been calling it something else... Grid Analysis, Pugh Matrix Analysis? Multi-Attribute Utility Theory? They all come to the same thing, really. It's basically an attempt to bring some sort of logic to what can be a very subjective process.' 'Well,' she'd teased him, 'if you can't even decide what to call it, maybe the concept is doomed to failure.' Oddly, he seemed not to find that funny, which she put down to all the stress he was under. What with his new module and everything, and the shock with her dad.)

Jess was surprised to find Matt's sister Zanna sitting in the back of the car, smartly dressed as ever but excited as a puppy and keen to know when they were going to name the day.

Matt smiled his mellow smile and said, 'That's my little sis, straight to the point. I've told her, all in good time. But I suppose we ought to start thinking about it.' He released the handbrake, and glided smoothly away.

'Maybe give it a year or so...'

'Yes, it takes a lot of time to arrange a wedding properly,' said Zanna in the back seat, as if she knew; then after a moment's seriousness, reverted to puppy dog. 'I'm soooo excited about this. You must be over the moon, Jess.'

Over the moon? she thought. *My dad nearly died and I'm meant to be* over the moon? At the same time, her mum's words were ringing in her ears. There had to be a chemical reaction inside herself. She had to act confident, and not get upset. She mustn't go off on one. Just explain.

'It's just... I'm not sure how long Dad's going to need to get better.' (Or if he would get better at all, or how much better he might get. For all she knew, there might be a funeral to deal with first. Maybe it would have to be a very quick wedding indeed.) 'To be honest, my head's so full of other stuff right now... the thought of organising anything feels a bit much. I couldn't even write a shopping list. Not that I would anyway.'

They stopped abruptly at traffic lights.

'Oh, totally.'

Zanna's high-pitched voice was right in Jessie's ear. Matt hadn't taken his eyes off the road ahead, but now he glanced in his rear-view mirror and flashed a broad smile at his sister. She went on.

'But look, this is what I was wanting to tell you... You really don't have to bother yourself with the boring bits. That's going to be my wedding gift to you both.'

Jess shot a look at Matt by way of a silent question. She felt just a hint of panic. Now he turned towards her, beamed and nodded. 'Yes Jessie, just listen to this… it's brilliant…'

'Yeah, like, incredible timing.' Zanna explained in a panting, tail-wagging rush: 'What it is, is, you know how I work in Events? For Bim Fox-Finch? Which is like, all totally brilliant and I love her to bits. Completely. Well, I'm just about to set up a business on my own. As a kind of sideline. Just to start, obviously. And my business is going to be… Wonder White Weddings. Ta-da!'

The lights changed and Zanna kept going.

'It's all online, see, so like, it's going to be www.wowee.something, and maybe spell it capital W little o capital N little d capital E little r, you get the idea. Anyway, online means no overheads and of course I've already got loads of contacts. So, the business model,' – she slowed down and lowered her voice so as to sound professional, and Jess had an inkling this was aimed at impressing her brother – 'the business model is, you tell me what you want and I arrange it for you.'

'I thought a business model was about how you make a profit?'

'That's a business plan,' said Matt helpfully.

The voice found a still lower register. 'Well obviously I'm doing this for free. For your wedding present.' There was a decent pause, before she started to wind her way back up the scale again 'And in a way you'll be helping me and you can like me and give me a nice 5-star review for the site and get all your friends and relations to like me too. For other people, obviously I take a cut because it's like a bespoke service?'

'With no overheads,' said Matt, eyes back on the road.

'Totally. No overheads.'

They were getting close to the hospital now.

'Does it have to be a white wedding?'

'Well I can't think of a better name. It's a great name. Why would I change it? Wonder White Weddings. WWW…'

'No, I mean, our wedding. Do we have to have a white wedding?' She looked across at Matt, hoping he'd query that too, but he was back in safe-driver mode, watching the traffic and checking his wing mirrors, with a funny little blissed-out smile that suggested to her he really didn't mind what his sister dreamt up.

Zanna momentarily stopped in her tracks. 'Well… if you want to be alternative… Oh I see! You've got some great edgy off-the-wall idea? Bring it on! Only most people go for white.'

'White is for a church wedding and I don't go to church.'

'Oh, nobody does. But their parents do sometimes.'

'Not mine. Do yours?'

'Well they go to weddings, obviously.'

Jess didn't know what to say. She caught herself fiddling with her engagement ring, which was not something she'd been aware of doing before; she liked to think she wasn't the ring-wagging type. Then Matt urgently needed her help to guide him into the car park, and the next thing she knew they were heading for the ward without the words *thank you* having crossed her lips.

Too late now. The moment had passed.

Bedside Manners

'You're looking much better than when you came in,' said the nurse who'd taken his blood pressure. It must be true, because he knew it was the second time they'd said that today.

'Have I really been here f-f-for-f-f-four days?'

'Yup. You'll be moving on to rehab soon. You're doing well, Joe.'

Today felt different. He felt a bit more like himself, although he couldn't get used to these strange formless limbs which didn't seem to be a real part of him, and which certainly weren't playing on his side. It called to mind a news item he'd once read about two Siamese twins, who'd grown up to hate each other. One turned out to be an alcoholic, the other was teetotal. Hmm. Maybe the dead weight half of him was in a drunken stupor and was going to wake up with an almighty hangover. Or ready for a fight.

At least he was alive.

And now in the late afternoon of a very bright spring-become-summer day, his heart jumped at the sight of Jess and Matt entering the ward. Jess was wearing a turquoise scarf over the pebbly brown frock, paying him the honour of a real colour for a change. They were holding hands and smiling at him, but in different ways, Jess making her whole face dance, Matt serene. A bit like the Mona Lisa. Or the Buddha. Behind them was a young woman who looked much more serious and who, unexpectedly, drew a third plastic chair to his bedside. She was extraordinarily small and slender and, unlike most short women, had an unusually small head, which in effect made her perfectly proportioned.

Joe had once seen a magician at the Moscow State Circus make ten such tiny women vanish into thin air. It had been his finale. One by one they had stepped into a suitcase in the middle of the ring. The magician had closed the lid, picked up the suitcase, bowed, and walked off, leaving the audience staring at the sawdust.

Jess leant down to kiss him. Matthew gripped his good, left hand, then introduced the narrow-hipped woman as his sister Zanna.

'Hi, Mr Faber.' She made an embarrassed gesture with her right hand. Of course, Joe had no handshake but he strongly suspected she didn't either. She looked alarmed by him, and who could blame her? You wouldn't choose to meet any of your future son-in-law's family three days after a stroke, or on the acute ward, and far less over dinner. His speech was slimy and sometimes words were missing. He knew that he looked all wrong. He was wearing peach coloured hospital pyjamas because they didn't go for nudity on Daffodil Ward. (The only pyjama equivalents he possessed were designed for winter wear, far too warm for hospital where they had to keep the heating up in order to encourage the microbes and save on blankets.) Since it was a mealtime, he had taken the grey cardboard urinal off the table, but it was still in the visitors' line of sight, on top of the bedside cabinet. The hospital food smelled good, but the plate in front of him looked awful; his dinner had gone through the blender, because he couldn't eat anything with corners, and this process extracted all the colour, so everything ended up as grey shepherd's pap. Like as not, some of it would be on his chin. He pouched stuff without realising because he lacked sensation in the right side of his mouth. He could only feel what half of his body was doing. All things considered, his person and the space around it were unlovely and at times unaccountably damp.

Jess squeezed his hand.

42

'You're looking brighter today. There's more colour in your cheeks.'

'So, are they looking after you, Joe?' asked Matt.

'What's for dinner then?' asked Jess, eyeing his plate.

He wanted to say, 'Irish Stew,' but it came out more like a sneeze.

'Oh god, Irish stew,' said Zanna. 'I remember that from school.'

'Oh yeah, said Matt, I knew that smell right away…'

'Did you have it at your school, Jess?'

'Think so. Only it was mostly gravy.'

He was all set to tell them, look, they can engineer gravy nowadays to make it a solid, but he missed his chance. They were on to steak and kidney pie now. He half listened but something else had grabbed his attention.

The best thing about being in the penthouse suite of the General Hospital was the spectacular lighting to be enjoyed at such heights. It now revealed the absolute precision of Zanna's make-up and clothing. The intensity of the contrasting shades of pink and blue she had chosen, and the clean lines of the tailoring – clever tucks, but not a crease in sight – all contributed to make her look hyper-real, a miniature painted on enamel with a two-hair brush. Perhaps she was a hallucination. Joe was genuinely fascinated by the sheer obedience of each garment. This quality extended to her hairdo. She had pin-striped shoulder-length hair that mimicked something casual but absolutely wasn't, because the fine knife-edge curtain which fell diagonally over her right eye was not seen to ripple and must have been held together by some sort of resin, he reckoned. The whole effect was delicate, stiff, and deliberate. A work of art.

They made a picture at his bedside, Zanna's shocked look as if her eyelids were somehow pinned apart, Matt open-eyed in quite a different, kindlier manner, and his lovely girl Jessica blurred between sadness and bliss. Joe wanted to tell her she had everything to hope for because she was brilliant, and she was getting married, and her old dad was fighting back. But somehow, he didn't.

They had done school puddings and got onto the hospital itself, how many nurses on the ward, what time do they wake you up and the colour of the walls etc., etc.; all talk of the particulars of his condition was somehow held back by the presence of this stranger.

'Oh, Mr Faber, I nearly forgot...'

'Joe.'

'*Joe*, I wanted to give you this...'

She drew an envelope from her bag, which she opened for him: *Get well soon.* Rather an old-fashioned card, he thought, pastel greens and blue forget-me-nots. She stood it on the table next to his supper.

'That's the first,' he said.

'Oh, Mum has a secret stash.'

He nodded, 'Ah. Thank you.'

Fran always said you could tell a lot about a family by their card giving. The Fabers were hopelessly lax in that respect. Immaculate card etiquette, which included timing, was as alien to their clan as food fads and obsessive hygiene.

'And I had a special reason for wanting to meet you. And Mrs Faber, of course. When Matt said he was visiting with Jess, I thought, great, jump in the car and you can start spreading the good news!'

She turned to smile at her brother, then at Jess, but Jess was showing her back. She was busy untangling his dead foot from between the horizontal bars at the bottom of the bed; only Joe saw the raised eyebrow.

'What it is, is… I'm going to be your wedding planner! That's my gift to the bride and groom. Although of course, it involves you!' She leant slightly back and opened her arms with a flourish, to conclude, 'Meet Wonder White Weddings! Ta-daa!'

Jess had sat upright now and placed her hands in her lap. The foot was back where it ought to be.

There must have been something about the way Joe said 'Oh!' that made his daughter's eyes twinkle into a smile.

This sister of Matt's really did have a very unusual physique. She ought to capitalise on it. He imagined her in a spangled leotard, as the magician's assistant. If she were double-jointed as well as petite, you could saw her in half. And she'd probably fit inside a suitcase.

The pause in the conversation lengthened, and as Joe made his attempt to fill it, everybody looked and listened, willing him on.

'Have we met before? Have you ever… worked… in a circus?'

She turned her head slowly to one side as she answered, 'Er, n-no. I'm in Events Management, actually.' Her sweet smile was offset by a look of terror about the eyes.

Her brother – who also looked a bit wary now – instantly smoothed things over: 'But it is a bit of a circus, metaphorically speaking, isn't it, Zanna? Hah, hah.'

'Oh… oh, yes. It's *totally manic* this time of year, what with all the summer weddings.'

'Thought so,' said Joe. 'Thought was something… in a tent.'

45

The grey eyes swivelled rapidly towards her brother and back again. This was great. He'd got her on the back foot already. They thought he might have gone bonkers. Only Jess was grinning wickedly at him, as if she'd recognised her dad, under all the dribble. Setting off on one of his ramblings. And now she seemed to gather energy and announced that she too had something to tell him, amazing news.

'I've got a gig, Dad,' she said. 'At this year's Frenzy. I've been offered an actual spot to play with Archie McNuckert on the Friday night. It'll be advertised and everything. It won't be free entry either. Eighteen quid a pop.'

The longer she spoke, the more she glowed, until she almost looked her old self. His daughter had been going to the Shetland Fiddle Frenzy since her teens, first as a rank and file participant, more recently in various combos and the odd solo spot. Joe watched her colour rise and listened as she explained to the sister that this was the biggest gathering of folk fiddlers in the northern hemisphere.

Yes, it was.

His Jessie.

The sister had opened her eyes wide and dropped her jaw a little, and was now slowly turning her head ever so slightly from side to side. Incomprehension, or a contortionist's warm-up? Jessie's whole body was swaying now as she impressed on her that this was not just any gig, but a chance to play with Archie McNuckert, *the* Archie McNuckert, a pupil of the great Tom Anderson; who'd played with all these great people, and now was especially keen to share a platform with the up and coming generation of women.

Joe was thrilled for her. God knew what fell out of his grinning gob.

'When is it?'

It was Matt who supplied the answer: 'First week in August. So, not long.'

Of course it was. Same as last year.

'Short notice,' said the sister.

'Someone else dropped out,' said Matt, and the sister nodded.

That was nearly two months away. Joe calculated: he was due to move on to another hospital, for rehab, any day. The man in the bed next to him had been completely immobile a fortnight ago, and now he was not only dressing himself and walking about but nipping downstairs for cups of coffee. There must be some reason they were moving Joe on so soon, when he couldn't even stand; maybe the research programme? Even in Joe's short stay, he'd noticed how quickly other people seemed to be recovering. Therefore it was entirely reasonable to assume he'd be better by August. He told Jess, 'We'll be there.'

She frowned and shrugged, 'Look Dad, it might not work for you. Don't feel you have to.'

Neither of them really knew. There was no point arguing about it.

'We'll see,' he said.

'We all need targets,' said Matt. So someone had faith in him.

Fran's Monday Morning

Monday dawned bright and clean, and Fran made sure she got in early. She knocked at the door marked Director of Laboratory Services, confident her boss would be ahead of her.

47

Behind the desk, Mairi beamed her toothy smile and her heavy features settled easily into deeply scored lines about the oblong face. Fran told her what had happened and watched this face fall as she pushed her chair back. A few short questions and answers – haemorrhage, no need for surgery, loss of dominant side, speech not too bad, vision and hearing intact – and the clinical picture was drawn.

'It's conservative treatment. Nothing to be done. Except physio. He's in the General. But they're talking of moving him on to rehab pretty soon.'

Mairi gave a tight shake of the head, so fleeting it was almost a tic, and pursed her lips.

'And how are you, Fran?'

'Yes. Well. I don't really know. But I thought I ought to see you. I need to tweak my hours, today, so I can visit. And I wanted you to know what's going on just in case...' She'd intended to say, in case I need to take time off. Now she was thinking, in case I burst into tears. She was conscious of feeling very wide awake right now, on the attack and ready to take on the world, just so long as that didn't involve actually talking to anybody she knew.

'I'm going to tell my section right away,' said Fran. 'I don't want everybody wondering what's the matter with me.' The sense of catastrophe radiating from her was so intense, it must surely be visible. 'So please don't feel you have to keep this confidential. The grape vine is fine by me right now.'

'You don't have to be here,' said Mairi. 'We'll cover. Take the time you need.'

'It's just visiting time. They'll let me in at 2 this afternoon. I can come back to the lab and work late, and then make evening visiting as well. I want to be busy.'

Mairi acknowledged that with another abrupt movement of her head.

'Any problems, Fran, just bail out. Whenever.'

'It feels like the whole world's vibrating. Ever so slightly, but all the time.'

'It's not the world, Fran, it's you.'

Was it?

'I'll talk to Harry and Madeleine. I'll ask them to keep an eye on me... maybe we should look at sharing jobs a bit differently. They'll understand.'

'Be careful,' Mairi said, and she smiled a broken sort of smile, as if she didn't expect her advice to be taken.

Back on the cool cream staircase of the fire escape, Fran wondered what Mairi had meant by that. Look after yourself? Or, mind you don't mess up? On Saturday, the ward sister had said Joe's inability to concentrate wasn't necessarily permanent: he'd be in a state of shock, because one minute he had complete control of his body and the next minute he hadn't. Now Fran wondered: am I in a state of shock too? Adrenalin was pumping. She'd worked out her survival strategy all right, and shared that with Jess; and she'd drawn up her to-do list to get through the practicalities of the week; but look how she'd fallen down on simple things, like the cauliflower cheese that turned out to be small comfort, minus the cheese. Yesterday she'd cried her eyes out for an hour before breakfast. Then in the afternoon there'd been a power cut – just a tripped switch, as it turned out – and she'd crouched in the cupboard under the stairs staring at the consumer unit and growling, 'Why don't you ever label anything?' as if Joe had made all this happen on purpose.

None of this was normal. Her mind was working fast but the thoughts kept flitting from one thing to another. She might make a mistake, and that was unthinkable given the nature of the work they were doing in Pathology Services. Every sample belonged to a patient. And every patient mattered to somebody as much as Joe mattered to Fran.

When she got back to the lab, Madeleine and Harry were both already busy and concentrating, so Fran waited till coffee time to sit down and tell them what had happened. From that moment, Madeleine stared at Fran with a look of horror that was hard to bear. Maybe it was pity, but that didn't make it easier. With her wispy hair falling over her temples, and her hand repeatedly drawn up to her open mouth, she resembled a cod soothsayer from some comic movie, at once ridiculous and earnest, and repeatedly begging the question, was Fran worried enough? Because if she wasn't, Madeleine would no doubt help. Straightforward Harry, the regular guy, with his tightly shaved black hair and immaculately transparent beard, black over brown, looked genuinely sorry and said, 'if there's anything I can do…' Fran was about to tell him that yes, there was something he could do, but Harry hadn't finished.

'He is going to be all right, though, isn't he?'

'I hope so.'

'What have they told you? I mean, he is going to be able to walk again, isn't he? How long do they think it will take?' There was a look of innocence about him: those flat cheeks above the beard, the eager, bright eyes, expecting answers.

'I mean, is it going to be weeks, or months?'

Why did he need to know so much right now? These were the very things nobody seemed able to tell her. There were people on the ward who seemed to have recovered overnight. They woke up one day and found they could move again.

However well-intentioned Harry might be, Fran was suddenly so annoyed by his badgering that she snapped back.

'How on earth would I know?'

Still open-eyed, he dropped his head a fraction and looked upwards at her, as if she were hiding under the brim of some childish hat.

'Are you sure you should be in work today?'

Thirty years old and no more tact than he was born with. OK, he might have a point. But even so... When Fran had raised her voice, Madeleine's shoulders had shot up to her ears, and the many parallel lines of her brow dipped and trembled. If those lines were an ECG, she'd have the crash team running.

Harry still hadn't finished. He asked, 'D'you think Joe will want to go on working when he's better?'

Fran took a deep breath and decided not to answer. His chestnut eyes were awake, and she could guess how far ahead the brain behind them was computing. If she needed to take time off, the rotas would have to be re-drawn, which was a task in itself, although there might be overtime coming his way. Bigger than that was the change of direction that had already been announced at the lab – there might be jobs changed and jobs lost, including her own – so he'd want to look keen and keep a straight bat if things turned out really badly.

'I need to juggle my hours, and I'd like us to look again at the job sheet. Joe's had the stroke, but I seem to be the one who can't think straight.'

She looked them both in the eye, hoping for a smile; Harry obliged. Madeleine was aghast.

'What I mean is, my attention span isn't the best right now. So there are a couple of things I'd like to hand over to you.'

That seemed to please them both; they'd be only too happy. When they all stood up, Harry went to wash the mugs and Madeleine moved to Fran's side. The pained expression hadn't left her, and her voice was breathy.

'I can't believe you've come in to work, Fran. This must be so awful for you. I'd go to pieces. You must be so worried. It's so terrible. Terrible, terrible news.'

Fran summoned some bland comment about not really knowing how you'll react to anything until it actually happens. Besides, Joe was alive.

She hadn't made it through the morning and already she was weary. Every day was going to be spiked with questions and assumptions now, like a field full of thistles, and if she was to make it to the other side, she'd have to learn to stamp them down.

The worst thing was, the medics couldn't or wouldn't tell her how worried she ought to be. It might not help to know.

When she returned from afternoon visiting, she found a creme egg sitting on her keyboard. Harry's doing. Then she noticed a new box of tissues underneath the one that was already open. That would be Madeleine, expecting the worst.

Joe's New Job

By the fourth morning of this new era, that is, the first Monday morning of the year 0 AS (After Stroke), Joe knew every fade in every fold of the blue fabric screen by his bed. Cornflower blue parched to ash grey in irregular stripes; bluest and best around the gathers at the top. He ought to be in his workshop now, admiring his model of the Parthenon. He asked himself a question. What was the most beautiful thing in this room right now? Take out the nurses, take out all the people, because that was cheating; take out the sky, because that was outside. Easy. The most beautiful thing on the ward was the extraordinary contraption they'd just used to get him out of bed and into this armchair. It was something he'd never seen before. Something between a camping stool and a shopping trolley. They called it an Arjo. It really was a thing of beauty and a design of genius. It had sleekly Scandinavian lines and a minimal number of parts. Gently curved blue plastic on a white tubular metal frame. They'd carefully manoeuvred him to sit on the edge of the bed. They wheeled the thing towards him and lined him up between two vertical flaps, which helped stop him slumping sideways; then he had to plant his feet – well, he had to plant one foot, they dealt with the other – on a little platform, and there was a rail in front of him to hold on to in order to hoist himself up to a stand. The care assistants kindly placed his useless hand on the rail for him and curled his fingers round. Once his bottom was off the bed (a scary moment because even with two people supporting him, he felt he'd topple over) they magically twisted the vertical flaps down and round to form a sloping seat behind him. He then sat back and could be transferred to his armchair, or better still – as he just discovered when he had been invited, at long last, to take a ride to the toilet – he could be wheeled around in an interesting Z posture, still holding the rail, and feeling rather important. Wait till Frannie saw that.

Being able to sit in a chair was opening up possibilities, too. A physiotherapist called Christine came up to visit him, and she'd brought with her another funny-looking bit of kit. It stood on the floor and had opposing handles which he was meant to grip and rotate, like the pedals on a bike. Christine put his right hand in position for him just as the care assistants had done earlier. They all seemed to think there was a point in pretending. Maybe there was. Maybe you could get better by sheer power of imagination. He knew his left hand could cope, and stared at the right hand willing the fingers not to slip off. They seemed stuck, so that was all right, in a way.

On the read-out in front of him, he could see two columns which were rising and falling, rather jerkily. One was his left side, the other his right. It meant he was pushing with both sides, even if one side was much stronger than the other.

'Your arm doesn't have movement yet, but your shoulder does,' she said. Incredible: how could you move, and not feel it? He couldn't feel his shoulder at all.

Then Christine performed a magic trick. She brought the bed table alongside Joe's chair and placed the towel on its smooth surface. Next, she laid the flat of his right forearm on the towel. He had to push from the shoulder and move it forward. And he could.

There was a lot to report to Fran when she and Jess came for the afternoon visit, although it was an uphill struggle getting them to understand about the hamburger-ham-back-handbag-hand bike. Nobody else was getting physio on the ward. Fran was bubbling with excitement at the way his face had improved since yesterday, whereas he was tiring fast. Then he yawned and she claimed that his arm had moved. She must be imagining it. As they talked, he yawned a couple of times again and in the end, he saw it for himself. With every yawn, the right arm would bend slightly at the elbow and the forearm would raise itself. OK, it didn't respond when he wanted it to, but at least this was a start. And it was no surprise that he now felt exhausted, because this had been his first day in a new job. The full-time job of getting better, so as to be in Shetland to hear his daughter play

Angela's Lesson

By the window, two beds away from her father, lay an elderly man who never moved. A wide tube emerged from his bed. The man's gaping profile haunted Jess; he'd come in a few days ago, had a second stroke and was now too ill even to sit up.

Jess didn't consider herself superstitious, but on that very first hospital visit, when she'd taken a wrong turn and found herself outside the mortuary, she'd been reminded that hospital was a place where people died. By Sunday evening, though, her father looked so much better and his speech was so much clearer that she was beginning to take heart and to believe in his recovery the way her mum did.

Which was just as well, because at half past ten on Monday morning the doorbell rang and there on the step stood her oldest pupil, Angela, in her trademark lilac leggings and grey rainwear, fiddle case slung across her back and stick in hand, straightening up to attention and jutting out her funny wrinkled little chin, ready for her lesson.

To get here, Angela had had to take a country bus, then walk a good half mile. What could you do but let her in? And put some proper shoes on.

After the lesson, Jess confessed, 'My partner was meant to call you on Saturday to cancel, and now I'm very glad he didn't.'

'Oh, that would be the flashy thing. It flashes to tell me someone called when I was out.'

'He probably left a message, then.'

'Probably.' Angela blinked. 'I never know whether it matters or not. Bad news finds you soon enough. But in any case, you were here.'

She looked very pleased with herself.

'That's started my week off on the right foot. I had a pig of a weekend, I don't mind telling you. The washing machine flooded and my cat's under the vet with his kidneys. It's the beginning of the end.'

'My dad had a stroke last Thursday,' said Jess. It must have sounded really random and she hadn't meant to diminish the sickness of Angela's cat.

'Ah!' said Angela, and checked herself only for a moment. 'How's he doing?'

Oddly, she really wanted to know, and Jess really wanted to tell her. It turned out Angela had had a stroke herself, ten years ago. She'd lost the power of speech for a while, and that was when she'd formed the wish to learn an instrument.

'And look at me now. But it takes time. Send your dad my love and tell him from me it's worth sticking at it.'

Jess drew several conclusions from this episode. One, people are tough, and they do recover. Two, a lesson cancelled is a lesson unlearned, and that might be for the teacher. Three, Matt thinks leaving a message is the same thing as communicating.

'You didn't mention that you hadn't actually spoken to Angela,' she told him when they caught up at the end of the afternoon to compare notes over the phone.

'Why did I need to? The answering service cut in.'

'She's a bit nutty, Angela. I don't think she picks messages up. But I love her. Anyway, how did the workshop go?'

'Yeah, good, real learning. I showed them a hypothetical example. Then we all did a simulation, you know the sort of thing, you've got a big purchase and you compare suppliers, so you score them against your objective criteria. Anyway, they worked out the maths, totted it up, and then – surprise, surprise – they didn't like the result. Picked the wrong supplier. Then they had to go back and change the priority scores so as to get the answer they wanted. Which of course was the main teaching point: you have to know what you want in the first place.'

'Why don't you just pick who you like and have done?'

'Because that would be completely subjective.'

'So, if I get the highest points score, but my company logo involves a swastika, I still get the contract?'

'You'd be insane to incorporate a swastika in a company logo '

'I would.'

'Also, if you're hiring, you'd embed social added value as one of your criteria.'

'If I was hiring, my idea of social added value would be this. The client actually gets to talk to a human being.'

The line fell silent for a moment. She imagined that confused look which came over his face at times like this; it was sweet, really, like a little boy struggling with long division. She couldn't be cross, when he'd done her a favour. Two favours, in fact: the official and the accidental. Seeing Angela had definitely helped.

Gill Oliver

As well as can be expected

Joe had been dumped in a strange place in the company of a man who groaned a lot and had the television on. There was another television somewhere outside this two-bedded room, tuned to a different station. Trees and the tops of parked cars were visible through the window to his left; he was on the ground floor now. He could smell the brightly patterned curtains crisping in the sun. The building must have been built from a kit, because the soft whoomp, whoomp of steps outside told you the floors were made of flat panels mounted on joists. So this was rehab.

He heard a familiar ring and took a while to recognise it as his own mobile. It was muffled and coming from a cupboard on his bad side. One glance was enough to know he couldn't reach it. Too bad. Ten minutes later, it rang again. Nothing he could do. When a nurse popped in to answer his room-mate's bell, he asked her to pass him the phone so he could at least see who had called. Perhaps Fran had been delayed getting back from work. But the caller's number wasn't recognised.

Probably a prospective client. He laid the phone on the blanket at his left side and gave some thought to what form of words he ought to use in order to explain that he couldn't take anything on right now. Nothing medical, a stranger wouldn't be interested. It was tricky, because he didn't want to put them off calling again at a later date, when he'd be up and running again. Only he didn't know what that later date was. The third time it rang, he almost didn't pick up; it was curiosity that made him fumble left-handedly for *answer.*

'Hello, is that Mr Faber?' It was a young woman's voice. It wasn't Jess. 'Look, do you think you can clear your diary for July 15 next year?'

Over a year away? With any luck he could be really busy again by then.

'Just for one day?'

Of course he could clear his diary, but what sort of job would be completed in a single day? Maybe it was the WI, wanting another of his World in Miniature talks. Amusing the first time, but he'd never been good at serial production. And it hadn't led to business. He didn't want to commit. It was too far off to know what other tasty things, including holidays, might be going on. And he didn't even know who this person was. Damned cheek. It all made him feel incredibly out of sorts. In fact, he didn't feel like talking to anyone.

'No,' he said. It came out nice and clear. 'I can't.'

The woman's voice rose to a whine, indignant: 'What do you mean, you can't?'

'I mean' – he thought carefully about where to place his tongue – my schedule isn't finalised.'

'What else will you be doing?'

'I don't know who I'm speaking to.'

'Yes, you do! It's Zanna.'

'Zanna.' In his mind's eye, he was back at the Moscow State Circus, and she had stepped out of the suitcase in the middle of the ring.

The voice softened and now she almost sang a lullaby, as though she were addressing an imbecile. 'Matthew's sister. We met the other day, in the hospital. Do you remember now?'

How could he have forgotten? But then, he hadn't paid that much attention to the voice when they'd met. Too engrossed in the spectacle. 'Ah. Yes. I r'member you.'

'So, will that be OK? 15th July.'

There was enough of a pause for her to backtrack. 'Oh, look, I'm sorry, I shouldn't have bothered you in hospital, it was stupid of me. I thought it would cheer you up. I'll try Mrs Faber again, and she can put it in your diary for you.'

'What?'

'The wedding! Only, I'm the official wedding planner, aren't I? So I'm planning it.'

His mind's eye presented a leaning tower of Pisa. Some planner. She didn't even know to start from the bottom.

'How are you, Zanna?'

'Me? I'm fine, thank you.'

And she rang off.

Not much later, Fran pitched up, looking a bit frazzled and apologising for taking so long to get there. He hadn't noticed. A lovely nurse called Jenna came to join them to do the paperwork, which meant a long series of questions. She tested him again on dates and prime ministers and suchlike, and it seemed things were getting back to normal now, although when Jenna asked did he know where he was, Joe had to say no. That was because he'd seen nothing from the ambulance and couldn't follow the route. They hadn't known this hospital existed until yesterday. He assumed this was Sheepcote Community Hospital, but its precise location was a mystery; which in his book meant not knowing where you were. Fran narrowed her eyes and told the nurse, 'This is what he's like. This is normal.' Then they were on to personal details all over again, but the general hospital had put someone else's address on his notes, so maybe it was just as well to re-cap. Jenna was surprised he wasn't on medication, because most patients of his age were. Obviously, this was proof that he wasn't fit to be ill. He'd seen the GP and had his blood pressure checked before signing on at the gym a couple of years previously, didn't smoke, definitely wasn't overweight, wasn't diabetic, drank in moderation, and hadn't been under any stress lately. So it really seemed to him that this stroke was one big clerical error, and the sooner they could sort it out, the better. When she said, 'It wasn't a thrombosis, was it?' Fran narrowed her eyes again and said 'He's a bleeder.'

By the time the questionnaire was over, he was exhausted. Fran pushed off to buy a couple of pairs of emergency pyjamas at the local 24-hour Tesco's. His room-mate had turned off the golf and was enjoying a very loud sleep. Joe drowsed, but jumped awake when Fran came back. She looked tense round the eyes. The only TV noise now was coming from the ward outside, but it still seemed to make her jump.

'Oh, that bloody racket,' she spat. 'We don't need it right now.'

If you didn't count the snoring man opposite, this was the first time they'd been alone since it had happened. He knew they ought to have things to say to each other, and she'd leant across the bed to hold hands, but bewilderment kept flickering across her face. Outside on the TV, some sort of drama was going on for other people's entertainment. She tried to recount her afternoon, wincing at every shout and every assault of the incidental music. From the look of her she hadn't enjoyed the drive to this distant hospital which neither of them had known about, and which he now learned was tucked inside a housing estate in a strange town. She'd had to make a couple of phone calls first to make sure which hospital she was visiting that night, in case they hadn't been able to arrange transportation. And it wasn't an ideal location.

'Nearly forty minutes each way! I could easily pop over to the General twice a day, but I can hardly call this a lunch break, can I? I'll only be able to see you once a day now, in the evening.'

She was down in the mouth about that, although Joe suspected one visit a day might be enough for both of them. She must be getting weary of all this racing around, on top of a day at work. How could he cheer her up? What funny thing happened today? Well nothing really, unless you put your daft-filter glasses on and looked at life through them.

So he said, 'Can you believe it? Some idiot rang me, trying to sell me a wedding.'

Instead of laughing, though, she clapped her hand to her head and said, 'Oh, I'd completely forgotten about that. She just got me in Tesco's. I was a bit short with her.'

'They have a date. We need an alibi, Frannie.'

'July next year. I'm not sure I can joke about this. I feel like we're all being steamrollered. Not just you and me, but Jess and Matthew too.'

'There's many a ship... many a *slip*... 'twix' – cup – and – lip. And I would know.' He gave her his best new idiot grin.

Fran smiled back and softened a bit.

'I sense panic on Zanna's part. Apparently, it has to be at St Cunegund's, and they book up so far in advance, she thought they might miss next year's season altogether.'

'Season?'

'Her words, not mine.'

'What's so special about St Cunegund's? Is his family r'ligious, then?'

'No, no, I doubt it. Apparently, it came in the top ten in Bouquet Magazine's *Venue for You* poll. It got five stars.'

'How does a church get five stars?'

'Dunno…. P'raps there's a pub next door?'

She shrugged and shook her head. But he could see her amusement was thin. The smile weakened as she breathed out slowly, and she was glum again.

'I just can't get my head round this, Joe. I'm happy for Jess, but I can't think about the wedding right now.'

She gripped his hands – one comfortably, one uncomfortably – and they looked hard at each other. Life suddenly so far apart was very strange. Apart not just because Joe was in hospital and Fran was at home, but apart because they couldn't have a proper hug, or even sit side by side. After a few minutes of saying nothing but frowning a lot, she seemed re-charged – at least, she began to fidget and swing her legs in the high armchair; so Joe said it was time to see these new pyjamas then. Tesco's finest. He could see this was to be the start of a new sartorial era: goodbye buttons, hello elasticated waist. He was prepared to hack it for a season.

Perhaps somewhere in the bashed-in tool box that was Joe's brain, there was a funny little torque wrench with a sense of purpose; it knew he was in rehab now, at vast public expense, so he ought to be getting down to serious work. At any rate, a couple of days after his arrival, something happened: he found he was able to raise his right foot. Not far, and not quickly; but seated in his armchair, he could raise the leg too, at least from the knee down. They told him this was a thing called spontaneous recovery; and it launched Fran and Jessie into a state of high excitement. But it wouldn't be complete. He didn't have much sensation yet. They said the leg would recover first, then the arm, and last of all the fine movements of the fingers. Last of all! These fine movements of the fingers were what had earned him his living. They said the most rapid gains would be in the first few months, but it was reasonable to expect continued improvement at a slower rate for years ahead. He thought for a moment about the acropolis and how he had destroyed it, then decided not to dwell on that. He could still speak, after a fashion, and his vital organs were all sound: he hadn't been left horizontal and hooked up to tubes, like the old man by the window back in the General. And he was more alert than his room-mate Eddie, whose wife had only monosyllables in answer to her conversation.

There was another milestone in his spontaneous recovery when he kicked Jenna in the face as the nurses were putting him to bed. Fallon was at his head, Jenna at his feet, and they'd done pyjamas. Getting comfortable was never easy; his right side was a dead weight, and in order to lie down and manoeuvre up the bed, he had to thrust his left shoulder backwards and kick off with his left foot in a series of jumps, hoping the rest of the body would follow. Fran said it looked like a seal trying to do backstroke up a dry shingle beach. Anyway, on this auspicious night, his right foot unexpectedly joined in, and jerked upwards. It lacked any real control, of course, and perhaps it was the sheer exuberance of unexpected movement which led it to wave up in the air and whack Jenna. Both nurses were visibly delighted. Jenna tucked a pillow between his over-excited and unfeeling foot – because he really hadn't felt a thing – and the bottom rails of the bed, to prevent arguments between them in the night, and told him how well he was doing.

Once they were gone, Joe pondered what *doing well* really meant for him now. Before the stroke, it would have meant having a steady flow of commissions, keeping the wolf from the door and avoiding boredom, with a decent holiday once a year. Kicking somebody unexpectedly in the face was not something he would normally have seen as an achievement. But then, the whole notion of acceptable behaviour had been re-defined.

They said you were meant to sleep a lot, after a stroke, and that was another thing he couldn't seem to do: sleep was there, somewhere, but always ahead of him. Tonight was no exception. His left side ached from lying on this bed too long. His thoughts spread and flattened until the modest triumphs of the day had disappeared and everything felt hopeless.

The night became a frozen ocean now. He was a massive ice-breaker all but trapped in the dark, with no other option but to plough slowly on, because there was no going back. From time to time, the fearsome echo of cracking ice reminded him he really had no business in this place.

In the morning, a trolley rattled him awake. He'd made the crossing, then. In time his mind cleared just enough for him to recognise that coming back from the dead was going to be a slow, slow business.

Joe Faber's Frenzy

Jess lay on her bed for a long time in the June twilight waiting for night to descend. That evening's visit had been hard going. Things were improving, but as far as his appearance went, her father was still someone she only half-recognised. Her ears were filled with the harsh sound of things that were all wrong: the random TV cackle at the hospital, the beepers calling for assistance, the washing machine running now at bedtime; and her thoughts were getting noisy too, chasing each other in relentless canon. What if he spent months in that hospital? What if he came out, but he couldn't travel? What if he could, but he shouldn't? What if he made the journey up to Shetland for the gig, but had another stroke because of the exertion: it would all have been her fault. She went to the door and looked down the landing where a low light came from her parents' bedroom.

'Mum,' she half whispered, 'I know it's late… Do you mind if I play?'

'No, I'd like that.'

There was a smile in her voice.

Jess picked up her fiddle and, in the gloom, started to play, music she'd known since childhood, pieces that she'd learnt for grades, exams, auditions. Tunes she'd composed. When her fingers couldn't remember, she lit a lamp and reached for sheet music. In a box file full of material from last year's Frenzy trip, she found manuscript papers in a familiar hand, arrangements by her friend Cath, things they'd performed together. It didn't matter that Cath wasn't there to play her line, she could feel her firm hug in the music. She worked down the box, picking only things she needed to hear now. There, like a jewel, was *Da Slockit Light*. She played it through several times, each time slower than before. It was a soulful tune, and now she burrowed deep inside it.

The next thing in the box was in her own hand, black ink on cream manuscript paper. It emptied her lungs of air. She'd forgotten all about this piece. It was something she'd written for her dad which had all started at a workshop in Lerwick last August, not long after her graduation, as a sort of thank you really, and she'd called it Joe Faber's Frenzy. It was wild and funny like him, a tight tongue-twister of a Shetland reel, syncopated, and made for the driven bow. It was music to dance to and to make you smile, and it ticked over at a rhythm which used to be his.

A rhythm which used to be his. Those words in her head shook her inside out. She sat on the bed and laid her fiddle down again. She let the silence in the house wash through her like a tide. Something gripped her throat, a sob perhaps, and with that sob came an idea which made her mind tingle and brought her to her feet again. She picked up the fiddle, and slowly brought her bow back up to the string.

To paint a portrait of her father would take a different music now. But it was already there, tucked safely in the centre of the reel.

First, she slowed the whole thing right down.

The obvious, text book move would be to put it all into the minor key, but that felt wrong; if you let it begin in the minor, though, it would be the shift to major that would open the heart. Her left ear bent to the music. If she stretched those first notes out, and smoothed away the stutter-rhythms, she'd have the makings of a fine slow air. Her fingers stretched up the fingerboard, feeling for the better line; if she just let it spread a little up the octave, instead of all that dainty stepping about; if she let that little knot unravel… if she just turned this, so… the piece found a new grace. As she played, she worked the tune like putty, re-forming it, re-shaping it, over and over until it was just so, until finally, at the very hilltop of the tune, the major key sang out. She couldn't put it down. Tentative at first, and conscious of her mother trying to get to sleep, she'd played at a whisper, without vibrato, but the closer it came to being right, the more tone she gave it, and the more she made it real. Her right arm stretched long and floated and danced easily on air, and her wrist coaxed the heel of the bow, no more, as the tune seemed at last to play itself. This was Joe Faber's Air.

Was she creating music, or was music creating her? She was grown bigger for it. She wouldn't try to write it down tonight.

She put the violin back in its case.

The silence of the house washed in again, but now it was a tide that had turned.

After a few minutes she heard light footsteps and her mother came to the door. She looked so little standing there.

'What was that, Jess? It was beautiful.'

'Oh… something old, something new.'

'It's Dad's tune, isn't it?'

She nodded. They smiled and hugged each other lightly, gently.

'Good night.'

'Good night, Mum.'

Long after the last stammer of the day was gone and the lights were out, Jess lay in bed playing it over and over in her head, imagining a performance, who knew when and who knew where – because it would be no time soon – but when her father was ready. Ready to enjoy it.

The Man in the Next Bed

Joe was wheeled into the garden soon enough and this confirmed his suspicion: the Community Hospital was one of those single-storey temporary buildings, beloved of the British public sector, which have become permanent. The bouncy floor meant that you soon learnt to tell what or who was approaching. A wheelchair, a patient walking with a Zimmer frame, the drugs trolley, the tea trolley – all soon became familiar. The purposeful step of the nurses was distinct from the easy gait of the Occupational Therapists and physios. One of the night nurses possibly had a day job on a building site, because she came in with what sounded like steel-capped boots, but most of the staff wore soft soles. Visitors, on the other hand, were a clattering lot, and could be slow-moving. Fran had a stomp out of all proportion to her size and Joe always knew when she was coming.

He never minded the footsteps and the busy noises. But he did mind the telly wars. The hospital Friends had charitably bought TV sets but no headphones. There was a set blaring right through the day in the communal ward around the corner from the twin room he shared with Eddie. There was one in the single room opposite, where the door was usually open. He and Eddie had one each, so whatever Eddie watched, Joe heard. It seemed a bit stupid to play his own at the same time and anyway, he'd never in his life watched daytime TV. The world expected it of him, now that he'd had a stroke. The best you could hope for was that everyone would be tuned to the same programme, and the favourite on the ward was one which seemed to feature a lot of people arguing, badmouthing family members and their boy/girl friends for lying, cheating, two-timing and generally coveting their neighbour's ass.

Eddie turned out to be partial to a bit of golf on TV, which at least was relatively quiet. This poor chap was in a bad way; anyone could see he wouldn't be golfing himself for a while. Like Joe, he couldn't walk, but much of the time he wasn't well enough for physio either, or even to get up and go to the bathroom in the morning. Then he'd soil the bed. He rang his bell often for help with everything, and explained his needs in a gruff voice and with much effort. His wife visited every day and sometimes took him off in the wheelchair to sit in the garden, but he was unable to hold a conversation with her. Joe's attempts to communicate had been barely acknowledged. He wasn't great company, but that wasn't his fault, and you had to feel sorry for him.

Then one evening a mate of his came round for visiting time and suddenly, as if by some miracle, he could talk. They sat watching some Open or another and chatting. Joe quickly learned a great deal about Eddie and his finances: the property deals he'd cut, the house in the south of France, the house in the Canaries, the work he was having done on the new build in Devon, the cost of everything. Including the cost of care. Once he left hospital, he told his mate, he'd be entitled to six weeks' social care on the state, after which he'd have to pay. Six weeks wasn't much; therefore, he reckoned, his best option was to stay in hospital for as long as possible. And in order to prolong his stay in hospital, he'd have to act sick.

The next time the nurse came to coax him out of bed for physio, Joe listened with a different ear. This man in his fifties obviously had a good handle on finance; but he was gambling his health away. Or perhaps he was one of those people who regarded sickness as a lottery anyway, with nothing to be done by the patient until it went away. Once again, his wife turned up to wheel him round the garden. Once again, he was limp and monosyllabic as the nurse helped with the transfer to the wheel chair. Joe got a glimpse of how life was going to be for Mrs Eddie, and promised himself it would not be so for Mrs Faber.

Hands Dirty

A whole working week had gone by, and the box of tissues which Madeleine had deposited by Fran's workspace was untouched. When Harry said, 'You still haven't eaten your creme egg,' she told him she was keeping it for an emergency.

'You might be needing it,' he said. 'Looks like they're going to take this place apart and put it back together again. They're definitely talking about flattening the management. That's the latest.' His voice was expressionless. 'I got it from Steve. Just this morning.'

'Steve from the Association?'

'Yup. He's talking to the Health Trust, trying to get assurances, like it's up to them, but...' He shrugged. 'Efficiency savings. Strip out the division managers, more section heads on a lower scale, one or two job losses, new contracts all round, change everybody's job description. That's what he thinks they're up to. Which I reckon means winners and losers.'

'You stand to be a winner, then,' said Fran. She stood to lose, being a division manager. Experience put you higher up the salary scale and made you expensive.

'Steve's not happy. I've got my own theory.'

'You're ready for more responsibility, though, Harry.' He'd been brilliant this week. 'You've proved you don't need me checking your work.' Not a flicker; he was more interested in his theory.

'The way I see it, they make everyone just that bit more responsible for decision making in their own area, which sounds great doesn't it, sounds democratic, on the face of things, to leave decision making to the people who know the job. Makes everyone feel good about themselves. But the beauty of it is, when someone makes a wrong call, or more likely, they haven't got the resources to meet demand, nobody can blame the Board. Hands clean, see?'

He shrugged and breathed out noisily, then stared at the floor as he said, 'Not everybody wants to be responsible for making decisions. Not when it comes to resources.'

His analysis was probably accurate. But Fran was surprised by the defeat in his voice.

'Surely though, Harry, you want to move up? You don't need to spend your whole life listening to people like me. You think for yourself. You're the problem-solver.'

Harry shook his head. 'Logic's one thing. Logic I can do. But since when were management decisions logical? Anomalies in test results, fine, I can sort that out. But people? Budgets? Seriously, Fran, between you and me, I'm not up for it. I don't want to get mixed up in that shit. Only I'm scared that if I tell them that, I'll be the one for the chop.'

'We're all expendable.' All this talk of change at work was about as badly timed as it could be.

'They're sending out another letter next week. And Steve's going to call a meeting.'

'It's wait and see, then,' said Fran. He neither agreed nor disagreed, but shifted his gaze from the floor and looked her in the eye.

'I'm not after your job, you know.' He volunteered this information in the same deadpan voice as before.

What was going on behind those eyes? She hadn't expected Harry to put himself in her shoes, or consider her feelings; was that what he was doing now? Or was he just getting things straight and clear? Although Harry was dark-skinned, there was a symmetry in his features, and a smoothness, that put her in mind of Matt; except that Matt was prone to flashes of enthusiasm, and he tended to mirror other people's distress; whereas Harry's brow was unlined and stayed that way. Harry was a few years older than Matt, but those years barely showed.

Maybe he was scared.

She said, 'It's new territory for all of us.'

'Right. But you can do that shit, Fran. You don't mind getting your hands dirty. You don't mind muscling in to fix stuff if you have to. Oh, don't get me wrong, I didn't mean… I didn't mean it in a bad way. Somebody's got to… I just mean, it's not my thing. No offence.'

It was as if his sharp eye had scanned her conscience and homed in on that one nasty little anomalous cell… She might as well tell him, if we were admitting our weaknesses now.

'You're right about me. I've just done something… well, I can't quite believe what I've just done.'

He raised his eyes and listened.

'I've wangled Joe an upgrade. He's getting his own room.'

'Why feel bad about that?'

'Oh, you know… Special treatment… It isn't fair to other patients. They don't all have bossy relatives who can come in and make demands.' She felt half-proud, half-ashamed, and flushed with surprise at her own behaviour. 'I just had to do it. Well, honestly. It's so noisy in there with all those TV sets blaring all day. I can't believe it doesn't bother some of the other patients, but they all seem to go along with it. He won't. So I explained to the staff nurse that Joe still had his mental faculties. And I told her he was used to a calm environment at home, and that for him, the telly noise was a form of torture. I told her if anything could be done, it would make a big difference to his wellbeing. Because it would.'

'Right. Course it would. It all sounds crazy.'

'And he's still Joe, after all. Same likes and dislikes. *They* haven't changed.'

73

Harry shook his head as he told her, 'Don't see what you're worried about. One man's single room is another man's solitary confinement.'

'I hadn't considered that.'

'Too wrapped up in your feelings,' he said, still shaking his head. 'But that's not surprising right now.'

He'd made her smile.

'I rate you, Harry.'

'Thanks.'

She thought about that conversation all the way home. Funny, wasn't it, that you could give up your seat and take your turn and sign petitions and vote responsibly and bang on about social equality and fairness and access and protecting the NHS; you could write to your MP and make the food bank a standard item on your shopping list and collect for every humanitarian cause under the sun and shout about the needs of the many not the few. But when it came to an individual she truly, truly loved, she'd pulled rank. She'd been articulate, and she'd hustled. She'd do it again, if need be.

A thought walked into her head. In his judgments of her, Harry was dispassionate. In fact, there was no passion at all in Harry's life. How different would things be if there were? Imagine: Harry plus a passion… A woman, a hobby… The thought walked away as she turned her attention to the list of things she'd need for visiting tonight.

Wee Bottles

It was inevitable that sooner or later he'd be rumbled and sure enough, one night, Fallon and Jenna found the secret stash of wee bottles. They never gave you enough. It was easy enough to hoard them during the day because there was always someone different on duty and Joe made sure he asked for two at a time. When actually, most of the weeing was nocturnal and one of the things that stopped him sleeping. The grey cardboard urinals were situated where they were meant to be, hooked to the side rail of the bed, and also where they were not meant to be, under the bed, in the cupboard behind the laundry, anywhere within that one-yard radius that he could reach with his tickling hand. Joe didn't like to call it his good hand because that was a bit harsh on Mr Right, made him the bad guy; and you couldn't call it the hand that worked, because it only really worked on its old left-hand jobs. It probably couldn't aim and thwack a hammer, for example, all it would be able to do was hold the nail and hurt when Mr. Right screwed up. One-handed peeing turned out to be its biggest challenge, in fact, because it had to control the aiming device whilst also supporting the increasing weight of the receptacle. All this with its owner flat on his back. So you were doing it uphill, really.

He told Fallon that one urinal was not enough for his prodigious piss, and he didn't want them to have to change the bed in the middle of the night just because they couldn't answer the bell in time. They underestimated his prowess. Anyway, far from confiscating his stash, they had a laugh about it. Fallon worked up the north end of Joe, sorting out his arm, while Jenna fearlessly went down south to attend to his right foot.

'So how are the wedding plans coming on?' asked Fallon.

'Major problems on the frock front. Bridesmaids can't agree. Jess doesn't agree with any of them.'

'Oooh, colours can be a touchy subject,' said Jenna.

'Matt's suggested a video conference. Or Skype, as we amateurs call it.'

'What does this Zanna do for a living?'

'Vents Management. Trainee.'

'Oh, she could have some handy contacts, then,' said Jenna, sunny as ever. Bless her. So pure in heart. He explained that Zanna's wedding present was, precisely, to organise the wedding. Jenna and Fallon had finished tucking him in and they both stood back from the bed to approve, whether this news or their handiwork, he couldn't tell.

'She's moon thing... moonlighting,' he told them. 'The boss doesn't know.' He had to concentrate on pursing his lips properly so as to explain, 'She's Wonder White Weddings, by night.'

'You're not exactly looking over the moon about that, Joe.'

'I'll spoil the photographs. Dribble on the cake and leave a dam-patch in the tent. Sorry, *mar-kwee.*'

'Oh, come on,' said Fallon, 'they won't be holding the reception in the middle of the night,' – she shook the nearest grey urinal – 'so at least you're in the clear on that score.'

She stood musing, too absent-minded to put the article down.

'What's he like then, this...'

'Maffew.'

'Matthew, yes.'

'Bootless.' Fallon and Jenna exchanged looks, and he explained. 'Came on a walking holiday. Wales. No boots.'

Fallon made a funny face.

'He's or-right though. Mad on Jess.'

'That's the main thing,' said Jenna.

'Means well. 'Sgot credibly shiny hair.'

'We nearly called our eldest Matthew,' said Jenna. 'It means gift of God.'

'Aw…' said Fallon.

'Only it was a girl'.

Gift of God. So, Matthew Harrington. God's Gift. Joe slipped that one in his pocket, for possible future use.

Targets

Before he'd even reached the threshold, Matt was ready to be excited by Joe's new room. For starters, Joe would be the only sick person in it, which was a huge uptick for the visitor experience. The General Hospital had brought on nausea. Their signage was a font that came straight out of your first reading book, and advertised scary facilities you hoped you'd never need. Multiple sickness options, all in your face. In comparison, the Sheepcote was less an institution, more a unit, with nothing threatening to distract you or to bring you down en route to the ward. Plus, patient-wise, they wouldn't admit you if you weren't going to get better. So this was strictly the winners' enclosure. They expected Joe to work, and according to Jess they made him go to the gym every day. It was all an education, really, because before this week, Matt had imagined 'going into rehab' meant taking it easy in a quaint old red brick building with shrubberies and lawns, where colourful people who'd overdone the stimulants wandered round in their silk dressing gowns, or got wheeled onto verandas where they could swap tales of life on the edge. This was not that.

'You've got your own washbasin now,' he said.

He cast his eye over Joe's new single room, seeking out the positives. The furniture – bed, armchair, tallboy, bed table, stacking chairs – was identical issue to that in the room he'd shared with Misery Man, except that now there was more space for visitors, and the wheelchair wasn't in anybody's way.

'Different curtains,' said Jess.

'Orange instead of blue. Less zen. More dynamic. It's good. That's what you need, Joe. A bit of energy in the room.'

Because Joe was definitely looking older. The mouth was no longer as grotesquely lop-sided as it had been in those first few days, yet there was still something odd about the face. He struggled to remember what it used to look like.

Jess drifted over to the window and looked out, then quickly turned her attention back to where her dad sat in bed. 'What can you see out of here, Dad?'

'Sky,' said Joe, 'flat wall, flat roof.'

'At least you can admire your cards now.' The get-well cards were no longer by his side but stuck with blu-tack on the wall opposite the bed. Matt watched Jess finger them one by one, inspecting even the ones she'd seen before; some had been up for over a week. Why was she doing that? Nervous activity, something to do? Then he realised: positive strokes. She was getting positive strokes from reminding herself about all the people who'd taken the trouble to send a card. You couldn't have enough positive strokes at a time like this. So he'd join in.

'You're getting a fan base, Joe.'

'Yes. I don't even know some of these people.'

'Madeleine works with Mum, doesn't she? She's found you a nice *man* card, Dad.' It showed golf clubs sticking out of a bag, with the message *Sorry you're feeling under par*. 'I can see you two have never met.'

'Nice thought, though,' said Matt.

'Yes,' said Joe. His voice switched from bright to serious: 'Anyway, something else happened today. Look. I can do... *this...*'

There was a moment's pause during which Matt wondered what. Then he realised Joe was staring at his right hand, clenched as it always was nowadays, and lying with the flat of the wrist uppermost on the bed. There was a funny, determined look on Joe's face, mixed with a very slight smugness, as if he was going to bend a spoon or something. Slowly, and with a few little jerks on the way, he lifted the hand from the bed and opened it enough to present a two-fingered salute. He bent the fingers back in and straightened them out several times, eventually allowing himself to look up at Jess, then Matt, for approval.

Of course, Jessie was ecstatic to see her father open his hand again. This was so what she needed. She whipped out her phone to video it, and she was grinning all over her face.

'Your message to the world. Nice one, Dad.'

'It happened this morning. Before the move.'

'You been practising?' asked Matt.

'Oh yes,' said Joe, 'I practised on Eddie. To pass the time. While I waited for the taxi.'

Eddie? Ah yes, the Misery Man in the other room.

'It's all looking good for Shetland, then,' he said, and he really thought he was being supportive. But Jess – who'd been all smiles a moment ago – growled at him.

'Don't add pressure, Matt.'

'It's not pressure, Jess. No pressure, Joe.'

'Let's just take it a day a time, shall we?' said Jess.

Oh, oh, oh, she was really touchy about the Shetland gig. He should've seen that coming. This wasn't about Joe, this was just classic displacement, wasn't it, because she was bricking it and she'd be only too pleased not to be going up north herself. She'd said yes, but she was struggling with the follow through. And he'd said to her, hadn't he, come on Jessie, you are what you do, not what you say you'll do. Call yourself a fiddler? Well fiddle.

He was very glad and not at all surprised when her father put her straight.

'*They* think I should go. The ferrapists. They say it's a goal.'

Ha, thought Matt. Exactly. He could safely leave this to Joe.

'They like goals. Physios. They pick up goals like a mango picks... like a... *magnet*... picks up pins. You have to have a goal, in here. Written down.'

Jess screwed up her nose.

'It's like your tariff. For a convict.'

She didn't look impressed.

'They're not like us, Jess. Oh no. They believe in targets.'

Joe stretched out his left arm to grip her hand, in a funny sort of pantomime gesture, and it was suddenly clear what was wrong with his face. His forehead was all crinkly. He might be doing his wicked smile thing, or he might be going to burst into tears: the point was, you couldn't tell. He was permanently on the brink of both.

'They believe you need goals for motivation. You need something to aim for. They say.'

'Joe, I couldn't have put it better myself,' said Matt. 'And... apologies for the jargon here... but isn't going to the Frenzy a classic SMART target? Simple, manageable, achievable and time-defined?'

'Well it might be time-defined, but I'm not so sure about the rest,' said Jess. The sunlight was catching the stray outer curls of her hair, and making them glow. Snaky. Angry. Luscious. She was still frowning.

He turned towards Joe and tried to find as neutral a tone as possible. 'What do *you* think, Joe? Is the trip to Shetland an appropriate goal for you? Is it a powerful motivator?'

'My motor…,' – Joe raised an eyebrow in amusement – 'my motivator…is the thought of getting off my bottom. Tomorrow'd do. Or the next day. Soon as I can.'

'Exactly,' said Jess. 'That's the point. It takes the time it takes. You can't start imposing deadlines on Dad's recovery, Matt.'

Maintaining eye contact with his future father-in-law in the bed, Matt nodded, and focused on regulating his breath, because this was a hard thing to hear. She might be right: he wasn't a doctor and he couldn't know. Also – and this was humbling, but you had to remember – some people did just have intrinsic motivation. Wow. Maybe his Jessie was wired that way too. Interesting.

Joe hadn't finished.

'About the Frenzy gig…Course I want to go.' Joe's lips were working hard, taking care to place each syllable. 'Look what I've lost. I don't want that taken away from me too. It isn't a goal. It's a need.'

'Oh Dad!' Jess went all teary. Matt drew a nicely pressed hanky from his trouser pocket and handed it to her.

'But look,' said Joe, 'if it motivates this lot to fast-track me out of here, great. I'll sign up to any goal they like. If it works for them, it works for me.'

'Win win,' said Matt, feeling he'd won, too. A world without targets made no sense.

Gill Oliver

Bad Liar

The deep apricot lipstick wouldn't fool Joe. It was brave face
stuff and Fran knew it. She knocked over a plastic beaker of
water and swore a bit, then put Joe's clean pyjamas in the
locker without first taking the laundry bag away, which was
her normal, efficient method. She thrust her hand back down
into the cupboard, too lazy to move round and look at what
she was doing, and set off a floppy battle between soft,
shapeless objects she could feel but couldn't see. Then she sat
down in the high-backed hospital armchair. Her feet barely
touched the floor, but she didn't feel like swinging her legs
today. Two weeks in, and she was weary. So she asked, 'Have
you got room for one more?' and slipped off her shoes. Joe
shifted as best he could and she moved onto the bed beside
him, carefully negotiating the side rail and lying on her side
so as to fit. He couldn't put his arm around her properly, but
she drew her left arm around him. This was new, and another
good thing about having his own room. They just lay quietly
for a while and she started to stroke Joe's disobedient hand,
then eventually they swapped notes on the day.

She usually came straight from work, but it was a Saturday
and she'd called in to look on the allotment. She hadn't
intended to tell him how it had made her feel, but couldn't
deliver the facts without giving herself away. The first reason
for her dismay was the state of the allotment itself. A
fortnight's neglect during the growing season, with one warm
and dry week during which she hadn't watered, followed by
five days of rain, had wreaked havoc. The brassicas were
spindly, victims of drought and flea beetle; weeds had overrun
the potatoes; and she blamed herself for starting off the French
beans too early, because now they were leafless and lifeless,

just so many snail-eaten stumps. They were past saving, she told him.

They agreed that maybe this year the best strategy for the allotment would be damage limitation. Fran grunted and stiffened her limbs in a spasm of bitter resolution. 'I'm going to hoik it all out,' she decided, 'and clear the lot. Maybe cover the ground with something. Unless we want to open a nettle farm.'

'Stop fidgeting,' he said.

'Was I?' She fell silent then twitched a bit more, on purpose this time, because she was doubly cross with herself for getting despondent and letting him see.

She hadn't shared, and wasn't going to share, the latest on the re-structuring at the lab, from yesterday's brief meeting, because nothing was definite; but she could see her job disappearing like the French beans, and come to think of it, maybe that was why the state of the vegetables had upset her so much. She'd invested a lot of energy, love even, into her work at that lab, but that was irrelevant to the people who'd make the decisions. She'd probably be able to negotiate the option of stepping down in terms of responsibility, or at least cutting back her hours, and that would give her more time with Joe, which was a big positive. Also, it might solve a few problems for her colleagues if she offered to go part time. Nobody had suggested this, of course; friends were too nice and management too careful. But it might be the right thing to do, for everybody. They'd have to manage a big drop in income.

'It's only one season,' said Joe. 'We've got to think long term.'

Deliberately now, she gave another shudder, so as to shake off the thought that if she did carry on working, and Joe's

83

recovery was incomplete, it could be the end of the allotment altogether.

'Maybe it'll do me good to chuck it all on the compost. I could do with expending a bit of energy right now.'

'Just don't spend it on me,' said Joe, ''cos I'm feeling a bit snail-eaten myself.'

And he told her about the Saturday physio, and how this morning his foot had turned under him not once but twice – painlessly, of course, but he was sure it must be sprained. The Saturday physio hadn't considered it a problem.

'I'll have a look in a minute,' said Fran, and she really meant it, but her immediate need was to snuggle closer. Soon Joe had to point out that his left arm was dead now. Either he'd had another stroke, or there was a ten-toed bed sloth sitting on it.

'Oh,' she said, 'that would be me,' and she drew away and propped herself up on her elbow. They'd need her income for the mortgage. The thought sickened her, but it wasn't a good idea to borrow trouble. She should wait until she had the facts. Then there was the wedding. Oh, the wretched wedding. She screwed her eyes up very tightly.

'You're making those noises again,' said Joe. He claimed she always made clicking noises when she was annoyed. 'What else is it?'

'It's Jess. This wedding business. It's just all happening too fast for her, if you ask me.'

'I thought Matt had the knack of calming Jess down.' Which Fran had to admit was true, however incomprehensible to her.

'He's not the one doing the pushing. It's his sister. Perhaps it's all just too fast for *me*. But she's got the Frenzy to think about first.'

No sooner had Jess said yes to the Frenzy gig than she'd got cold feet. Fran had been sharp with her. *You can be anxious or you can be excited, that's your decision. If you were a bloke, you wouldn't think twice. You'd get on with it.*

It was nice to be lying on the bed with Joe. Still, comfortable, cushioned. Everything outside this room felt so precarious now. All the hurrying and the jolting. Fran had already given away her glumness about the allotment and she really mustn't worry Joe further.

She'd picked up a juicy piece of gossip, though. He'd like this.

'I bumped into Marjory at the allotment. She knows Zanna from singing. Apparently, she's got a bit of a reputation. She's been through every unattached man in the choral society. Or at least that's the rumour. Marjory says they probably exaggerate but there's no smoke without fire. Marjory reckons it's like a form of collecting with her.'

'*I-Spy Book of Blokes*, eh?'

'Mm… She doesn't exactly dress like a nymphomaniac, though, does she? So neat and tidy and… prissy, really.'

'They're the worst sort,' said Joe. As if he'd know.

Fran snorted. 'I can't imagine her getting over the hygiene issues.'

'There is another 'terpretation.' Joe had recently taken to pruning unnecessary syllables. 'Perhaps she's looking for Mr Right. Hence the obsession with weddings.'

'So, you're a psychologist now.'

'No, seriously. Think about it, Fran. What sort of a man could live with Zanna for more than a weekend?'

'A stud who doesn't mind his whole life being scheduled.'

'Then we have to find this bloke. We need a decoy. Give her something else to think about besides Jess and Matt.'

'What do we do? Set up a blind date? Pop a small ad in the local paper? I'll leave the wording to you.'

Joe started to giggle and it took him a while to spit it out. But when he did slowly deliver his text, he hit the nail on the head.

'Wanted. Partner – with brains – but no drive – for career woman – with drive – but no brains.'

'Must have own car.'

'Sense of humour unnecessary.'

Fran stretched out and luxuriated in the fact that Joe had made her laugh. Better still, he'd started building one of his crazy wobbly towers of fantasy again, just like he always used to. This stuff and nonsense was the best thing she'd heard all day. All week.

No Tomato Sandwich

By the third week in hospital, the get-well cards numbered three rows stretching all the way from the washbasin to under the telly. But their rate of arrival was slowing down. People expected him to get well soon, and he was letting them down. Even Fran, who was taking his recovery with apparent stoicism, told him, 'I can see how things are going to be. You're going to sit there like Molière's invalid while we all orbit around you.'

Of course, this was a joke. When Joe had been training in set design, back in the eighties, he'd been given the brief from hell, as he saw it. The play in question was a farce called *The Hypochondriac*. French. There wasn't much to do, scenery-wise; the main character barely moves from centre stage. But he's visited by a long list of idiots. Joe thought he'd cracked it by picking up the idea of the motion of the planets, and he placed the eponymous Hypochondriac in the middle of a 17th-century orrery, which was a sort of brass model of the universe with moving parts representing planets in their orbits. In Joe's model, the characters made their stage entrance on gyrating saucers, and the maquette looked fabulous – you could make it turn by cranking a little handle, and everything. But apparently it wouldn't do, because if you were to scale it up for construction in an actual theatre, it would need some serious engineering, lots of metal, and power. Also, the elegant tilt of his ellipse meant the actors might fall off. To his tutor's relief, Joe had given up stage design and stuck to models ever since. Anyway, the point Fran was making was that though he had no movement, Joe had acquired phenomenal density, and his own gravitational pull was beginning to dictate the motion of others around him.

Joe took an interest in his visitors while they were in the room, but he didn't have the energy to be bored, so their absence was OK too. He was fully occupied trying to make sense of himself. He realised he must be coming round to normal ways of thinking, though, when he challenged himself to recall the people who'd actually walked through that door in the last fortnight.

Fran came once a day after work, swapped laundry for clothes, and left at bedtime. Always wearing lipstick these days. She was here most. But she was mostly not here.

Then Jess – either in a complete rush, or apparently catatonic. Sometimes with Matthew.

Ah, Matthew. He was nice to Jess, obviously besotted, and that was a good thing. Giving a lot of advice for a young man, though. His latest was that apparently visualisation promotes healing. Let's just try that, shall we. Imagine: your right hand grips that plate of trifle and lifts it clear off the table. When Matthew says the phrase *another technique you can use,* your arm moves back then forwards so as to smash the trifle in his face.

He was less aware of other people's visitors now he had his own room. Eddie's mates were still very much in evidence, and he caught snatches of laughter and loud talk about his various properties, what to keep and what to sell. Eddie remained silent whenever his wife visited. No jokes for her. She was sentenced to a lifetime caring for a selfish, graceless bastard. He despised this man.

A reverend: it was his job to visit every other Wednesday. Seen twice.

Doctor? What do you mean, doctor? There was nothing for a doctor to do, no wonder drug. It was down to him and the physiotherapists now.

One speech ferrapist. He'd read out her list of five-syllable words well enough for her never to come back.

The most extraordinary visitor of all, and a complete one-off, was the Psychologist. (Apparently. Because she hadn't told him who she was, at the time.) Their conversation pretty well summed up where things stood in terms of his recovery, and the memory was hard to shake off.

She was thin, pale, and with the sort of slight face and figure you could imagine crouched behind a loom in some Victorian mill. Dark clothes, black bic biro, file, packet of tissues. She wore that blanket magnolia makeup – the colour and texture of masonry paint – that told you a young woman was scared of something. She asked did Joe mind them having a chat because it was three weeks since his stroke. She had a list of questions to which she would have known the answers if she'd read his notes. It was clear that she was dreadfully unhappy.

Whiny hair, and a lank voice – they sort of blended together. She had an unhealthy interest in stuff he couldn't do. Could he get out of bed on his own? No. So, he couldn't get to the bathroom then? No. Could he walk with a frame? No. But Joe told her he was a whizz on the parallel bars. (OK, so it took one therapist to place his feet correctly one in front of the other, and another at square leg to watch the wobble.) 'Not walking yet then,' was her cheery comment. Was he getting about with the wheelchair on his own?   No, he couldn't steer, and didn't have a lot of power in the right side. Could he write? No. Was he reading? No, he couldn't concentrate. Using the same left hand to hold a book and turn the pages wasn't easy, either.

And before the stroke, what did he do? Joe told her. 'You made models? That's unusual,' she said, although she looked more disappointed than interested. Then it was hobbies and did he still enjoy them as much as before. No, he said, because he couldn't do them. Playing the piano, the allotment, obviously not. His favourite music was on the phone but touchscreen turned out to be useless because, as he explained, touching wasn't enough, you had to learn to let go. Not a glimmer of a smile from his young friend; in fact, she just looked pained. Still, she said, he had the telly, didn't he? Joe put her straight on that: other people's deafness plus daytime TV equalled toxic reaction. Hence the single room. Did he like being with other people? That depended on the people. The nurses were lovely. Joe tried to cheer her up by telling her, still, there's Radio 3 on this telly, you're never more than eight feet from a requiem, so it's not all bad.

On it went. Did he mind not being able to do things, or did he find he didn't feel like doing much anyway? He minded a lot. So overall, how was he feeling about what had happened?

Well, overall, he was quite cross really. So, he'd say he was angry then? Yes. And did he let this anger out in any way? Joe nearly said, oh, so they told you about me assaulting the chaplain, but thought she might take him literally. You ought to nurture the young, not take the piss. Besides, she was trying to be sympathetic, and she looked so unhappy in her work. So he suggested the anger made him want to get better. And she sort of sang, in a weird atonal kind of way, 'So, anger, but quite a useful anger then?' Yes, useful anger. That was it. Now she gave herself permission to smile. Evidently the interview was working towards a resolution: she raised her black bic biro and read her final question from the sheet: when he left hospital and got home, what was Joe looking forward to doing first? A stupid, impossible bloody question and none of her business anyway. So he said, 'Hall, stairs and landing. They really need a coat of paint.' She wrote something down and looked concerned.

When he told Fran about this visitor, he wondered aloud why they would send such an obviously depressed and depressing young woman to annoy the patients.

'Sounds to me like that was a psychological assessment. Only she was meant to be assessing you.'

His wife seemed to think this was funny.

'Well I'm very concerned. For her welfare. And annoyed. I don't need to be reminded. About everything that's wrong.'

His right hand lay there on the coverlet, good for nothing much. The long fingers looked swollen to him, and ever since movement had started to return, they hurt like hell. His left hand moved across to rub them.

'Just feel,' he said, and lifted his right arm. 'Like ice. But to me, they're hot.'

Cold to the touch, they burned, ached and throbbed. The index finger and thumb repelled each other like opposing magnets. He must refuse to get used to this.

Fran chafed his hand. 'It's never a good thing to cast yourself as a victim, though. That's why they talk about stroke survivors, these days, not stroke victims.'

But he had to take issue with her there, because running through that questionnaire had made Joe realise that a victim was exactly what he was. The stroke wasn't something he had caused or wanted. One minute he was healthy and happy and the next he was like this.

There was plenty else for Joe to be usefully angry about. Matthew's bloody mother for a start.

Matthew's mother had called Fran to introduce herself and to discuss the wedding. Which was a nice gesture, she said. Joe asked how she sounded on the phone, and a blank look came over her face as she gazed into the middle distance.

'Big,' she told him. 'She sounds big. Much bigger than her daughter.'

'You can't tell a thing like that. Come on, I want hard facts. What did you find out about them?'

Fran re-focused and made proper eye contact again.

'Her name is Janet and she comes from Cheshire. Her husband's called Derek. She's very well spoken, and she says *Derek and I all* the time. *This is wonderful news for Derek and I,* that sort of thing. We'll find out about them soon enough, because they want to invite us round for dinner once you're out of hospital, so that we can all get to know each other. She's not up for visiting, by the way. She says she's got post-viral syndrome and she'd hate to bring that into a hospital. I think Zanna warned her off. *She* hasn't been back, has she?'

Joe accused Fran of being shrewish and she said, 'Yup.' They agreed it was early days and they ought to give the Harringtons the benefit of the doubt, because they might be a charming couple for all anyone knew. But after Janet had called four times in as many days, there was no doubt at all. The woman was turning out to be a pest.

'Honestly, love, I'm sure she thinks I'm giving her the runaround, because I'm always on my way out of the house when she calls, and I tell her it's visiting time, but that doesn't seem to register. And today she had the nerve to say, *Isn't he better yet?* Because her friend's husband had a stroke, and he was back at work a fortnight later.'

'I told you I was a lingerer.'

'Yes, you are. And no wonder, when you're surrounded by women waiting on you hand and foot. Literally.'

In fact, the question of Joe's leaving date was already under discussion. The Health Authority was trialling a thing called Early Supported Discharge, which sounded a bit like early release for good behaviour, or like being let out on parole, because if you didn't shape up they'd take you back. Instead of using the hospital gym, the physiotherapist came to your home. A cynic might say it was a way of freeing up a bed; the therapists said the home was a more stimulating environment for rehabilitation. Joe subscribed to both theories. It made no difference. He didn't feel equipped to move on.

The optimistic half of his therapy was about being able to do things in a genuine way, re-wiring the brain so that the body re-learned how to make movements it had done before, and that consisted of pure physical exercises such as bringing each fingertip in turn to touch the thumb. There was a simple elegance to all this, like playing scales: boring, but essential for fluency. But they also had to teach him how to cope with *not* being able to do things properly: always putting the first sleeve on the disobedient arm, the first trouser on the disobedient leg, that sort of thing, stuff which hadn't mattered before. This was what they called *strategies*, which was the sort of language Matthew used. In fact, Joe reflected, it wasn't just Matthew, it was everybody. When Joe first encountered the word *strategy*, as a lad, it was all to do with military cunning: it was a masculine, muscular, heroic word, about how to win. Nowadays, most of the time you heard that word, people had in mind a coping mechanism, in which some sort of defeat was implicit. At any rate, there was a lot to come to terms with, and a lot to learn, and he knew he hadn't mastered it yet. Although he'd probably be as terrified about going home in eight weeks' time as he would be about going home next week.

Back to the wedding. Janet's concerns were, according to Fran, 'All farty faffy stuff about the difference between ivory and ecru.' Zanna had presented her outline plan for the couple's consideration: church wedding at St Cunegund's, white wedding (or maybe ivory or maybe ecru, but definitely not cream because that could be yellow and yellow didn't really work for an English rose complexion), reception at Highams Hall which was virtually next door to the church, Smarts for the caterers, a sit-down meal. When Fran warned her that Jess had been thinking of the Jolly Roger, she'd made an '*eow*' noise in disgust and asked would they need to limit it to 100 guests? Although of course when you gave birth to a baby girl you knew you needed to start saving for her wedding. (Fran made a most unbecoming gagging mime at this point of her narration.) The thing was, did they know how many guests there would be from the bride's side? Fran had suggested that it was surely for the couple to decide who or whom they wanted to invite. Of course, said Janet, so maybe they could discuss that with Jess, because she didn't seem able to focus on the matter and as for Matthew, well, you knew what men were like.

'It's over a year off,' he said.

'I know,' answered his wife, in a mock patronising voice, 'but you wouldn't understand, dear, because apparently you're only a man. There's so much to organise. For example, Janet tells me we'll need to coordinate our outfits at some point in the future.' She might have suggested fascinators, fishnet stockings and alligator handbags, from Fran's grotesquely brittle grin.

'Oh, and they haven't decided between morning dress and lounge suits for the gentlemen, and she wanted me to sound out your views on that. She's for morning dress, but Derek prefers lounge suit, so you might've had a casting vote there. But don't worry, I told her you'd stick with the kilt.'

'You what?'

'Well honestly. It'll keep her off your back.'

'Wasn't she spicious?'

'She said, *Eow, I didn't know there was a Faber tartan*, so I made up some rubbish about there being Campbells on your mother's side.'

'Because of the soup.'

'No,' said Fran tartly, 'I chose the Campbells for their legendary fierceness. *The Campbells are coming, hurrah, hurrah.*'

At that point, almost as if she had a sixth sense, Fallon popped in to take Joe's blood pressure – they did this three times a day – and commented that they sounded to be enjoying themselves. So they denied it and told her what it was all about, and she said she could just see him in a kilt. But he'd

94

have to learn to stand up first, in order to put it on. He thanked Fallon and told her that was all the motivation he'd need. She cocked her head to one side and made a long 'mmmm' noise, then said he was 179 over 110 again. They liked your blood pressure to come down naturally after a stroke, but if it was over 180, they'd normally suggest medication, because of the high risk of a having a second one.

'The thing is, you're hovering just under 180 all the time. I don't feel happy with that, Joe. I think we ought to talk to Dr Dean and get her to look at these numbers.'

She looked across at Fran, who looked at Joe, and they nodded agreement. After she'd gone, they were quiet for a while and Fran said, 'I'm glad she said that. It would have been easy for her not to, if you're within the guidelines. But it's better not to take any risk.' They told each other that Fallon, like all the nurses there, seemed to have experience and her gut instinct was probably right.

The thought of a second stroke when he hadn't yet recovered from the first was chilling. They went over once again how this had all come out of a clear blue sky. Ten years ago, when life had been much more stressful, and they'd had all those problems with Jess's schooling, and Joe had been chasing work all over the country because they were so worried about money, it might have been less surprising. But recently things had settled down and life had been ticking over very happily, with proper holidays and time for the gym as well.

Fran said, 'You know what's difficult to come to terms with? Up till now, being ill, for you, meant three days in bed taking headache pills and having nothing to eat, then on the third day you'd ask for a tomato sandwich, and I'd know you were on the mend. But with this, there isn't going to be a tomato sandwich moment, is there?'

They didn't say it, but Joe knew they were both scared that he might not even make it through the night.

He did, however, and woke up with an irritating tune in his head.

The Campbells are coming, hurrah, hurrah…

He wasn't beaten yet.

The Jolly Roger

Zanna had eventually ground Jess down. It was time to get serious about planning this wedding, she insisted, and if she really was going to help, they all needed a proper meeting. Jess persuaded her best friend Annie to come along too, for moral support, and it was time she met Zanna, if they were going to be bridesmaids together. Annie had refused the role, of course, because of her deeply held beliefs and principles. But Jess didn't fall for that. Annie always made a big thing about scruples, that was all, and you just had to put the shrimp net behind her, where she couldn't see it. Make her jump backwards, and you'd have her.

The Jolly Roger, about as far from the sea as any pub in Somerset could be, was a big favourite with the Faber family; the obvious venue for this meeting, and of course for the wedding reception. It wasn't just that it had a function room *and* a skittle alley. It was where Jess and Matt had first met, at one of their folk nights, where she was a regular player, he a chance member of the audience. Zanna had her eyes on something more formal, but surely once they brought her here and showed her how lush it was, she'd understand. The place oozed atmosphere, with its old beams and modern colours; it was a coaching inn with tons of history, practically National Trust really, so how could she not be smitten? They all pitched up at the Roger after work on Thursday evening, early enough to nab that great place in the corner of the bar, with the fat old leather sofas and the low table.

Most of the pub was laid up for meals anyway, and they needed a fair old acreage of table space for the pile of glossies that Zanna had brought with her. *Bride and Groom, Your Wedding Magazine, Big Day, Hitched!* – they were all there. The wedding venue had become a top priority not only because the booking needed to be confirmed, but also, apparently, because you couldn't even begin to *style* the event until you'd sized up the potential.

'That's why we're doing a site visit,' said Zanna.

Annie grimaced into her pint glass. 'I thought we were having a drink.'

'We are,' said Jess. She was determined to enjoy it. Matt had prepped her for this. He'd told her you shouldn't go into a meeting unless you knew what you wanted the outcome to be. Also, he'd told her that in this meeting, she was a thing called the Decision Maker. She sat back into the soft thick leather and rocked her head from side to side. 'I love it here. Thing is, Zanna, we all do. We know this place really well.'

'My parents came here for a meal. Once. But this is my first time.'

She wasn't sounding smitten yet.

'The food's great. The beer's great. And there's tons of room.'

'Oh yes. Wait till you see the function room, Zan,' said Matt. 'Where we come for gigs. It's just off there.' He indicated a doorway a few feet away, and his sister immediately set her white wine down and stood up, smoothing her skirt as she did so. Nobody else moved.

'Well come on then,' said Zanna.

Matt hovered for a moment, neither sitting nor standing.

'We've spent hours in there,' said Annie. 'Weeks, years of our lives. We don't need another look, do we Jess?'

'Not really. I already know what I think about this place. You go. Matt'll show you.'

She watched as Matt walked his sister across the bar and disappeared through the door. Annie leafed through a back copy of *Somerset Bride* with one hand and was working through a packet of cheese and onion crisps with the other. She'd got a good steady rhythm going. Something was absorbing her, but it was hard to tell what, until she spoke.

'Holy Moly Jess. Have you seen this? This place here advertises *Hen and Stag Retreats*. What do you s'pose that means?'

'Prayer and meditation?'

'It says here they've got *stunning private grounds in which to frolic and play.*'

Jess sniggered to herself for a bit then Annie read aloud: '*Sample menu...* blah blah... *Breast of Guineafowl with aubergine terrine and a walnut jus* ... How the heck do you get jus out of a walnut? I mean, that must *hurt...*'

'They're not like lobsters. They're already dead.'

'I mean for the cook.'

'I'm guessing you take them out of the shell first.'

'No but really... All these posh country house hotels rely on an underclass of minions on zero-hours contracts. There'll be some poor soul in the kitchen who earns their living bashing walnuts for weddings. On half the minimum wage I bet.'

Annie gave a look of disappointment and surprise to find the crisp packet empty and for a moment it became a glove puppet. Then she sucked her fingers and read on.

'*Confetti allowed*. A lot of them say that. Not sure about the dyes they use though. D'you think they use vegetable dyes in confetti? They bleach the white bits, definitely. Hmm... Maybe good old rice is best. Or lentils. Seriously, Jess, whatever you do with this wedding,' – she looked up from the magazine – 'it's got to be ethical. Like a woodland burial.'

'Cheers. You mean as long as I bury my previous life in a wicker coffin, that'll be OK?'

'No, no, I didn't mean that... oh... It's a happy occasion... I just meant the principle, you know...'

These magazines were mostly advertising. How was Zanna ever going to make her mark with Wonder White Weddings all on her own, faced with such competition? But then, musicians practically grew on trees as well.

'Have you ever thought of having a humanist ceremony?' asked Annie. 'They're ever so good.'

'Matt's mum thinks humanism's a sect.'

'It isn't though, is it?'

'No. It isn't.'

They sat in comfortable silence for a while. With Matt and Zanna out of the room, she could have another go at persuading Annie to be her bridesmaid. The real bridesmaid. The one who did stuff.

The thing you had to understand about Annie – the thing which she'd stupidly forgotten first time round because she'd been so one-track excited about getting married – was that Annie was a political animal. She had loads of ologies. And a truckload of theories about social convention. Symbolism and stuff.

So now Jess took a deep breath and settled herself before broaching the question again.

'Look, Annie… please… You've got to be there, at my side. At the wedding.'

Annie pushed out her lower lip. 'You've already got a bridesmaid.'

'Zanna? Oh please!'

'I mean, maids, honestly, what sort of language is that? There's no such thing as a maid these days. Straight out of D H fuckin' Hardy. It's tribal.' Oh God, she'd gone off on one again. This time, the important thing was not to react. Annie examined the empty crisp packet and folded it neatly and deliberately in two. 'All you're doing is parading candidates for the next wedding. You're saying, hey, all you single guys, there's bad news and there's good news. Bad news – Jess is out of circulation; good news – all these lovely girls are still available! Here's your chance to watch them move in a tight dress and swipe right.' She smoothed down the packet with the palm of her hand, pressed her fingers down the edges and folded it a second time. '*And* people play spot the virgin too. They do, at weddings. And virgins are getting younger, so you ought to think twice before you draw attention to that. Sorry Jess, I love you lots, but I don't want any part in it.' She drew her hands back into her lap with a brisk movement, and there was a slight rustling sound as the shiny packet sprung open and jumped to one side. But she was no longer staring at it. She looked Jess in the eye, her lip still curled under.

'Oh Annie, come on. Don't be such a puritan. I'm pleading with you. If a stranger like Zanna can blag her way into this, how can you not be involved? You're my best friend.'

'More fool you for letting a stranger take over your wedding,' said Annie. Harsh. But true. 'You don't need me,' she added.

Ah... was that what all this was about...

'Of course I need you. Look. She means well, Zanna, but she doesn't really get me, you know? She's like a... an alien. Dad calls her the woman from the end of the alphabet. Because she's that far out. I need someone on my side. I need some *support* here.' That was a master stroke: Annie wouldn't be able to resist the S word.

'Mmm... Depends... What are we wearing?' Annie tilted her glass thoughtfully, while Jess considered her red-haired friend. She was looking stunning right now, in that emerald T shirt. People didn't like green at weddings.

'Dunno. Any ideas?'

'Not pink.'

'Oh, definitely not pink.'

They both nodded. That was a deal, then. The glass was drained and placed decisively on the table.

'Not a bad dance floor,' came a sharp, high voice. Zanna and Matt had reappeared. Jess shifted a little to make room for him alongside her.

'Not bad? It's great,' said Matt.

Jess smiled at everybody, because Matt had told her this thing: studies proved, smiling signified consensus, so consensus was what it generated too. That was another useful thing to know.

'Good. So that's OK then.'

'Except you're a million miles from St Cunegund's, and you've got to think about your guests,' said Zanna. Also smiling. Same trick, probably learnt from the same person. Oh Jesus, did it really make you look that insincere?

'She *is* right about that, Jess,' said Matt. 'It's gotta be a good hour away. And will people find it?'

They were right, of course. She hadn't thought about it really. He put his arm around her shoulders and patted her forearm.

'Change the church?' she offered.

Zanna had another observation.

'The question is, what's your style? And your theme? Because you have to admit, you're very limited here.'

She nodded to the four corners of the pub. A worn-in, traditional building with powdery hops wound above the bar, a darts board, a stone flag floor, a proper fireplace, unvarnished wooden tables of irregular shapes and sizes and window seats. See. Perfect.

'Doesn't country pub count as a theme?'

'You certainly can't do fairy-tale wedding in a venue like this,' said Zanna.

Annie winced and shot Jess a look which said, you did warn me and now I see what you meant.

'Look. Stop there. You know what the danger with a fairy-tale wedding is? You start off with a fairy-tale wedding, and you end up with a fairy-tale marriage. Built on complete fantasy. Next thing you know,' said Jess, surprised at her own rhetoric, 'the handsome prince has turned back into a frog and there's a gurt big pumpkin blocking your drive!'

Annie's eyes widened. 'That's a bit hard on Matt.'

'I'm not getting at Matt, he knows that, don't you babe?' said Jess and gave him a big hug and a nuzzle. Ooh, she loved that smell.

'I know that,' said Matt good naturedly. 'But hey, don't disrespect my car.'

They all laughed. He was such a sweetie, so easy with everything. None of this seemed to bother him at all and maybe Jess would do well to take a leaf from his book and approach the wedding a bit less seriously. And stop seeing his sister as the enemy. There was no point in being pig-headed. Zanna was right about one thing, you did need to think about your guests.

'OK,' she said, 'I'm not against looking at another venue...'

'Like Higham's Hall,' said Zanna. Far too quickly.

'...Only I think my parents ought to see it too. As they'd be hosting it, technically.'

Annie rolled her eyes. Oh God oh God it did sound paternalistic when you played it against Annie's backing track.

'I can easily arrange a visit. We can go with your mum.'

'No, both my parents.'

'But we might lose the date if we wait for your dad to come out of hospital.'

Matt sat up straight and said, 'So what?' He squeezed Jess's hand and told her, 'Whatever's right for you. I don't mind.' *That* put his irritating little sister back in her box.

'Whatever. And I'll haggle for that discount, don't you worry,' said Zanna.

This reminded Jess there was one other thing that definitely needed nailing down, before this bossy-boots tried to take it over.

'Oh, and Annie, can I ask you to organise the hen do?'

Annie pulled down a triumphant fist. 'Oh *yes*.'

'Something short and sweet and uncomplicated, please.'

'Yes ma'am. I can promise you short, sweet, uncomplicated... and... *ethical.*'

Transit with One

Joe hadn't planned to be caught like this, mid-limbo. The door had opened on him just as he was slithering off the armchair, his torso at a 45-degree angle to the floor, his right leg folding neatly under him, and his bottom quivering in mid-air. His left hand still gripped the armrest in an attempt to haul himself back up, but he was losing the battle with gravity. Every muscle – at least, every muscle he could feel – was straining.

The scuffed boots just a foot or so from his nose belonged not to a nurse, but to his daughter. Those turquoise laces were unmistakeable. He heard her breathe in, then without a word she stepped forward and bent down to put her arms under his oxters in such a way as to take some of his weight. She held him fast and gently lifted him just enough for the legs to sort themselves out. With a series of slow, careful movements, she helped him manoeuvre back into the chair, then stood back and dusted her hands with a cheerful smile.

'Hi, Dad.'

It was as if she dealt with this sort of thing all the time.

'Where did you learn that?'

'Oh… On my course. Sort of. There were these brass players I knew at the College, and I'm telling you, those guys could *drink.*'

'It wasn't all arpeggios then.'

'What happened, Dad?'

'I wanted to get myself into bed. I thought I could do it.'

'If you never try, you never will,' she said with a grin, and went off to find a nurse.

Joe felt a certain pride to hear his catchphrase in his daughter's mouth. Swiftly followed by panic: roles might be reversing here.

She came back with Fallon, who got him where he wanted to be, and it was obvious from the way Fallon dealt with it that Jess hadn't grassed him up. She would probably tell her mother eventually, he reckoned, but she'd wait till he was better and they could all laugh about it properly.

Jess now occupied the high-rise armchair as one who'd usurped the throne, flexing her fingers round the wooden arms, pushing her spine into its back, stretching her legs and surveying the room with her chin up.

'Mum's behind, talking to the Sister. Good day? Apart from the floor show, I mean?'

'Oh yes,' he said. 'I've unlocked a whole new level. I've reached *Transit with One.*'

'What does it mean?'

'I was on *Transit with Two* before. But now it only takes one nurse to get me from the bed to the chair. So that's *Transit with One.* I can swivel on my good leg. Want to see?'

'No.'

'And I've been to Torquay. Up and down that Fawlty Towers staircase like a man possessed.'

In the hospital gym, there was a small right-angled staircase, three steps up to nowhere and two steps down again to where you hadn't started. Dan and Emma were teaching him to step up and down. Joe was a long way from Basil Fawlty's windmill of arms and legs, moving as he did very slowly, but nevertheless he reckoned his own expenditure of effort was probably the greater.

It occurred to him that his daughter looked much more at home in that hospital armchair than his wife, whose feet swung some inches from the floor. It seemed to fit Jess better. But then she was bigger. And unlike Fran, Jess didn't fidget. Today she seemed to have regained something of her habitual poise, as she used to be before all the excitement of the last weeks. She would make a good artists' model; in fact, he'd love to draw her now. But look, no hand.

'D'you know, Dad, I've had the whole day to myself to practise, and work out my set for the Frenzy. No interruptions. Bliss.'

A rhythmic noise drew closer and he felt the floor shake. That would be Fran, stomping above her weight again. Sure enough, she appeared, kissed him, then settled on the grey stacking chair by the other side of the bed, looking unusually flushed and fizzy. She had news.

'Your discharge meeting is on again for Wednesday of next week. Emma's going to do a home visit so they can see what accommodations they need to make. You know, aids, grab rails and such like.'

Nobody knew why this meeting had fallen through the first time, although it sounded as though a lot of personnel were involved, and perhaps they hadn't all been available. And anyway, it seemed incredible that today had been the original date suggested for him to leave hospital under this new early discharge scheme.

'Look at the state of me,' he said. 'Would you want me back in this condition? I wouldn't get through an MOT.' It was going to take more than a spot of WD 40 and a new set of windscreen wipers. Yet the hospital seemed to think he was an ideal candidate. Based on what?

Your attitude, they'd said. They trusted him to do his exercises. It was true that things were looking up; the physio sessions with Dan and Emma were going well. The swelling on his sprained ankle – so callously ignored by Fran – was starting to go down, and it was actually beginning to give him pain now, which might be a good thing, because at least pain was a form of feeling. Pain in the foot, and pain in the back and shoulder. As sensation crept back, the discomfort in bed was becoming a constant nag, and kept him awake at night. Now, if everything was OK – *OK?* – Joe could be coming home next weekend.

'I'm going to be up on bricks for ages, waiting for wheels. Cluttering up the drive and lowering the tone.'

'You stick to what you do best, Dad.'

Fran focused on practicalities. 'The main thing will be to get the spare bed down into the dining room. Harry could help, he's already offered to help with anything. Harry at work.'

'Matt could do that,' said Jess.

'Have they had you on a Zimmer yet?'

No, they hadn't. Joe had to watch a 92-year-old expert speed past his door to the washroom twice a day. But on the bright side, he told Fran about achieving Transit with One, and explained the concept again. Fran said 'Oh. And I suppose I'm the one?'

Joe and Jess exchanged glances, because her brow was knotted. Fran went on: 'Look, I so, so want to have you home. I so want you home. But you're so big and I'm so little… and… what am I going to do with you?' She may be laughing, but his fierce wife was scared.

'Mum's right, it might take two to scrape you off the floor, Dad,' said Jess; then, more helpfully, 'But one day soon, you won't need anybody else at all. And the bed downstairs is only temporary, isn't it?'

They all looked around the room for a moment, and Joe stared at his cards. Get well, you lingerer. Get well.

'I had another call from Janet,' said Fran to Jess. 'She's very focused on the big day, isn't she?'

107

'Is she?'

'She's full of it, Jess. Surely you've noticed. She talks of nothing else.'

Jess smiled and looked surprised. 'Really? Well that's lovely. I didn't realise she cared. Do you know, she hasn't said a thing to me about it?'

They agreed that people were funny. 'But I expect Zanna's busy making plans.'

'Oh, no,' said Jess. 'Why would she? She's not coming. Why would she be?'

'Not coming?'

'She'd never get time off. And it's so far to travel. And she's more into classical, isn't she?'

'Not the Fiddle Frenzy, you idiot, the wedding. *That* big day.'

'The wedding? That's over a year away,' said Jess with a shrug. That's my girl, thought Joe.

'Janet would like an idea of numbers, so they can start thinking about who or whom to invite. From their side. Who or whom do you want to invite? Family, I mean, from our side?'

'She asked me that question the other day. This sides thing is funny, isn't it?' said Jess. 'As if it's a contest.'

'What did you tell her?'

'I said everybody, of course.'

'Sooner or later we'll all need to know who everybody is, Jess.'

'Oh Mum. You know. Grandma, grandpa obviously, Shetland lot, obviously: Uncle Tam and Auntie Nell, the cousins. Maybe Mark's lot. Emma's lot. Uncle Norrie and Auntie Mavis, … and our friends. But our friends are almost all double agents. You know. Working for both sides.'

Her mother clicked and pointed out they'd have to think about where all these people were going to stay.

'Don't you start,' said Joe. 'It's a year away.'

'True,' she answered and laughed at herself.

But he could guess what Fran was thinking. That spare bed was coming downstairs, and none of them knew how long for.

Bridesmaids

It was not merely in alphabetical terms that Annie and Zanna were distant from each other. Annie knitted. Zanna ironed. Jess suspected that if you examined their current wardrobes, you might not find a single item in common. Throw in the Shetland cousins, and the bridesmaids became even more of a muddle. What on earth would they look like?

On the way to hospital visiting, she shared these thoughts with Matt. He drove the way you were taught to drive, both hands gently on the wheel at ten minutes to two, barely moving as he turned a corner or negotiated a roundabout; she watched the wheel spin.

'Look, sweet thing, the bridesmaids are your team. They're there to support you. But equally,' – he negotiated an awkward junction at a perfect speed – 'you're the boss, and that means *you've* got to manage *them*.'

She balked at that. It was all just too much and maybe she shouldn't have any bridesmaids at all. He kept his eyes on the road ahead, and checked his mirrors regularly. He was too careful to look at her. But he tried to reassure her.

'How do you eat an elephant? Hm? One bite at a time.'

Was this wise or just weird? Surely, she said, eating an elephant was a really horrible idea. And how would you cook it? And even supposing you could eat elephant without sicking up, it would go off before you got very far. He conceded it was a bad analogy, environmentally dodgy and very un-PC; he'd have to think of another one... But the point was, Jess had to keep on building her team, which meant it was time the whole team met. All she needed to do was to agree a time, get Annie and Zanna together again, and Skype the cousins. Easy. OK, she said, she'd do it.

'Throw in a pizza afterwards and everyone'll go home happy,' he assured her.

Except that when the day came, Annie texted to say she'd come off her bike at a pothole, and was dealing with a punctured tyre. To make matters worse, the tea room had been short-staffed, and Jess arrived home late, with a thumping headache and itching all over from tiredness, desperate to strip off the black uniform and jump in the shower.

Jess knew something was up when her mum ran to meet her in the hall with her hands in the air and her shoulders up round her ears. It was followed by a vigorous apology: 'I couldn't stop her'. There was a voice coming from Jess's bedroom. She ran upstairs to find Zanna actually sitting on her bed, opposite the dressing table desk. Unbelievable. She had only made herself at home, opened the laptop and set the Shetland Skype session off. It was all well under way as scheduled. Without the bride. Since when was punctual more important than polite? And it was surreal to see Zanna transported here, clean and well-defined in pale blue amidst the clutter and the dust which Jess hadn't really been aware of before. Perhaps she might do a Mary Poppins and clean the place up.

'Hi, hi! Hi Jess!' sang the Shetland cousins as Jess moved into shot and joined Zanna on the edge of the bed.

'Hi. I suppose you've all met, then.'

The pair on the screen chorused yes and Zanna explained she hadn't wanted to keep anybody waiting. But they wouldn't make any decisions without Jess, obviously.

'Obviously.'

'Christ Jess you look awful shite,' said the fourteen-year-old blonde.

'Cheers, Ella. Been a hard day.'

'I always thought black was your colour. But today I'm not so sure.'

'It *is* Ella's colour,' said her elder sister, smiling ironically.

'Black or white. Or Navy. Or Cream. Or Grey,' said Ella.

'We need a colour that tones for everybody,' said Zanna.

'But we don't tone with each other, do we? Just look at us,' said Ella. She had that razor edge to her voice which, combined as it was with the straight lips and the narrowed eyes, told you that she'd already taken a dislike to Zanna and was established on the offensive.

She had a point, though. The screen shot was a study in disharmony. Ella was thin as a blade, horribly elegant for her age in pale grey jumper and leggings, with long and lustrous fair hair and naturally thick black lashes; Freya sat alongside her, leaning in to the camera in a friendly way, a rosy brunette, pretty, upholstered in parrot-coloured layers of frock, vest, T-shirt, hand knitted cardigan, with something like a ribbon in her hair and earrings which were large, bright, and unmatched. At the side of the screen, in the little mirror inset, Zanna stood out in her tidily tailored blue dress, looking demure. Next to her sat something resembling a dull bin bag with a butternut squash for a head poking out, topped by a pantomime wig. That would be herself. It occurred to Jess that Zanna was the only one of the lot of them who looked like bride material.

'Why not have a rainbow?' sang Freya.

'There's only four of us and you need seven colours,' said the younger sister, apparently talking to the mobile in the flat of her hand. But that was it. The two of them were off.

'So... we need Bess and Jake. Gets us up to six. They can have a coloured collar. Or a dog waistcoat.'

'Bess is a girl!'

'At least she doesn't have to worry about skin tones. I mean, everything looks good on a black lab.' Freya had dimples when she laughed and she was enjoying herself.

Zanna fidgeted as if she was about to say something, when Freya exclaimed, 'We could all have a tat!'

'Oh yes!'

'But what?'

'But where?'

'Shoulder is nice. Not arms. I don't want everyone looking at my BCG scar.'

'You could get a tat on that. To disguise it.'

'What of?'

'Whatever it looks like.'

'It looks like a sprout.'

'Well a rose then, that's true love and dead weddingy. And a rose looks like a sprout.'

Jess felt it was time to stir the mix herself. 'But what about your *other* tattoos?'

She could feel Zanna stiffen as Freya began to roll up one sleeve, explaining to the outsider, 'this one's my Fair Isle bracelet,' then gave up because the layers of clothing meant the sleeve wouldn't roll back that far. 'Ach, pish. But have you noticed my new piercing?' and she turned her head so that the silver nose stud caught the light. 'And... have you seen my hair? I can wear it down for work, like this, kinda normal, but when I go out, I can wear it up like so...' and she pulled her hair over her head to reveal a sunshine yellow arc about the neckline. 'Discreet, see?'

Zanna's face had frozen some time ago but now the effort was starting to show. She said, 'We have to fall in with the bride here. It's what the bride wants.'

'Oh yes,' said Ella, looking away from her phone for a moment to eyeball the bride with the killer question. 'Will it be a long dress? Or a short dress for the dancing?'

'Short for the dancing,' said Jess. Ella grinned approval.

'What?' Zanna had gone off like a rocket. 'You can't get married in a short dress!'

The Shetland cousins improvised a wild duet on the theme 'What about the ceilidh?' which resolved on Ella's firm statement that you can't dance at a ceilidh in a long dress.

'It just gets in the way,' she said. 'You have to pick it up and hold it and prance round like a numpty all night. It's *stupitt.*'

'Two dresses, then,' said Zanna. 'That's the thing. A lot of brides have two dresses now.'

This could get expensive.

Freya was trying to smooth things over by changing the subject to ask, 'And who's baking your bannocks?'

'What's a bannock?' asked Zanna.

Jess hadn't thought about that. 'They don't really do that south.'

'You don't have bannocks at a wedding? Bannocks and soup?' asked Ella, incredulous.

Jess shook her head.

'So... you'll be having fancies, though? Who's baking *them*?'

Jess shrugged. 'Dunno.'

Maybe it would be a laugh to have tattie soup and bannocks with reestit mutton, and fancies to follow, Shetland style. It would be worth running with this idea just to give the caterers a challenge and wind Zanna up. Source that, smart arse…

'We're getting off the subject. We're meant to be thinking right now about what the bridesmaids are going to wear,' said Zanna. That could be Matthew speaking. Brother and sister were very alike when it came to conversations. If there was an agenda, he didn't like to stray from it for long, and Jess knew she was capable of exasperating him. They were good foils for each other, which was what you needed in a couple. It tickled her, though, that her cousins were really messing with Zanna's head. She must be hating the way they got excited about something then let it drop, so as to chase whatever new and daft idea had just loomed into view.

'It all starts with what the bride wants,' Zanna reminded them. 'So, Jess, what sort of look were you thinking of?'

'How do I know?'

'Every bride knows. Every bride knows what her dream wedding dress would be. Just tell us your dream.' Zanna had turned to look her in the eye, and was smiling encouragingly.

'I know I'm not wearing a long dress,' said Jess, although she hadn't known that till just now.

'But that's not fair to Matt!' said Zanna, pleadingly, as if there were an important dimension to all this that Jess hadn't considered. She still couldn't work out what it was.

As if on cue, the wails of the cousins were cut off abruptly, and the image of them, hands upraised, faces caught in the snarl of exclamation, froze on the screen. Then it pixelated into overlarge squares, before disappearing with an electronic plop as of water into a bucket.

There was an awkward silence. Jess and Zanna were both more comfortable looking at the inert laptop than at each other.

'Thing is, Zanna, I really do want to marry your brother. But I'm not sure I want to be a bride.'

'Oh, that's just nerves,' said Zanna. 'Poor Jess. You're a bit back to front really, aren't you?'

The hand on Jess's arm might as well have been poised on the nuclear button. She closed the laptop in as controlled a way as she could manage.

'It isn't me that's got it back to front,' she said. She observed an appropriate silence after the electronic click sounded, before picking up again: 'It's you. Look, if you don't mind, I'd like to have a shower now.' As much as that shower, what she wanted was to race to her violin and practise very hard and very loud, until she made Zanna's ears bleed. But then she heard Matt's footfall on the stair. He entered the room with a broad smile. Not a care in the world.

'Got the pizzas. Oh, no Annie? So, how's it going? Progress?'

'We're not sure about the dress,' said Zanna, and her whole face creased as if she were making an apology.

Matt looked so innocent, as he nodded towards the laptop. 'They've signed off already? I was looking forward to saying hello.'

'We lost connectivity,' his sister explained.

His brows arched in surprise as he glanced at Jess. Oh yes, she told him with a look, they'd lost connectivity all right.

Best Man

Matt was cross with his sister about the big Skype usurpment, but he couldn't be surprised, because she'd been like that ever since she stole his giraffe. No sense of boundaries. His toys were her toys; same with his friends. When they were small, it used to annoy his mates, the way she tried to boss them about, but at least it was easier then to shrug the kid sister off. By the time they all hit their teens she had become one huge distraction, and it was Matt who suffered the most as she lured his mates over to her side. It was simple really. She was one of those people who needed to be important precisely because she wasn't. You couldn't expect Jess to understand any of this, or forgive. And she was so knackered as well, at the moment. There was plenty to grind her gears. Zanna was a train smash, Annie was a nightmare, and that was quite enough for anyone to handle, without the two oddballs from the arctic circle who sounded so wacky he was really sorry he'd missed meeting them. He had reason to feel just the tiniest bit smug, though. He'd got his best man recruited by text within twelve hours of the Big Decision, immediately after he'd phoned Parent Central and before he'd done the Bonding Mountain Walk with Jess. There wouldn't be any trouble from that quarter. Aidan didn't really do style, either good or bad, and he never wore a suit anyway, so he'd accept whatever you hired for him.

Aidan Barry was a shoo-in for best man. Matt had known him since school, but they'd only become friends late on in the sixth form when Matt, to celebrate his eighteenth, launched a pub quiz team. They'd got hammered three times in a row, which pointed up the need for a nerd. It was a defining moment, his first controversial management decision, made when they were still at school: Matt acquired Boring Barry to do flags of the world and the periodic table. And to this day he maintained, if you just looked at that decision in terms of outcome, it worked. Aidan was never going to be flavour of the month with the rest of the team, admittedly, but he did know a ridiculous amount about all that unimportant stuff that nobody cared about, yet which came up surprisingly often: history, geography, science, politics, books, paintings, that sort of thing. It had been fine at first. But when he started answering the music questions too, and the cinema, the sport, and then the TV – in other words, all the important trivia – the other lads felt he'd overstepped the mark, and they took it badly. Which was a pity. Matt had stood by his signing, but the team became a handful, and in the end the whole thing fell apart. Which was purely and simply because he, Matt, was the only one who understood how a team worked. The rest of them were just playing at it.

Fair was fair, and you had to give credit where credit was due: Boring Barry knew more than he was hired for. It was funny really how their friendship continued through the years. Aidan didn't say a lot, but he was steady. Always home in the holidays and up for a pint. Someone to go out with. The women went straight for Matt, of course, because he was the extrovert, but Aidan never took it in bad part. And when Aidan came out to him about the bird-spotting, Matt realised he wasn't surprised and ought to have guessed sooner. It was touching to think Aidan had shared that with him, and it made Matt feel somehow closer and almost protective of his geeky friend.

Crucially, though, it was Aidan who had given Matt his first in with Jess, all because of the Shetland connection. Aidan never really left university – Matt had always suspected he was a bit scared of the real world – and he'd recently gone out to Shetland to carry out some sort of research into birds, which was surprising because he'd done physics not biology. It involved recording them, apparently, which was his thing. Aidan, the quiet one, had come back home for Christmas and something must have flipped in his head because he couldn't stop talking about it. He was full of it. Unzipped. He managed to get Shetland this and Shetland that into every conversation. How the birds were amazing. He'd reel off lists of the species he'd seen and a mad look would come into his eyes, like he was high, or in love. It was almost embarrassing and in fact there was one evening when it got so bad that Matt had just to say, *Mate, maybe you shouldn't be telling me this.* But then one day Matt met Jess at a gig, and she was so… oh, so… Jess, and he tried to chat her up but could see she wasn't biting; then she mentioned playing fiddle Shetland style and her Shetland family, and Matt turned out to be the first guy in Somerset who really did know where that was and how you got there; next thing he was telling her how he'd heard that the landscapes were beyond photography and the birds were amazing and how lucky she was and he'd just love to go there and see it for himself. Her eyes lit up. They connected. And the rest was history. He owed everything to Aidan, really. Aidan could be trusted to make it work.

Own Two Feet

This felt worse than any fairground ride.

'Right Joe. Hands flat on the edge of the bed first to steady you. Feet in line with your hips, flat to the floor. Head forward.

No, further than that. Head right forward, push your head down, lead with the chest and swing your upper body forward. Go on.'

It was like abseiling – scarier the second time because you knew what was coming – and it took a few goes to believe he wouldn't end up head-first in a heap on the floor. He had to learn to stand on his own two feet, even if one of them was completely untrustworthy. It was strange to think that he was being taught how to stand up by a student, and made him feel suddenly old, as if his place in the universe had shifted.

Andy was a trainee, young, slight of build, fair, blue-eyed, friendly and respectful, in fact you could easily take him for a beginner. But he'd already acquired the two most important physio skills so he must be close to being qualified. One, he'd quickly sized up Joe's abilities and limitations. Two, he insisted on nagging away at them until they shifted, in a manner which bordered on sadism. So tender, and so hard! Now that Joe was almost certainly into his last week in hospital, Andy was taking him through the stuff he'd need to be able to do in order to be ready to go home: washing, dressing, walking with a frame. Learning to stand up unaided was far and away the most disconcerting. Joe was once again as clumsy as a toddler. But whereas it was OK for a toddler to learn by falling over, that was not such a good idea when you were 6' 2" and your bones had set. You lacked bounce.

Andy wheeled him to the washroom and they went through ablutions, then dressing without help.

'What about the laces?' asked Joe, contemplating his trainers.

'Most people switch to Velcro,' said Andy.

He bristled. If they made everything too easy, he'd never grow stronger.

'I've got to be able to tie my laces.' Those words belonged to a time where he was maybe four or five years old and in his first school uniform.

'OK. I can teach you to tie laces one handed.'

His right hand was much, much clumsier today. It could be used to steady one lace whilst he worked with the other. But it mattered to him just as much now as it had then, to learn this trick of adults, to get it right and be like the other kids. By the time he was dressed and wheeled back to his room, Joe was exhausted. Not ideal, when he was going to be up in front of the medical board that afternoon.

Fran and Fallon had arranged the GP visit between them, so as to sound out the feasibility of making the Shetland trip. Joe had no idea at all whether the decision would be thumbs up or thumbs down. In the event, the doctor seemed rather nonplussed about his role in the whole thing, as if to say, why would you want to see *me*? Dr Stewart turned out to be a calm young man, with fine sandy hair, grey eyes, and a fresh complexion, who listened carefully and kept his eyes trained on Joe while Fran did the talking. She looked tense about the eyes. Joe didn't like that.

'First, I'd like to know how you feel Joe's doing. He's being discharged soon, but I haven't spoken to a doctor since the day it happened. We saw the consultant, Mr Shah, in A and E. But of course, Joe doesn't remember much of what he said.'

'Oh?'

He looked surprised, but why should he be? Once the consultant had made his diagnosis, the machinery had started to move – nurses, physios, OTs, everybody except Joe seemed to know exactly what they were doing – and it was whirring along at a lick now, about to push Joe Faber off the conveyor belt and deposit him in the outside world. If doctors were part of that machinery, they were hidden from view. Even the blood pressure medication had just appeared as if by some automated process.

Dr Stewart set off at a perfect pace, explaining the stroke and summing up Joe's condition whilst leaving plenty of space for them to interrupt. He had a pleasant, musical voice, easy on the ear, and he glanced across to include Fran from time to time. He didn't move at all. It was a strange relief to be hearing nothing new; it was all as Fran and the nurses had told him. It had been a bleed deep in his brain, not a clot, hence conservative treatment, which meant no real need for medical intervention, other than controlling the blood pressure; the site of the damage was the left basal ganglion, which had created disruption to communication between brain and movement down the right side; movement and sensation were coming back in the order they'd expect, the leg would be first, then the arm, and – hopefully – the fine motor skills of the hand might return eventually. The swiftest gains would be over these first three months, after which recovery would slow down, but improvement could continue for years to come, so long as Joe continued to work at it.

It was all beginning to sound so normal. In his sluggish state, he was happy to let Fran raise the whole flying business, but not before he had seized his big opportunity. There was a doctor in front of him, so he could ask the question that had kept him awake at nights.

'Why did it happen?'

'We can't really say.'

Joe thought he ought at least to thumb through his theories for the doctor's consideration. Because he really wanted to know. He had to place the beginning of each sentence carefully, and couldn't rush at elaborate explanations in the way he used to.

'I used to get migraines. All my life. But not since the stroke. Maybe there was a fault in the wiring all along. What d'you think?'

'It's hard to say.'

'Also, I've had thumps.'

Fran stepped in to translate. Acci-thumps. Road accidents. He'd had three shunts in the space of two years, none his own fault, and walked away from all of them. Which was incredible luck, given that in one case his car had rolled onto its side, and the last time, the car that had run out of road as it attempted to overtake him had ended up in a ditch. Nobody hurt, supposedly. Not even an X-ray taken.

'It could be that. A series of accidents, that's possible. We'll never know. The good thing is, since there's no obvious medical cause, and you don't smoke, there are no real lifestyle changes you need to make.'

Apart from getting used to doing nothing.

Fran nodded gently. They were quiet for a moment. She glanced at Joe. He'd run out of things to say.

Now she asked, 'Would it be safe for us to fly? Only, we had a trip planned.'

The doctor answered slowly, weighing his words.

'I don't know of any problem in principle. I'm not aware of contra-indications, once you've reached a month after the stroke.'

Why the repetition? Was he a bit of a cold fish, this bloke? Or was he just being cautious, and kind, in giving them all the time they needed? He sat very still, knees together, hands upturned in his lap, and added, 'Airlines nowadays are used to dealing with passengers with much greater disabilities.'

That word felt like a slap in the face. He could see Fran's eyes re-focus momentarily before coming back to the room.

'When were you planning on travelling?'

'First week in August.'

'That would be…'

'Five weeks, yes. Five weeks from the stroke.'

Fran was edgy, cutting in like this. She was doing that a lot lately.

The doctor scrutinised Joe, his grey eyes fidgeting, uncertain. It occurred to Joe that it was Fran who had raised this question, so perhaps the doctor was trying to work out whether this trip was something that Joe himself really wanted to happen. After all, Fran might be a selfish bully or an idiot or simply complacent, for all a stranger knew. Add to this the fact that Joe's face couldn't be trusted to render any meaningful expression faithfully these days, fake or real. Maybe he was looking scared. In fact, he *was* scared. But he was still sure he wanted to go.

'That would be… heroic,' said the doctor. 'I can't say it's impossible, but it would be very demanding, so soon. Couldn't you delay it for a while?'

'No, we can't,' said Joe, as forcefully as he could.

'Where are you off to?'

'Shetland.'

The young man's head moved. He must be impressed. Joe started to explain about his daughter Jess and her big gig at the Fiddle Frenzy, and he listened so patiently that the words just came. Fran explained about the family, and her sister Nell who used to run a dementia centre, so there would be plenty of support. They told him about the concerts, and how Jess had been going to the Frenzy since she was a girl. And this year's line-up.

'Oh,' said Dr Stewart, in a reverential, that-changes-everything voice. 'Archie McNuckert... Well, good luck to you. And congratulations to your daughter.'

Insect Life

An ant can carry several thousand times its body weight. Fran glanced in the mirror and realised she now had biceps. She was turning into an insect. However strong she was getting, though, there was no way she would get that double bed downstairs on her own.

The biceps had appeared as a result of modest jobs like carrying all the shopping from the car herself, but also from the shifting of objects and furniture which was now necessary in order to make space for Joe to sleep downstairs. That was the easy part. Emma the OT had told her that the bed needed to be higher – 26" from the floor, if Joe was to get in and out easily. You could put the frame on blocks, but there were only days in which to fix them and no carpenter in sight. The mattress on the spare bed was beginning to age anyway, so she had the idea of getting a topper made of that magic foam stuff instead. It would add the necessary inches and also upgrade the bed. According to the advertising blurb, this magic foam would remember the contours of Joe's body, which was more than she did, she thought with a grunt. And she could order it online and have it delivered the next day. Simple.

When the topper arrived in its vacuum pack, however, it weighed a ton, and the instructions said it had to be opened out and left to breathe and to find its proper shape for 24 hours. Where to put it? She pushed the sofa and the armchairs in the sitting room against the wall, in so far as she could, and imagined she'd just roll the shiny fat sausage out of the hall and into place, but it didn't want to move. The foam had shrunk to a cosmic density milliseconds from the big bang, and she had to push and grapple the leaden weight from the hallway into the room. When she ripped open the plastic and allowed it to begin its unfolding, it became even more intractable, forcing her to dance around it, pulling and pressing and flattening, now this side, now that. Hands, knees, bottom, elbow, there was no part of her which hadn't wrestled with the monster and tried to beat it down, and the only consolation was a soft landing when she lost her balance. It was never going to fit in the remaining floor space, and one corner curled stubbornly upwards against an armchair, like an upturned finger saying, sod you, missus.

Harry came over the next day after work to help move the bed. Once in the house, he quickly sized things up.

'Right. First question, where's it going?'

She showed him the dining room. He raised an eyebrow. People always reacted to that wallpaper. Joe loved telling visitors that Prussian blue was a poisonous pigment. Harry made no comment, however, and scanned the room. She'd already removed the top from the Edwardian table and slid it against the wall, and its central cluster of legs was pushed to a corner for the time being. It was too heavy to take upstairs, but it could be pushed into the workshop once the chairs which she'd stacked there yesterday had gone up for storage in the bedless spare room.

'Right. Next question, where is it?' As they went upstairs, he looked about him, eyeing up the dimensions of the staircase and the turn of the half-landing like a pro. He scanned the spare room in a second.

'Right. You've taken it apart already. Good. Base first.'

They got it downstairs in a couple of journeys, and he helped her put it back together again in its new position, looking onto the garden. The same decisiveness she'd seen so often in the lab was visible in his every movement now, and although he wasn't a particularly big guy, he made light work of it. They went back for the mattress. Together they eased it down the stairs with Harry at the lower end, supporting the weight and working backwards. He'd just made it to the bottom half landing and was about to negotiate the turn into the hall when the doorbell rang.

'Right,' he said. 'Let it rest for a minute. Down. Gently does it.' They leant it against the wall, and Fran kept one hand on it to prevent it toppling. Harry answered the door and from her perch halfway up the staircase she could see two legs in navy drainpipes and loafers, and orange socks. Matt. She heard him say 'Oh, so you've started without me,' and she let out an involuntary *Oh shit.* She thought she'd been pleasant but also firm when she'd told him not to bother. Because she'd seen him put up a tent once. And she knew Jess was the one who'd assembled the bookcase in his flat, when it turned out he couldn't tell up from down. He wasn't clumsy as such, simply unaware of how the world of 3-D objects worked: what bent, what didn't, what balanced, what collapsed, little things like that.

Matt stepped inside, lighting the hall with a glow of knitwear, and she introduced them. Under his neatly-trimmed beard, Harry's smile was verging on a smirk. She could guess what he'd be thinking: we've got a proper young fogey here, therefore a complete wuss, has he ever shifted furniture before, probably not, therefore get him out the way and keep him there.

Matt, however, seemed to have slipped into a management role.

He told Harry, 'You've got to get it round the bottom of the stair and into the hall.'

'Right.'

'But it's too long to turn this way.' He was standing below her now with his hands on his hips. Not one hair out of place, she noted.

'I know,' muttered Harry, whose eyes were firmly fixed on the mattress.

'If you lift it, you can flop it over the bannisters.'

'What, and you'll catch it, will you?'

'Sure.' He sounded confident.

'Lampshade?' The light was in the way.

'That needs to come down first, of course,' said Matt.

'Hall table? '

'You need to move that in case. And you need to move the phone and all this stuff.'

'Do I?' said Harry. 'As I see it, there's just one big thing in the way.'

Matt didn't answer and she guessed he was puzzling it out.

Harry called, 'OK Fran, just support your end now.'

It was a joy to witness the ease with which he picked up the mattress and rotated it at an angle so that it sat over the newel post. Matt jumped out of the way, ran along the hall and took a step back into the sitting room, whose door was wide open. There was a shout of surprise and a thud. He'd fallen over backwards. Harry raised an eyebrow but didn't halt in his manoeuvre, and in seconds the mattress was standing on its side against the opposite wall.

'Well at least he's found the crash mat,' said Fran. 'We're big on Health and Safety in this house.'

Harry grinned up at her.

It all ended amicably enough. She really did wonder sometimes about Matt, though. It was thoughtful of him to turn up; he was willing and sincere, and so good-natured. But if his idea of help was telling other people what to do… Imagine being married to that. Their Jess, married to that.

Although who could say what made a marriage work? Who would have backed the artist and the lab assistant to make it to 24 years?

Own Goals

Saturday morning dawned bright and Matt's apartment was tickled awake by filtered sunlight. Jess stretched out an arm and pulled on the cord of the venetian blind to let more in.

Matt swung out of bed and headed off to the kitchen.

'I'll miss this place, once we set up house together. God knows where that'll be, though,' she said.

'Yeah,' he answered from the other side of the open door. 'Me too, in a way.' The room became instantly bright. A series of taps and clicks and a brief grinding noise told her he was attending to the machine which she couldn't be bothered with and which made such great coffee. 'What do you like about it most? After the happy memories, that is.'

'The space.'

'But there isn't any!'

Technically, of course, he was right. His flat was arranged so that you could fit everything in, provided you left your childhood in storage back at your mum's. She looked around at cool walls, simply painted in shades which reminded her of the white sand and turquoise sea at St Ninian's, with just a couple of prints for decoration. Smart venetian blinds instead of curtains. No stray items of clothing hanging about the place – Matt was disciplined about his clothes. He didn't overstuff the wardrobe, either. In fact, he had the sort of wardrobe you read about in magazines, balanced, everything matching everything else. There was no room in this flat for anything you were only hanging onto in case it might come in handy.

'It's just so different from home.'

He brought her drink and padded back for his own. Bliss. She still tingled because he'd loved her so well, and the memory of last night's music was every bit as sharp and commanding of attention as the smell of coffee. The room had been full, the applause genuine and warm, and if there were imperfections which had troubled her, the audience hadn't seemed to notice. No Tea Room today, either, because every fifth Friday was off. More percussion in the kitchen, a short wait, and he was back in the doorway. He beamed at her and she thought for the thousandth time how sweet his two little eyebrows were, how neatly their arcs balanced the cup of his smile. He slipped back into bed. She sat up and they drank together, staring through into the living area.

'Yeah,' he said, 'it *is* different. Your mum and dad do have their own style, don't they? They've put their mark on the place. It's a big old house, they've got the scope to make a statement. Whereas this flat just has to be functional.'

'Far as I'm concerned, functional is the new exotic. The main statement our dining room makes is *Daddy got a great contract in the noughties.* That's when he splashed out on block-print wallpaper and matching curtains. It ought to be in the V and A, really.' Every friend she'd ever brought home from school had said 'oh!' when they caught an eyeful of Prussian blue.

'I like it,' said Matt, and put an arm around her. They snuggled down, and he said, 'I hope your mum and dad get on OK tonight.' It was to be her father's first night back home. Matt had juggled his schedule so as to help transport all the kit.

'Oh, they'll be fine.'

'Only I remember, my mother had a sort of an operation, once, and she was in a chair for a couple of days. It was a bit of a mare, round the house.' He suddenly checked himself. 'Don't let on I told you, though.'

'Was she very ill?'

'No. It wasn't that kind of op. Forget I mentioned it.'

Ooh, thought Jess, varicose veins? Ingrowing toenails? Maybe *cosmetic surgery*? Liposuction? Something hidden and staying that way. Janet Harrington kept the sort of house where few objects were naked. Tupperware reigned in the kitchen, loo rolls were covered up in a holder, magazines hidden in a leather rack. Even paper hankies were dispensed from a padded box. Who knew what had gone on under the upholstery? No, no… Think about something else, Jess.

She mulled over the set she'd planned for the Frenzy, and the email she'd had from the great Archie. He said he was thinking of a duet on a slow air, and had suggested a few tunes for her to pick from. She seldom got to play with another fiddler since she'd left the College, so it would be fantastic, but daunting. What if she let him down? What about nerves? Playing a few tunes at the Half Moon was one thing. The Frenzy was another. A folk club in Somerset meant, mainly, a bunch of guitarists – who'd be content if you just played all the notes in the fast pieces – and singers, who appreciated a sweet tune but wouldn't even notice your technique. Round here, fiddlers were a bit of a novelty turn, and it was easy to impress; the music and the instrument did it for you. The audience at the Fiddle Frenzy would be supportive, yes, for sure, but knowledgeable too. She knew these people as friends and teachers. And some of them would be thinking, I can do better than that.

Eventually they got up, and put breakfast together side by side in the narrow galley kitchen. In the fridge she discovered a bagged-up meal deal from the supermarket and a tidy stack of plastic containers. Leftovers. This man not only shopped and cooked, but when he ate, he still had bits *left over.* Amazing.

Matt moved his laptop off the table so that they could sit down with their toast.

'I've got to do some more work on this Module. You know, the one they've asked me to re-engineer?' She knew the one. 'So, every time I come up against *Goal Setting*, I drift off task.'

She said 'Oh dear,' and looked out of the window. Down in the street, a bin wagon was screeching horribly as it tipped a wheelie bin and set it down again.

'So, I've devised this process diagram… You know, *if this, then that…* Look, I'll show you the format.' He hoisted the laptop from the sofa back onto his knee and opened it up.

'It looks like a form you have to fill in?'

'Well, yes, kind of. So, I thought, walk the talk, Matthew, try working through it yourself. As if you're the client. That way I'm inhabiting the process, right? So, the first heading I've got is Organisational Goals. OK, I'm good with that. Then… see…? There's Societal Goals. Bit more tricky, because you have to do some defining there and I'm trying to avoid cultural bias? In fact I nearly cut that out because it's kind of fraught but in the end I thought, you've got to be holistic across the whole piece. In today's global world. So, OK, so far so good. But it's the third heading... Look...'

She read from the screen: 'Own Goals?'

'That's *Own* Goals. So, my own, not what my boss or my organisation wants. And that's the problem.'

'Oh. How?'

'The bottom line is, my own goals are subverting this whole process. Because they are one hundred and ten per cent divergent from my Organisational ones!'

'Let's see, then.'

He brought the document up and waited for her to put her toast down before handing her the laptop, cautiously, as if it were an infant. Hmm. The Organisational Goals were gobbledygook. No, he assured her, they were fine, he could be sure of that because he'd cut and pasted them verbatim from the most current version of WayUp's Business Development Plan. Matt's Societal Goals included Paperless Commerce, World Peace and the strengthening of Marriage as an Institution. Quirky, or Disney? wondered Jess, still only half-interested. His own, personal goals came next, and that was what she felt most curious about.

'Mmm. "Living with the woman of your dreams" – that's really lovely, Matt. But would you be sharing all this with your boss – sorry, the organisation?'

'Oh, no, this last bit's confidential to the client, of course. You're just asking them to reflect. But you see, the thing is, this section turns out to be the aspect of the whole process that I'm most interested in.'

She read on:

Launch independent consultancy
Net revenues to outstrip WWWeddings by end year 2

Make myself useful.

Coach J in self-affirmation / confidence building before FFrenzy

Oh, she thought, he means me. How sweet. He's right, that's what I need. Someone to help me assert myself.

'So, my problem is, it takes time to do all that. Time I don't have, because the Organisational Goals which are imposed upon me are *pulling in the opposite direction.* I can't achieve for WayUp and for myself. I mean, we're talking a complete 360 degrees of variance.'

'So what you're saying is, you'd prefer to be doing something other than what you're paid for?'

Matt bit his lip and nodded.

'Isn't that most people's definition of work?'

Now he shook his head, acknowledging the hopelessness of his situation.

'I know. I know. What I'm realising, more and more, is that I don't want to work for them. I've got to strike out, Jess. I've got to have space to express myself. For my work to be creative. More like play. Just like yours.'

A click and a dry rattle came from the toaster.

'One thing at a time,' she said, 'if you still want that pay cheque.'

He smiled and the platinum hair almost sparkled for a moment as he shook his troubles away.

'You're right. What am I like? I'll park the *Me* stuff and get back on task. Although maybe I ought to talk to your dad. He's always been his own boss, hasn't he?'

'Mmm. Why not.'

'It's just that this morning I've woken up with so much creative energy, it feels like I can't contain it.'

133

'Same! Last night went well, but it's left me itching to do more. I just want to play better.'

White lie. It wasn't creative energy, in her case, it was terror. Well, the only medicine Jess knew for nerves was preparation. She'd best crack on.

'Oh, you were brilliant,' he said.

'Look, why don't we both work for a bit this morning? We've never done that together. We're going to have to get used to it, when we're living together all the time.'

'You're so right, Jessie, Jessie, Jessie. My Jessie. Wise woman. What would I do without you?'

They cleared the table and Matt repositioned his laptop, while Jess took herself to the bedroom. She even made the bed so as to make it all feel more purposeful. With a sweet expression, he closed the door on her whilst she was still tuning. Fair enough. But she was barely warmed up, half an hour into practice, when he appeared at the door pleading, 'Jess… Do you realise… 'you're playing the same thing over and over again?'

'Ooh. Yes. Well I have to, really, sometimes. That's how you do it.'

'Totally. Yeah, that's how you do it. Only… I'm not used to this yet… Is there something else you could do? I mean, just for today, because it is our first time, and everything.'

Oh dear. She was just in the mood for the technical stuff. But she wanted this to work.

'OK, I'll play whole tunes. Would that be better?'

'That would be better, yes.' He kissed her lightly and returned to his seat.

She played a couple of slow airs, behind a closed door. No reaction; maybe he'd be getting used to the sound now. So she struck up *Lasses Trust in Providence*, trying to decide how fast to play it. It was one of those tunes in 4 that risked a lumbering effect if you took it too steady. She tried again at a good lick; it might make some of the traditionalists frown, but it felt a lot more fun, and she was prancing along with it happily when the doorbell rang. It was the guy from the flat downstairs who wanted them both to know that number one, you weren't allowed to keep a cat under the terms of the leasehold, and number two, torturing animals was wrong and if they wanted to avoid a call to the RSPCA they'd better shut the f*** up. Right now.

Home yet not Home

This used to be Joe's favourite comfortable armchair. It wasn't comfortable now. He tried to relax and hoped that the jangling vibrations in his right arm and leg would stop. The house was quiet. All the rehab paraphernalia – perch stool, commode, mystery tubing, washing up bowl and such like – had been offloaded and was sitting quietly in the dining room, and the scraping and banging and shouted instructions were over. The only noise came from the kitchen, where Fran was preparing his first meal back in his own home. He played the journey backwards in his head, following the tumble of events upstream, trying to seek out the last time he'd sat still.

Getting the wheelchair through the house had been tricky. They had to bring him backwards up the new ramp to the front door. That was a nifty bit of metalwork. He had no idea how it had got there; he must have a good look at that one day.

Jess had taken over the wheelchair after poor Frannie had rammed it against the kerb, which had sent the reverberations of pain up to a new level. It sounded like she'd hurt herself too. And she'd been so upset about it, close to tears. She was strung out. A good job Matthew had been there to help fetch and carry.

Getting out of the car, Joe's right leg had got caught behind the sill, but he'd lifted it over with his left hand, and all things considered that particular manoeuvre had gone pretty smoothly. At the start of the drive, too, he'd managed the transfer from wheelchair to car pretty well considering he'd only done it once before, a couple of days ago. Fran had asked them to teach him how to do it, at the discharge meeting. Typical Frannie, never liked to wing it. Always had to read the instructions first. Turned out to be just as well, though, because starting with your back to the open passenger door was completely different from the way he would have done it before. His left hand had to work on its own to find the seat before he lowered himself down, then it had to steady him, then it had to lift the right leg into the car before his left leg could follow. The strain had shifted from place to place, muscle to muscle, as he eased himself in.

So how had he emerged from his coccoon in the first place, and got outside the hospital into the fresh air? Pushed along by Fran; there had been just the odd rattle over uneven ground. That wasn't her fault.

The last time he'd been completely still, then, must have been in the hospital lounge, where he'd sat for ages waiting for them to come and get him. Most of the staff were in a meeting and there'd been no opportunity to say goodbye. Now he wouldn't see Jenna or Fallon at all. It would be a new good night regime.

The food was better at home, of course. When Fran emerged from the kitchen, it was to announce minted new potatoes. Brilliant, worth the effort of getting up from this chair. She wheeled him to a small table she'd laid in the sitting room, from where they could see the front garden and the quiet street. Everything had grown strong and green whilst he had slumped indoors in hospital. There was a glass of red wine on the table, because, she said, this was a celebration. Yes, it was. In a way. But it was hard to be in your own home yet not to be able to take your usual place in it. Fran was anxious, her almond eyes never still, her smile never quite whole. He'd seen that expression once before. It was exactly as she had been on the day they'd first brought Jessica home from hospital, a snuffling, dusky little thing whose tiny fingers flexed and closed, as if signing incomprehensible messages for them in her sleep. Now, gradually, as they ate, he watched his wife relax. Perhaps it was the wine.

'I'm so glad to have you home.'

'Me too. I'm scared, though.'

'Oh yes, me too,' said Fran.

'I'm surprised they let me graduate.'

The discharge meeting, three days ago, had felt a bit like a dodgy parent teacher meeting, where it was full marks for effort and full marks for attitude and what a great sense of humour Joe had and how much they all loved having him around, but nobody liked to mention the fact that he'd got a big fat zero for attainment.

'I can't even drive the Zimmer frame. I mean, I crashed it into the wall for God's sake. And I never got further than the first set of double doors under my own steam.'

'True. But they all seem to think the home is a much more stimulating environment for rehab. There's more to do.'

Joe kept to himself the observation that he wasn't so sure. All he could see around him were the things he *couldn't* do.

137

Lay the table. Walk to the toilet. Open the door. Cut his own food with a knife. Even to pick up an object with his right hand, though beginning to be possible, took all his powers of concentration. Their furniture had become jumbled and pushed to the walls in order to make room for the wheelchair, whilst the pictures he'd arranged so carefully looked completely wrong from this low vantage. A glimpse down the hall had shown him that the door to his workshop was shut and likely to remain so. But you couldn't give in to these thoughts. When Fran told him that Dan would be round for physio on Monday, Joe reminded her he was meant to be starting the decorating, as he'd promised the depressed psychologist. His intuition was right: Fran needed to laugh. And to see that he still could. At the discharge meeting, they'd learned that his release – which felt precipitous enough – had been delayed (delayed!) partly because the psychologist had reported that Joe was a danger to himself. He was likely to take unnecessary risks, she'd written, because he didn't fully understand his vulnerability.

Whatever had brought him here, whatever accidents of fate and man, whatever gaffes, whatever plans, deliberations and arrangements, the fact was, he was in his own home now and he needed to think himself forward, and establish his new place in things.

'Right. We can't put it off any longer. Let's work out how we do bedtime in this house,' he said at last. Fran wheeled him to the downstairs bathroom, where he brushed his teeth left-handed, then to the dining room, where the spare bed had been set so as to give a view of the garden. The room was furnished now with all his new kit – a shiny white plastic and chrome commode on little shopping-trolley wheels, the perch stool which would support him so that he could almost stand to do things, and the Zimmer. They looked odd against the dark blue wallpaper. Mysterious blue, he called it, but now he wondered why they'd ever chosen it. She'd placed his favourite reading light, a slender stalk, at the headboard. The laundry basket, on its folding legs, also stood beside the bed. It was better than a bedside table, she said, because nothing could fall off it.

Together, they worked through undressing and putting on pyjamas, and finally, Fran pulled back the quilt so he could sit on the side of the bed and she could help him swivel in, exactly as Jenna had showed her. He got to a stand, and tried to get to a sit, but the bed was too high. Suddenly everything was moving. He lost balance, fell half sideways, then backwards; his legs were off the floor, but he felt as though his bottom was going to slide off the bed. The mattress seemed to be bouncing, and Fran must be straining to support him. He couldn't right himself and felt almost sick. Somehow, she helped him to get three-quarters on, then fully lying on the bed. But it felt terrible, frightening, because of the way it gave and moved. It wasn't just too high, it was too soft, too wallowy, and he had to tell Fran that he couldn't stay there.

She was perplexed, because in her perception, the surface of the bed was level and firm. There was nothing for it but to take the magic topper away. The bed would be a couple of inches lower, and with a bit of a sag in the old mattress, but that would be the best they could do for tonight. They got him off the bed again, and she wheeled him into the sitting room so as to have space to heave the offending item off and haul it out. He listened to the bumps and grunts. There wasn't the smallest thing he could do to help. She just needed him out of the way. By the time she'd re-made the bed and got him into it, they were both exhausted. He wondered guiltily if he had just panicked, earlier. Fran arranged pillows to help him get as comfortable as he could. But the pain in his shoulder and his arm meant he couldn't tolerate his wife lying beside him for more than a few minutes. When finally they said good night, and she left him to go upstairs, he felt as wretched as he had ever been.

PART TWO

Arrivals

The terminal buildings at Sumburgh looked like an animation studio prop that someone had improvised out of a couple of painted cereal cartons, small, low, and with something so makeshift about them, you couldn't believe that year after year, the airport hadn't blown into the sea. The sunlight was intense. Out of the cabin window, he could see the white ambilift waiting, one side in deep shadow. For lack of an available one at Glasgow, the ground crew had ended up using an evacuation chair to haul Joe backwards up the eight or nine steps into the aircraft, with a dreadful lurching jolt on each one which sent every nerve down his right side ringing again. This must be what Dr Stewart had meant when he'd described the trip as heroic. But here he was, and there below him on the concrete was his own personal nerve-jangler, his wheelchair with its green LSI tag, safely out of the hold.

Once he was on dry land, the wind smacked him good-naturedly about the head as if to say, hello there, welcome back, well, well, well, look at you, what sort of a scrape did you get into? He could hear skylarks, invisibly high in that huge sweep of sky; he'd forgotten about them. After the battering of engine noise, it was a relief to hear nothing but the natural world. And it was dry; they might have flown through rainclouds, but he had his back to them now.

He'd done it. He'd got there.

Fran had been excited and excitable all day. He'd never had any trouble reclaiming baggage, being so tall; people saw him looming overhead and actually got out of his way. Now he had to watch his little ant of a wife zigzagging her way through the travellers, moving wherever she could find a space, then hurling herself at the conveyor and, from the look of things, making an inappropriate number of apologies as she dragged each item back to the trolley, by the wall where his charming young handler had parked him. One day, he promised himself, I'm going to walk through here. And drive away, too.

As things turned out, though, they did end up sharing the driving, because the cheap deal on the hire car had come at a price. The small car had an aroma of stale cockleshells with top notes of sheep. Worse, the gearbox looked like the sort of 3-D puzzle that you found in the corner of the sofa at the end of Boxing Day, and Fran kangaroo-hopped all the way round the car park trying to get out of first. He felt certain that if only it were him in the driving seat, he'd be able to work it out from the feel of it. He leant across with his good left hand and found it took all his strength and a fair bit of waggling about to make the gear stick move. But it did, and they gathered speed with Fran doing the footwork and Joe in charge of the gearstick. It was painful to stretch, but everything hurt anyway.

Once they'd looped around the terminal and crossed the airstrip, Fran relaxed; or maybe it was tiredness tipping into hysteria which gave her the giggles.

As they headed north towards town, the rich pastureland round Dunrossness swept to a wide horizon, licking up to a ridge far to the west which was left behind them soon. The sea was always at your elbow. Every now and then, to their right, they glimpsed the Isle of Bressay, moody and blunt-nosed, over the sound; and you couldn't help being stunned by the sea at Channerwick, which today was navy blue. Fran read out every road sign with glee: Spiggie Loch, Quendale, Bigton and St Ninian's, magical places tucked away and waiting for their next visit. A good job the road was empty, given the way her eyes wandered. She was magnetically gripped by the emerald spathes of an iris bed or the bright yellow of marsh marigolds. It was all particularly fresh and bright and open to greet them today.

'We'd make a good pantomime cow.'

'You can be the back end,' she said.

'I'm the brains. I got this working. I'd be up front.'

She snorted. 'That wouldn't be aerodynamic, would it?'

He conceded with a sniff.

As they drove, he scanned the blue above the moorland for birds. Nothing much.

'Now we've actually got here,' she said, 'we can start to get excited about the concert. I've been so busy thinking how unthinkable it would be not to be there, that I haven't thought at all about what it was we were being at. If you see what I mean.'

'Easy for you to say.'

'You know what I mean. I really haven't given the concert a moment's thought. Which is ridiculous.'

'About time we saw a return on our vestment,' he said.

'Yup. Fifteen years of lessons. Growing out of fiddles faster than shoes. And the bows…'

'Spensive things.'

You didn't stumble over *them* down the charity shop, in amongst the plastic firemen and My Little Ponies. Fran

143

wouldn't catch that over the engine noise, so he didn't share the thought.

'We couldn't miss this. I'm so glad you're here, Joe.'

She stretched out her hand and let it rest on his thigh.

She'd never said to him, don't worry Joe, there'll be another time. Nobody had said that. There would be another time for Jess, but there might not be for him, because there could easily be another stroke. Fran knew that. His sister-in-law knew that. And they both knew that he knew.

Near the show ground at Cunningsburgh, maybe twenty minutes from their destination, they had to slow down for a tractor. Joe attacked the gear lever, which resisted as before, then suddenly clicked happily into place. And that was it. He had no idea what he'd done, but from then on, the car was unmistakably in automatic mode and gave them no more trouble at all. Apart from its quintessential odour of low tide, lanolin and disinfectant. Perhaps he'd be like the car. Perhaps one day, if he kept on rattling it, something would just click in his brain, and he would simply glide along the road again as if nothing had ever happened.

Tested

'For the price of these flights, I could be on the receiving end of three days' valuable management coaching myself. Just saying.'

Jess wasn't going to dignify this with eye contact, let alone an answer.

'Instead of which I'm losing three days' pay. And I'm using up my holiday allowance.'

Nope. Let him stew.

'And we want that for the honeymoon.'

The engine, which had been idling since the plane had come to a stop, cut out. Rain lashed the cabin window. Matt lowered his voice.

'So, it was essential, I mean, essential, to negotiate this work-from-home deal. Although obviously I'm not at home. So, I couldn't, I just couldn't do the Full Frenzy, and I don't think I can do the Half Frenzy really, if you add an evening out with Aidan. Not with the price of the ticket, I wouldn't be getting our money's worth. And anyway, I'm not a fiddler, am I?'

She wasn't ready to look at him and continued staring out of the window. The pale grey of the runway met the pale grey of the rain; the horizon was a blur, and just below, the ground crew in glistening back waterproofs and gloves were bending their heads against the wind.

'And anyway, how can there be any such thing as a Half Frenzy?'

At this point, Jess answered. 'Maybe they created it specially for you.'

It wasn't a good start. He was going to hate this, she thought. Cold, monochrome, and wet. Like him, today. Matt's first time into Sumburgh and he wasn't going to see anything, not even the lighthouse, or the rise of the cliffs over the bay at Fitful Head.

She had to give herself a quiet talking to. Look at the positives. That's what he'd say. So. At least Matt was there. Even if he'd just announced he wasn't up for even the Half Frenzy. Plus she was back in Shetland. Plus she had a great gig and tomorrow she was going to meet Archie, her childhood hero, not to beg a signature or seek advice or do a masterclass this time, but to work with him, almost like an equal. And her mum and dad would be there for the concert.

So get your cagoule on Jessie, and be grateful for that rolled-up woolly hat in the pocket. She'd warned Matt he needed one but he wouldn't be told. Ha. Served him right.

'Come on,' she said as she turned towards him and gently tapped his arm.

Once in the terminal, Jess spotted her Auntie Nell straight away, striding across the hall, smiling broadly, elbows out ready for action, pushing an empty luggage trolley.

'Is that her? What has she got on her *head?*' asked Matt.

What she had on her head was a brightly coloured Fair Isle hat with ear flaps and trailing woolly pigtails. All grin and glasses, as usual; but he did have a point, it wasn't fashion's finest moment and it was hard to imagine that hat looking good on anyone. The cowboy boots were boring in comparison. They hugged, and Nell turned to say, 'You must be Matthew. Welcome to Shetland. Oh, but look at you! You look like you've just hauled yourself out of the ebb.'

Jess sniggered. 'Oh Matt, she's so right. Your hair's kind of stuck to your head.'

'Ach, it'll pass. It was fifteen degrees and sunshine when your mum and dad flew in three hours ago.' Auntie Nell nodded to the conveyor belt which had just chugged into life and was bringing a chain of damp suitcases through a hole in the wall. 'Will I help with the luggage?'

Matt said, 'Thanks, can you stay here with the trolley,' and went over to the black belt.

Nell linked arms with her niece and they snuggled for a moment as they watched him go.

'He seems nice. I see what Ella meant about the big brown eyes. Adds to the wet seal look.'

'Yeah…'

'They got in safely, right on time. You're dad's OK. They're just settling in. He'll be cream crackered, though.'

She'd forgotten how short Nell was. Like her mum, only slightly more substantial.

'We're off,' said Nell.

Matt had leaned in and deftly picked up his black leather holdall by its proud handles. Their next item was Jess's backpack which he swung rather more awkwardly in the air, but Nell and the trolley were perfectly placed to receive it. She took it from him smoothly and handled it with ease.

'Ella wanted to come with me, but I told her to get onto that homework straight away,' said Nell. 'I'm not having stress on Sunday night. She's so excited about meeting you, Matt. If she gets in your way, just tell her where to go. She's a right nosey madam at the moment. She's at that awkward age. But then, aren't we all?'

Jess wondered what Matt must make of her Auntie Nell. The silly grin and the cod philosophy. Nell's eyebrows worked hard under the joke hat. She wouldn't take to anyone who didn't share her good humour.

Matt promptly flashed his lovely white smile and said, 'Yes, aren't we all?' and Nell beamed her approval at them both. He'd passed the test, then.

Trial and Error

The first you saw of Nell and Tam's home – one of the great granite houses on King Harald Street – was a steep and imposing central flight of steps leading high up to glossy red porch doors. The house had been built in a bygone age with money from the catch, constructed into the side of a brae; and like the herring, it was dappled grey and likely to be glistening wet. It had four storeys, and you might not even notice, on either side of this stone staircase, the narrow windows of a basement flat. A puffin burrow, really. It was tucked away and dark, but it had easy side access and Joe, who used to take the front steps two at a time, was grateful to be on the level this time.

Nell had picked up a Zimmer frame from the Gilbert Bain and found a ramp for the back door so that the wheelchair could come into the main floor of the house proper. And now the family was gathered in the high-ceilinged Edwardian sitting room which overlooked the Flower Park, eating cake.

'So here we are. Alone at last.'

The eight of them were packed into the sitting room. Nell stroked Joe's good arm and beamed round at everyone. She was brilliant to have fixed all this. Although her hair was looking a bit funny, squashed on top and frizzy round the edges. Hat damage.

Everybody started talking at once and Joe sat back to look and listen. Fran was rattling through an account of the journey and the dodgy hire car. Jess and Matt occupied the smaller sofa, and Freya had chosen an armchair alongside Jess, where they made a woolly huddle, talking Frenzy. Tam, the only quietly spoken member of the household, was trying to engage Matt in conversation and Matt was smiling and nodding slowly with something Joe now recognised as his all-purpose listening look, a look which might equally signify *I know exactly what you mean* or *I have no idea what you're talking about.* But he wasn't saying much himself, and he hadn't repeated a single word of Tam's, which was significant, because Matt always repeated what you said so as to work out what to say next, like a pilot lining up with the runway. It was a sure sign he hadn't yet tuned in to the shushing accent of the Shetlander.

Ella, meanwhile, hadn't taken her eyes off her cousin's fiancé. She perched forward on the edge of her low stool, looking cute, or trying to. No luck, kiddo, you won't catch his eye, he's too busy lip-reading a letter box. You could see that Matt needed the whole of his brain to figure out whether whispering Tam was telling, enquiring, offering or threatening. Joe had been in that situation often enough himself.

The girl suddenly gasped as if she'd just realised something truly astonishing, interrupting her father's conversation.

'Matt, d'you want to see the puppies?'

She made huge eyes.

The word puppies was like a gavel hitting the board. The whole room fell silent. 'You're not bringing them in here,' said her mother.

'Oh please!'

'Oh yes, please!' Freya joined in. 'Just one!'

Nell ignored their pleas and addressed Matt from the other side of the room. 'So, Matt, I hear you're wanting to start your own business? And what kind of business would you be in?'

Everybody turned to watch as the handsome young man took centre stage.

'It's kind of coaching.' For the first time today, so far as Joe could see, Matt began to look confident.

'I'm still at the planning stage, just doing scoping exercises, if you know what I mean.' Nell's right eyebrow was lifted in anticipation, which only seemed to encourage him. 'My psychographic niche is people who work on their own, sole traders, people in a company of one. Family firms.'

149

'That's me,' said Tam, 'I run the business on my own. With Nell.'

'More a psychopathic niche really,' said Nell.

'Oh, right, well, people like you, yes. I offer my bespoke services and work with the client as an enabler.'

'Enabling what?'

Matt nodded vigorously, bright-eyed and ready in the slips to field that very question. 'Decision making, for a start. Because it's lonely on your own. So, my mission is to accompany the client in decision processes. Which is why I want to call the business Quorum.' His smile expected applause, and there was a faint echo of it on Jess's lips. She was looking hopeful too.

'What does that mean?' asked Ella.

Fran cut in. 'A quorum is when you've got enough people in a meeting to put something to the vote and make a binding decision.'

'That way there's always someone else to blame,' said Nell, 'like in a democracy.'

Oh dear, both eyebrows were involved now. Irony was never innocent. Also, when his sister-in-law's eyebrows were raised like this, it was usually a sign that her internal crapometer had been triggered. Things could turn nasty. But Matt hadn't noticed.

'It's for the client who might not want to do the big things and make the big decisions on her or his own. It's about empowerment. I'm a reflector and an amplifier of the client's decision-making instincts. I want to coach people and help them tune in to that inner voice.'

'Would that be the same inner voice as tells you there's ice cream in the fridge?' said Nell.

'Is there?' said Freya. 'What kind?'

'Mint choc chip,' said her little sister casually. 'I looked.'

'Did that involve opening the tub and eating some?'

'Might've.' She grinned and threw her glance to the corner of the ceiling.

'So how far have you got with your planning?' asked Fran. Joe wondered what his wife was playing at, shepherding everyone back to the Quorum discussion when puppies and ice cream were so much more interesting. Matt picked up the baton fluently, with that same nod he'd used before.

'So, with the planning, I've already got the killer, niche-defining name, obviously…'

'Quorum.'

'…Quorum, right. Because the letter Q is cool isn't it? And I was thinking… You know how you have, say, the four Ps of Marketing…'

'Marketing begins with an M,' said Ella, rolling her eyes and shaking out her long fair hair.

'I know, it's rubbish isn't it? But you do. Anyway, with Quorum, it's Q for Quest, because we're on a journey together towards a distant goal; and it's Q for question because you have to ask the right questions to get there, and it's Q for Quality, because… well obviously. But I'm not sure three's enough. Quantum's good because it sounds cool, only it doesn't mean anything; or it could be Qualification if I give them a certificate. But I don't know if I want to give them a certificate. I mean,' – he turned to Tam – 'do you need that kind of validation?'

Tam looked startled and shook his head vigorously, as if he'd been asked whether he beat his wife.

'The one thing I'm sure is, it's got to be the four Qs.'

'Four Qs?' said Nell, with her head in her hands, 'Oh my lord,' and her shoulders shook as she made an asthmatic sawing noise.

In the blond corner, Matt really had gone a bit pink now.

'So, Ella,' he said, 'what about you? What have you been doing in school today?'

She'd been gazing up at him for ages, waiting to snap up a biscuit, and gave him her most winning smile.

'Today we did learning styles. What is your preferred learning style, kind of thing.'

'Very good,' said Matt, 'Very useful.' He nodded slowly now to show he was taking her seriously.

'Yeah, so there's four of *them* too. Visual, auditory, kinaesthetic and naturally intelligent.'

'And which are you?'

'Naturally intelligent,' she said, cocking her head to one side and blinking.

'Hey Joe,' asked Matt, and looked across the room, 'have you ever worked out what type of learner you are?'

It was nice of Matt to draw him into the conversation. The answer was easy.

'Right now... a slow one.' Everyone laughed. Good. 'Perhaps that's because there's too much on the... irrational curriculum.' He'd had to pause there because his ace joke word *irrational*, which he was rather proud of, didn't want to come out, it was sort of stuck behind his teeth.

'I just wonder if the therapists think it might help to know your preferred learning style?'

'I don't feel very kinaesthetic right now,' he said carefully, and wanted to add: or any sort of aesthetic for that matter. But that was another expression that would strip off the tongue, wouldn't it? People were listening though, and every member of the family was smiling encouragingly, so he followed up: 'Trouble is, moving is ninety p'cent of the course.'

Everyone understood.

'Bummer,' said Freya. She stood up and smoothed down her printed skirts, picked off a few balls of fluff which she dropped onto the carpet, then slipped out of the room.

At his elbow, Nell was making a low growling noise. It was a protective sort of noise, the sort of noise Bess might be making with the puppies. 'Mm,' she said, shaking her head, 'you've just got to keep going. You made it here.'

'I wouldn't miss this for the world.' Although if he'd known how beaten-up he was going to feel after the journey, he might have done. But he couldn't have put Fran in the position of having to decide whether to come up without him. He wasn't going to tell anybody that, either.

'You're getting better by the day, Joe,' said Matt seriously.

He snorted. 'They said I'd be able to drive after a month. But I can't. I've been deceived.'

'They said you *couldn't* drive *for* a month.' Fran rolled her eyes then sent him a cartoon frown.

He sent one back. He wasn't sure if it would come out right, but you had to try. She was so pernickety about accuracy. What you needed to hear was not what they needed to tell you, that was all.

Freya reappeared, pink cheeked, with a black puppy in each hand.

'Who wants first go?' she asked, and Jess reached out straight away. Nell took the other one and held it towards Joe. The puppy squirmed and jabbed his muzzle in Joe's direction, lifting his nose and sniffing excitedly at the prospect of a good lick. Joe bent his head to oblige, and Nell turned around to hold the silky black wriggler over his lap. To his good hand, it

153

felt just like a puppy, lovely and soft and warm. He wouldn't try with the right hand. He knew it would feel like a bag of spanners, and if he tried to stroke it, he might poke it in the eye by mistake.

'What's his name?' asked Fran.

'Oh, they haven't got names,' said Nell darkly. 'You don't give them names if you're going to eat them.'

'Five hundred and fifty pounds each. Six hundred for the females. Pedigree,' said Tam.

'Very entrepreneurial,' said Matt, making steady eye contact.

The signs were promising that they would eventually establish a common language.

'Spider's a good name for this one,' said Freya. 'He's that sprickly.'

Matt asked Tam, 'Where will you sell them?'

'We've got buyers already. Mostly word of mouth.'

'And it must be an easy way of making money?'

'Well I wouldn't say that,' said Nell.

'What I mean is, as a business, it's straightforward. You're working from home, you've got no staffing costs as such, you just have to feed them.'

'And clean up after them,' said Freya. 'You're mucky peerie pups, aren't you?'

'Yeah, sure, it's work, but it's not rocket science,' said Matt. Oh dear, the golden boy was taking a wrong turning. Joe could sense his sister-in-law bridling.

'And weigh them. And take care over their diet. And make sure they get exercise,' she said, as the puppy she and Joe were handling made an unexpected leap and half-slid, half-ran down Joe's leg and onto the carpet. 'It's a full-time job.'

Matt spoke to the animal now.

'It's got to be a lot more fun than creating another problem-solving exercise, hasn't it, Spider?'

Jess looked around the room. 'Matt's writing a module for WayUp,' she said, as if she were explaining something.

'Yeah,' he said with a sigh.

People nodded. The puppy was snuffling around at Matt's toes, so he picked him up and gave him a good stroking, playing with his floppity ears the way Joe would have liked to. There was nothing quite like a puppy's ears.

'I'm writing a module. It's about Constructing a Procedure. Define your outcome, break it down into tasks. Create a system, evaluate, improve, fine-tune. You know the sort of thing.'

Joe caught Fran's eye and wanted to say, '*She* does.' Their whole life seemed to be about systems now. He couldn't even get out of bed without following a prescribed sequence of moves.

But Nell's voice rang out first, triumphant.

'Well that's brilliant, Matt. You can do the puppies!'

Matt's open face lit up with enthusiasm and his white teeth positively sparkled with innocent excitement.

'Oh yes. Fun idea. I like it,' he said.

Sucker, thought Joe.

Deep Water

Strong morning light streamed through the deep-silled window of Cath's mum's kitchen and hit the washed wooden table with such force they'd had to push their chairs back. This close to Archie, Jess had more permission to stare. He was a wild-looking man, gruff even, with thick-tufted eyebrows and deep-set eyes, and wrinkles that lent themselves to dramatic studio lighting and made for great album covers. Spare, narrow-chested, and with so little flesh on him that his wrist bones seemed enormous. But he was animated in conversation, tender-hearted and quick to smile, so when you met him in the flesh the first thing you noticed was that those eagle eyes flashed an unreasonably pale and gentle blue. He had that Shetland way of speaking where all the d's and t's were close together, soft, as if dampened down. There was a sweet whistle to his s's. He rolled his r's and said *oot* for *out*. It was so tuneful, you could listen to that voice for ever.

It had been kind of Rona to lend them her kitchen for the morning by way of a rehearsal space. Cath herself was up in Lerwick right now setting up for an event, and that had made it easier for Archie to decline her Peat Shed Studio with its spiders and its rickety furniture, and opt gracefully for daylight and warmth. The kitchen was lined by purposeful clutter, with dishes drying, tea towels draped over the Rayburn, an empty pot on a chopping board, waiting for something to happen. Loads of great players had sat right here, relaxing in the faint odour of salmon scraps. These cats knew how to live all right.

They'd tuned up first. As they drank their tea, Archie was interviewing her, as if she were the interesting one.

'Faber's not a Shetland name, is it? But you've been playing here for years.'

'It all goes back to My Auntie Nell's wedding. I was only four. She came up to work in Mid Yell, and she married a local.'

The eyes flashed. 'They're wild on Yell,' he said, and she laughed. He was a tease, like Uncle Tam, like her dad.

'Three days at a wedding is a long time when you're only four. I thought the whole of Shetland was like that – people eating and drinking and dancing and making music. Everyone seemed to be on holiday. Everything had different rules from home. I wanted to be a musician from that first day I watched the band.'

'Do I know your uncle's family?'

'The name's Croot. He's Tam. But they're none of them musicians. They're on King Harald Street. I've stayed with them every Frenzy now for years.'

Archie nodded. 'And I've been watching you come on. And now here you are. So let's play.'

Jess was caught off balance when Archie picked up his fiddle and struck up a reel, because he didn't seem to draw breath between speaking and playing; but if this was how it was going to be, she'd have to up her game; and by the end of the first eight she was ready to join in. It was a tune she knew but she couldn't recall the name. She warmed up quickly as she bent into the music. Then, without pausing, he went on to another, and another, and she'd never known an audition so brisk. He put a harmony in, then on the repeat nodded to her to do the same, while he took the tune himself. It was a fine strong sweet sound from his Scandi violin. The two instruments blended well enough but he hadn't really opened out in the kitchen, and she wasn't sure she'd be able to match his tone once they got to the hall.

He stopped as suddenly as he'd started, and sat his fiddle upright on his knee.

'If there were nae music at a wedding, what would you have?'

His pale blue eyes, under their wiry, sandy brows, demanded an answer.

157

Jess had to shake her head.

'A fight. That's what you'd have. A stramash.' And he picked up the fiddle again and attacked *Lasses Trust in Providence,* which at least had been on her list.

'I've been trying that a wee bit faster,' she ventured after a run through, and played a couple of lines. 'What d'you think?'

'Aye. Go on then, you start this one and I'll just hitch a lift.'

But it didn't feel like he was hitching a lift. Speed was effortless, and he was somehow adding notes where there was no room for them to be. He seemed to be driving her faster and faster down a narrow winding moorland road with pools on both sides and no passing places. She waited for the look that would tell her, now we're coming to the end, but no, he was back at the start and heading once more down the winding lane. When they ripped their bows away to end the double-stopped final cadence, they both laughed, and she slumped back into her chair.

'I nearly ended up in the voe!'

Archie sat up straight and eye glinted as he said, 'Right, that was the warm-up.'

The wicked look soon faded.

'Now let's get down to the serious stuff.'

He began *Da Slockit Light,* the slow air she'd learnt as a child, but only really heard a few weeks ago. In Archie's hands it spoke a very grown-up language of love and longing. He played it with such gravity and tenderness that the arc of the music seemed to start and finish deep in the heart; and if ever she was going to achieve that herself, she dare not stand too long in awe. This was no time for nerves. She had to get down to work, listen and learn, and do the best she could to match the sweetness and the richness of his tone.

'Come on, Jess,' he said.

She was caught between wanting and not wanting. 'It's such deep water, Archie.'

'Don't be scared. Let yourself float.'

When you float, you have to tell your limbs what not to do. You tell your shoulders not to tense, your arms not to struggle, your hands, your legs, your feet to relax. You tell your head, this water is a pillow. You trust the water to hold you up. You breathe as slowly and as easily as you can.

She picked up her fiddle and looked across for his sign, the sign of his ribcage widening as he took in the breath, the eye, the heel of the bow as it descended to the string. Then she settled into the music.

They'd been playing for the best part of an hour when Archie asked her would she have a tune of her own she'd like to share. In a rush of excitement, and feeling rather juvenile, she told him about Joe Faber's Frenzy Reel, and the stroke, and how Joe Faber's Frenzy had become Joe Faber's Air. And that her father was in Lerwick now, and had been a complete hero for making the journey north to hear her play only ten days after leaving hospital.

Archie listened and leaned forward slightly.

'My sister had a stroke last year. She couldn't speak properly. She couldn't knit, either, for a long time. She used to have all the patterns in her head, you know? She has to have them written down now.'

Immediately, they compared notes: speech, mobility, memory, coordination, personality. Archie's sister Aggie had become prone to tears – music, a story in the paper, even a sentimental advert on the telly could set her off. Jess explained how her dad was funny as ever but he just couldn't jump in to conversations any more – his lips were slower than his imagination – and anyway, his humour wasn't always recognised as such these days. People didn't expect you to be funny in a wheelchair.

Jess played Archie her original tune, Joe Faber's Frenzy Reel, and did her best to show him how jaunty and quirky her dad had been. Then the slow air, with the syncopations smoothed away, and time to linger on the leaving of each note. She gave it all the space it demanded. It was as different from the reel as Archie's *Slockit Light* had been from her childish nyeetling on an ill-tuned half-size.

When she finished, neither of them spoke immediately. Behind her, she heard the light inside the stove pop into life. *Pah*. Like a blown kiss, or a dandelion clock launched on the air.

'You've opened it right out,' he said. 'Your Frenzy reel is music for the feet all right. But the way you play that air… It's music of the heart, Jess, and that's what sorts them out. Play it again. We'll do this together, for an encore.'

She had to stop herself from blurting out her first thought, that they might not get one.

'There's a message in this music, Jess. Your da's life has slowed right down, and he has to *take it peerie ways*, as they say here. But even taken peerie ways – with little steps – life can still be sweet.'

His smile was generous, and under the thick mad eyebrows, the pale blue eyes sparkled clearer than ever. So, the music conveyed something to him… a sweetness, and a meaning. A moral. Something beyond her sadness on the day of its creation. Now that she had a listener, her music took on a new and fuller life.

Duff Notes

Some mate Aidan was turning out to be.

So, technically, in the day time, Aidan was working on his research project. No problem with that. Matt imagined his best man standing in a bog, drenched, trying to take sound checks in a gale, for the sake of a few little brown feathers a normal person wouldn't even notice. But one evening out together wasn't much to ask, when he'd travelled all this way. I'll come over to yours, he'd said, I'll get a cab, we can go to the pub, maybe get a bite to eat. Oh no, Aidan had told him, there isn't a pub. Come round with some beers if you like. Only he wasn't really available anyway because it turned out most nights this week he was doing the sound board for a bunch of kids in some village hall out in the sticks. Volunteering for the Frenzy. So he'd been sucked into it too.

Matt had coaxed him, come on bro, how about volunteering for me? And you've gotta meet Jess. Well, that was different, wasn't it, suddenly he was interested, because she was a fiddler and they were bound to bump into each other at the Clickimin. Matt went along to the hall at the leisure centre as Aidan suggested, and had to endure an hour and a half of wall-to-wall fiddle playing. He'd never heard so much at one sitting, and it turned out to be tougher than he'd ever imagined.

You were talking whole fiddle orchestras, made up of kids and grannies, just sort of jogging along with plonky piano accompaniment, woom-cha woom-cha; woom-cha woom-cha, and a set of drums that could only do one thing, thum, tsss, thum, tsss. The hi-hat sawed into your brain after a while and left you desperate for a blast of Ella's gangsta rap. Jess did a set with Cath and the girls, and they were definitely a cut above. But there was something he'd never noticed about the fiddle music before: repeats could get very close to monotonous.

At one point it got so bad that he had to get out for air. Aidan Barry was manning a stall at the back and jumped up like some sort of warder. Asked him where he was going. He had a bit of a go at him about not coming to any gigs which was well out of order but Matt put him right on that score.

'Do you hear what I hear?' he'd said in the end.

Scratch scrape screech.

'I rest my case.'

When it was over, they all met up in the cafe where the only seats left were low stools. Aidan's long thin legs were forced to bend absurdly at the knee, and his upper body swayed about. Then he whacked Cath with a leg and decided to stand, which looked even worse. Red-haired Cath, Jess's childhood accomplice, turned out to be even noisier off stage than on. She congratulated everybody loudly, Matt and Jess for getting engaged (OK, that was appropriate), Jess for improvising like a jazzman (was that a compliment?), Aidan for sorting out the buzzing PA system (totally over the top, no big deal). She had a laugh you could hear a mile away, too, a bit like the sound of water gurgling down a plughole. And the worst of it was, before he, the groom, even got a chance to open his mouth, Cath had jumped in and introduced Jess to Aidan. Woah, butt out, lady. In fact, she acted like she knew Aidan pretty well and completely monopolised his attention, addressing everything to him. She gabbled on. You couldn't get a word in edgeways.

Not that Aidan ought to have a problem with that. He was one moody guy, never said much, just loomed over everyone, listening, like a bloody great aerial mast. So skinny, so vertical.

Except that suddenly, he was jammed on transmit. Of course Jess should be pleased to meet him, but she didn't have to sound so curious about his boring research. She asked some random bird question, and it was like turning on a tap: suddenly, Aidan gushed away, and she was standing there going 'ooh really' and 'wow' and 'how amazing'. Matt had completely lost her now. She was fixated on the pole. She raised her eyes to stare at him, and her head made micro-movements that followed his every statement. He'd liked Aidan better when he was antisocial. Even Cath glazed over and went off to get another beer, then never came back, because honestly, all this bird talk was so much white noise.

There was something about Aidan's posture, now that he stooped over Jess to tell her stuff, that was unsettling; not just the closeness; he was doing that thing a lot of tall guys do when they realise their head is in the wrong place for women to hear them properly: he lowered it engagingly to one side. Too cute by half. It was exactly the way her dad used to talk to her, in the days when he could stand up. Which made this particular use of body language an outright threat. Matt drew his arm around her waist and waited for her to press towards him. Which, eventually, she did.

Puppy Training

It was almost an industrial process. Fran watched as her sister picked up a biro to note in a small red exercise book the weight of the white plastic box which sat on her kitchen scales. Inside it something shadowy was moving. Then Nell lifted the two-week-old puppy out and set him down on the floor to eat, before letting the next one through the makeshift gate between the kitchen proper and the dining space. A barrier had been made using parts from the puppy pen, a cardboard box, and a huge bag of kibble that slumped against the wall. The second puppy headed for the feeding bowl but Nell scooped him up and put him into the plastic box on the scales. Then down to feed, and on to the next. One by one, she took them to suckle from their mother. The puppies were identically black and sleek, but each wore a differently coloured collar.

'There's a lot to be said for routine,' said Fran. 'Me and Joe are both in training.'

She'd left Joe in the puffin burrow, in an armchair with the paper, recovering from the exertion of breakfast. For him, every day began with ranging exercises for his arm, which had to learn to stretch: contraction of the muscles was the enemy. Getting up was slow, likewise getting dressed, and the days of flitting between bedroom and bathroom, washing, brushing teeth, shaving, and dressing as the mood took him, were over.

'We put the Zimmer outside the bedroom door.' There wasn't room inside; the door of the holiday flat opened straight onto the foot of the low bed. 'He can just about make it that far. Honestly, Nell, I can't do right for doing wrong. He needs me to be there in case he wobbles. But he needs me not to be there because I'm always in his way.'

'It's all learning,' said Nell. She was wearing pale old jeans and flip-flops, with the sleeves of her loose blue shirt rolled up. Obviously acclimatised. Whereas downstairs, Joe had a fleece over his jumper and the heating on full.

'We started off thinking the big question was whether he ought to fly. Would it make his brain explode, do brains that have popped once go pop again at high altitude, you know? But I realise now the real issue about travel is how and when they haul you on and off the plane. And I never realised how uncomfortable he'd be sitting in a wheelchair. I'm trying not to think about the journey back.'

'You can only live life forwards,' said Nell, 'and you can only understand it backwards. Or something.' She looked over the top of her glasses and added, 'Steve Jobs. Or was it Aristotle? Some bloke on a TED talk.'

'I'm seriously thinking I ought to go part time,' said Fran. 'There's a big re-structure going on anyway.'

Nell stopped moving, held the puppy she'd just weighed against her chest, and looked her sister straight in the eye.

'A year from now, he might not need you.'

'They've allocated carers three times a day, at the moment, while I'm at work. And what happens after the six weeks?'

'All I'll say is, be careful what you sign yourself up for.'

'I signed up the day I got married.'

Fran's resolve soon wavered, though, as it did every time she imagined a life without work. She saw in her mind's eye a long dark corridor with many rooms off, from which, as you walked past, you could hear gossip, laughter, music, raised voices, but whose doors were firmly shut. Perhaps her world was going to shrink to this.

'Ach, it's early days. See how it works with the carers. Don't burn your bridges.' Nell put the puppy down to feed and picked up her former rhythm. 'It sounds like he's doing fine, and the main thing is, he's keeping positive.' And she began to sing, in a silly voice, and bobbing from side to side, as if entertaining a child: 'You've got to E-liminate the negative, ac-centuate the positive, latch on, to the affirmative, don't mess with Mr In-Between!'

'You've frightened him, he's going to wee.'

Fran looked down at the floor, but Nell was there already with the puppy pad, and plonked the little sniffer down on it, telling him 'It's Frannie's got you frit, coming here with her great big feet in your way.'

'I have not got big feet.'

Ella pattered in daintily and placed a mug and a plate in the sink. Her hair was up today.

'Hello Auntie Fran,' she grinned, then her voice turned to mock seriousness: 'Mum, you were singing again. I've told you about that.' She looked across at Fran with a shrug which apologised for her parent's bad behaviour. 'How're they doing then?'

'This bruiser here is fine. That little chap in the blue isn't so good. He's not gained since yesterday.'

'The runt of the litter,' said Ella. 'So I've got a soft spot for him, Auntie Fran.'

'I did him first, so he could get a good feed before the heavyweights muscled in.'

With the bruiser in her right hand and the other arm held out for balance, Ella swung one slender leg then the other over the barrier to join the pups in their playground. All eight had been weighed now. Some were feeding, others racing about. The object of this game, as Nell had explained to Fran, was to keep the floor as clean as possible, so that the puppies learnt to expect cleanliness. You had to wipe up any accidents quickly and preferably behind their backs, so they wouldn't grow up thinking it was your job to clean up after them. Although of course it was. Ella sat on the floor in pale grey leggings and bare feet, swivelling round on her bottom, playing with them and watching out for poopers. They ran around, then they got a bit tired, and then would be the danger time. You had to get them onto the pad, then screw it up and get it out of the way before they walked through their own mess and spread it round the room.

Fran's eyes followed their unpredictable zigzag movements across the shiny floor. She had been intending to ask her sister whether she missed the health service, but a look of such satisfaction had spread across Nell's face as she gazed down at the dog ballet that it seemed a stupid question. Besides, if you didn't want to emigrate to the land of regret yourself, you shouldn't buy anyone else a ticket.

Nell put the plastic box away in a cupboard and pulled up a chair.

'Of course, this is how I trained all my children,' she said, and Ella rolled her eyes.

Fran tried a different question.

'So, what's it like, working with Tam? Being together all the time?'

'Well, at least I haven't got an idiot for a boss.'

Ella looked at her mother from the corner of narrowed eyes.

'You called Dad an idiot only yesterday.'

Nell shook her head and guffawed, 'Yes, but I didn't call him boss, did I!'

She laughed so loud that Bess, who'd been stretched on the floor with her pups, tensed her front paws, lifted her head and turned it over her shoulder to see what was going on.

'Seriously, though,' said Fran once they'd all calmed down.

'Ach, you find a way of working. Tam has his jobs, I have mine, and it's up to me how I do them. In a way it helps working from home. If I get fed up, I can take it out on the hoover, can't I? But sometimes you need somewhere to go.'

'So she walks the dog,' said Ella, pursing her lips. 'If she takes the dog out at unpredictable times, you know they've had a mazanter. And if she takes the pickup, it's *really* bad.'

'Yessirree!' Cowboy Nell slapped her thigh. 'Sometimes I just head for them thar hills.'

Bess gave a couple of woofs, wagged her tail and looked like she was ready to go.

Light Bulb

Their time in Shetland was fast running out, with the Frenzy coming to its final weekend, and Matt was looking forward to being warm again. There was one place to shop, which everyone called 'the street', where you could buy chocolate. You could also buy framed photos of local sunsets and bad weather, and any amount of antiquated knitwear, too, but what would be the point of that? He ought to take his mother something and opted for a pincushion in the shape of a puffin.

He had ventured beyond Lerwick. Nell had taken the pair of them down to St Ninian's, and that was, admittedly, spectacular: the white sand of the double-sided beach-with-no-land and the turquoise sea looked positively tropical. But walking on the beach meant getting out of the car, and the minute you did that, the illusion was shattered. The Frenzy organisers put on outings for the visitors, and he'd joined Fran on a minibus trip to three places with -*sting* on the end of the name. He saw a man wearing a veil, strimming a churchyard. The veil was to keep the midges off. There was a lot of nice scenery but otherwise nothing much, although Fran seemed to like it.

Then there was the Shetland family. The house in King Harald Street was not an easy place to work. Freya was home from uni, too cheerful by half and with time on her hands which she spent painfully writing and rehearsing songs on her ukulele. Awful plucking noises. In the evolutionary scale, the uke was one up from the elastic band. If you allowed yourself close enough to hear the lyrics, some of the skits were funny – *I sat on the range / When my pockets were full of loose change* – but she was putting a lot of time into a song with the chorus *He's a waster, oh yes, he's a waster.* Matt had a horrible feeling it was about him.

Sometimes the uke was drowned out by the rap from behind the closed door of Ella's room. A fat bass line, and on top of that turntable squeals like nails down a chalkboard, and vocals which came at you like well-landed punches. It racketed up and down the staircase and bounced off the quarry tiles in the hall. Jess shrugged and said at least the kid had music in her life. But he was troubled by what he saw when he asked her to turn it down. It took a lot of hammering before the door opened, and actual mime in the doorway, before she ran inside to switch it off, leaving the big old door wide open. He wasn't ready for what he saw. The wall above her bed was covered in neatly aligned sheets of A4 paper printed with targets, each one bearing a hole where the gunshot had entered. The consistency of her aim was impressive; she must have spent hours perfecting her technique. In the middle of the rectangle formed by these paper tiles was a poster of two black Labradors. The sudden silence felt more brutal than the music.

'Oh, sorry about the language. Mum keeps telling me the words are really bad, but I've told her, I don't listen to the words.'

'I'm due to talk to a client, but it's, um… quite loud?'

'Oh,' she said. 'Right. You're upstairs. Sorry. Sorry,' and she scrunched her shoulders up to her neck and did a special frowny face with a tooth-gritting grin, to underline the apology.

Then there was Jess's Auntie Nell. He had a feeling she'd been having a laugh at his expense, with her problem-solving challenge. He had a whole flow chart coloured in felt-tip pen, showing how to get the puppies weighed, fed and exercised, which worked on paper. It was not his fault that the delivery had been, well, OK, clumsy, because she'd hidden his clipboard. Well, put it on a chair where he couldn't find it, same thing. If he'd had it to hand, the floor would have been pristine. And two of the puppies hadn't actually needed a bath, so it wasn't all of them like she said. Then when he asked Nell how she'd developed her own process, she told him it all came from *The Book of the Bitch*. Which was one training manual he hadn't ever come across.

As the week went on, Matt had come to realise that Boring Barry was something of a celebrity round these parts. A big fish a small pond. Yet Freya thought Aidan Barry was seriously hot and she was dying for him to come round to the house; she said the wedding would be an excuse to get to know him better. What was there to know?

The night before Jess's big gig, surprise, surprise and out of the blue, Aidan texted to suggest they meet up in the bar after the fiddle session. The venue had a dialect name: Mareel. You weren't meant to say *the* Mareel; it was an arts centre, not a pub. Although people did. This invitation was a little bubble of golden sunshine, a chance to get away from the weird women up at King Harald Street, to offload about the weather and the flickering broadband, and to impress someone with his otherwise great life. Also, it was time to claim his ten quid.

Extensive reading of the inspirational bios of sports celebrities taught him one thing: you wouldn't be a winner unless you set yourself challenging targets. You needed something to aim for in life. Even if you didn't achieve it – that wasn't the point; success, and therefore happiness, was all about a disciplined mind set. Aidan, on the other hand, was one of those people who simply didn't get it. His only strategy was to hang around and wait for opportunity to knock; according to him, you just had to be ready to jump at a good thing when it came by. Fine, except he was obviously delusional about what constituted a good thing, so it was no wonder he'd ended up here in the back of beyond, racking up a student debt as big as a house. Whereas the first thing Matt had done at the very start of his career in management training was, sensibly, to re-visit his own list of life goals. Aidan had taken one look at the Life Plan and scoffed. He'd bet Matt a tenner that he wouldn't achieve any of these objectives, because, according to him, life wasn't like that and life would get in the way. Which made him one sour, glass-half-empty, sad loser.

OK, some of Matt's goals had fallen off the list, not because they weren't achievable, but because he'd changed his mind about them. There was no point being specific about what model of car you'd drive, for example, because let's face it, specs kept changing and so did your needs. But one of the things that had always been there on the list, well before the management career and secretly for as long as he'd been into girls, was to live with the woman of his dreams. And now he'd achieved it. Good as. Which meant Aidan had lost his bet.

The Mareel bar was packed, but he picked Jess out straight away in the midst of the crowd. It was her amazing head of hair: so big, so golden, so frothy and unpredictable. It never looked quite the same twice yet you knew it could only be her. She returned his wave then turned back to her fiddly friends who were all gassing away; she'd promised to give him and Aidan a bit of space. He bought two beers and sat down quickly as low seats became free. Aidan appeared but it took him some time to make his way across the room, because he had to say hello to everyone – which was not the Aidan Matt remembered from their quiz night days. Then it turned out to be surprisingly difficult to hold a conversation, with all these people wanting to say hi, who's your friend. One of the interruptions came from a curvy young woman called Iona, who was wearing a low-cut top and goggled at Matt like he was fresh meat in a famine. So he did his best to blank the bosom looming over him, and practically shouted out the news that Aidan was going to be his best man, actually.

'Am I though?' said Aidan, and gave him a funny look. Once this Iona woman had drifted off in search of the next meal, Matt came back for clarification. What did Aidan mean, *Am I though*?

'The way I remember it, you sent me a text. "Getting married, want you for my best man. PS you owe me a tenner".' He swallowed some beer, all the time looking beyond the bottle at Matt.

'And you said yes.'

'I said... just a minute, I've got it here...' and he actually got his phone out and started scrolling back to find the evidence. Anal. 'I said Congratulations. I didn't actually say yes, did I?'

Matt felt like his weary brain was balancing on a log, trying to work out whether to take his friend seriously or not. Aidan's angular face was deadpan, but then, it always was.

'You're having me on. Nice one. Very funny.' Aidan wasn't known to be a practical joker. So maybe he was changing, coming out of his shell. What did they put in the water round here?

'Course I'll do it, mate, but first I need you to answer one question.'

'Go on.'

'Why me?'

What sort of a question was that? He should be flattered to be asked. His tone was definitely borderline aggressive, too, so the answer needed to be something that would de-fuse potential conflict.

'Me and Jess… it's all thanks to you, in a roundabout way. Because, well, you got me into the whole Shetland thing.'

Aidan's clever glasses made him look like some guy off the telly, even more sceptical than usual.

He wasn't blinking.

'Are you sure it wasn't because you didn't have anyone else to ask?'

'Oh, mate…' That was harsh. He had to recover, and looked away for a moment. Someone had strung a row of old-fashioned lightbulbs across the ceiling, which he'd not noticed before. 'Look, I'd do the same for you.'

'OK. Only Christ, Matt, a *text*…'

'What's wrong with that? It's not like I was dumping you.'

Aidan actually smiled. 'Look, for future reference, right? It was a bit casual. A big thing like that, and no follow up.'

'I sent you the date!'

'And be honest: you've always taken me for granted. You did right at the start, with the quiz team.'

'That's history, Aidan, I mean…' But Aidan cut him off.

'In fact, you do that with people, you know. You cross your fingers and hope they're OK with whatever you want.'

There was this sort of buddha look on his skinny face, like he was imparting some special wisdom. Nobody had ever said anything like this to him before. So obviously, it couldn't be true. All Matt could do was shake his head.

Aidan went on, 'Just be careful when it comes to Jess. Check in with her before you build your plans.'

Now he gasped. That was out of order. It was easy enough to defend himself; he had stacks of ammunition.

'I'm only here because of her. I'm the support team here. It's my job to cheer her on and give her a bit of faith in herself.'

Aidan opened doubtful eyes, and let him go on talking.

'I'm the one who talked her round when she'd got cold feet about the gig. I'm the one who made her think career trajectory. I've given her the tools to visualise her own success! I helped her with her website. And it's me that's nagging her about getting an agent.'

Aidan frowned, shook his head and took another sip of beer. Which was annoying.

'Look, Aidan, Jess is fair and square right slap bang centre stage in the very middle of this relationship. In fact, she dominates my activity log.'

For some reason he couldn't fathom, saying all this just seemed to be making Aidan madder and madder. There was an urgent conversation he still wanted to have with Aidan that he couldn't have with anyone else. He'd wanted to talk about getting married. To tell someone how much it meant. How brilliant Jess was, and why they were absolutely made for each other. Somehow, it wasn't coming out. Aidan threw his shoulders back and stared at the ceiling, then took his glasses off and placed them carefully on the table. He pinched the bridge of his nose and blinked a couple of times. His eyes, without their protection, looked like little round dark nuts. Beads. Proper beady eyes. They didn't look short sighted at all, they just drilled into him as he said, 'You really think you're good for her, don't you? You think you're doing her a big favour.'

This was crazy talk.

'No, Aidan, you've got it all wrong. *She's* good for *me*.'

Because yeah… she was…

Everything wobbled. All the lights in the bar seemed to be waving – the trad white bulbs strung in a row suspended above their heads, the dotted line of red LEDs that followed the window frame from ceiling to floor, and all the jazzy reflections dripping down the shiny plate glass. Perhaps it was an illusion set up by the choppy waves in the wharf outside, which were suddenly gripping the light from the bar now that it was starting to go dark. Shaking it out. Waves… waving!

It was as if the actual *universe* was excited.

He'd never had an intuition before. He hadn't even been sure it was a thing.

This was an incredible moment and it made the whole room glow. His head was pulsing now with the knowledge he'd just landed a knockout punch, and not just in the argument with Aidan. He *just knew* that Jess could only ever make his life better, could only ever come first. He'd always been sceptical about gut feeling, because he suspected people used it to justify their own partiality. Perhaps he'd been wrong all these years.

Aidan set the specs back on his nose.

'Now you're talking. Tell me more.'

Matt's eyes darted about the room. He was never going to forget this bar. Or this moment.

'She's totally brilliant. In every way. I mean, she's lovely.'

'I want specifics, Matt.'

Aidan was smiling, like he'd stopped being snarky.

'She's…'

Aidan stared comically over the rim of his glasses, waiting.

'I can't imagine life without her,' was all he could manage.

'Well, good. Good!... Just be careful.'

He found himself laughing. His best man shook his head in a forgiving sort of way and brought the bottle back to his lips.

Mareel

They hadn't managed to get seven seats together, and it had tickled Joe to see how smartly Freya and Ella had shepherded Matt along with them into the stalls, leaving their mum and dad to join Joe and Fran in the gallery at Mareel. From here, Joe had a perfect view of the stage and the whole of the auditorium, which was bathed in an otherworldly purple. Also, the elders could also keep an eye on the younger half of their party below. Freya had hung back for a while to talk to a gangly young man in glasses, identified by Nell as Aidan. Matt sat between the sisters, and all of them were in a huddle which swayed like seaweed in the tide, now this way, now that, over one mobile phone or another. In front of them all, a huge blue and white projection of the double f of the fiddle frenzy logo filled the backdrop. *Fortissimo.* You had to take your hat off to the designer who'd introduced those lovely fiddle shapes into the lettering, the scroll and pegs.

Nell stood before him, leaning against the gallery rail so that she could turn to make eye contact with everybody. She was in fine form and regaling them with stories of some bloke on Unst who'd sprayed the undercarriage of his car with fish oil, so as to protect it from the sea spray. Nell reckoned that with all that Omega 3, it ought to be twice as effective as other oils. She laughed shamelessly at her own joke. It was hard to have a proper conversation when you were parked on the end of a row, and Joe's upper body, neck and shoulders, were so

176

sore and aching that he couldn't really turn around to face the others on his left. He knew that down on the end of the line, whispering Tam – who must have heard this story a few times before – would be adding his own brand of salt. There was no chance of catching these cryptic asides over the piped music. It was getting to be a way of life, half-hearing things, now that the wheelchair meant his head was at everybody else's elbow. Fran, the heartless minx, told him now he knew how *she'd* felt all these years, but he reckoned she wouldn't be joking about it if she thought the wheelchair was going to be permanent. And it was not going to be permanent. He'd make sure of that. Even if he still had no sensation in his weak limbs, he'd proved to himself that you could walk with a Zimmer frame without actually feeling the pavement. Besides, the physios were teaching him how to walk, and they wouldn't waste their time if they didn't think that one day it would work, would they?

He fell deep in thought about the whole walking business. *A walk in the park.* Not so easy now. *A walk on the wild side.* If only. It came up a lot in songs. *Walk on by. Walk tall, walk straight, look the world right in the eye. Walk on, walk on, with hope in your heart, and you'll never walk alone*. He was surprised to find himself getting more sentimental these days. Getting soft in his old age. Just about all his favourite people were here at Mareel tonight, and in an hour or so his Jess would be on stage, and he was here to see it. The sense of his own good fortune hit him like sunshine.

'Oh look, he's waving at us,' said Fran. Across the auditorium Matt had turned and seen them. She waved back.

'He always looks so innocent,' said Nell, following her gaze and glancing over her shoulder in his direction. 'Oh jeez, *Ella!*'

Down in the stalls, Ella was trying to take a photo of them all and had knocked an elderly woman seated in the row in front on the head. Freya looked like she might be apologising for her little sister, who'd brought her hand up and was shaking with giggles, and Matt... well, you couldn't see any of their faces, but Joe reckoned it was a safe bet that he'd have that winsome seal pup look that Jess seemed to like so much. The woman was talking to him now and positively beaming. She got to her feet and turned around, and seemed to be offering to take Ella's photo for her. See, he was a charmer.

'I think he looks innocent because innocent is what he really is,' said Fran.

'Yeah, he knows nothing. He means well,' said Nell, 'but he couldn't kick a hole in a wet Shetland Times.'

'He's more nervous than Jess,' said Fran.

'Oh, she'll be just fine,' said Nell.

'Oh yes,' said Joe. 'Matt's had her visualising success for the last four weeks.'

'There you go then,' said Nell with a full eye-brow somersault.

'He tried it on me once.'

'Visualisation? Any success?'

'Mmm... Sort of. I kicked a nurse in the face.'

Turn of the Tide

These were great seats near the front of the stalls. But they made you realise how big and draughty that platform was. Matt had terrible butterflies. He was just too impressionable. In a way, the cousins were a welcome distraction. They weren't that bad really, just a bit young and silly. They meant well, but they knew nothing.

Wedged between them, he was caught in a battle of two scents: Ella was wearing something sharp-sweet, expensive, mainstream – a *fragrance*; whilst Freya had a single something which reminded him of Glastonbury High Street. Herb, spice, or dope?

She nudged him and passed over an envelope.

'Aidan wanted you to have this,' she said, and stared, shamelessly waiting for him to open it.

He could feel the folded ten-pound note inside: a sweet moment. So he just said, 'Thanks Freya. It's OK, I know what it is,' and allowed himself a ripple of smugness as he tucked his winnings into his pocket.

Everybody's mobile pinged more or less at once. Zanna had shared a set of pictures of herself modelling her latest inspiration for the bridesmaids' outfit.

'Jeezuz,' said Ella.

Freya made the sort of noise that went with pulling a sticking plaster off slowly.

'Oo-h-h-h-h, I don't think that's a good idea. I don't think that dress is ethical.'

He didn't follow. 'I like it.'

'It's not good wedding etiquette,' the little one explained. 'Out-bumming the bride. When Uncle Joe walks her up that aisle, everybody's eyes should be on Jess. Not the bridesmaid's arse. Although it's probably her best feature, I'll give her that.'

Yes, thought Matt, Joe is going to walk her up the aisle one day. In all the time he'd been staying with Nell and Tam, it wasn't something that had ever been up for debate. This whole family shared a kind of confidence in the future, which was something he recognised and respected, all the more since he expended most of his professional energy trying to persuade the faint-hearted to embrace change. Turn the music down, and in the long term, he could get on with this lot.

'I guess it's up to Jess,' said Freya, with a sigh and a shrug.

Matt agreed. 'Of course, it's up to Jess. Jess won't mind about other people's bottoms.'

She wasn't unreasonable and it just looked the same as a hundred other dresses to him.

'It won't show for the photographs, either,' said Freya. 'The back, I mean. So it won't be there for posterity. Or maybe I should say posteriority.'

'It's a braw dress, don't get me wrong,' said Ella. 'Only a wedding shouldn't be an arse competition.'

'Yeah. We're planning an eightsome reel, not a twerk. And anyway, I'm not wearing that,' said Freya.

'No way. I'm not wearing that either. It would be disloyal,' said Ella, thin-lipped.

While they were taking the moral high ground, he was reading on. 'So, she knows the designer and he's offering an amazing deal...'

'Check him out,' said Ella. They did.

'Woo-ooh-ooh,' said Freya. 'I like the look of him.'

'Oh my *God,*' said Ella. 'Look at this one. The two of them together.' She leaned across Matt so they could both see the photo on her phone. 'Your little sister is *into* him.'

'How can you tell?'

Two girls rolled their eyes at each other.

'It's just the way she's looking at him. She is *so* into him,' confirmed Freya, nodding. 'Mind you, so would I be. He's kinda cute.'

The nodding went on.

'Mmm,' said Ella, 'He's more your type than mine. Skinny. Specky.'

Matt turned to fix Freya's eye.

'A bit like Aidan Barry.'

She blushed crimson, then dimpled and said, 'Maybe.'

Freya laughed so easily at herself, he was warming to the idea that these kids might one day be family.

Joe Faber's Air

By the time they got to the interval, Joe's bones were weary, and he had to keep wiping the wet from his half-feeling chin; he seemed to have been sitting there for hours. Before it came, though, he already knew that the second half would be something he'd remember for the rest of his life. Archie played a brilliant set alone, then introduced 'the very talented Jess Faber'.

In walked a young woman that he'd never really seen before. The electric blue of her dress was mesmerising under the lights. Blue, Joe had read somewhere years ago, was a powerful colour for an artist because the human brain somehow had to make more of an effort to see it... something to do with wavelengths. It meant you might either miss it completely, or, given the right quantity and intensity, you might be absorbed in the contemplation. And also gratified. That was how it worked now. Suddenly, too, the pinned-back hair made sense: everyone could see her face. Which meant she wanted them to. Something in her had grown up, and she was taking her place in the world. Once she began to play, Joe knew that it would all go well, because this was where she belonged. Something in the way she held her head, the stillness of her stance in the fast passages, and the little easy movements, a slight dip, a look across at Archie, told him she was more than ever swimming in her own familiar sea. Fran held Joe's hands, stroking the poor one to wake it up, and squeezing both whenever the music was particularly exhilarating or particularly soulful. He could feel the way his wife held her breath, and he could hear the audience listening. Archie and Jess might have been playing together for years, they were so well in step with one another. At last, after a crazy run through *Lasses Trust,* they came to a stop, and Joe laughed and cried to hear the applause, which seemed to go on and on. His own inept clapping was as vigorous as it was unpredictable, which gave him the giggles, and he laughed out loud, louder and louder. Nothing could top this. But of course, there would be an encore.

Archie stepped forward and everybody fell silent as he leant into the microphone.

'We have a very special encore for you tonight. It's a first performance with a special history, and it all started right here, last year, with one of those Frenzy workshops you all like so much. Some of you might remember that this talented lassie here wrote a cracking reel, and she called it Joe Faber's Frenzy, because it was kind of a musical description of her father.' All eyes were on Jess for a moment, and in the pause, Joe heard Fran gasp; she hadn't been expecting this any more than Joe had. Then, down in the stalls, people nodded and one or two exchanged glances with their neighbours.

'If the music's anything to go by, her da's a bit of a nutter.'

'You're right there,' said Nell. Typical soothmoother, calling out in the theatre. She and Fran were all smiles as they turned to acknowledge him. The hairs on Joe's head stood up.

He well remembered this piece. So, they were going to give his reel an airing at the Frenzy, and Jessie hadn't breathed a word. It wouldn't be a first performance, though – Archie was wrong about that. Then Archie was suddenly talking more about Joe. The microphone left no room for doubt.

'Now, Jess's dad had a stroke a few weeks ago. He's still atween da bed an da fire, but he's made a special trip to be here today. Aye, aye, Joe!'

He actually waved up to him in the gallery, and everyone turned around.

'It's a slow business, learning to walk again, which is what Joe's doing right now. But for the time being, Jess has re-written her tune. So, it's not Joe Faber's Frenzy Reel, it's Joe Faber's Air. And this is for Joe, and for my sister Aggie, and Dorothy the stroke nurse and the support group. Because we all know someone who's battled with stroke, don't we?'

He heard Fran gasp. It seemed unbelievable. When had she written this? The whole audience took in a deep breath as Jess stepped forward and raised her bow to the fiddle. Joe recognised the old tune not far under the surface of the new, but where the original reel had bumps and corners, and jolted you about and spun you round and changed direction till you were giddy, this air was smooth and clear as the wing of a gliding bird. Jess played it through first, then Archie took over the tune and made it his own, with Jess lending a thoughtful harmony. There was sadness in it, but warmth and strength too, and whilst it caressed the deep notes, it ended resolutely on the high. Now his face was wet again, this time with tears.

The music met a long hush before the clapping started again. Down below them in the stalls, somebody stood up – it was Matt – it was lots of people. All standing for his daughter's tune. Clumsily, and weeping for all he was worth,

Joe held his arms out and swung his body forward, his left hand feeling for the rail of the balcony, so that Fran could help him up.

At last, he was on his feet.

PART THREE

Back to Earth

Other people could be perplexing.

The care package was in place, and Fran had come back to the lab this Monday morning with the expectation of a normal week. Things were looking up. She was still on a high after Frenzy. When they all went down to the staffroom for morning coffee, Madeleine had been keen to hear how the trip had gone, and Fran thought she'd just given an honest account of a series of triumphs, both for Jessie and for Joe. It was all good news. Yet Madeleine sat opposite with a mouth curved down like a mushroom cap, and eyes filled with pity and horror. As she listened, her head was making funny clicking movements from side to side; her heavy-lidded eyes were half-shut, her cheeks flushed an intense pink, and her long hair clung to the sides of her head. One hand sat limply on her breastbone, and from time to time she would take a sharp intake of breath, give a little *oh,* or worse, a barely whispered *no*... When Fran told her about Joe Faber's Air, and how the audience had loved it, she said, 'Oh Fran, I'm so sorry.'

'But it was a fantastic moment.'

'Oh Fran, I don't know how you keep going, I really don't.'

Which left her wondering how to begin to answer. After coffee, Fran worked through a tray of samples, injecting each with the reagent. Madeleine was hard work. Her emotional magnet clung to half the elements of the story: the man struck down, the husband in the wheelchair, and a jolly piece of music which had to be chucked away. She simply ignored the rest. The best. Madeleine thought Joe was never going to get any better. And yet this was an educated woman, a scientifically educated woman no less, who ought to know enough about the brain to know it could re-wire. Perhaps she thought the effort and the time involved were not justified. Which was insulting, when Fran could see him getting better every day. Although nobody else was looking that closely. She was extravagantly proud of Joe these days. Madeleine probably thought she was putting on a brave face. Which she wasn't. Or that she was delusional. Which she might be.

Fran's view of things and Madeleine's were simply not calibrated. They could work side by side in the same lab, and keep on running the same experiment of life, and they'd never, ever, come up with the same results. The trouble about this sort of heavy conversation was that when Madeleine rounded it off by saying, 'We're all thinking about you,' it begged the question, just what were they thinking?

A deliberate and uncompromising hygiene had taken hold of Fran, which treated unwelcome thoughts like microbes with the power to infect everything, and which therefore had to be eliminated. She was lucid and energetic about this, and becoming aware that discourse with others involved a series of rational, clinical decisions: there were some people you just didn't talk to about certain things. Because look what had happened with Madeleine just then, when really it was all good news, and she hadn't mentioned the bad things, the pain and the being manhandled on and off the aircraft.

The same scrubbing process went on with her own thoughts. However, she couldn't push back the memory of the airport checkout, where she'd stood behind him, hands on the chair; the sight of his curly head lolling to one side, his right shoulder dropping, his tall strong body just snapped in half like some twig, had brought tears to her eyes and throat: her husband was in a wheelchair now. They had to use the special queue. People in the other line glanced across. Some would be envious that they were fast-tracked, some would be making their guesses about what was wrong with him. Perhaps the tears had formed because she'd known he couldn't see her.

It didn't help to think about the allotment, and yes it registered with a twinge of pain that she was having to buy her French beans from a shop this year, but that was hardly a big deal.

'What happened?' asked Harry, looking down into the waste bin at the end of Thursday afternoon.

'What d'you mean?'

'Something made you eat that creme egg.'

It was true, she'd not only eaten the sickly confection, but actually enjoyed it. He must have spotted the foil wrapper.

'How d'you know it wasn't Madeleine's creme egg?'

'She doesn't do carbs on a Thursday.'

'So, your Cornish pasty... what's that about?'

'Oh, I always have a pasty for lunch on a Thursday.'

'Since when?'

Harry grinned his beautiful grin again. 'You're changing the subject. How's Joe?'

'Mm. *He's* OK. It's *them*.' Oh, for heaven's sake, thought Fran, she could tell Harry what was going on without him reaching for the tissues. Out it came in a torrent.

'The whole point of the care package was to make it possible for me to stay at work. But they can't tell you when they're going to turn up. Mornings could be any time between seven and eleven. I shouldn't leave the house later than 8.30. And I can't just leave him in bed! So I can't see how we're going to get into any sort of routine.'

He frowned. 'Tricky.'

Strangers had a key to her house and were dashing in for three short visits a day. Joe was waking up early and in pain, because he couldn't lie comfortably. By the time the carer had arrived that morning, she had already helped him get up, wash and dress, given him his breakfast and checked on the painkillers, so there was nothing left to be done. Four days in, and she was mentally exhausted. She hadn't felt like this since her first days at big school – disorientated, unsure what happened where and when, or who was responsible for what. She pondered on the creme egg. Joe would say this was the thin end of the slippery slope. And she hated being late for work. What if this lifestyle went on, and she was late every day; and what if creme eggs led to Mars bars and Mars bars led to giant Toblerones? It didn't bear thinking about. She'd end up looking like the Michelin man.

'Madeleine's very disciplined,' she observed.

'If you say so. Back to Joe. I might have a set of wheels for the old man.'

'Wheels?'

'Mobility scooter. It works. It's one of those you can take the battery out and it fits in the boot of a car. My Uncle Pete had it and my Aunty Bren's trying to get shot.'

'Doesn't your Uncle Pete need it anymore?'

'No,' said Harry, closing his eyes in a way that made her not want to ask why.

When she got home, she told Joe about the offer. He said, 'Ah. What happened to Uncle Pete, then? Trip to Lourdes? Or dead man's wheels? Oh, what the hell. How fast can it go?'

Table Etiquette

Round to the Harringtons for dinner. Just the four of them, the parents. To get to know each other.

Joe already suspected they must be the sort of people who did everything properly, from the way Zanna had eyed up his tea towel napkin back at home. Well honestly, an ordinary napkin was just not big enough; food might end up anywhere. They'd told him at the hospital he had to use his wrong right hand even if it was just for a few mouthfuls, which meant anything involving a spoon was doubly hazardous, because neither hand could do it. Since he had very little feeling on the right-but-wrong side of his face, the mouth didn't always receive food as graciously as it should. He couldn't cut up a slice of roast chicken, or even hold the knife properly, but he could use it to pin the bugger down whilst making shredding motions with the fork. Bits might fly off anywhere. At home, accommodations were made; red meat was sliced up daintily, and on a good day nothing on the plate was bigger than a sprout – it was real *fine dining*. Fran had a special smirk that meant, darling, you have food on your face. This always made him laugh. But Zanna hadn't seen the joke and looked hugely embarrassed.

189

Matt's parents' house was magnolia-with-a-hint-of cream – carpets, curtains, everything – which put you on your guard from the start. He was in a foreign land, and the Zimmer tracks were going to give him away as an undesirable alien. There was a good bit of pale knick-knackery around, and Joe's eye was particularly drawn to an opalescent porcelain bowl of silvered pot-pourri which sat on one of those radiator shelves, just asking for a cuff to sweep it along and off the end, sending the contents deep into the Wilton carpet. It didn't, though. Janet Harrington turned out to be nothing like Matt, and nothing like her daughter Zanna either. She was much larger and better upholstered, with a sturdy pair of cabriole legs and good, wide-fitting shoes. Her hair was assisted auburn, huge and wavy, her jewellery discreet, her make-up flawless. She wore a daring pastel pink which, as Joe told her, made a charming counterpoint with the oatmeal curtains. And she was, in fact, friendly and chatty now that you met her face to face, he thought. At first. Then there was Derek. He was all right in his way. Once they got talking about the A303 Joe realised he did have quite a lot to say. He had two facial expressions. One was *now I'm talking to you*, and featured slightly raised eyebrows in anticipation of a response; the other was *I'm not talking to anybody at the moment* and involved brows, eyes, mouth in a series of straight and parallel lines. Very steady chap, Derek.

They got through the sherry and nibbles without mishap – Joe knew not to go into nibbles territory; anything dry and biscuity ended up decorating your whiskers. He was really making an effort, for Jess's sake. Fran wasn't exactly blending in, though. When Janet explained that she hadn't worked since having the family, because there was so much to do at home,

Fran said, 'Ooh, gosh, how many you got then?' She knew damn well it was just the two, she was being a minx.

Derek said, 'Matt tells me you used to make models for a living.'

'I do.'

'Did it start as a hobby, then?'

'I went to art college. Four years hard labour.'

This was generally a tricky moment, when people realised you were an artist not an engineer. Derek remained inscrutable, but it registered immediately with Janet. You could see the war in her brain between *things I know about Art* (the renaissance and all the lovely impressionists Turner and Constable trips to the National Gallery holiday in Florence that nice man on the telly a better class of Christmas card) and *things I know about art college* (drugs hippies mess paint punk bands mess more drugs nude models paint in coffee cups scary people who failed Maths).

'Is there much call for that line of business round here?' asked Derek.

'Oh, t'riffic,' Joe lied.

'Only I thought, what with the state of the economy…'

'Oh yes. We're speshly busy in times of' – he placed the words carefully – 'austerity and doubt. People can't afford the real thing. The multiplexes and the malls and the luxury 'partments. We just knock 'em up a miniature. Something to show their customers – planned developments. This project's currently in the pipeline, sort of thing.'

Derek's face had settled back to horizontal lines. Joe sighed and stared into the middle distance as wistfully as he could, to add, 'I'm in the business of dreams, really.'

Not a glimmer of a reaction. But Fran actually kicked him under the table, which was a pretty rotten thing to do to someone in his condition.

'Actually, he does a lot of work for museums.'

Now that impressed them for a minute, until Joe tried to explain how the Parthenon had literally flown through the air and ended up in a big black bin. Janet was aghast.

'How simply terrible.'

'You wouldn't think it had… aerodynamic… prop'ties, though, would you?'

Janet gave a restrained shake of the head. Derek said, 'It didn't. That was a freak accident.'

'I'm only sorry I didn't see it happen,' said Joe with complete honesty.

They made it to the dining table. It was correctly laid, a symphony of right angles – credit where credit's due, one of these two had an eye as true as his own. The only thing aslant were the smoked mackerel fillets which lay across each plate, and even they were purposefully so, poised between a *frisson* of lettuce and a precisely dosed blob of horseradish. He had always liked smoked mackerel, and could see it wouldn't be hard to cut, so the strategy was clear: he'd take his time and use his knife, and eat like a gentleman. He'd always been good with fish, being fascinated by their basic construction. All he had to do was keep looking and stick to the guide lines helpfully indented on the flesh – one delicate tap on the long straight line would split each fillet lengthways in two, whilst the lateral chevrons acted like perforations which could break it into politely sized morsels. Slide it off the silky skin, hold the knife still as you can while you ram it against the blade, and Bob's your uncle. Beautiful things, mackerel.

Drinks were poured and Janet checked with Fran, was he allowed wine.

'Only by the glass' said Joe.

'I was wondering,' ventured Janet as they all began to eat, 'about the reception.'

Fran smiled amiably and cocked her head to one side, expressing her readiness to hear what the question was. Joe took her cue and did the same.

'Zanna tells me you've booked the Jolly Roger at Nuttiswood.'

Fran nodded. 'We've been going there for years. Haven't we, Joe?'

'Years.'

'Zanna's recommendation was Highams Hall. Was there a particular reason you didn't go for them?'

'It's not really up to us,' said Fran, 'it's Jess and Matt's decision.'

'Of course. But you know how they are. I wondered if they'd really thought this through. Highams is so close to St Cunegund's. Much more convenient.'

'People will be in cars,' said Fran with a shrug.

'Ah, now, you're right there,' said Derek, suddenly animated. He turned to Joe. 'Highams Hall has a car park that can accommodate fifty-six vehicles comfortably.'

'Gosh,' said Fran.

Watching Janet, you could see where Matt had got his enthusiasm from.

'And you know, they put on the most wonderful wedding breakfast. You can even have vintage bone china to eat off, and honestly Fran, it's just so pretty. It's a lovely little rosebud pattern with a gold rim, just like our grandmothers used to have. It's quite the thing. And they put lovely ivory covers on the dining chairs with big bows on the back.'

'What's the food like?' asked Fran.

'Oh, enchanting, very, very dainty. They do these lovely lovely canapés and gorgeous gorgeous nibbly bits, because there's always a lot of waiting around isn't there, so your guests do need something straight away with their fizz. And for your main course, they can do chicken several different ways.'

Joe was tempted to ask her preference between tikka masala and Kentucky fried, but Fran got in there first with a mischievous 'Do they do chips?'

'Um... Well, yes, they do... I'm sure they would, anyway. If that's what you want. Although I don't think Jess and Matt will be wanting chips for their wedding breakfast.'

She gave a genteel laugh, somewhere between light-hearted and half-hearted. Dainty as a canapé, thought Joe, who was studying his mackerel for fear of catching Fran's eye, because he knew if he did, he'd corpse like an amateur.

'The thing is,' said Janet, 'the Jolly Roger is absolutely fine for what it is. Which is a village pub with a perfectly good kitchen, lovely hearty food – Derek will remember, won't you dear, we went there once for Sunday lunch, you had the pork with that crackling, Derek. I had the beef. And they do have a very serviceable reception room. But on such a very special occasion, do you not think we ought to be... well... raising our sights?'

There was an awful squeal of knife against plate, followed by a gasp. With painstaking care Joe had worked to slide his mackerel from its coppery-silvery wrap, and had succeeded, but at the last moment sent the oily and crumpled skin flying across the table and into Janet's lap.

194

'Oh,' she said, and gave that dainty laugh again.' Well, I suppose that's what a napkin is for.'

'Flying fish,' said Fran and grinned from ear to ear.

'At least I saw it go this time,' said Joe, realising he now had a serious case of the giggles.

Derek remained unmoved. 'No. That was another freak accident.'

Hmm, thought Joe. Some accidents were meant to happen.

But later that night, when Joe was getting ready for bed, Fran told him something truly awful and not funny at all. He was prepared for the worst because she prefaced it by saying, 'I wasn't going to tell you this.'

Apparently, while Joe was in the loo admiring the African violet and its mother-of-pearl cache-pot, which exactly matched the soap dispenser, Janet had taken the opportunity to have a quiet word with Fran. The wedding could turn out to be a terrible strain for Joe, she said. Everyone would understand if he didn't want to make a speech. Although of course it was early days. And would he be giving the bride away, if he couldn't walk her down the aisle?

Now, thought Joe, let's just put to one side for a minute the fact that 'giving the bride away' is a borderline offensive concept and one which belongs to a more primitive age. Let's just park that thought and go along with custom. But why would anybody ever think he wouldn't be able to make a speech at his daughter's wedding? And who was she to decide that he wouldn't be walking by then?

'What did you say to her?' he asked his wife.

'I said of all the people round that table tonight, you would be the best after-dinner speaker, hands down. You're so clever with words and you're so funny, and you've got so many stories about Jessie, and she's so stupid not to realise, and not to think… Well. Honestly. So I said, perhaps she didn't realise but you were much in demand on the after-dinner circuit. And she went *e-ow*, and she said no they didn't. Anyway, I said not to worry, you wouldn't be asking your usual fee. Only it's no joke really. How could she?'

That night, Joe turned this question over and over in his mind.

Perhaps it was the way he looked. Perhaps his mouth was a bit more crooked than he realised, and he'd failed on Artistic Impression. Failed Janet's decency test.

He used to be clever and funny. He used to tell a good story and people used to laugh. Nowadays he had to rely on Fran or Jess acting like a conversational snow-plough and clearing the way for his set pieces, subtly or not so subtly warning people to shift out, shut up and listen.

But a speech would be OK because at a wedding, everybody *would* be listening, and you could write it down. Perhaps he'd be able to write by then.

Imagine if all those years ago he'd believed what his teachers had told him, that art college would be the gateway to ruin – or worse, a life in advertising. It had taken a certain cussedness to resist, but he had then, and he would now.

He wasn't prepared to let this woman define his limitations. People who told you what you couldn't do should never, ever, be trusted. In fact, you had a duty to prove them wrong.

Stroke Gym

Jess was curious to see what her dad's Stroke Gym sessions at the General hospital were like. He always came back knackered, but mellow. So what did they get up to? This week, her mum had a meeting about the re-structure, and whilst Matt was really being very sweet in offering to take her place, Jess suspected it was an excuse not to buckle down and do some work. Whereas she, as Joe's daughter, surely had first dibs on any truanting opportunities. Besides, she was the only one who had nothing in the diary.

On the drive out, she seized on the opportunity for a good old gossip.

'Zanna came into the Cherry Tree yesterday for a panini...'

'Stop. You can't have a banini. That's like having a pence.'

He expelled the P of pence with huge volume, as if to make up for the banana / panini mashup.

'Whatever, Dad... Although can I just say, *they* called it a panini.'

'Customer's always right.'

'Dad, you keep interrupting me.'

'You interrupted yourself.'

This banter was a very good sign; maybe he was starting to get back to his old, annoying ways. He was sounding a bit the way her mate Annie got before a gig. Excitability due to nervousness. Aha. The gym was her dad's chance to perform in public, and these might be performance nerves.

'Anyway, she was in town to have her nails done, she said, because she's going out tonight. And I just realised, she's always dressing up and going out, but I've never met a boyfriend. Or girlfriend. Although I do wonder if Freya was right about that designer bloke...'

'What does Matt say?'

'I haven't talked to him about it, Dad. I mean, this is all just malicious tittle-tattle.'

Inside, a cheery white-haired chap dressed in civvies greeted them. His moustache was immaculately trimmed, and there were neat creases down the short sleeves of his pale summer shirt. His ID swung from a lanyard round his neck: Volunteer. Ted Doubleday. Was Doubleday really his name or was it some weird hospital code? They sat on plastic chairs and he wheeled his blood pressure monitor to her dad. There was nothing much for her to do, other than spectate.

The surroundings were grim; it was a flimsy looking box, really, with high windows tucked under the ceiling such as you sometimes saw in school gyms, no colour to speak of, and hard surfaces everywhere. But the thing that stopped it being an ugly place was a look on the faces of the people using it. For some of them, like her dad, this was probably a level of physical activity they didn't achieve during the rest of the week.

Ted Doubleday guided her father from rowing machine, to bike, to arm bike, to pull-downs, to steps, all the time standing by and offering encouragement, even bursting into song at times. She reckoned she'd been right about the performance nerves.

She scrutinised every member of this tribe her dad had joined. He was progressing from Zimmer to stick, but lots of these people were walking around unaided. Some of them were much younger than him, some much older. Some were seriously overweight, others trim. Nobody as tall and spindly as her Giacometti dad, mind you. Some were alone, some needed a helper, like the young man who couldn't speak properly and had a person who seemed to be a carer from social services with him, or the woman about her father's age who had lost the sight of one eye, and whose husband she got talking to; he enthused just like her mum.

She also got to meet Linda. Linda, the stroke physio, was a bit of a legend for her mum, because they'd spent all that time together the day it happened. Linda turned out to be small and spare – not much taller than her mother, but definitely more athletic – and dressed in a practical blue trouser-suit uniform whose short sleeves revealed sinewy, tanned arms. Short haircut – no time for messing. Jess was struck most of all by her hands. She talked with her hands all the time, using them to explain things, yet without ever waving her arms about; all her movements were strong and controlled. Doing hands. Square and flexible, with fingers that took her father by the shoulder or placed his foot on a pedal and seemed to command, stay there. She had one gesture which was a bit like demonstrating the way you held a violin bow, wrist raised, fingers dropped down and slightly apart. But in Linda's language, this wasn't to do with holding anything lightly; on the contrary, it meant *solid*, it meant contact with the ground. You could imagine her sculpting or potting or kneading bread.

The gym began to empty and they were directed to another room full of chairs for the talk. Helpers queued for coffee and tea, and a tin of biscuits was passed round. Jess recognised Charlie as the sister on the Stroke Assessment ward. She announced today's topic as Goals. Blimey, was there no escape from this obsession?

One by one, participants volunteered information about what their goals were and how they were achieving their ambitions. A really nice-looking guy, slim, dark skinned, maybe thirty, in black jeans and a neat, dark fitted shirt, said his goal had been to ride his motorbike again. And last weekend, he had. But Charlie had to feed him questions, to get any further than that.

'Can you just tell everyone how you were after the stroke?'

'Well, at first I couldn't move.' His tone was almost indignant, as if everybody ought to have known.

'So, you stuck to your exercises?'

'Well yes, or what's the point?' His face wrinkled in a scowl, like a troll in a children's picture book.

Charlie kept smiling. 'So that must have been very difficult, at first. Getting back on the bike.'

'Well yes. I kept falling off.' The same frown. He's quite proud of himself, thought Jess. He thinks this should all be obvious, so what's to talk about?

'And how did you deal with that?' Charlie wasn't going to give up.

'Well it's simple really. I wouldn't have it. I just kept on trying.'

'But didn't you hurt yourself?'

'Oh yeah. Loads of times.' Now it was as if he was beginning to see the point of this conversation, because for the first time he looked around the room and spoke to the others.

'The way I see it, I don't want to be disabled. I don't see myself as a disabled person, and I won't let anyone tell me that's what I am. I just decided, I don't want it. And I won't have it.'

At her side, Jess heard a deep sigh from her father. She knew he was trying so hard. The young man's combative manner intrigued her; he wasn't angry with Charlie, he was angry with *it,* the stroke. There was a grain of arrogance in implying that all you needed to do was to get a grip, exert mind over matter, and you too could be riding the lanes of Somerset on a motor bike. But cussedness was definitely an advantage, and her dad had that. Meanwhile the room congratulated the biker: *good on you fellah, that's amazing, well done.*

Next to speak was an elderly woman who sat behind a walker, at right angles to her father.

She started quietly. 'I don't leave the house much these days. So, my goal was, to come to the gym with my friend here, because my friend can help me on the bus.' Suddenly her voice gathered surprising strength and her face was all excitement when she said, 'And here I am!'

The room was full of chuckles and ahs.

Her dad leaned across to tell her, 'What about a lift on that bloke's motorbike next time? I... I... I can see you in black leather!'

She let out a big ooh, her friend whooped into laughter, and although his voice didn't carry far, there was a definite reaction from the people sitting near them who'd heard him, too.

A few more weeks of this regime, thought Jess, and he'd soon be back in full heckling mode.

In the car going back, she told her dad how incredibly energising it had been just to sit and watch them all.

'Ted was nice.'

'Mmm. But he would insist on helping me.'

'What did Linda make of you then? You were having quite a conversation there while I was queuing for coffee.'

'She said I'd come a long way since she last saw me on the ward and did I have any questions. So I said yes. Why is it that all these other people who've had strokes like mine seem to be doing better than I am? When I'm doing everything I can?'

'And I bet she said, *every stroke is different.*' They all said that, all the time.

'No. She said: Joe, most people who've had a stroke like the one you had…' – he paused – 'are dead.'

He'd timed that delivery – he was such a *performer,* her dad – and now he waited again for it to sink in, before adding nonchalantly, 'So I'm thinking maybe it was serious.'

Jess sat back to grip the steering wheel straight-armed, glanced at him – he was silly-faced – and blew out her cheeks. 'Blimey, Dad.'

She'd been so afraid when it happened, then as he got further into recovery, she'd blamed herself for having an overactive imagination and dramatising the whole thing. But this was official, then. He *had* nearly died.

Ten minutes down the road, she decided to look to the future.

'Targets, then. Got any, Dad? Now you've done the Frenzy?'

'I could ask you the same question.'

Ooh, that was a surprise. Had he noticed she was drifting a bit? She did feel she was in a bit of a dither. It was about time someone put her on the spot.

'Cath's been on at me about going back up to record a disc. Aidan's offered to do the sound.'

'I thought you young people did all this in your bedrooms these days.'

'Well you can, of course. I'd rather not, though.'

'Perish the thought. You'd have to tidy up.'

'I could stay with Aunty Nell and Uncle Tam, that'd keep costs down. But it's still going to be an expensive trip. I'm not sure.'

'What does Matt say?'

The fact was, Matt had smiled his cherubic smile and said, Whatever. *Whatever you want to do, babe. – No,* she'd said, *I'm not asking permission, Matt, I'm asking you whether you think it's a good idea. Is it a justifiable expense, in terms of time and effort as well as cash?*

'He said it was my call. Which doesn't really help me make my mind up. It's a business decision, after all. I thought he'd help me figure it out. With one of his *if this, then that* things. His decision analysis tools or whatever they're called. I mean, it ought to be right up his street. I said to him, forget it's your girlfriend, imagine I'm a client. Didn't help.'

'OK. Now *you* imagine: it's next year and you haven't made this CD with Cath. Because Shetland's too far away and it's too much trouble. Now. How will you feel about that?'

'Same way you'll feel if you don't make a speech at my wedding,' said Jess.

So that was that. Decision made.

Wheels

They were like kids. Standing in the driveway behind Harry's gleaming orange Mini Cooper, Joe, Matt and Jess were practically fighting over who'd be first to assemble the mobility scooter, which sat in three pieces in the boot. When Fran knew full well she'd be the one who'd need to do it most often, so it clearly ought to be her. Now Joe, hovering uneasily behind his Zimmer, told her the battery would be too heavy for her to manage.

'Look Joe,' said Fran, 'for your information, right? Hands up all those who have a certificate to prove they can lift and shift.'

She and Harry raised a hand and the others exchanged perplexed glances.

'All right you lot. Of all the tasks on my jobs list this weekend, this is the only one I'm actually formally qualified to do. Right, Harry?'

'Right!'

She was extra careful to do it by the book, with no awkward twists. The battery was no heavier than a bag of potatoes, the chassis and the seat were light. The assembly was straightforward.

When Matt asked, 'Shouldn't we charge it first?' and Harry said, 'Done,' she remembered the mattress incident.

'What are you smiling at?' asked Joe.

'Me? Just looking forward to the practice lap.'

'All right,' he said.

Joe brought the Zimmer alongside the little blue scooter and used his left hand to swivel the seat round. It looked like an effort, but once he'd lowered himself onto it, he easily returned the seat to the forward position and checked both his feet were solid on the plate. Harry bent down on his haunches to show Joe how the controls worked, and Matt paid serious attention too. Joe tried forward and reverse.

'The lever on the right side sticks a bit,' he said, and Harry fiddled with it and said, 'Mm, it is stiff. But it's working.'

There was a sound like a lazy sewing machine, and he glided down the drive, with Matt alongside; the turn into the road was negotiated brilliantly, with just a slight bump as the scooter adjusted to the pavement. It went on juddering, so maybe the flags were uneven. They had lived in that house for the best part of twenty years and until the wheelchair had arrived, she had never really noticed that the pavement sloped towards the gutter; as she watched him glide behind the garden fence, one shoulder was a lot higher than the other. Joe used the neighbour's drive to reverse, then sailed back home looking pretty pleased with himself.

'That's great, Harry, thank you. If ever there's anything I can do for you... I'll be very surprised.'

'Right. No worries,' said Harry, and shook him by the hand. Somehow.

How had he managed that so deftly? Usually there was a lot of masonic arm-wobbling first. Must have been a power shake, like politicians do. Without you realising it, they take you by the forearm and assert their dominance by controlling the whole movement, she'd seen that on telly. Harry had a firm grip on things in general.

Back indoors, Joe and Harry had a long conversation about getting the mobility scooter properly serviced. After all, it had been in Harry's Aunty Bren's garage for over a year. Apparently it worked a bit like a golf buggy. Joe was getting on with Harry like a house on fire and had started telling him all about the time he'd recovered from a blowout on the M25 when the doorbell rang. Matt was onto it: that would be Zanna with the next lot of brochures, he said.

When she appeared at the door of the sitting room, it was with a sickly 'Hello everybody!' as if she were sure they would all be glad to see her. She bent across to hand Jess a weighty pile of magazines and brochures: 'For you.' Then she looked around the room and let her gaze fall on Harry.

'So, whose is that fabulous car?'

'It's Harry's,' said Fran. 'Harry, this is Zanna.'

With a rapid gesture she swept the curtain of her hair aside and stared at him, clearly very pleased with more than the car.

'Harry. Harry,' Zanna said, as if making an effort to memorise his name. 'Harry who works with Fran.'

'He's just brought the scooter round for Dad,' said Jess.

'He shifts furniture as well,' said Joe.

'I've heard a lot about you, Zanna,' said Harry.

'Ooh,' she said, with a different smile now, one that reminded Fran of popcorn, in the way it blew up and jumped about in the pan for a second. Zanna had a whole repertoire of dodgy smiles but Fran had never seen this one before. And another thing was happening that she'd never seen before. Harry – matter-of-fact, tell-it-like-it-is, you-can't-surprise-me, been-there-seen-it-bought-the-T-shirt Harry; Harry the human algorithm, Harry the flawless and odourless and super cool – Harry was glowing.

'So, Harry… you can actually fit a mobility scooter in the boot? Wow, I'm impressed.'

'It's a great little car. Does everything you need and looks pretty as well.'

'Good things in small parcels,' said Zanna.

'It punches above its weight in every department.'

'Mmm.'

'I'm getting 40 miles to the gallon.'

'Love the colour.'

'I bet you'll like this,' said Harry, thrusting his hand into the pocket of his jeans. He produced his iPhone, gave it a couple of strokes and handed it to her. 'See? It tells me everything I need to know.'

'Wow.'

'I can search my optimum journey route online and programme the satnav directly.'

'What's the upholstery?'

'Yeah…' That was an odd thing to say, thought Fran. There was a moment's pause before Harry went on, 'Cream leather.'

'Naturally.'

Fran saw Jess exchange a glance with her father, and now she was staring at a corner of the ceiling with a definite smirk on her face. Matt filled the silence with 'Well this is nice,' and glanced at his watch.

'Right,' said Harry eventually, 'I'll leave you all in peace. Enjoy your day,' and he got up. Zanna slipped through the door in front of him.

'Could you just show me something?' she said. 'Only I was thinking of changing my car...'

'Sure, right. Bye, everyone.'

'Bye'

'Cheers again Harry, bye.'

'Bye Harry.'

Fran was surprised to realise she felt protective of her young colleague. The last thing she noticed, as he turned his back to leave the room, was a visible pulse on the clean-shaven side of his neck.

The Trouble with St Cunegund's

It was only a matter of time. You couldn't have a church wedding without involving the church. Jess was well aware that Zanna could only shield them from this for so long; she'd wangled a provisional booking for the ceremony and twice re-made their appointment with the SuperRev, as she called her, with whom she was friends on social media. The vicar turned out to be a regular, decent woman who introduced herself as Sandy, and somehow managed to mention chocolate three times in the course of their conversation. Perhaps this was like men vicars talking football. Except that she both talked and looked as though she knew something about chocolate. Was this what they did to put you at your ease? At any rate, Jess felt Sandy got the measure of them pretty quickly and could see that regular church attendance was not remotely on the cards. Sandy set out the practical side of things and gave them a useful leaflet, which amongst other things outlined the things you do and don't agree to in your vows, and the optionals like being Blessed with the Gift of Children and Promising to Obey. On that last issue, Matt, bless him, actually asked couldn't they *both* promise to obey? Which was sweet but obviously stupid. They would meet again, said Sandy, to talk through the nature of the commitment they were making to each other. Jess came away feeling very awkward and wrong-footed by the vicar's sheer niceness. The big mistake was agreeing to *touch base* with Zanna immediately after the meeting she'd so proudly brokered, because once they were out of the vicarage and ushered into the conservatory at Chateau Harrington, Jess found that what she really wanted to do was to run straight back home and scream for a bit.

'So,' said Zanna, 'I told you the SuperRev was lovely. Isn't she lovely?'

'Oh, she's lovely,' said Matt.

'I liked her,' said Jess. 'She seems really…' She nearly said *honest*… why had that word popped into her head? Of course a vicar would be honest, that would sound odd… so she opted for 'down to earth.'

'Great. So, we're all set then.' Zanna looked mightily pleased with herself, and started fiddling with her mobile. Sharing, no doubt. Matt wore that cherubic grin that Jess now associated with his matrimonial dream world. How could she disappoint him? On the other hand, disappointing Zanna was much easier and infinitely more appealing. Jess was still weighing up whether to share her mind now, or leave it till later when she and Matthew would be alone, when Janet came in and plonked herself on the peach-cushioned cane armchair immediately opposite them. She leaned forward, feet apart, hands clasped in front of her lap, looking a bit like a very eager wicket keeper, wide-eyed and expectant, and said, 'So how did you get on? Isn't she lovely?'

'She's very sweet.'

'And isn't St Cunegund's simply divine?'

Janet might have been talking about a dessert or a new frock. There was only a short pause, but in that time a lot happened in Jess's head. First it was a sort of squirming for an answer, a mental wriggling between *of course it's divine it's a bloody church* and *no it's not, as a matter of fact, it gives me the creeps.* Then a voice telling her, if you can't say something nice, don't say anything at all. Then a terrible sense of shame that she was treating the church, which embodied the meaning of life for Sandy, like a function room or a restaurant.

'It feels dishonest,' she said.

Janet straightened her neck and gave Jess a piercing, questioning look.

'What I mean is, it feels dishonest to be married in a church. When I don't go to church.'

Zanna shrugged.

Janet softened and tilted her head. 'Oh Jess, you really don't need to worry about that. If every bride had your scruples, well… There'd be no white weddings.'

'Exactly,' said Zanna, 'and that would be ridiculous. It just isn't going to happen.'

Matt clasped her hand, though. At least *he* understood.

'When we make our vows,' said Jess, looking deliberately into his big brown eyes, 'it will be the most serious thing

209

we've ever done. I don't want there to be anything about that moment that isn't completely sincere.'

'My Jess,' he said, and put his arm around her.

'For God's sake,' said Zanna, disgusted. 'You might as well get married in a registry office.'

'Fine by me,' said Matt.

Zanna's annoyance was only momentary.

'Oh my God!' she exclaimed in delight, and suddenly she was swivelling in her seat to target everybody in turn with her great idea. She began with Jess, then right round the coffee table and back again, and she flashed bright eyes. 'Oh my God! We can do the whole thing at Highams! The ceremony and the reception. I don't know why we didn't ever think of that in the first place. They're registered and everything.' Then she lowered her voice, and also her painted-on eyebrows, to emphasise, 'It makes *so* much sense.'

'Perfect for your guests,' said Janet, nodding now.

Jess turned to check Matt's reaction. He appeared to be on the verge of a mmm-maybe, and his look was quizzing her, too.

She had the notion that she'd somehow won a victory only to have it snatched away. Her first thought was a simple *no*. They already had a perfectly good venue for the reception. But what she heard herself say was, 'Perhaps it's worth a look.'

How had she ever got herself into this muddle?

To the Mantelpiece

It's a cartoon classic: the road runner speeds along over the edge of the cliff, and carries on sprinting through the air in a dead straight line. It's only when he looks down that he falls like a stone. Joe was experiencing exactly that static, hovering split-second of realisation now. Without thinking, and driven by hunger, he'd taken three steps from his armchair to the mantelpiece, in search of a biscuit. Without the Zimmer.

Terrified, he was now clinging to the shelf and wondering what to do next. There was only one option really. Logic suggested that if he'd walked this far, he could walk back; and at least he had one good leg, which gave him a hopping chance. So he took a minute to pivot round and steady himself, and resolved to make the three steps back in as controlled and deliberate a manner as he could. After all, something had electrified him just now. He could tap into it again. All that mattered was to get to the chair without falling over, so he planted each foot heavily, with the tree trunk steps of Frankenstein's monster. The packet of biscuits was gripped like a weapon in his wavering right hand, whilst the shield arm was outstretched for balance and emergencies. Three steps with the packet of Digestives wobbling uncontrollably left and right. But you couldn't let that distract you. His toes met the solid upholstered edge of the armchair. He pivoted again to present his back to it, and lowered himself down slowly, the left hand searching for the seat. A slight sideways topple as he landed, which the judges would have noticed, but you had to put that down to sheer relief. All things considered, it had been a pretty successful manoeuvre.

Once he'd got over this and his heart rate had started to calm down, he attacked the biscuits. By biscuit number 3 he realised that good stuff was happening.

He hadn't fallen. He had taken six steps unaided, three of them intentionally. He'd proved he could manage without that panic alarm thing that the social services had wanted him to wear around his neck at all times. *What would you do if you*

211

had a fall, they'd asked. He'd put them straight: *I'm not planning on having any falls. I've seen loads of photos of these things being modelled by June-who-knows-that-help-is-coming and her like, and trust me, they are never worn by anyone in a vertical position. Which makes me spicious.*

Right now he was waiting for his lunchtime carer. He'd forgotten who was meant to be coming next. He hoped it would be one of the really great ones, someone with whom he'd want to share news of today's exploit, and not that wet young man Thomas. Thomas was empathy in wellies. He'd quizzed Joe yesterday at embarrassing length on how he was feeling, and seemed to believe in the healing powers of tea. Incomprehensible to a coffee drinker. It was a dialogue of the deaf from the start. Their conversation always began the same way.

Thomas (slightly whiny voice): What can I do for you, Joe? Shall I make you a cup of tea?
Joe: Please don't.

Then there was Hayley who only ever served up half the food Fran had left for his lunch, and whose signature dish was the virtual ham sandwich. He worried that she and her children were malnourished. All because she was underpaid and in the habit of eking things out. They had to work so hard for so little, these people. You only got glimpses of them. A bit like speed-dating. Life was so empty these days, and every human contact was at a premium, so the stakes were high; but you had only minutes in which to gauge the likely success of a relationship, and that in turn gave the dangerous illusion that minutes were all it took to decide how much you liked someone. Of course, this was wrong and selfish. The fact remained that a successful visit added up to a good day, and a bad one brought you down. And he was incredibly lucky, really, to have not one but two absolute smashers as blind dates. There was Amy, a slight woman with wisdom way beyond her years, who just knew what he needed and was always smiling. She'd broken her back as a teenager and been through years of rehab herself. Then there was Sian, with her Glasto take on the uniform: punk hairdo, nose stud and tattoos. Her young husband had been left unable to walk after a motorbike accident. Like Joe and Fran, they now had separate bedrooms because he couldn't get comfortable and needed lots of equipment; but whereas Joe's situation was assumed by everyone to be temporary, Sian's man was not expected to recover. She worried what would happen when their children got too big to share a room. Sian always treated Joe as if he was special, which was humbling when you considered that at the end of the working day, she would be going home to care for someone with much greater needs.

In general, the days were long and boring, spent doing endless reps of his exercises – gripping a tennis ball, Hitler salutes, the armchair hokey-cokey, that sort of thing – and waiting for visits or for Fran to come home. Parked in his comfy chair, he got so bored he'd even started to watch TV in the afternoons, bits of sport which he only half understood, and a programme he'd re-named *Crap in the Attic*, in which you never saw the attic but you did see an awful lot of crap, and real people sold their old tat for, ooh, pounds.

Finally, the key turned in the latch. But at two o'clock, it still wasn't lunch. It was Emma the OT, ready to put him through another session on the naughty step. She was very focused on training him to climb stairs, and so far he'd made it up and down the three steps to the half landing, which was the equivalent of base camp. He told Emma he'd already run a short marathon that morning so could she please treat him gently, and explained about the biscuits. It was hunger that had driven him to it.

'Well done you. Bodily needs make good motivators,' said Emma.

'Very true. That's how I weaned myself off the commode.' The first time he'd used it, Fran had nearly sliced his balls off by trying to withdraw the potty while he was still seated. Once was enough. Come to think of it, *that* was straight out of *Crap in the Attic*: the glistening combination of chrome and shiny white plastic suggested it might have belonged to Elvis.

They did their usual hour, and finished in the kitchen, where Emma helped Joe assemble his lunch. If the carer hadn't come, it probably meant that he or she had walked in on some emergency – June-who-knows-that-help-is-coming, moaning on the floor. Or worse.

Emma left. A couple of hours, and Fran would be back. She was talking about going part time, if they let her, under this re-structuring business. Every fibre of Joe's being told him this was not a good idea. There was a lot of pain and frustration and anxiety that had to be got through. It wouldn't help either of them if he had to act happy all day every day. He'd remind her they needed the money. He'd have to persuade her that he didn't need a minder. But now he could say, look, he'd just walked across the room! As far as progress was concerned, this was a red-letter day. Something to report, at last. She'd be impressed: she always maintained that any competent person ought to terrify themselves at least once a week. Well, that was job done, and it was still only Tuesday.

Plans

The next planning meeting at the Jolly Roger ended up girls
only because at the last-minute Matt had to deliver a telephone
mentoring session. Same table, same glossy mags, but it
wasn't the same without him; they all ran out of energy, and it
became an excuse for a drink. Gradually, and to Jess's
amazement, Zanna began to unwind and even started to take
an interest in Annie's knitting – a multicoloured hairy thing
which she was making up as she went along, she said,
according to the principles of the Free Knitting movement. It
did rather draw the eye, with its multiple conflicting colours.
By the end of their third drink, Zanna was getting expansive
on the virtues of powder blue for men.

'Pastel shades are very now for weddings too. Ties, cravats,
cummer-bands.'

'Cummerbunds,' said Jess.

'Yes, cummer-bands, those things men wear round their
waist? They have them in orchestras,' said Zanna.

'With a waistcoat and sporran? Not a good look.'

Annie's jaw dropped.

'Oh yes,' said Zanna. 'I'd forgotten we had to integrate that.
I always think the pastel thing is to do with letting men express
their feminine side? Which is nice.'

'Funny you should say that, because my dad's latest design
inspiration is dolly-mixture tartan.'

Jess and Zanna had evidentially reached a new level of
understanding, because even if she hadn't twigged about the
kilt yet, this last comment was recognised as a joke.

'Your dad's such a tease,' she said.

'Putting the camp back into Campbell, hah, hah!' said
Annie, as she hauled the beast around to start a new row.

Suddenly Zanna flopped back into the armchair in a gesture of despair. The glossy Bride magazine in her lap was open on a feature entitled Grooms and Dads, which involved a double-page spread of photos of future in-laws bonding by modelling various wedding outfits for men. Because you don't just let everyone wear what they want.

'Mind-blowing, isn't it?' said Annie.

'Mm? Oh. Yes.' Zanna glanced at the photos and said, 'It's not that. It's just… First they show you their masculine side and you're like, ooh yes, give me more. Then they show you their feminine side, and you're like, aaah. Then once you're hooked, they show you their total bastard side. Why are men such bastards?'

'Are they?'

'Well not my brother, obviously. He's an angel. But… how do you do it, Jess?' She was beginning to sound upset and her tiny hands searched every pocket until she found a hankie, which she then sniffed into. 'How do you hang on to a keeper?'

Jess could only stammer, because she had no idea, and hadn't even been aware that that was what she'd done.

'What I don't understand, Jess, is the same thing keeps happening to me over and over again. I find a fit guy, I think he's the one, the chemistry's just *right,* you know – and honestly you wouldn't believe the number of men who've told me the chemistry was right, so there's nothing wrong with me chemistry-wise. And it's like, fireworks, and I think yes, this is the one. And then they dump me. Do you think I need a boob job?'

'I don't think anyone needs a boob job.'

Holy Moses, thought Jess, what had happened to the patronising know-all sister-in-law? She was a lot easier to stomach than the drunken bosom pal.

More out of curiosity than concern, she asked, 'Was it the dress designer?'

Zanna gripped her nose in the hankie and her head bobbed up and down, then from side to side as she cried, 'It turns out…. It would seem… that he was more interested in getting the business. All he ever saw in me was a potential commercial transaction.' She ended on a wail.

Jess winced. 'Better to find out now…'

'Oh, I don't blame *you*,' she said, quietening down professionally. 'If beaded satin isn't your look, that's completely your prerogative. Only – sometimes I think no-one's ever going to marry me. Always the bridesmaid, never the bride. That'll be me.'

'Sometimes, if a guy thinks you're coming on too strong, they get cold feet.'

'You mean they have issues with commitment? Tell me about it.'

That wasn't exactly what Jess had meant, but she let it go.

'Except my brother again. He's the only man I know who doesn't have issues with commitment. And he's not available. Obviously.' She snuffled and remarked in an offhand way, 'Matt was always going to be married by twenty-eight.'

That sounded very specific.

'Blimey. How did he know?'

'He decided, of course. It's on his Life Plan. He drew that up… ooh…first year at uni. You know what he's like. He always knows where he's headed.'

'So, this Life Plan… What else is on it?'

'Degree by twenty-three, *check*. Job and car by twenty-five, *check*. Own place by twenty-six, *check.* Well, rented, obviously. Married by twenty-eight. Well he's on target for that, obviously. Own business by thirty. Actually, he's a bit annoyed I got there first.' That thought seemed to perk Zanna up.

Annie had stopped knitting and her eyes were trained on Jess.

'Anything else I should know? Children?'

After all, Jess was directly concerned.

'Oh, I'm sure that's flexible in terms of time-line. I mean, there's no detail on that. How many, what sex. I mean, there are some things even the most positive thinker can't control.'

Jess brought her hands up to her head and considered the ceiling, whilst she tried to work out just how she felt about all this. After all, she'd already been privy to Matt's latest personal goal-setting document, hadn't she? *Living with the woman of my dreams.* It had seemed so sweet at the time, so romantic, so what was different now? The answer was plain. It was the disconcerting notion that Matt had been shopping for a wife, and she, Jess, just happened to come along at the right time, and he thought, she'll do. If that was all it took to qualify as the woman of his dreams, it was a fairly meagre achievement. Because the dream was there before the woman.

Annie was frowning, and her expression now – lips parted, teeth together – was the parody of a smile, closer to an *ouch*.

Zanna too must have realised the Life Plan hadn't gone down well.

'It worked for my dad,' she pointed out, plaintively.

Jess had always thought that Matt and his father Derek were as dissimilar as any two people could be, and not just in looks – Matt's face oval and gilded, his father square and leathery from all that mowing and daisy-worrying. Matt was so open and frank and warm-hearted and such a huge enthusiast, Derek a cold fish. But if you thought for a minute about the world they lived in... Derek, the auditor, was the sort of person who never left anything to chance; he even had his lawn care regime on a spreadsheet. He could tell you the correct way to do anything from replacing a tap washer to drawing up a will. Just like Matt. Also, look at Matt's apartment, which made her feel so calm because there wasn't any mess... Derek was clinically tidy and never lost the Sellotape. And whilst the colour scheme in Chateau Harrington - shell pink and uncooked pastry – was down to Janet, Derek was the one who famously enforced a clutter ratio of 3:1, shelf to shite. (Shelf to chinoiserie, Janet had said; *nicknackersoiserie* was what her father called that sort of stuff.) Give it ten years, even ten days, and this could be Jess and Matt. She'd want a home for her lucky dancing dahlia (pink plastic tat but it just made you smile) and he'd be, like, no, babe, we've got the amethyst geode and the pencil pot you made in year 11 on that surface already.

There was definitely a crack in that ceiling.

The Venue

"A Palladian villa set in 200 acres of parkland, Highams Hall is the ancestral home of the Earls of Bunn. It was visited by Royalty in the roaring twenties, and is now in public ownership and the county's premier wedding venue." The photo on the home page of the website showed a pink stucco facade lit by a sunset, which faded into a bride and groom in soft focus.

The index finger of Joe's left hand had done a reasonable job in firing up the computer and typing slowly. He reckoned it wouldn't take him long to get used to using the mouse left-handed. But it felt odd to be sitting at the keyboard in the corner of the workshop again. This room, the scene of the crime, would carry an unwelcome memory long after the shrouded corpse of the acropolis on the bench was removed, as it must surely one day be. Frannie's idea, covering it in a sheet to keep off the dust. She was as hopelessly optimistic as Joe was. It would have to go. Nobody wanted it now. During his time in hospital, the client – a regional museum with national ambitions – had changed the exhibition floor plan and hired a capable young woman to do a 3-D computer graphic in place of his model. The space they immediately gained would allow them to include a bronze age piggy-bank, they said; no doubt that would go down a storm with the punters. Which all went to prove, it's an ill wind that blows nobody any good. He sighed.

What would the first Earl of Bunn have thought of his family seat being turned into the County Council's wedding factory? They advertised four separate venues for the ceremony and several different reception rooms. At least they were prepared to publish their tariffs, though. A bit less expensive than he'd expected, although once you got to the evening do and the things that were additional but compulsory (how did that work?) it began to mount up. *Doormen.* This was another word for bouncers, which made him wonder about their clientele. For a hundred quid he'd expect a flunkey in gold braid to announce the entrance of every guest.

Sinisterly, a disco plus house DJ came into the *additional and compulsory* bracket. Jess might balk at that one.

The site menu on Highams home page included the key word *Access.* This was promising. He had to be as objective as possible about the venue, and the fact was, although he loved the Jolly Roger, the tables would be close together, the floors were uneven, the loos were tucked away down a side passage... It was just a fact of life that perfect pubs meant imperfect buildings. Perhaps Highams would be more practical. A click on *Access* brought up a photograph of a huge flight of stone steps, which he recognised as part of the building's grand entrance. Perplexing. Hmm. Would they put beans on toast on their catering page? But you had to keep an open mind.

How to be Depressed

Fran was indignant. The talk at the Stroke Gym had always been an upbeat affair, marked by good humour; but all those smiles had been wiped off by the guest speaker, a quietly spoken woman in lilac who worked for an important medical charity. Fran recognised a sequence that was becoming familiar. 'You can't work, you can't drive, you can't play sport...' A long list of reasons to be miserable, from physical and practical difficulties, to fears for the future, to other people's lack of understanding. All real. All familiar. All awful. This time, though, they were being listed explicitly as the reasons why both you and your carer will probably be depressed.

Ten minutes into the talk, and the therapists – who not so long ago had been bouncing around next door in the gym –

were strangely subdued; the patients uncharacteristically silent. Hyper-attentive. For the first time she wondered how many of the regulars, under the usual jokey exterior and the bluster, must indeed be clinically depressed. Whereas Joe had self-diagnosed as pissed off. Carers too? Was this a compulsory part of the package, then? No, she wasn't up for that. It may be entirely appropriate to be depressed. But it would be bloody unhelpful.

I know what this is, she thought. This is the Toxic Litany. I'm free to reject this creed. She was bubbling inside. She could feel Joe shifting on the plastic seat next to her, and hear his impatient breath.

It seemed to Fran that all the therapists' efforts in the previous hour were being undone. They invested so much energy and care into acting and talking positive; they never said 'you can't' without adding the rider, 'yet'. You can't walk unaided yet, you can't balance properly yet. The discipline of their language was faultless.

But then again, she told herself, you had to be fair. If you were battling to keep your spirits up, it would be a tremendous comfort to be told, officially, that what you were going through was normal. These would be comforting words. The healing message you most needed to hear.

Rationally, she understood all that. Yet her heart was racing, and she wanted to shout: just stop it. Stop it.

From the memory of a dull limbo of misery, when she was still a young woman, she knew what depression was like. You only realised how serious it had been once you were well clear of it. What they were experiencing now wasn't the same, for her. Maybe deep depression was just around the corner. But she didn't have to run to meet it.

Her thoughts were at a rolling boil, while the lilac voice droned on.

To tell yourself *I am depressed* was like saying *I'm a victim*. You had to be really careful about uttering those words, because they changed everything: both the way other people saw you, and the way you saw yourself. They changed your mental and your social chemistry. That chemical reaction would be mightily hard to reverse. You had to be sure you'd hit the bottom.

Come on Fran. Wasn't there some small part of her that would find it a huge relief to say, that's it, I admit, I'm stressed out, I need help because I feel so low?

Briskly, she rifled every file in the cabinet of her conscience. Nothing. So long as Joe's condition was improving – and it definitely was – there was no reason to be anything other than upbeat and excited. It wouldn't help him, to underscore the misery.

The lilac woman was still talking in a meek voice, as if she didn't want her breath to trouble the air. What had she been saying? Fran tried to tune back in. She knew this voice was gentle, kind, compassionate. Soothing, even. But she hated it for its seduction.

Joe breathed out loudly through his nostrils, and they exchanged looks.

She whispered, 'Do we need this right now?'

'No,' he said, and they scarpered. Albeit slowly.

Once inside the car, where nobody could hear them, Joe shook his head.

'I felt like saying, I know I'm a sad bastard. I don't need you to remind me.'

Fran started up the engine and edged her way out of the car park. Once they'd successfully made it onto the dual carriageway, and out of the town, she could speak her mind.

'Did you see how that woman drained all the energy from the room? What do you think happened after we left?'

'I wish Gary had been there. The guy I told you about, with the motorbike, you know? The one who refuses to be disabled. He'd have told her.'

'Perhaps we ought to have stayed, to support the others.'

'No. Thanks for getting me out of there. I couldn't listen to that. OK, I might be miserable, but I don't have to turn it into a hobby.'

'Yes, but… For some people, that's probably going to be the most valuable talk of the lot. We're the ones who are out of line, Joe.'

'We're in denial,' said Joe.

She shot him a glance. He was staring, expressionless, at the road ahead.

'Well, Joe, it's working for me. What about you?'

'Yup,' he said. 'There are some tunes that don't improve from repeating.'

'I just hope somebody in that room says, *Yes, but, the point is, they're alive*. I can see Ted Doubleday breaking into a chorus of *Look for the silver lining*. Because *he'll* make sure they don't all go home on a downer.'

Even to her own ears, she sounded snappy, and increasingly loud.

'Maybe that was going to be the conclusion,' said Joe.

Hmm. Maybe. She didn't feel that generous. It was time for a shout.

'I should have *testified,* you know, like people did with Billy Graham in the Gospel Tent? I should have stood up and said, Hallelujah, brothers and sisters, hear my witness! I wish with all my heart my husband had been spared this terrible affliction, I wish with all my heart he hadn't had to suffer like this. You may say it has made our life poorer, but I say, I am a rich, rich woman. Because now I have living proof that Joe Faber is the man I thought he was. Which is, a COLOSSUS. Ha! How many women can say that? Mm?'

'We've been lucky,' he said. 'Mind that bus.'

And her thoughts turned to the testimony of another regular at the stroke gym, a couple of weeks back. A quiet, tidy man in his sixties, who came alone, and told how his wife of thirty years had grown angry with him for all the things he could no longer do. He didn't say so, but you could see, by the perplexed expression on his face, that it wasn't his brain but his heart that was broken.

It shakes your life, she thought. Stroke shakes your life to see what rattles.

Site Visit

Highams Hall turned out to be more welcoming than Joe had expected, even if he did have to approach by a side entrance. Squarely enthroned on Harry's Uncle Pete's mobility scooter, he simply glided up the wide and gently sloping ramp to the side of the facade, where the modern, plate glass door opened automatically, as if operated by some hidden butler. Less decorously, Matt kept running ahead and filming everything on his phone, because you had to think about how the pictures would look. They came to a high-ceilinged vestibule, light and echoing, which was dominated by a huge equestrian portrait. Rider and horse gazed down at Joe on his scooter. This vestibule connected with the main entrance, with great doors open onto parkland.

As he advanced along a smooth, stone-floored corridor, Joe could see that Zanna had got there ahead of them, and was already talking to a tall man in a suit. She was standing just a bit too close; twice the man took a discreet step backwards, twice she took a step in his direction. He moved to his right, she moved to her left. When he turned to welcome Joe and his party, Zanna turned too, mirroring his movements exactly. The man was well into his thirties, a bit old for her, surely? Zanna introduced him as *Damian, the Events Manager*. Ah. Maybe what he was witnessing was not the smouldering start of a *paso doble*, but a purely professional schmooze.

Damian the Manager was charming and generous with eye contact; bride, groom, the parent on legs and the parent on wheels were all equally blessed with his attention. The one area of life in which there was absolute equality of opportunity was that of stumping up your cash. Well, you'd rather buy from an intelligent salesman than a bad one, thought Joe. You felt less of a schmuck yourself.

Damian confirmed that one of their rooms was decorated for a reception to be held that very afternoon, which would help them envision their own event. Up somewhere above his head, Joe heard Matt give an excited and not very manly 'Ooh.' Damian, with Zanna clicking along on high heels at his side, led the way through double doors towards the Vitoria Suite, named for the cavalry charge in which the first Earl of Bunn had so distinguished himself.

It takes a while for man and vehicle to act as one, but so far, Joe was pretty happy with the scooter. Steering was no problem at all, provided that function was delegated to his trusty left hand, and progress was smooth enough, the speed regulated by a lever underneath the handlebars – squeeze right side for forward, left side for reverse. Like most portable mobility scooters, Harry had explained airily, it had no brakes. If you released your grip on the paddles, it would simply glide to a stop. But it did have a horn. So that would be OK then. By now, Joe's right hand was much more obedient; it had learned to let go as well as to grip, and he had been able to compensate for a slight sticking in the forward paddle which arose very occasionally, at one particular angle (and therefore speed). It might be worth taking the scooter apart one of these days, and trying to fix that, before he passed it on to some other needy soul who might not be so phlegmatic about its shortcomings. Assuming, that was, he could one day talk his hand into cooperating with a screwdriver.

His confidence wavered, however, when they reached their destination. The panelled double doors were wide open on a truly breathtaking sight. The room was decorated in a pale, unmistakably heritage grey, and was full of round, white-napped tables, sparkling with glassware and cutlery, each with an unfeasibly tall and slender centrepiece of glistening crystal, topped by a huge and fulsome bouquet. The flowers alone were a serious piece of handiwork. Pink and white roses both large and small, white daisy things, and a lot of those green flowers, the *jolies laides* of the floral world, whose function was to show the real beauties off. At the far end of the room was a longer table swagged in satiny stuff and with a lower, similarly themed floral tribute at its crisp centre fold. A young woman in a suit stood behind it and was writing something on a clip board. To either side of this table, awkwardly filling an awkward space, were a couple of silver birch trees about nine feet high, in Versailles planters. Now they were just *odd*. Tall windows ran along one side of the room, which Joe took to be north facing; the grudging daylight was balanced with good, warm spots and lamps, just enough to add sparkle to the tableware, from walls and ceiling. Impressive. Driving around these obstacles to penetrate the room, though, would be tricky.

A sensible voice told Joe not to attempt it. A more optimistic voice told him this was what mobility was all about, a good opportunity to hone his skills, a challenge, a sort of indoor rally. A third and louder voice, belonging to Zanna, who must have been just behind him, told him to 'use the aisle.' Aisle? What aisle? 'There, to your left. See?' Sure enough, space had been cleared to make a narrow path which ran the length of the room, on the side opposite the windows. So, while the others advanced in random fashion inwards, lingering to inspect the place settings and the flowers, Joe made his way carefully and directly to the top table. The gentle, even hum of the motor formed a drone to their admiring gasps and twittering approbations. There wasn't much room for driver error, though, and as he skimmed the side of each table along the way, he was particularly wary of the bouquet-on-a-stick, with its ambitiously high centre of gravity. One nudge and you might bring the whole lot crashing down. And this wasn't a dress rehearsal. In a few hours' time, the room would be full of guests for some lucky couple's real live fairy tale wedding.

As he approached the end of the straight, there was a temptation to speed up, but Joe was careful to keep it steady and steer into the best racing line; a skid on the parquet here could slam him into the tyre wall. Well, the tree. Its bottom branches were at nose level and had a funny smell, reminiscent of 70s vinyl upholstery. A bit of whitewashed twiggery and a couple of white peacock feathers sticking out gave the game away: the whole thing was a veritable fountain of fakery.

Joe glided to a well-judged halt at the end of the top table, where Damian was introducing the clipboard carrier to everybody. This was Sylvie, the wedding coordinator. She was cheerful and had nice round edges – face, smile, bobbed hair, everything – and she looked pretty relaxed about the whole clipboard thing, setting it down immediately to shake hands. Nose first, Zanna's whole face sharpened, and she pitched in straight away with the question which would of course be uppermost on Jess's mind. This was all fabulous, but what about room for dancing? Sylvie explained that if you took out some of these tables, you had a good-sized sprung floor right here. You could still fit eight tables of eight round the edges. Plus the top table of course. Unless they were talking bigger numbers, in which case would they like to see the ballroom?

'I don't think so,' said the bride.

'Where would you put the band?' asked Annie, looking around doubtfully.

'How big is the band?'

Zanna turned to her brother and said, 'Nobody mentioned a band.'

'How do you have a ceilidh without a band?' said Jess.

'You could shift the trees I s'pose,' said Annie.

'That would be my solution,' said Joe, trying to sound affable, and thinking, send in the lumberjacks.

'What's wrong with recorded music?' asked Zanna. She was doing her body language thing again. Squared up to assert dominance over the wedding coordinator, and with confident hands palms-upwards to emphasise her reasonableness. 'I mean, *you* record stuff, don't you, Jess?'

'Oh, yes!' said Matt, with an excited in-breath. 'We could use your tracks, babe!' Joe sensed imminent disaster. This was Matt all over. Wide-eyed, innocent, and so resolutely solution-focused, he couldn't see that what he took for a stepping stone was actually a man-trap.

'Ooh, so you're a musician yourself then?' said Sylvie, rosily, and in apparent awe.

'The thing is… Matt…' Jess turned towards him and looked him straight in the eye. 'I know imagination is very important to you...'

'Very important, totally.'

'So, there's something you need to know right now.' Jess spoke slowly, breaking the words up as if for a child: 'Call it a deficiency on my part if you like, but there's one thing I just can't get my head round. I *cannot* imagine my wedding without live music.'

'No?'

'No. I can imagine somebody else's wedding without live music and that would be just fine. But not mine.'

'Oh. Of course, you're right,' he said and drew an apologetic arm about her shoulders.

'There'd be an insurrection,' said Annie, leaning towards Sylvie to explain. 'There'll be loads of musicians on the guest list. People will expect to jam.'

'Gosh,' said Sylvie. 'How lovely.' She looked like she meant it.

'But there *is* room for a band, surely?' asked Fran. 'Think of all the ceilidhs you've been to in much smaller rooms than this.'

'And the Jolly Roger is hardly the O2, is it,' remarked Zanna.

'Mum's right,' said Jess. 'People will manage. It's not a problem unless we make it one.'

Annie grinned, with a that's-my-girl look, and shrugged in good-natured agreement.

'The last thing you want is a room that's too big,' said Fran.

'People do need proximity for successful interaction,' said Matt.

Joe agreed. You didn't want your guests rattling around like peas in a colander.

Damian invited the tour to move on, indicating a door almost behind one of the trees. Sylvie smiled at Joe and warned him it might be a bit tight in there for the buggy, so he hung back for a minute with Matt, who in any case wanted to get footage of the view from the exact spot where the bride and groom would be sitting. This felt like a good moment to park the scooter, stretch his legs and walk for a bit. He was getting pretty nifty with the collapsible stick drill and had it re-assembled in seconds. Matt helped him up from the scooter and offered an arm.

'Thanks, Matt, but I'm trying to fall over all on my own. It's a bit of a goal right now.'

Matt grinned. 'Yes, of course.'

Joe uncurled his back as best he could and took a few juddering steps to reach the others, who were gathered in the doorway.

'So, ladies and gentleman,' said Damian proudly, 'this is our Cake Room.'

'Did he say coke room?' hissed Annie, who was just being deliberately silly now, picking up Joe's riff.

'The cloak room's just down the corridor,' said Zanna. 'If you need it.'

Bugger, thought Joe, did you have to bring that up? And he tried to make himself think of the desert. Because these days, if he had to go, he really did have to go.

As things turned out, the Cake Room was distraction enough. The women gasped as they entered. A huge tiered confection ascending in ever deeper shades of pink icing stood in the centre of the table, which itself almost filled the room. Trays of cupcakes decorated in pastel colours, and flowers of similar hue in bowls and vases, were arranged symmetrically around the cake tower. The overall impression was one of tasteful opulence. And yet, Joe thought, it was comparatively intimate after the function room; it was more the size of a normal sitting room. It had a real fireplace and quasi-antique, wannabe mahogany chairs in the available niches. A space for genuine conversations. The place you'd put the coffin at a wake.

'Can you recycle those?' asked Annie, who had noticed that some of the roses in the smaller containers were made of silk.

Zanna explained, 'The whole idea is to re-use them.'

'Do these come with the room?' asked Fran.

'You can hire additional decorations, certainly,' said Damian.

'I've never seen a Cake Room before,' said Fran.

'It gives your guests a talking point. And another space.'

'A kind of break-out room,' said Matt.

'Somewhere for a crafty fag,' said Annie. 'Well, no, obviously not literally. Maybe a crafty snog with the best man though.' She giggled.

They all filed around the table. Matt was exercised by the difficulty of finding a good vantage point for photography, with all these people in the way, and started dodging about, phone in hand. He was excited and frustrated all at once, and getting animated. This, for Joe, was disconcerting. He could walk with a stick given a clear path ahead, but his balance was not good and an emergency stop this close to the confectionery could mean somebody ending up with a face full of currants and wrecking a blameless stranger's big day. So he stepped back and hung on to the doorway.

'Who's doing your cake?' asked Annie.

Fran said, 'I thought I was, but now I'm not so sure. Can you see a normal-sized cake in here? It'll look like a pimple on a brick.'

'Do a fake bottom,' said Zanna, with a practised plumber's nod.

'A fake bottom?' Annie made it sound like a joke.

'You just make the first tier out of cardboard. Lifts the whole thing.'

Joe was on home ground here and glad to have something to contribute.

'If you do a square cake, you can use an ordinary box. That would be the easiest option. Provided it's strong enough. You'd have to build it up inside. Pack it with something. Polystyrene.'

'I'm not decorating it though,' said Fran, and her eyes, mouth, fringe and folded arms drew a series of resolute parallels.

'Leave that to me,' said Zanna. Everybody, even Matt, looked a bit shocked and worried for a moment, because they all knew that those little hands could barely decorate a piece of toast with a slice of cheese. 'I'll source you a cake decorator,' she explained. 'All part of the service.' And she turned to Damian who possibly didn't realise that was the sort of thing Wonder White Weddings would take care of.

Damian glanced at his watch. 'I'm very conscious that we're doing all this back to front, because normally we'd start with the place where you'll have the actual ceremony, but that was still in use when you arrived. It should be empty now. If

233

you'd be so kind as to follow me this way, I'd suggest we take a back route and avoid bumping into the guests.'

'Good idea.' Fran was first out of the next door. She didn't even look round to check Joe was following. Or vertical. In a way, that was a relief. A sign of trust. He went back for the scooter, collapsed the stick and shoved it in the basket, swivelled the seat and backed himself onto it, swivelled it again to face the front, got arm rest down, and turned the key, all gloriously unaided. That lever was catching again and it was almost exciting to be moving with unintended speed through the door. The cake table was to his left, leaving a clear passage in front of him, along the window side, to the open door by which everyone else had left.

Except that Matt suddenly jumped back into the room and made towards him saying, 'Oh Joe, sorry we nearly forgot you there, are you all right?' Joe released his right hand from the lever, but the paddle had stuck and he had neither the strength nor the dexterity to release it. The right hand couldn't turn the key to switch the motor off either. He daren't divert his left hand from its steering function. What was he going to hit first?

The terrible thing was, he couldn't shout out, these days, least of all in an emergency. That particular sort of spontaneity in speech was impossible now. It seemed an age before Matt correctly read the situation, stepped back and, in a movement that put Joe in mind of a toreador, lifted and flattened his whole trim body against the door and stood on tiptoe just in time for the scooter to glide gracefully past. When, inevitably, it crossed the corridor and bumped into the wall opposite, the lever was released, and the motor stopped.

Had he imagined it, or was that a faint rustling noise from the Cake Room behind him, a noise as of petals falling? He had no intention of looking back to find out.

Once they'd got over the surprise, Joe and Matt found themselves helpless with laughter, like two schoolboys mucking about behind the teacher's back. Joe guffawed and snorted till his nose streamed. They swapped explanations and re-lived their experience all the way down the long corridor. In this swashbuckling drama, they were both heroes, and they were both idiots. Following voices, they came to a smart pastel blue room filled by rows of white chairs, and found a much more serious conversation going on.

'So how many weddings do you have booked for today, Damian?' Zanna was asking.

'Only the two. One, as you know, is under way. They had the ceremony here. The other is just a reception – that was the room you saw. We had a last-minute cancellation. Very unfortunate, sad for the couple, obviously, and too late for us to re-book.'

'Do you get many cancellations, then?' asked Jess. Joe cocked an ear: this was the first real fact-finding question which his daughter, the bride, had asked all day.

'The odd one. Usually it's because of an accident, or a death in the close family.'

'Do people ever just… change their minds?'

'Ooh Jess, what a terrible thought!' said Zanna, laughing it off.

'It's not unknown,' said Damian 'In fact we got a cancellation only this week for a wedding four months from now. There's no guarantee we'll fill that. Which is why we do, I'm afraid, have to ask for a non-returnable deposit.'

'Presumably you'd offer a discount on a cancellation?' said Zanna. 'I mean, that would be in your interest, to maximise occupancy, as it were.' She was standing a bit too close to him again.

'We might consider it, certainly,' said Damian.

Zanna sighed.

'Less than four months' time, though... That would be pushing it, to get the invites out and everything. As a wedding organiser, and even more so as the happy couple, I'd expect a big reduction for that. So, Damian... you'll be lucky to fill it, then?'

'Mmm... maybe. You never know.' Damian was smiling a different smile now. Irritation? Calculation? Cogitation of some sort was definitely going on.

Matt went up to greet Jess. 'Sorry, sorry,' he said, with a wide grin. 'We're back. You haven't shaken us off. Your dad and I had a bit of an adventure back there, didn't we, Joe?' He was still overcome by hilarity, and looked round, appealing to everyone to share it. 'Honestly, guys, you should have seen this man! He went for me! He was like a demon on wheels.'

'A bull in a cake shop.'

Jess smiled at her father and shook her head. 'What are you two like?'

'Come on then Jess,' said Matt, linking his arm in hers. 'I'm going to practise walking you down the aisle.'

Damian discreetly backed off to take up position in the doorway. Annie, Zanna and Fran watched the happy couple for a minute, then splintered apart, pretending to look at things in a room which offered nothing much to look at at all. Joe had a distinct feeling that something was going wrong. Too many little signs. The wrong people gushing about the venue. That question of hers, out of the blue. Just at the very point where Joe, after his unpremeditated attempt to run Matt down, was really beginning to feel more fond of his future son-in-law

236

than ever he had before. Matt was an idiot, but he was such a kind, loyal, good natured idiot. Fran came up and laid her hand on his shoulder, then bent down to kiss him on the cheek.

'She's not sold on this place, is she?' she whispered in his ear.

'No.'

They both stared at the couple who had reached the place where there wasn't an altar. They watched Matt run back to make the walk again, this time filming it on his camera.

'So, what happened back there, with you and Matt?' asked Fran.

'Ah. Scooter. The lever got stuck again. Nearly ran into him. It took him a while to react.'

She chuckled. 'He can be a bit slow on the uptake.'

'He was a bit slow at first. Then he was pretty damn quick.'

'No damage?'

'Naaa,' said Joe, wistfully.

Zanna strode up the aisle. She engaged the couple in a hushed conversation which quickly became animated. The only thing Joe caught was Jess saying *no*, at regular intervals, and each *no* was louder than the one before. When Jess abruptly turned on her heels to stomp back, the other two flanked her, apparently trying to persuade her of something. Matt was waving his arms about, looking ecstatically happy and insisting it was a great idea. Zanna's eyes kept darting towards Damian who was still waiting in the doorway with a set of marketing portfolios in his arm – because it really was time the pack of them moved on – and as they approached Joe heard her hiss in an urgent whisper, 'Four months' notice is *plenty,* trust me. Leave it to me. I can get you *such* a deal. I promise, it'll be worth it.'

237

'Oh yes, please babe,' said Matt. 'Yes, I completely get that it's someone else's misfortune, but hey, it's our luck. Bring it on. What are we waiting for?'

'What do you think, Mrs Faber?' said Zanna as they drew level. 'Don't you think it's worth going for a cancellation? I could save you *thousands,* after all.'

'It's not a decision anybody needs to make right here and now, is it?'

Fran's tone was sharp and she'd folded her arms again.

'Exactly,' said Zanna. 'We don't want to look too keen. You just sleep on it, Jess, and I can call him tomorrow.'

Jess exploded.

'I don't need to sleep on it.'

'You're not sure what you want, is that it?' Zanna was wheedling now.

Jess squeezed her eyes tight shut, let out a strange sound a bit like a gargle, and exhaled slowly through gritted teeth.

'I *do* know what I *don't* want,' she wailed, and she looked close to tears. Then she positively shouted, so that nobody, neither Matt nor Zanna nor Damian was in any doubt.

'I don't want someone else's second hand wedding... or a cake with a fake bottom.'

And with that she ran. She ran right past Damian and out of the door at such a lick that one of her pumps fell off. Matt followed, scooped it up and went after her, waving it in the air. You could hear the alternate clop, thump of her feet on the stone floor outside, then a change in rhythm as they grew more distant, and the surprised voices of wedding guests for whom the entertainment had started early. Zanna rolled her eyes and smiled. But the middle fingers of each delicate hand were tapping compulsively.

'Wedding nerves,' she said to Damian, who was the only person in the room to remain unfazed. 'We'll take these, then, shall we? I'll be in touch.'

She picked up the glossy folders and led everybody out to the vestibule.

A small crowd – a waitress, two men in morning suits, and Sylvie minus clipboard – had gathered by the grand entrance, and were peering down the steps. It was impossible for Joe to see what was going on, but he tuned in to the commentary of all these strangers. 'Is he hurt?' – 'He's fallen on the steps.' – 'He went to give her the shoe, and she threw it straight back at him!' – 'No, she didn't, she dropped it and he tripped on it.' – 'She threw it at him and he lost his balance.' – 'She tried to put it back on, and she dropped it.' – 'She chucked it!' – 'No, she dropped it.' – 'She chucked it all right.' – 'Ooh, look, he can't stand up.' – 'Can't put his weight on it, can he?' – 'Ooh, that boy's in pain.' – 'Blimey, guys, is this what happened in Cinderella?'

The Tortoise and the Hare

'Yours is quite a bit longer than mine.'

'I'm quite a bit taller than you.'

'It's fully extended.'

'Ah well, you see, it has to touch the ground. Otherwise it doesn't really work.'

Fran had been listening to their conversation without comment. Although Matt snorted quietly to register amusement, he still managed to look doleful. He lay on the Fabers' sofa, with a surgically booted leg propped up on one of its arms, and the other foot dangling listlessly to the floor.

Jess had already told him he needed to watch out because this sprained ankle was having serious side effects on his face, and right now Fran could see exactly what she meant. A look of mingled surprise, pain and sheer affront seemed to have settled there and forty-eight hours after his visit to A and E, it couldn't be dislodged.

She watched as Joe tried to coax him into humour with his routine on the basics of stick drill. He'd laid his whole collection on the carpet in front of the sofa where Matt reclined, and from the comfort of his own sit-up armchair opposite, used his least preferred, hospital issue stick as a pointer for the naming of parts. Handle (these come curved, straight, or formed to fit the hand); carrying loop (be cautious of these, they can have your arm off); stock; extension mechanism; ferrule (no lad, never call it the pointy end, it isn't pointy; a good ferrule makes full contact with the ground; in fact, look at this special bendy one which allows you to pivot and minimises shock to the arm. Ah. See.) Next, their uses and comparative merits. First up, the classic bent wood. Best design, a perfect fusion of form and function. Best look, for an intellectual. Top score for hooking objects, e.g. carefully pulling a chair towards you by the leg, adjusting vertical blinds with a view to their later destruction, etc., etc. Top score for environmental credentials. Heavy, though, and therefore a low score on safety, in the event of third-party contact. Matt stopped him there.

'What do you mean, third-party contact?'

This was Fran's cue to interrupt. 'You have to remember, one of the main purposes of a stick is for the random pointing out of objects, ideally in the way of other pedestrians. It's only blokes with sticks who do this. Otherwise pointing is reserved for Victorian melodrama and ballet.'

'What?'

'Nobody points in real life.'

'That's true,' said Joe. 'And of course, a veteran stick waver gives no warning. Or where's the fun?'

'So, you get a smaller bruise from contact with an aluminium stick, then?'

'Correct,' she said. 'Although an aluminium stick sounds really tinny when it falls on the floor.'

'God, they do fall over a lot, don't they?' said Matt with a rush of feeling. 'You can't leave them anywhere. The least touch and they slide over. It's just the most annoying thing.'

'Oh yes,' She said, 'That noise. You tune in to it. You know, the first time you hear the sound of a stick falling, you run to help. Then after a while you learn to wait for the thud of someone falling over. In the end, you just think, *bloody stick.*'

'Two weeks! And longer before I can drive again,' said Matt. 'No meetings. No trips to meet the client. It's all going to have to be the on-line stuff, and honestly, that can be such hard work. Staring at a screen. And of course, my boss thinks, great, just the opportunity for Matthew to write us another module.'

'I thought you liked the creative jobs. You said.' Jess walked in with tea for everyone on a tray.

'But you know, sweetheart, I need a balance between things and people. Not just things. I hate spending hours hunched over the keyboard. And all that formatting…'

'What's your topic this time?' asked Fran. A gleeful anticipation passed over Jess's features, which said, *wait till you hear this*.

'What's my topic? Well… Their first suggestion was Dealing with Difficult Situations. I mean, it's not funny is it?

And in any case as a topic, that's much too vague. Too inclusive.'

'Vague, oh yes,' said Joe gravely, shaking his head.

Jess chuckled and said, 'Oh come on, Matt, it *is* funny.' He shrugged.

'But anyway, I managed to negotiate it down to Conflict. I'm OK with Conflict.'

Fran had a sudden realisation. 'Do you know Matt, I don't think I've ever heard you have a real argument with anyone. Ever.'

'Well thank you, Fran,' he said. 'I don't think I *do* argue with people.'

He and Joe went back to the stick discussion. So what was going on here then? She'd made a neutral observation – free of any value judgment – and Matt had taken it as a compliment. Interesting. Was it a good thing never to argue? It took milliseconds to compute that it was not. On the contrary, it was a sign you were a coward. Or soft in the head. Now she stopped to think about it, this young man was borderline irritating. He'd lain there on their sofa, whining on about his inability to work properly, when Joe was having to face up to the fact that he might never go back to work at all. If Matt didn't get a grip soon, he might be in for his first real argument earlier than he was expecting, and his future mother-in-law could be ideally placed to provide the opportunity. Maybe even bill him for the coaching.

Someone ought to tell him that a mild sprain, however painful, was only a temporary incapacity. He didn't seem to recognise how much harder things were for Joe, who really needed to walk with a stick supporting his right side but whose right arm and hand were too weak to cope with that. Whose whole posture was thrown out by the simple mechanics of walking with a stick. Her eyes stung at the sight of this fine tall frame slowly becoming more distorted, shrinking and crushed by pain. And he needed both his hands. That right hand hadn't just switched switches and written letters, and fixed just about everything round the house; it had fashioned so many things. It had helped re-create the acropolis of Athens, for goodness' sake! For which he'd never been paid because of course, it was never delivered to the client. She had to watch her husband caught in a quandary – whether to train the left to take over and learn to live one-handed, or persist in the optimism that one day, with the right effort, the right magic, the sleeping beauty on his right would wake and live happily ever after.

It was a quandary of the intellect but not of the heart. Optimism was a habit and sometimes a folly, but the whole family habitually gambled this way, because if you didn't expect things to work, they sure as hell wouldn't. In fairness to Matt, he was an optimist too, and perhaps that was his saving grace. Mmm. Perhaps.

'Right,' she said, and stood up straight. 'Tea's too hot to drink. Let's make a start. We can get this thing out of the box, at least.'

She looked across to Jess who said, 'Sure. Let me at it.'

They left Matt and Joe to their masterclass and headed for the workshop.

The treadmill had been delivered in a flat cardboard pack which Fran had dragged along the floor backwards, all the way from the front door through the hall and into Joe's workshop. She'd cleared a space for it by collapsing the small workmate table and stashing the vice on a shelf.

'Your father has completely recovered the ability to buy stuff on line.'

This was perhaps the only area where, in terms of outcome, the left hand had now usurped the right. A bargain at a hundred and ninety-nine quid – because it had been superseded by a new version – the treadmill was supposedly a lightweight model, but then so was Fran, so that particular advantage had cancelled itself out. She stared down at the box and wondered where to start.

'OK, Jess. I need to get something straight. So. Matt's just told your father and me that you're both "reframing the whole wedding thing." When you're off to Lerwick in a couple of days. What does that mean?'

Jess screwed her nose up and shrugged. 'That's what you call a form of words. It's something to tell Zanna so she'll take me seriously and butt out. A truce. No more site visits for the time being. Personally, I need to stop thinking about it. I've told Matt he can research all he likes while I'm away, just spare me the updates.'

'Scissors. On the shelf.'

Jess handed them over. The instruction booklet was with the invoice, inside a plastic sleeve which had been taped onto the box.

'Your father wouldn't approve of me reading this,' said Fran. Immediately underneath *open the packaging and take out the treadmill* was a message printed in a red box. '*NOTE. Fold up and SAVE* – that's in capital letters – *SAVE packaging...* It's not exactly hopeful, is it?'

'They just mean in case you move house ever, Mum.'

'I meant, you not thinking about the wedding.'

'Oh, that.'

'And what do you mean, a truce? It shouldn't be warfare. Who's in conflict with whom?'

'I'm in conflict. With everyone.' This girl was avoiding eye contact. She tipped the box up slightly and laid it back down on the floor. 'OK, so we open one end. But I didn't throw my shoe at him, honest. Maybe I over-reacted.'

Jess knelt down and cut the plastic thongs with a Stanley knife from her dad's collection, then prised out the staples at one letterbox end with a screwdriver. Beneath the cardboard was a tight wall of white polystyrene foam. It was difficult to get hold of it.

Fran nearly asked, *You do still want to marry him, don't you?* but checked herself. That form of words was far too sloppy. Too subjective, loaded, unfairly designed to prompt the answer *yes*. Instead she said, 'I'll hold this end, you pull.' But the white packing wouldn't be gripped.

'If we insert something flat between the box and the polystyrene, and shush it around a bit, it'll flatten the foam and give you a bit of play.'

'OK.' Jess got up and looked around the workshop. 'Anyway, I'm taking up Cath's offer. At least I'll come back with something to show for it.'

'You'll stay at Nell's?'

'Yup.' She found a ruler and inserted it between the foam and the cardboard. 'It's something I need to do. I don't think I'll settle till I've done it. Right now, I need a creative project.'

'He'll miss you. If you're going on your own.'

'M-hmm.' Jess's lips were tightly pursed as she tried a longer, steel rule.

'So he's really going to have to fend for himself, then. With that bad ankle.'

'M-hmm.' Now it was the blade of the widest knife she could find. The only thing that came out of the box was a series of horrible dry squeaks.

'It's no good,' said Fran, 'we're just creating static and making matters worse.'

They changed ends. No better. Finally, Jess said, 'This is a bit pointless, isn't it? We've got needlessly hung up on vaginal delivery. We're going to have to cut the sodding box. Pass me the Stanley knife, I'm going in.'

'Listen to me, Jess. You'd be the first to say, the rest of your life is much more important than your wedding day. So you need to apply your mind to *that* creative project too.'

The cardboard cut with a pleasing, positive note. After a couple of squeaks and a feeble shower of plastic hailstones, the pre-formed white packaging was easily cast aside. Jess sat back on her heels and finally looked her mother in the eye. Her fists rested on her thighs and the Stanley knife pointed harmlessly at the ceiling.

'You're right. I do.'

Unmistakably, there was the regular beat of Joe's stick, and the less predictable sound of his footfall. Now he loomed in the doorway, just as they were getting somewhere.

'Your tea's going cold,' he said and gazed at the long dark object which was bound, mummy-style, in layers of transparent plastic bandage. 'That's holding the belt to the upright. You need to stand it up now.' He waved his stick and said, 'That's the top.'

'No, it isn't.' Fran hoped he wouldn't notice the open instruction leaflet on the shelf behind him. 'It faces this way round, and *that's* the top. It folds up for storage. Like this. Here's the joint.' She pointed authoritatively, thinking, all we need now is for Matt to come and read the instructions aloud to us as if he knows what they mean. This interruption was maddening. She needed to pursue this conversation. And she'd hoped they'd get the treadmill up and working on their own.

'Use the knife,' she told Jess, who'd made a move as if to start unwinding the bandage. 'Slit it.'

There was a bag of bits – an Allen key, a black knob, screws, nylon string and suchlike – which Joe emptied onto the workbench and sorted out left-handed. Fran passed the booklet to her daughter, who read each step. Joe sat on a stool and watched his wife's clumsy efforts at inserting pins and screws, handing her things and offering suggestions. She was getting annoyed on account of both her own cack-handedness and his scrutiny, until she caught his eye and realised the depth of his frustration. He was leaning forward, willing her on; he knew exactly how to do this, which screwdriver to reach for, what pressure to exert and where. He had the look of a little boy whose dad had hijacked the train set, and who was waiting hungrily for his turn.

'I know, I know, I'm making a pig's ear of this,' she said.

'You're brilliant.'

Disarmed, Fran was thoroughly ashamed of herself now. Jess must have read something in the look that passed between them, because she said in a serious voice, 'Mum, Dad... Can I ask you a question? Is it normal to get on each other's nerves?'

They answered with one voice.

'No,' said Fran.

'Yes,' said Joe.

A plaintive voice came down the hall.

'Is everything all right? What are you all doing?'

Foot in it

After a few days laid up, Matt had grown tired of his own four walls, but God it was even more boring here. Poor Joe, to be stuck on his own like this, most days. Matt's eyes searched around the Fabers' sitting room and lighted on a dark box that overhung the bookcase. Scrabble. Something his mum brought out in times of trouble to facilitate interaction, say if boring Uncle Nige came round, or if his dad was being an arse. Not his favourite game, but Joe was good with words and hey, it wasn't about winning; process was everything. By the time they finished the game, Jess and her mum would be back.

Joe was up for it. The coffee table was too low, the dining table next door had lost its legs and been squashed flat against the wall because of the whole bed thing, and the table in the kitchen seemed to be covered in abandoned shopping today, so they decided to play in the workshop.

'You lead the way,' he told Joe, 'I'll hobble along behind.'

Matt's hobbling style might be slow but it was consistent. Studied from behind, Joe's way of walking was something else; almost a dance, only less predictable. His right leg kicked out conga-fashion from time to time, or he might suddenly raise the knee, which was more morris-dancy; when he picked up speed, though, the front of his right foot suddenly stuck to the floor, forcing them both to a jarring halt.

The workshop had never been so gloomy and cold. The weather didn't help – they needed the light on – and the sheet over the smashed-up model on the big workbench made the room look a bit like a slightly dusty morgue. Spooky. Under Joe's direction, he moved a few little gluey bits and bobs from the small table by the window, blew off the dust, and pulled up a couple of chairs. Rain spat at the pane. Joe sat with his back to the obviously horrible memories.

The Fabers had the De Luxe version, but the lid didn't sit properly. This turned out to be because inside, under the square board, was what looked like a soft toy, made of printed fabric, and designed to look like a fish. A big round flat one, brown with orange spots. He held it up by its tail.

'Ah. So that's where she put it.' Joe smiled.

'What is it?'

'That's the fish. Smeant to be an oven glove. Try it on.'

He slipped it on and looked at it. One fish eye stared back at him, the other swivelled towards the window.

'What's it doing here?'

'You've never played hide the fish?'

'No.'

'Oh, we all do. The person who finds it has to hide it somewhere else.'

This was a new one on him.

'Can I put it somewhere for you?'

Joe pursed his lips and waggled his head from side to side.

'Mmm… In the hall cupboard, Fran's big white coat. The puffy thing.'

'The ski jacket?'

'Mm hm. Roll it up like a cigar. Shove it up the sleeve.'

'She won't find that for ages.'

'That's how it works,' said Joe, and peered over the rim of his wire-framed glasses. Sometimes he really was the mad professor.

Respectfully, Matt took the fish to the coat sleeve, then came back and let his future father-in-law start the game. He was working one-handed and managed to knock the tile-holder thingy backwards, so it was only fair to begin again.

Joe's first word was DOLIANT.

'Oh. *Doliant*. Right.'

'It means how I'm feeling right now.'

Matt had never come across this word before, but Joe specialised in words nobody used. It earned 24 points plus an extra 50, apparently, for using up every one of the seven letters. That rule was new to him as well.

Matt's running total showed that after four goes each, he'd scored 38 to Joe's 100.

There was an awkward passage early in the game when they were both in a hurry to use up their special letters. Matt started it all off with his QI. His next move was a majestic YING.

Joe said, 'Don't you mean *yin* without a G?'

'No, it's ying. You know, ying and yang.'

'Ah. *That* ying.'

And he only went on to use Matt's G, and set down ZIG right on the triple word score.

'Is that a word?'

'Zig. The opposite of zag. You know.'

After a while he wondered if maybe Joe was cheating.

That wasn't the only dubious call. Joe laid down CUSS, and Matt, brilliantly, was able to extend it with PER and ION to make percussion, which was one of those moves which deserved bonus points for genius, which you don't ever get, which is an inherent unfairness in the game and probably its greatest flaw. Joe was impressed; only, later, he tacked an S onto the end.

'PERCUSSIONS? You can't have percussions plural.'

'You can. I'm having percussions right now. Stroke painless, percussions painFUL. That's why I'm on the cetamol.'

Repercussions, paracetamol… Joe had his own language now and maybe it was churlish to argue.

So he answered, 'Me too. I'm on the cetamol. For the ankle.'

'Legs, arms, shoulder. All my aches in one basket.'

He laughed. There was no point treating this as a zero-sum game. Playing Scrabble with this guy was entertainment. Joe was in his element, and found something to say about every word. Silly rhymes, puns, reminiscences, no word was innocent. Matt decided to join in and play by Joe's rules. And it was all going swimmingly, until the bag was empty and they needed to get rid of the last few letters, and he plonked his last O alongside a vertical D and, thinking he was entering into the spirit of Joe's game, sang, 'DO. Three points. You *are* what you *do.*'

'But I don't,' said Joe.

He stopped admiring his superbly placed tile and looked up. Oh shit. That had been the wrong thing to say. Joe's expression was one he hadn't seen before, and he wasn't sure how to read it: the eyebrows said surprised, the mouth said disapproval, and the muscles round the nose were active, almost sneering.

'I don't. I don't do anything, do I? What does that make me? Does that mean I'm nobody?'

'No, no, I didn't mean… I mean, it's just a thing people say, isn't it?'

No answer. The horrible expression had set.

'I can tell you what I don't do. I don't work. Not any more. In fact, today, I turned work down. Recommendation. Some woman. Wanted a dolls house for Christmas.'

'Oh Joe, that's tough, mate.'

Christ, thought Matt, let the floor open up and eat me... It was as if he'd forgotten everything he'd learned on that Empathy course back in March.

'She said what about next year. I referred her to Santa. So I'm pissed off today.'

It was all coming back, though, what they'd said on the course. You just had to shut up and listen. And Joe continued.

'I don't go out, apart from once a week to the stroke gym. I don't garden. I don't play the piano. I do my exercises then I get tired. I rely on other people to entertain me. Books, radio, internet, and you, right now, playing scrabble. Which I appreciate, thank you.'

A brief nod, and the frown released. Phew. But he'd never seen Joe so hacked off. And it was all his fault for being tactless.

'I used to have hobbies but no time. Now I've got time but no hobbies. I miss the allotment. I miss being outdoors.'

Oh, the allotment... It was hard to understand, but Jess's parents were as emotionally attached to their vegetables as other people were to their pets.

'Fran's worried about it, isn't she?'

'Course. It's going to be in a state. You have to keep on top of it. Needs covering up for the winter, really, to control the weeds. Get some old carpet down. It's a bad lookout if we don't.'

'Maybe I can take care of that!'

OK, he didn't really know how... But it was the least he could do to make up for being so incredibly insensitive just now. It couldn't be difficult. You only had to google it. Allotment, cover, winter.

'Where do you get old carpet from, anyway?'

'You buy a new one, and let it mature.'

Joe still looked bloody miserable. It must be sarcasm, maybe irritation.

'Sorry Matt. I'm not good company right now. Thing is, I'm getting well enough to realise how sick I am.'

'I'm so sorry.'

Joe shrugged and raised his eyebrows with a tight smile.

'S'oright.'

There was something important about this empathy thing that Matt had only recently found out. It was a lot more fun to push a wheelchair round for a couple of hours than to sit in one for ten minutes.

3-Month Checkup

I came a proper cropper at the Acropolis apocalypse. To be practised in front of a mirror. Well that just stripped off the tongue, didn't it?

Joe reckoned it was no coincidence that the word *Acropolis* now came out as *apocalypse*; after all, his problems had all started with a horrible conjunction of the two. His appointment with the speech ferrapist had come out of the blue. He was less affected than many stroke sufferers; in the rehab hospital, they'd made him read out lists and seemed quite impressed that he could manage five-syllable words. This appointment was a luxury really given the state of NHS finances, but this time next year he was going to be giving the speech of his lifetime, and maybe it was best to take a long run-up.

The therapist was a friendly woman with an interestingly creaky voice. She quickly homed in on his poor lip closure; the right side of his mouth lacked sensation and he had a definite dribble, which apparently would be helped by sucking boiled sweets and drinking through a straw. Or blowing bubbles. She also identified a slight problem there with his plosives. At any rate, they agreed there wasn't much wrong and she didn't really need to see him again.

Nobody really needed to see him again, when it came down to it. He didn't speak as clearly as he used to, but he spoke well enough for them. He walked a bit like a zombie with a stick, but he walked well enough for them. His right hand didn't work, but after all, nobody expected it to. So that was all right then.

The exception was the researchers back at the General Hospital. They definitely did need to see him again, because it was time for the three-month questionnaire. All part of the research project Fran had signed him up for when he was incapable of making his own decision. The two interviewers were charming, still in their summer frocks, brown-armed and bonny. One asked questions, the other scribed. They both smiled a lot, but nothing could disguise the fact that the object of the exercise was to chart the outline of the funny little island he now inhabited. Or reiterate the list of things he couldn't do, or couldn't do properly; it came to the same thing. At least these two had the grace to be apologetic about it.

The more helpless he felt, the more Joe found himself teasing them. Could he make a cup of tea? Yes, but that was like forcing an old lady to cross the road. Make a meal? He could make a meal of anything. Could he stand on one leg? Which one, yours or mine? The worst thing was the list of 'who does' questions, which he'd never been asked before. Who shopped: you, yourself and someone else, or someone else? Who prepared food: you, yourself and someone else, or someone else? Who did the housework: you, etc.? How many times a month did he do the following outside the home: shop, visit relatives, leisure activities such as cinema etc., etc. Apart from a great day out last week, when they'd taken their future son-in-law to A and E, he wasn't going out much at all. Going out was tiring, and such a palaver.

Fran reminded him about Shetland, and the researchers were impressed by that saga, but spoiled it all with the stupid question did he still enjoy the things he used to as much as he did before.

'No, because I can't do them. I can't use a hammer, or go for a walk, or drive, or garden.' He didn't need to add, o*r have sex or sleep in the same bed as my wife. Or even do a two-armed hug.* They were sliding into mental health territory.

'Fran, would you be able to leave Joe to look after himself for a week?'

'She wouldn't,' he said.

Fran frowned, naturally.

'Why would I leave him for a week?'

'Say you'd already booked a holiday in Spain,' the scribe suggested. They were desperate to get something out of her.

'Is she going to Spain?' he said, and turned to face his wife. 'Are you going to Spain?'

His idiot routine was going down well. Both the interviewers were giggling.

'Right,' he said. 'My wife's going to Spain for a week. *Now* I'm anxious.'

They were apologetic about the cognitive test. He had to listen carefully.

'What do these two things have in common: an orange… and a banana?'

Tough one. 'Now you've got me there. Even in a fruit salad, I don't think they're compatible. Wrong chemistry. The acid

255

from the orange makes the banana go brown.' He appealed to Fran: 'This is a trick question.'

Fran's head was in her hands. The interrogators loved it.

The half hour interview took forty-five minutes, and he well knew that was all his fault. Back home, once they'd finished laughing about the whole thing, he found he was exhausted and pretty fed up really. Because it wasn't good, was it? He was undergoing the very commonplace metamorphosis which turned a normal middle-aged-to-mature man into an old codger. The codger, par excellence, makes something of nothing. He hasn't got a whole lot to contribute to the smooth running of the world so he compensates by playing the irritant or the fool. He distracts attention away from his incapacities in the here and now, in favour of an elaborate fantasy world of his own building. All very amusing, but leading nowhere.

That night, Fran jumped into his bed for a bit of a cuddle. A bit being the operative word, because what with the shoulder pain and the hopeless arm, most of the cuddle was missing. And she had her own question to ask him.

'Does kissing hurt?'

'It tingles. But not so much as before.'

'You just need to do the repetitions, then.'

She sounded mightily smug about that. Every cloud had a silver lining.

Mairi

After the Friday briefing and across the chaos of Mairi's desk, Fran recounted Joe's approach to the questionnaire. Mairi laughed toothily at the funny bits, and listened to the hard facts, before pushing her chair back and telling her, 'He's not going to need full time care, you know. He doesn't now, does he? Don't talk yourself out of a job here, Fran.'

'But someone's got to go.'

That much seemed obvious, both from the letter they'd all had from the Healthcare Trust, and from what the rep had said just now. A transfer would be possible. A part-time post in one of the hospitals could be negotiated. So there'd still be an income, of sorts. She could have more time for Joe.

It was impossible not to stare at Mairi's face; it was strong-boned, square-edged and straight-lined – Joe once compared her to a lino-cut – and seldom adorned by anything much. This was a woman who was never troubled by the way she might appear to others. Unexpectedly, she now leaned so far forward that a sheaf of papers buckled as they brushed against her woollen jacket, and she looked more long-faced than ever as she asked, 'Why does it have to be you?'

'I know he doesn't need nursing. But it's so lonely for him.'

Mairi dropped her head. 'What makes you think your being home will help?'

There was a funny thing going on here. Mairi's tone was pretty much the same as the one she herself had adopted with her daughter when she'd announced she was having a break from wedding plans; or earlier, when she'd almost talked herself out of the Frenzy gig because her father was in hospital. The inference being that she really hadn't thought this through. Mairi was an old-school feminist and probably thinking – as Fran had been about the gig – that a bloke wouldn't be reacting like this. Although plenty of men did care for sick wives.

Fran tried to justify herself.

'There's this pattern of behaviour…You could call it half-day syndrome, because that's when it happens. When I leave him in the morning, he's bright and cheery. So all morning I'm thinking, great, today we can have lunch together. Maybe we can do something together this afternoon, walk round the garden, play a game, you know. Then when I come home something's happened. He's a misery. Really low. So although we've finally got a nice block of daylight leisure time together, he doesn't want to use it. It almost feels like he's punishing me, for having been away. I think he needs company.'

Every week, the same sinking disappointment, the same process of wrapping her frustration up in sadness, then pulverising that sadness by means of some physical activity. Weeding the garden. Cleaning.

Mairi said, 'Have you challenged him about that?'

Challenged was an interesting choice of word there. Although in fact she had.

'He says sometimes he needs to be miserable. He says it's hard work entertaining the healthcare industry. But that's all going to dry up soon, anyway, because he'll be discharged in a couple of weeks.'

Even before he could wash and dress unaided, they'd both grown so disillusioned and confused by the unpredictable timing and content of the carers' three short visits a day that they'd started cancelling. Other people's needs were greater, let them have the time. And now that Joe was tackling stairs with more success, visits from the OT and the physio would be stopping soon. When his right hand still couldn't tell a sphere from a cube.

'Once Jess gets married, he'll have no company all week. You wouldn't leave a dog in the house alone like that.'

'Your staying at home isn't going to help his independence,' said Mairi, rather harshly, it seemed to Fran. They let it hang in the air for a moment. Then she softened. 'Anyway. There was something I wanted you to know. It'll be all round the place soon. We've worked together a long time and I wanted to tell you myself. I'm off, Fran. It's time for me to move on. It's the right time. That's one less manager, isn't it? They're going to need your expertise.'

Fran sat up. She hadn't been expecting that. There were huge things going on in other people's lives that were completely lost on her now.

You wouldn't insult a woman like Mairi by telling her to hang in there; she wasn't one to back down from a fight. You could only ask what she was planning. More time on the bench, she said, with a nod; she needed a change. She'd reached that age. Ah, yes, the bench. She'd forgotten her boss was also a Magistrate.

Stretching way into the future, Mairi would be involved in a lengthening series of judgement calls. Saints and sinners, innocents, low-level miscreants and weak, misguided people whose fate could be decided in an afternoon. Maybe she was flexing those muscles now, when she said – with such aplomb, such certainty, and such a *nerve*, as if she had absolute authority to say it – 'It's the right time for me to step down, Fran. It isn't the right time for you.'

Fran chewed this judgement over. How could Mairi be so sure? Joe was her priority now. In a surprisingly fluent movement that had started last June, her centre of gravity had moved. She could carry home and work, in fact she might need to work in order to stay sane; but her weight had shifted towards Joe's care. Time was precious. Who knew how long they'd have together? And it could never be enough.

PART FOUR

Equinoctial Gales

In order to book the flights, Jess had hammered her credit card. As September wore on, the weather in the south west was growing more and more windy and Matt was growing more and more whiny. He'd be off the crutches completely by the time she got back, but he was still ridiculously sorry for himself.

Her dad, meanwhile, was better than before but nowhere near recovery. Some days he too was downright grumpy. Now her mum had started saying unthinkable things, about going part-time at the Lab, maybe even having to give it up, because her job might be disappearing anyway. Jess overheard her talking it through on the phone with Aunty Nell. This was a big deal for a workaholic. Everything – no, not everything, *everyone* – was upside down. It was only when she fastened her seatbelt and turned her brain to flight mode that she realised how relieved she was to leave them all behind for a while. What she needed was exactly this: a climb above the grey into a cloudless, open sky.

At Aunty Nell's, though, she found the memory of her last visit with Matt and the family overlaid like a film or a clever piece of projection on everything she saw. The stone step at the entrance to the puffin burrow was where Nell had given her mum a few tips on how to manoeuvre a wheelchair. Her dad had learnt to drive the Zimmer up that garden path. And of course, the attic room in King Harald Street in which she'd played hide and seek as a girl was now the room she'd shared with Matt. He'd spent all his time cooped up in there, hunched over his laptop, while she was out at the Frenzy, apart from that one trip to Lunnasting with her mum which he'd been so rude about. Which was weird, because ever since the day they'd met and she'd told him about her Shetland family, he'd been mad keen to visit. Apparently.

Shetland had been one of the first things they'd ever talked about. She and Matt had met at a folk night at Odd Down. He was in the audience with a whole bunch of friends. She'd played a Shetland tune. He came up to congratulate her during the interval, they got talking, he'd told her about his best mate Aidan, who'd just gone to work up there; she told him she went there every year, he said what an amazing place it sounded, and asked what was it really like, so she told him, probably at some length. And he'd always seemed really interested. Until he got here.

It didn't add up. While they'd been in Lerwick back in August, Matt hadn't even spent much time with Aidan, who'd done all that volunteering for the Frenzy, helping with recordings. Spindly Aidan, the human radio mast, always hopping around, playing with his cables and his gaffer tape. They were supposed to have been best mates since schooldays.

Did she really know the man she was going to marry? She wondered what Aidan might be able to tell her.

Over supper in the kitchen, Jess let slip that Cath had Aidan lined up to produce the disc.

'Freya fancies him,' said Ella, then asked, 'You do know, about the big bust-up? Only we were wondering, was he still best man? And now you and Matt are on a break, well...'

'I'm not on a break from Matt. I'm on a break from his sister and her wedding plans.'

'The plans are meant to be the best bit!' squealed Ella, and reached for more pasta, whilst Auntie Nell raised both eyebrows and said it would be a bad look-out for a marriage if that were true.

'Anyway, what big bust-up?'

'Aidan and Matt. They had a huge set-to when you two came up for the Frenzy.'

Nell shot an angry glance at Ella for giving this away. 'You don't know that,' she said. 'You weren't there.'

'Yes, but Dougie Halliday was there at the back of the hall in the Clickimin standing next to them when it happened and he told Kirsten and she told me so then I got it straight from him. So all right, I didn't see them but we know what he said.'

'You're makin' dirt again,' growled her mother.

Jess cast her mind back. 'This was the afternoon the juniors played? And I did a set with Cath's lot?'

'That's right, it was while the wains were playing. So, Matt slopes off to get a drink and Aidan stops him at the back of the hall and says how he's come all this way so why couldn't he just turn up to more of the events and Matt says no way José. Because *the music's a bit like the knitting*. He says. Scratchy and repetitive. Scratchy and repetitive! And Aidan was like, how can you say that, and Matt was like, don't get me wrong, I love what she does but this is just all too much...'

'Ach, Ella, did you have to?' said Nell with a frown fit to punch rivets.

'What? What?' Ella, wide-eyed, took off her scrunchie, shook her hair out and drew it back into a long ponytail again. It was nice and sleek as she half closed her eyes and put on a simpering voice to mock her sister: 'Then when you all came home Freya said, "Oh Hi Matt, how's Aidan?" because let's face it she fancies him. And Matt said...'

She stopped dead as she caught her mother glowering at her over the table.

'Well it wasn't very nice.'

This was a lot to take in.

An early night was what she needed. It was almost too quiet in this house. Even Ella had taken to using headphones while she did her homework. Freya and the uke were back at Uni in Aberdeen, Aunty Nell, Uncle Tam, and the telly were two floors down. Unpacking, Jess heard every note of the town hall clock chimes, which meant there was still no wind. Where had it gone? It had been dead calm ever since she'd landed, when the autumn equinox was really meant to be a time of gales. It had been wild when she'd left home. It was a special period, repeated only twice yearly, when the daylight hours in the farthest reaches of Britain coincided, and day and night were of equal length. From this week on, the discrepancy between the two would widen as the northern isles raced into darkness. Darkness like a commitment.

She didn't know how literally to take Ella's account. It was like the shoe incident all over again: complete strangers putting their spin on things. Because it wasn't even first hand, was it? People made stuff up.

She'd be seeing Aidan Barry tomorrow. Aidan wasn't the most forthcoming of men, but if she could coax him out from under the headphones, he might be able to tell her a bit more about the real Matt Harrington.

It was true that when it came to her musical life, Matt was turning out to be pretty clueless. He had no means of telling a good performance from a bad one, other than by looking at her face. Picking up visual cues, he'd say.

Scratchy and repetitive, though. So unfair. Could she live with someone who thought of fiddle music like that? Assuming that really was what he'd said.

Because Matt *had* been the one who led the standing ovation after her big gig. He'd been more than enthusiastic after the performance. Ecstatic, in fact, and they had tumbled happily together and rolled around and around each other like a pair of otters, making love that night.

On the other hand, applause wasn't always a simple expression of enjoyment. Sometimes it was a sign of relief that the performance was over. A section of the audience would be thinking, *everybody's clapping, that means we're done with this, and in a minute we can get off these horrible seats and hit the bar. Let's clap some more.* Hmm. That could be him.

The doubts gathered momentum. Perhaps she was just a cog in the wheel, a part of Matt's grand plan. It might have been anybody.

And she'd seen his recent to-do list: *Coach J in self-affirmation / confidence building before FFrenzy.* So what had this coaching consisted of, in the end? Liking her website and telling her to visualise success. Correcting her use of language so that *I'm no good at* became *I'm challenged by.* That irritating routine where if she said *I can't,* he gave her the third degree: are you *sure* about that? What makes you say that? What does it take to say *I can*? Plans, goals, affirmations, mantras, a shedload of bollocks to think about and stuff to do.

Anything to distract her from actually picking up her fiddle and *practising.*

He didn't understand. Even supposing Ella had got it all wrong and he did like the music, he didn't understand where it came from.

And another thing. Nature. The outdoors. He hadn't really been back to visit it, had he? He claimed to love it, when they were all on that holiday in Wales. But she was starting to suspect he didn't need it. He'd raved about their mountain walk, but he hadn't scheduled another one. And this was damning, because let's face it, in his world, anything that mattered got *scheduled.*

In fact, that was another thing, there was nothing spontaneous about this man at all.

There was not a shred of romance in him.

Maybe they *should* be on a break. A break from each other, not just from the wedding plans.

Maybe they were too different. Full stop.

As soon as she got back, she'd tell him.

Only first, she'd make sure she got her dad's walking boots back.

And that was another thing: he'd only had to borrow them in the first place because he didn't possess any of his own. Why not?

She'd go round to the flat and say. 'I'm not staying. I've come to pick up Dad's boots.' And he'd say 'What, right now?' and she'd say 'Yes, because you're not going to need them, are you?' And he'd say, 'What d'you mean?' and she'd say, 'Yeah, because you're dumped.'

No.

No. Maybe not go that far.

That would be so awful. As soon as she imagined a life from which Matt had been subtracted, all the things he added suddenly sang out. It wasn't just moral support; he *did* stuff. If he said he was going to post a letter for you, he did, and her parents had pronounced him kind and considerate long before there'd ever been a wheelchair to push. He had this talent for thinking ahead: the wine was always chilled, the tickets always booked. Whereas she was famous for her 'oh we should have...' moments. And as for not doing the Full Frenzy or even the Half Frenzy... well, look at it the other way, she wouldn't want to spend a week watching *him* work, would she? Also, he was absolutely gorgeous... In fact, when it came down to it, maybe everything about Matt was exactly right.

The irritating monotone she could hear right now was her telephone ringing.

'Jess? You OK?'

See? She loved his voice. It was never harsh, always warm. He already knew she was safely arrived, though, they'd only spoken a few hours ago. It must mean something bad had happened.

'Is everything OK?'

'Oh yes but it's just... It's nearly midnight. And you know what today was? The equinox. So, where you are, and where I am, the dawn rises tomorrow at the same time. It's kind of magical, isn't it? And it's gone so quiet here all of a sudden, the winds have dropped, and I just thought, where's my Jessie? What's she doing now? And to tell you, when you wake up, I'll be thinking about you.'

'Me too,' she said. And she knew in her bones she wanted this to work out.

'So that'll be approximately 6.48 am. Sunrise. Seeya there. I love you, Jess.'

After they'd rung off, she realised she was smiling to herself and decided to put the whole thing under her pillow. It would all be clearer in the morning.

Mother knows best

It had been ages since his mum had come over to the flat. She looked out of place, at war with the decor, in her mumsy patterned cardigan and her sensible shoes. She'd brought a jam roly-poly pudding with her, for heaven's sake, because she still clung to the belief that it was his favourite. When in fact it was *hers*. This gross pudding reminding Matt of the terrible Friday evenings of his childhood when boring relatives came round. Baked pudding and no TV, and an evening spent trying to beat his sister at cards.

His mother set about decanting a huge bag of Tupperware pots into the fridge, occasionally tutting about the things she was finding inside. She held each object she had brought in her hand for a moment, to explain what it was. She announced a steak and ale pie from Marks and Spencer and a lasagne for one. A bag of miniature carrots that didn't need preparation and would cook in five minutes. A frozen portion from the fish pie she'd made when Derek's friend Clive from the Rotary came over with his wife, 'who believe it or not barely said a word all evening. A diminutive woman, and she ate like a horse'. She always said all that about Mrs Clive. She waved a big box of chocolate biscuits at him, the sort you buy at Christmas or for a special occasion like being poorly. He nodded graciously from his place on the sofa through to the kitchen; ooh yes, thanks mum. Well, he could agree with her on one thing. He needed cheering up. She picked a small half-opened package from the door of the fridge and grimaced.

'*Mushroom pâté?* Well you don't have to eat that now, darling. Shall I just bin it? It'll only go off.'

She was very down on Jessie's food choices, unfairly, it seemed to Matt. But he did hate mushrooms so, yeah, sure, she should bin it.

She put the kettle on and came to sit beside him on the sofa. He could sense her scanning the room. He knew it was all a bit minimalist for her taste because she'd told him so, on many occasions. Why was there room for that lump of rock on an otherwise clear surface, and none for the lovely vase she'd bought him as a housewarming? Why indeed, mother. They'd agreed to differ.

'I still think you ought to come home and stay with us for a bit.'

'Makes no difference where I am, Mum, it's going to hurt just the same.'

Because it really was painful, not just to stand on, but if he touched it.

His mum knotted her brow in sympathy and held that look for a moment.

Then she said, 'Well at least I've got you on your own now and we can have a little talk.'

He'd thought as much. She was sitting at a slight angle to him, hands in her lap, one ankle neatly tucked under the other. The way she would for an interview, or a formal portrait. Composed.

'Matthew… Is everything really all right between you and Jess? Only from what Zanna says, she got herself into quite a state, and now she's disappeared.'

'She hasn't disappeared. I know exactly where she is. I spoke to her only this morning.'

He felt warm and cosy just thinking about their equinoctial phone calls.

'But what was it that made her so hysterical? Zanna said it was because she didn't like Highams Hall. I can't believe that. How could anybody not like Highams Hall?'

Of course, she hadn't seen his little sister in action.

'Zanna was too full-on. Over-selling. She doesn't read the signs. She never knows when to back off and let the client work out for themselves how much they want the product.'

She tilted her head slightly; a sign of concession.

'She's never had your objectivity, Matthew. Your rational detachment. But my goodness, your sister puts her heart and soul into everything she does. You can't fault her for that.'

'*I* put my heart and soul into everything I do,' he protested, but went no further. The fact remained that if Jess had been cross, it was with Zanna, not with him. This was an important insight, but his mother would think he was being petty if he voiced it, so he kept it nobly to himself.

'I do wonder, though, if poor Jess was maybe just a little over-awed by it all. I mean, they're... informal, her lot. A touch Bohemian?'

'Oh, come on Mum, she hasn't been raised by hippies in a commune.'

'No, but... I can't help wondering... Look, Matthew. Do you think they've got money worries now? The Fabers? Because Joe shows absolutely no sign of going back to work, does he?'

'Money worries?'

He had never stopped to think about that. She might be onto something there. One of the things he'd found out, now that he was researching setting up his own business, was that if you were self-employed, like Joe, you didn't get sick pay or anything much. If you didn't work, you didn't earn.

His mother's tone was grave. 'And for all we know, the Fabers might have a huge mortgage to service. Based on two salaries. And *she* might have to give up work to look after him.'

The only thing Matt had taken in about Fran's job was that she worked in a pathology lab alongside a bloke called Harry. Harry didn't act like her boss. Fran was a boffin, with her radio four and her crosswords. But she might be one of the people who cleaned the test tubes. For all he knew.

'I'll tell you what *I* think. I think poor Jess knows her parents can't pay for a proper white wedding now. She must be crying inside.'

Matt recalled how their early attempts at a budget-setting meeting a few weeks ago in the Jolly Roger had ended in a hangover.

'Honestly, Mum, I don't think Jess is that bothered about the wedding. Her dad reckons if we left it to her, she'd probably knit her own frock.'

'Does he?' She sat bolt upright and the strain on the sofa sent a sick echo right down into that sprained ankle. 'Does he now? Hm. That's exactly what I feared. I'm sorry, Matthew, but you deserve better. And Zanny's making such an effort, you know. She's cut a brilliant deal with Damian, at Highams. It's there for the taking, Matthew. They've got a date four months from now, they're offering a whacking discount for a cancellation. You need to grab it before somebody else benefits.'

'How? Jess isn't here to decide. And anyway, she *has* already decided. It was a definite no.'

His mother sighed noisily and placed her hand on his arm. 'Matthew, Matthew,' she said, 'you can be so... literal sometimes. Jessica is a kind person of very high moral probity. Can't you see what she's doing? She's sacrificing her own interests to spare others. She must be so disappointed by what's happening to her father. It's terrible timing. Catastrophic, for a bride. She's trying to protect her parents – all credit to her – and she's much too proud to tell you that none of them can afford a proper wedding.'

Wow, his mother just said that Jessica was a person of very high moral probity. How did she know that? Was it obvious? And perhaps Joe's stroke did go some way to explain Jess's recent... wobble. His Jessie would never dream of playing the grasping little madam. That was more Zanna's bag.

'I don't see what we can do, though,' he said.

'Well, I do.'

She sat back, drew her mouth into a sort of zipped purse, stared into the middle distance and took in a huge breath through her nostrils.

'What if... and I've talked to your father about this... what if we helped? We can pay that deposit *tomorrow*. It would at least take the pressure off.'

'Take the pressure off? So, she'd come back from Shetland and we'd say, *surprise?*'

She nodded silently.

It all made sense. Rational analysis, plus logical solution. So why did it feel like a terrible idea?

She tapped him briskly on the thigh.

'Sleep on it. That's all I ask. Now: fish pie or steak and ale?'

Ill Met by Frozen Fish

'Watch that van!'

'I wasn't planning on hitting it, Joe.' He heard the smile in her voice as she gave a sort of harrumph, warning him he was getting annoying, but in an endearing sort of way. She'd already told him she liked to think of their little sessions in the car as a series of masterclasses.

He was longing to drive. He'd apologise for over-reacting, once they'd reached a good straight stretch. His wife was particularly twinkly and upbeat, today, because this was a landmark outing. He could now walk well enough with a stick to be ready for his first supermarket sweep. They'd earmarked a store with particularly wide aisles, and their plan was for Fran to bring the trolley to the car so that he could use it like a baby walker to help him round. She seemed absurdly excited not to be doing the shopping on her own. It was months since they'd visited any sort of shop together, unless you counted parking a wheelchair near the museum gifts in Lerwick.

In his previous existence, Joe had assumed that disabled parking spaces were intended for people in wheelchairs or who couldn't walk very far. Now he'd discovered that a wide space was also essential if he was even to get out of the vehicle. No more shimmying about and congratulating himself on his svelte physique – he needed to open the door every bit as wide as if he'd been a sumo. But the catch was, no blue badge application until you'd been disabled for six months. By which time he hoped he would no longer need it. Also, you had to promise to stay that way for the next year or so, which with any luck was out of the question.

At twenty past two on a Monday afternoon, the new out-of-town Lidl offered plenty of spaces and a choice of trolley spec.

Joe opted for the saloon version, the biggest on offer. The stick fitted easily down one side and the steering was perfect. The pavements and the floor were level. Wide glass doors opened automatically into a bright lobby where you could pick up a huge bag of compost and a sack of daffodil bulbs for under a tenner. Well, Frannie could pick them up, seeing as she was getting surprisingly muscly these days. Daffodils, though. A sign you were heading for winter but planning for spring. It was important not to be scared. Who knew what he might be able to accomplish by the time those dry brown onions were blooming yellow? He'd take it nice and steady today and see how far he could get. The shop wasn't busy, so he'd have to be pretty determined to collide with anyone. Although, like the learner driver he now was, Joe's eyes were never focused very far ahead.

Right from the start of the first aisle, however, Fran had a good long view of two familiar figures bent over a fridge.

'Look,' she hissed, 'by the frozen fish.'

He stopped to have a look, and took the opportunity for a good stretch of the neck. There was no mistaking Janet Harrington's opulent hairdo. Give her a moustache and you'd have Charles II on a bad day. Only Charles II famously had better legs.

'Well I'll be… What are *they* doing here?'

'*We're* here,' Fran pointed out.

'We're shopping. They'll be doing undercover ops. To see how the other half live.'

'She's seen us,' said Fran. 'She must have.' Janet had uncurled to put something in their trolley, and was now facing them. Derek made a movement to look over his shoulder which was quickly checked, and they stepped around the corner into the next aisle.

It turned into a game. Fran and Joe made their way around the store, and every time they caught sight of the Harringtons, the couple turned their backs and disappeared.

Fran tutted. 'Pretending they haven't seen us.'

He disagreed. 'Modern manners. Seriously. Lidl etiquette. Because some people don't like to be seen shopping here, do they?'

She flared her nostrils by way of response.

'I like to think the best of people,' he told her. 'If we catch up with them, I bet they'll tell you what they've come here to get. Organic milk. Pistachio nuts, say. You know, staples. Then we have to do the same. Because by sharing consumer tips, you're actually establishing a state of *I'm OK, You're OK*. As Matthew would say.'

Inevitably, they met. After threading a logical route up and down the first two aisles, Fran wickedly jumped ahead and caught them in contraflow by the random crap. Everybody loved the random crap section. You might pick up something really useful in amongst the plastic storage, the long johns and the socket sets. Such as, for example, a magnet on a telescopic stick, or a clipboard with integral solar powered calculator. It could be high tech. And cheap enough for you not to be too disappointed if it didn't work.

Fran's hello was loud enough to imply, don't pretend you haven't noticed me.

'Oh hello!' said Janet. 'We've just popped in for some dried mango. And my friend told me they do this amazing Halloumi which actually comes from Cyprus.'

'Cod,' he said. 'We're here for the cod. Aren't we, Fran?'

'Oh yes,' said Janet. 'I've nothing to say against the fish. You can't go wrong with a vacuum pack, can you?'

'Yet nature abhors it.' No response. Fran asked after Matt: how was the ankle coming on?

'Oh, fine, but he is getting a bit sorry for himself all alone in the flat. It's such a shame Jess has to be away, at the very time when he needs a bit of TLC.'

Derek's eye had wandered back to the counter where there was an intriguing selection of metal brackets and things called *tool tidies*. His blank expression indicated he wasn't in conversation mode, but he might be weighing up the options to improve his garage.

Fran nodded and made some bland remark about Jess's work being important to her, then Janet nodded back and said she was surprised they didn't need her at the Cherry Tree Tea rooms. Joe prickled. This woman seemed to think music was a charming hobby. A suitable accomplishment for a young lady.

'How's his module coming on?' asked Fran.

'Conflict,' Joe chipped in to show he had taken an interest.

Janet gave a feeble titter. 'Conflict doesn't sound like Matthew's bag, does it, Derek?'

Derek was examining a pack of sanding discs. He looked up to tell Joe, 'You want to get some of these. Very handy. You never have one to hand when you need one.'

'You haven't seen me with power tools lately, have you Derek?' said Joe, thinking, the man's an idiot, but it adds to my motivation. If I keep up with the physio, maybe one day I'll be able to take a hedge trimmer to his topiary chicken.

'Matt's a sensible boy,' said Janet. 'Very steady. He hasn't got Jess's artistic temperament, I'm afraid.'

Joe attempted to draw himself to his full height. He was beginning to stiffen up from standing in one place so long. The devil on his shoulder goaded him.

'Funny expression, *artistic temperament*. Never got to the bottom of it myself. What do you think it means, Janet?'

Fran blinked hard, signalling to him not to pursue this.

Janet Harrington bridled and looked from side to side for help from Derek or Fran. As if she were about to cross a busy road.

'Of course, Jess is a lovely girl, and she's so creative. And it goes without saying, with all that imagination, she's bound to be highly strung. But Joe... Fran... Running away like that... you must admit it was a bit... volatile.'

'Which particular running away are you talking about?' asked Fran.

'Highams Hall, of course,' said Janet.

Oh, is that all, he thought.

Janet's tone modulated to become conciliatory.

'But anyway, Joe, what about you? How are you doing? It's good to see you out and about.' And she turned to tell Fran that it must be very tiring for him, he was bound to feel out of sorts, and was he doing his exercises. Because look at that chap on the telly, back interviewing the movers and shakers, and you'd never know there had ever been anything wrong with him.

Derek put a tool tidy into their trolley, and held another one out to Joe, as if to say, don't you want one too? Joe declined it with as little effort as he could muster, a sort of reverse auction-room twitch.

'It must be a worry for you that Joe's not working now. I mean, with all the expense of a wedding coming up.'

Fran seemed to be mimicking Derek's expressionless listening mode.

'And what are your plans, Fran? Workwise?'

At that, Fran's face dropped. Right. Time to jump in, Joe. 'Business as usual,' he said.

Fran's mouth opened and closed a couple of times and she stared at him.

Janet tutted in commiseration and said, 'You must be feeling such pressure. You're very brave, Fran. But I'm a great believer in providence. In fact, it could be providence that we've bumped into you like this. We'd like to help. Wouldn't we, Derek?'

'Oh yes.' Derek spoke without moving his lips, a technique which might be worth emulating – after all, it was Joe's rubber lips that kept tripping him up.

'We'd really like to help with the finance. Because I'm sure your lovely girl is just trying to save your feelings, and your pocket. Don't you think that's why she's run away to lick her wounds?'

Fran looked as though she was biting on something now, but she let Janet carry on.

'Put yourself in Jessica's shoes. Every bride wants a fairy tale wedding. She may not admit it, but she does. And it doesn't come cheap. Now, as it happens, Zanny has managed to get a fantastic deal if we fill their cancellation slot. Forty per cent discount! Forty per cent. Derek and I are more than willing to put up the deposit.'

She turned to face Joe. Nice to be included. 'And there'll be no need for anyone to worry. You can pay us back in your own, good, time.' She tapped him three times on the left forearm as she spoke, as if uttering a magic spell.

The flat line of Derek's mouth had lengthened by a good five millimetres: this must be a smile. Janet looked excited, expectant, even hopeful.

It was tricky to know how to respond.

Fran had been so feisty a minute ago, but now she was ashen faced, as if all her vigour had drained away.

'What does Matt think?' asked Fran.

'Matt's for waiting till Jess gets home to tell her, although I have to say, time is of the essence here. But perhaps *you* could get alongside her. She'd listen to you.'

'So, Matt thinks it's what she really wants? He thinks it's a good plan?'

'Oh, you know Matt,' she answered. 'It's been, *don't worry Mum, it'll all work out* for months with him. I said to him yesterday, yes, Matthew, it *will* work out. *And this is how.* Only now he's waiting for a green light from Jess.'

Joe stiffened and stretched again. 'Well… thank you. It's a very kind offer…'

'Is it?' said Fran in a voice so pale it was possible they didn't hear. They certainly didn't acknowledge it.

'…But I think we'll be OK. Thanks anyway.'

'Sleep on it.'

She tapped his arm again.

Nobody seemed to know what to say next, until Janet remembered something else she wanted to buy and gave them an excuse to head in opposite directions.

Fran looked terrible. Literally gutted, collapsing from within.

Joe didn't believe for one minute that Janet was right about their daughter; Jess was incapable of hiding her feelings. But what if the only thing holding his wife back from seeking part-time work was the fear they wouldn't be able to make ends meet? Janet had touched a nerve. Her interpretation of Jess's actions made matters worse. He wanted to sit Fran in the car and drive her straight home. He wanted to be the capable husband who'd carry the shopping indoors and put it all away, then wrap her in his arms and convince her that everything would work out right. All of which was impossible, now that even their marriage was lop-sided.

Square One

Janet Harrington had taken the rug from under Fran's feet, but in the space of the drive home from the supermarket doubt had sublimated into anger. She was annoyed with that woman. And even more annoyed with herself for being so short-sighted. As she entered the house Fran was thinking and moving at speed, re-playing everything that Jess had said about the trip north, looking for clues as to her deep intent. She was aware of Joe behind her as she walked briskly into the kitchen, where she began emptying out the first bags of shopping. Anything that couldn't break was slammed down on the counter with relish, packets of rice and coffee, jars, tins. Before she'd had time to go back for the rest of the groceries, though, she heard a thud. It was accompanied by a flurry of other noises, knocks, small objects falling from another carrier bag; but unmistakably, the thud was the heavy heart of it.

Joe had fallen.

He lay crumpled against the staircase and close to the hall table, with one leg folded under him and the other bent at the knee, the weak foot scrabbling for a hold. He was trying to get up. His shoulders were hunched in the effort, his head down, his weak arm beating out awkwardly as he tried to balance. A carrier bag was looped around his left hand and its contents were half-squashed under him. The table was in his way. The first thing she needed to do was to help him unfold from this awkward position without toppling the lamp or pulling the table over, and that meant taking care about the way she extricated his stick; she had to check nothing was broken, to help him up, guide him across the two steps into the dining room and over to his bed, and then get him into it. All the time being careful to lead him by the strong side.

Hardest, though, she needed to stop herself from interrogating him whilst all this was going on. Can you move this, where does it hurt – those were sensible questions. But she must hold herself back for the moment from asking the question that mattered to her most: why? What was it that made you fall?

She assessed every component of every movement: the speed with which he got up on all fours and to a stand, the weight with which he leant on her in each step of each manoeuvre, the grip of his elbow hooked around her neck, the way he placed each foot; she measured the degree of certainty with which he sensed the height and contours of the bed. He sat, and she had to help him swivel, she had to lift his legs up for him.

Only now that he was flat and comfortable on the white pillow could she stare him in the face in an attempt to work out whether he'd had another stroke.

His slack features had fallen back to that collapse over three months ago. Almost exactly, but not quite. Almost as bad, but no worse. She left him propped up on pillows and phoned the surgery.

To Da Boat Shed

Cath's house was out towards Hamnavoe, some twenty minutes' drive from Lerwick, so Jess was grateful to Aunty

Nell for offering to drop her there in the morning. The wind was up again; a storm had rolled over during the second half of the night and was already on its way out. By the time they hit the road sometime after ten, the last big white rainclouds were breaking up, with long ribbons of dark grey, fray-edged cloud unravelling, pulled at speed across a pale blue sky and heading southwards.

The route took them upwards and Nell pulled in for a moment at the lay-by at the top of the hill so that Jess could take in a favourite view: a mile or two below, the pierced outline of the ruined keep of Scalloway castle against the silver water; the haphazard mixture of sea, islets, inlets and land, the pale roof of the Marine Centre far away across the harbour. And in the foreground, the Shetland signature, a thread of orange baler twine which had snagged on the fence and which now drew a rippling horizontal line in the wind. She wound the window down a millimetre to let a sharp slice of air cut through the smell of damp dogs that lingered in the pickup. Next to the car was a roadside litter bin and a sign: *Dunna chuck bruck*. The original yellow lettering had dissolved to the point where it now met the green of the background. From the squat metal bin, the edge of a black plastic bag snapped back and forth, and every now and then a cardboard coffee cup popped up like a bird in the nest, threatening to fly.

'See that bin? That's me right now.'

'Full of crap?'

'Yeah. Something like that. Full to bursting. I feel like everything's going to spill out and if it does it's going to make one unholy mess... But I shouldn't be fly tipping in your back yard.'

Of course, she was going to end up telling her Auntie Nell everything. The only question was where to begin. They drove down the steep hill, which was bald and brown like so much of the land here, until they dropped to where the green grass grew, then round the sharp left turn before Scalloway, and past the bright red and blue Scandi houses that overlooked the voe. The land to the west, to their right, was low, the sky huge. They had to stop for a car travelling towards them before they could cross the long and slender bridge to Trondra themselves.

'Don't hurry this bit.' They were hanging over the water, where a car shouldn't really be, and she opened her eyes as wide as she could, so as to take this all in and keep it safe for future reference.

'Bloody tourist,' said Nell.

You couldn't see it, but Jess knew from poring over maps that the bank opposite was the nearmost of three islands set in the sea like dates in a box, with the route forcing the traveller west in order to go east: Trondra, West Burra, East Burra in that perverse order, because that was how they were linked by a set of low, flat bridges, which were modern, simple, and elegant in their way. This first bridge was a couple of hundred yards long, and sent them skimming over the rippling grey of the voe.

'So. One thing is, I can't stand my mother-in-law. And that's not going to change.'

'Janet with the beige house and the cabriole legs.'

'Janet, yes.'

'Because?'

'She's horrible to my dad. She thinks he might dribble on her. She'd airbrush him out of the wedding completely, if she could. Or park him in the disabled loo and barricade the door.

And I overheard her telling Matt that my *artistic temperament* was something he'd learn to live with. He just laughed. But can you believe it?'

Nell tutted.

'And the irony is, I completely reject the artistic temperament fallacy. Because it's just something people use as an excuse for behaving badly.'

'*Have* you behaved badly?'

'Prob'ly. In her books.'

'Specifically?'

Her dad always said there was something in Nell's nursing background that prompted her to fumble around for any spot that might hurt. Palpating, they called it. Prodding, in layman's terms.

'Specifically, I *did* run screaming to get away from my future sister-in-law. Who was trying to sell me a second-hand wedding at the time. So it *was* my fault he sprained his ankle. But I wasn't hysterical, just angry. And I didn't throw my shoe at him.'

Maybe Nell hadn't heard that part of the story before, because the eyebrows danced and she asked, 'Why would you?'

'Exactly. Some random bystander just made that up.'

They were on land again and travelling down the well-made road parallel with the sound, which was on their left now. The emerald pastureland sloping down to the water was scattered with sheep, and the gouged hills beyond flashed bronze wherever the cloud parted.

'What does Matt think?'

'He says love conquers everything.'

'It does.'

'Hmm. Yeah.' Like life was a game of paper, scissors, stone.

They drove in silence until they were within sight of the next long, water-hugging bridge.

'How *are* things with you and Matt?'

There she was again. Nurse Nell. She'd started ripping plasters off. No notice of the exact moment, except you knew it was coming.

'He's been a complete arse about his ankle. I think he might be a hypochondriac.'

'Hypochondriacs aren't immune from illness and injury, you know,' said Nell.

'It isn't that serious, but it's the only thing that's ever really got him down. I suppose that's been a surprise to me. Because he's usually so upbeat about everything. Nothing much ruffles him, you know? He's one of those people who floats through life on a happy cloud. Usually.'

'Makes it more of a shock,' said Nell.

She might have something there. Her own ascent through life had been a bit like bouldering really, mostly clambering about, hopping from rock to rock, zigzagging up the mountain. Whereas if you'd spent the last twenty-seven years confidently *moving forward* – to use one of his favourite expressions – in a straight line to the top, well, any obstacle would be much harder to negotiate. So she could just about forgive him this.

It was possible that her mind was clearing, because now, out of the irritating background hubbub of the wedding noise came one supremely discordant note, the single thing that was troubling her most.

They reached the second magical bridge, with a clear road ahead.

'The thing is, a while ago, I found something out about Matt. Maybe it's nothing, but it's really bugging me.'

'Uh-huh?'

'Turns out, when we met, he was actually looking for someone to marry.'

Nell said, 'Isn't that how it's meant to happen in the fairy tales?'

'Is it?'

'Yeah. Cinderella. Prince Charming's dad holds a ball which is basically a speed dating opportunity. The whole point is to find Mrs Charming.'

'I found out from his sister, he drew up this plan when he was at uni, with all his life goals written in with dates, and he's worked through it, and now he's got to 28: get married. And ever since I found this out, I feel like I was just the one he happened to be talking to when the music stopped.'

As they came to the water's edge, Nell slowed the car down and they both took the opportunity to scan up and down the narrow voe.

'The crazy thing is, I don't want to tell Mum and Dad about this Life Plan, because I know they'd think the worse of him. I mean, in our family, you might plan a picnic or a holiday, but you wouldn't plan your life.'

'Do *you* think the worse of him?'

They were half way across, and the water to the left and right was a silvery shudder. The flat, straight lines of the narrow bridge and its low parapets presented a perspective quite at odds with everything else that she could see.

'It's more that it's… alien.'

'So why did you get engaged?' asked Aunty Nell. 'And I don't mean you two. I mean you personally, Jessica Faber.'

This was an easier question to answer now. Jess knew the things she liked about him. The way he looked, his open, honest face. His voice. The lovely smell he had about him, like no-one else she'd ever got that close to. He was kind and caring. To everybody. And there was that incredibly strong feeling that even if he didn't always understand what was going on, he was on her side.

'I've always felt he brought out the best in me. And that he's rooting for me, cheering me on, you know? And he knows all this stuff about how to believe in yourself and how to make things happen. I mean, that's his job.'

'And your problem is?'

'I don't know if he really gets the music. I mean, long term, can I live with that?'

'Don't you mind what Ella said. The less he knows about the music, the more his focus is on you. Besides, what do you think your Dad knows about cytology? Bugger all, is my guess. It's all stuff down a microscope to him.'

They reached land. The pickup sailed past the East Burra turnoff, and on towards Hamnavoe.

Jess admitted, 'There's always more to people than what they *know*. Matt and I have always had... you know... chemistry.'

Nell took her eyes off the road long enough to turn and give her the benefit of a raised brow.

'Is this bedroom chemistry, or does it work in the rest of the house?'

'Oh, I love staying at his. Although... He does sort of tidy up after me. Which suits me down to the ground, right now... Only I can see that, in the long term, it might get on my nerves.'

Nell grimaced and made a silly humming noise; then shook her head and said, '*Nnn-ope.* That's not the sort of behaviour that would *ever* get on *my* nerves. In case my children ever ask.'

Eventually they reached that bend in the road from which you had a glimpse of the destination, across shallow waves of green fields: a fine white farmhouse of two storeys caught the sun; but what held your attention was a curiously shaped dark object close by. It was the pitch-black roof of a low outhouse: an outhouse with no gables, and a roof which curved and downturned at each end. From this point of the journey, they would lose the landmark and pick it up again a couple of times, when the hollows of the land were right. It always provoked the same reaction. Jess's heart strained on tiptoes, eager to be there.

Da Boat Shed was a peat shed, but nobody called it that, because its dry-stone walls were crowned by an upturned sixareen. It was the blackness of the hull which made it stand out, and from a distance it seemed flat and insolent. Only as you approached – and then only if the light was good enough – was your eye drawn to its contours, the keel wide and shallow, with a graceful symmetry that came from being double-prowed in the Shetland way, the whole turned with such elegance. It was basically a Viking ship, designed to be strong yet nimble in heavy seas. In its day this ancient boat had carried six oarsmen, a skipper, their tackle and the catch far out to sea. Now it was the lid of Cath's music box.

Jess had always stood in awe of Cath Isbister. She picked up instruments the way other girls picked up boyfriends. She'd had a head start, because the music in her family went back generations; her mother taught violin and piano, and her dad played every style of guitar, as well as mandolin and even banjo. In their living room there was a framed photo of a chubby baby Cath, sitting on the floor with two drumsticks in her raised arms and the huge base of a jam pan in front of her. Also, Cath in school uniform, with her fiddle, her recorder;

287

playing duet with her grandad, in some hall or other; with her brothers' band, pounding the keyboard, or wielding a bass guitar. She had flirted with the bodhran, and even had a brief fling with the Northumbrian pipes, which she claimed was the dodgiest boyfriend of the lot.

Aged fifteen and up one summer for the Frenzy, Jess had been surprised and flattered to be invited to Cath's birthday party, which also turned out to be the official opening of Da Boat Shed. She was even more proud to be invited back there to make music. At the time she thought the Isbisters were the coolest parents in the world, to give their daughter the boat shed as her own practice room. By then Cath had discovered amplification, though, so maybe Rona and Tom needed to ease her banging, squealing, plucking and scraping out of the house.

As they all moved through their teens and into that choppy water where schools kept asking you what you were going to do next, Da Boat Shed become a serious project for a while. Cath saw it as a potential recording studio which she could let out to supplement her future living as a musician, and if Jess already knew that music was a calling, it was probably Cath and her parents who showed her how it might become a profession. Cath scraped the money for equipment together from birthdays and Christmases and holiday jobs in the fish factory, investing in herself, she said, which must surely be a catchphrase she'd picked up from some business thing on the telly. But only a teenager could believe the venue had commercial potential. It wasn't just that Da Boat Shed was big for a shed but small for a recording studio, or that the location was well off the beaten track. The rain hammered on the clinker roof, and even on a dry day nothing would stop the wind whistling round the door and through the dry-stone walls. No amount of dead quilts, expanding foam and old socks and tights – poked under the gunwales with the help of a butter knife – solved the problem. Cath had experimented with making that infiltration of the wind a signature sound on her own recordings, a way of bringing the landscape into the music. But ultimately, she got fed up with people asking what was that noise and telling her she had a bad hiss there, hadn't she noticed. There'd been no argument about hiring the studio at Mareel this time for the actual recording. They had all grown up, and so had their music. Yet even with Da Boat Shed relegated to rehearsal space, Jess knew that the teenage haze of optimism hadn't quite cleared for Cath. Last August, the same old throws and hangings had been draped about the place, because Cath still hadn't noticed they had faded. When people said, wooh, it's dark in here, she'd answer, theatre lighting. The earth floor meant it was seldom completely dry, and tuning needed a lot of attention as the place gradually warmed up. The peat shed had trained their ears and fingers. It did no favours at all, never flattered any sound; it was a place of spiders and trembling cobwebs full of peat möld. If a piece worked there, it'd work anywhere.

Nell pulled over on the rutted drive in front of the big stone house, and wished her luck. As Jess stepped out of the car, she met a roar of wind, and for a moment it was as if her head were under water, because the air had stopped her nostrils. By the time she had righted herself to wave goodbye, the car was turning and on its way. The wind wanted to tear the fiddle case from her grasp, so she clutched it to her chest; her feet sank into bright grass that felt like sponge, and with zigzag steps, head down against the gale, she made for the shed. The wide door was centrally placed, half way along its length. It was easy on the eye – on a day when you weren't squinting – but it did mean you trod into the middle of everything when you stepped inside. No porch, no vestibule.

So when Jess tipped in, she already knew the weather would come in with her. What she'd forgotten was the intoxicating smell that would rush to greet her in this exchange of air: a deep scent of peat, with top notes of instant coffee and dust burning on the electric fire. She'd carry this home on her clothes tonight, fixed by the damp air. Inside, grey and barely lit by the autumn morning, two grinning faces welcomed her in.

Lifeline

Fran had woken early and came down to find that Joe was awake, too. She helped him get comfortable and brought breakfast on a tray, pulling up a chair to eat with him. He wasn't chatty. She had to force herself to observe and take things at his pace, rather than irritating him with the questions that were backing up in her mind. His speech, his movements, the way he ate and drank, everything had slowed down; he remained ashen-faced as yesterday, wet-chinned, his mouth a smear again, his right eye almost closed. There was no question of him getting out of bed today.

She was desperate to hear her sister's voice, but forced herself to wait until late morning so as to be sure that Jess would be out of the house, because it would sabotage Jess's whole project to worry her needlessly; although this rationalisation wasn't the whole truth. The fact was, she didn't feel up to telling Jess about the fall. There wasn't meant to be bad news now. This wasn't meant to happen.

The mobile emphasised the slight echo of the big kitchen in King Harald Street. Fran tracked her sister's movements round the room, talking greedily all the while. Clearly, Nell had set the phone down at one point whilst her hands were busy with something else. Clicking, opening of packets, scrabble of paws; then she seemed to have sat down and picked it up again.

There was a lot to tell. Fran started well enough: how the good thing was that the doctor wasn't troubled. There were no new symptoms, only a return of old ones, and it hadn't been another a stroke. How Joe had told her himself what had happened, that he'd tried to carry a bag full of shopping through from where she'd left it in the front doorway, but it had caught against the edge of the table, and he'd overbalanced. No harm done, said the medics. The prescription was not to worry, and to wait to get better. Wait! A whole week before they'd have the results of his blood test. When she could have gone in to the lab and done it herself that very day. Once that frustration was out, Fran felt a visceral, involuntary release. A sort of incontinence. And she told her sister how, suddenly, Joe seemed to have no strength at all; no appetite for anything, food, radio, conversation. He'd lost heart. As if someone had flicked a switch. Also, look at the time he'd lost! You made the biggest gains in these first six months, but now he was completely out of action. No more re-wiring in his brain. And forget exercise. He'd be losing muscle mass again with every day in bed. It all felt like a cruel game of snakes and ladders. He'd worked his way up the board, with so much effort, and now he'd slithered down a horrible fat snake right back to square one.

When at last Fran stopped speaking, it was not that she'd run out of breath, but that the ground had opened up in front of her. In this place of silence, she was left guiltily clutching the thoughts she hadn't shared, because these were the thoughts she couldn't bear to utter.

For three months now, she'd watched him getting better, and cheered him on. For three months she'd stuck to her Manifesto. She'd been scathing in the face of pity, militant in her optimism, and that had all seemed justified, hadn't it? Not any more. She'd been wrong.

Throughout the monologue, Nell had been murmuring, uh-huh, uh-huh. Now she took her own deep breath.

'It's going to happen, Fran. Sooner or later, rehab means injury.'

'A few random bruises, that's all there is to see. Only he says everything hurts. Everything's jangling.'

'A fall's a shock, for anybody, any age. It'll only take a small thing to send him out of kilter. And it's still early days.'

Early days? Was it really? It seemed a long, long time.

'The worst thing is, even on the day of the stroke, he had a smile for me, you know? He tried. Not now. It's as if he's lost all faith in his own ability to recover.'

'Well just make sure *you* don't doubt it.'

'Is that how it sounds?'

Nell took a heavy breath, in, out. 'You're shit scared, Frannie.'

She was right. And Joe was going to need to borrow Fran's confidence, in much the same way she was borrowing her sister's now.

'Look,' Nell came back, 'none of this is unusual. It's what happens. He'll get over it, you mark my words.'

'I haven't told Jess yet. We text, but I haven't told her. I don't want to pull the plug on everything she's doing. But I don't want her to get a fright when she comes home, either.'

'Is this an emergency?'

'Well no, not any more.'

'There you are then. But Jess will imagine it is, if you let her. Look, it's going to take a while for him to be back to normal. The chances are, though, these first two or three days will be the roughest, so with any luck she won't see the worst of it. He's just having an off week, isn't he? That's your press release.'

'I've had to take today and tomorrow off work. Sometimes I think I ought to give the whole thing up, or at least go part-time.'

Nell made a low growling noise and told her, 'Don't do anything in a hurry. He's not going to stay like this.' Fran made no answer. She went on: 'This isn't the same problem as when he had the stroke, is it? You're up against chemistry this time, that's all. I bet his blood test shows something's out of whack. His potassium could plummet after a fall, or his sodium. Or whatever... He's probably got a big wobble in his electrolytes. That can be fixed, if it doesn't sort itself out first.'

She knew that... but why had she not analysed it that way herself? If she hadn't seen the obvious here, how badly compromised were her other judgments, her judgements in the lab? Which was just another reason to think that maybe it was time to call it a day... Something told her to put that thought to one side, shut up and listen.

When Nell picked up again, her voice had brightened.

'Anyway, it's great that he felt able to carry the shopping for you, even if it did go pear-shaped. It's great that he wanted to.'

Hm. She was clutching at straws now.

'I don't think I helped. I was such a crosspatch at the time! Bloody Janet Harrington, met us in the supermarket, offered to pay the deposit for the wedding reception because she thinks we can't afford it and Jess doesn't want to be a financial burden now that Joe isn't working.'

'What?'

'She could be right though! About everything. What if I haven't seen the truth under my own nose? Janet thinks Jess has run away to Shetland *to lick her wounds*. I quote.'

'That's not the vibe I'm getting,' said Nell.

'You know, I've been so high for so long. Watching things get better. Then yesterday I hit a wall. It's as if... suddenly... I don't know anything about anything...' Her thoughts gathered. 'I do need to talk to her, don't I? I need her in the same room.'

Nell said, 'That can wait a couple of days, can't it?'

'I suppose.'

'Christ Fran, trust me, for the time being, as far as Jess is concerned, just stick to texts. Any cloth-eared idiot can hear it in your voice. You need to look after yourself. Stop beating yourself up.'

'OK. You're right, there's no urgency.'

Perhaps it would help if she could find something pleasurable to do... 'Maybe, if it stays dry, I'll do a bit of tidying in the garden.'

'And don't worry about Jess. You know what they say up here, about the trows?'

'The trolls?'

'Yeah, the trows. The peerie folk.' Nell's voice was nothing short of gleeful. Now what? Some daft story was on the way.

'So, the trows are great music lovers, and if they hear a really good fiddler, they carry them away! And three days later your fiddler comes back and they can't say where they've been but they've learnt all this fairy music... So. Think of it like this. Right now, your little Jessie has been kidnapped by trows. She'll come to no harm. And she'll come dancing back with all kinds of fancy tunes, you wait and see.'

Fran had to smile. Who wouldn't want this nonsense to be true?

Kidnapped by Trows

'Rrright,' said Cath, waving a piece of cardboard – the back of a cornflakes packet? – on which a wonky list of song titles had been written in thick felt pen. 'So, this is what we've got.' She held it up in front of her so that Jess and Aidan could see, once Aidan had angled the wry-necked lamp to illuminate it.

'Where d'you want to start?'

'*Lasses Trust in Providence*. Gotta be,' said Jess. She set her fiddle case carefully on the rickety card table, took out the instrument and rosined her bow. Aidan started to unwind a cable that was dumped spaghetti-wise against the stone wall. He placed a microphone stand in front of Jess and adjusted the boom.

'Let me see you stand,' he said. He stared at the violin as if it was going to speak. Cath meanwhile had set up her own microphone, but Aidan stepped forward to tilt it slightly, and her voice came up an octave as she protested, 'Hey! Fusspot!' Aidan backed off but misjudged the fall of the roof and bumped his head.

'Mind your head, you great rafter!' said Cath with a wide grin which revealed the gap between her otherwise even teeth.

295

The whistling gap, she called it, and she really could whistle through it.

'This is no place for grown-ups,' he muttered. 'It's a play pen really.'

Once everything was connected, Aidan folded himself behind the tiny mixer desk, on a stool which bedded itself into the earth floor. His knees stuck out at crazy angles. He ran his handkerchief between the faders then round the top and sides.

'Right,' said Cath. 'I've got a second fiddle line here, and I worked out something for guitar. So, if Aidan works his magic, I can be in two places at once.'

Then she interrupted herself. 'Oh, but listen. First, what d'you think to this, for your Frenzy Reel?'

She picked up a mandolin and started to play. The thin sound died quickly, as if pulled through the gaps in the rough stone walls; but the line was brilliant, nice and spiky, precise, nippy. In a proper recording studio, it would be fine.

Cath was all generosity, and she led them on a romp through the morning. She'd mined each tune for counter-melodies, and come up with so many that their first problem was deciding which to use. On the guitar, her harmonic progressions were never quite the ones you expected to hear, because, as Aidan pointed out, she knew too many chords. And she insisted, in the faster pieces, that they add some mischief to the music. That might mean stopping it dead with a pause like a sudden gulp of air, or a few bars which switched from four to three then back again. Mad stuff, but it worked. The best thing about playing with Cath, though, was the way she listened. She took your music and handed it back to you, polished.

At last Cath looked at her watch and announced, '12.30. I'm hungry.'

'We ought to take a look at my dad's air.'

Jess regretted her suggestion immediately, because Cath's face fell; the set of her eyes suggested ill temper on the way.

'Here's the thing, Jess. I don't have the first idea what to do with it. Archie was so brilliant that I don't want to touch a fiddle. I can't follow him. But I can't get his version out of my head either. So there you have it.' She leant back and threw her empty hands into the air. 'I'm out of ideas.'

'At least we could play it through,' said Jess. Panic was threatening to rise: perhaps the truth was, Cath didn't like Joe Faber's Air. And even if she did, the most important piece deserved the most rehearsal time, and they'd never so much as looked at it together before. They'd worked on everything else back in the summer.

Cath held up the flat of her hand. 'I won't play fiddle on this. And you need to stand right out on this track, Jess. If you have a backing, it's got to be something warm. Flute would be tacky. Maybe the Spanish guitar.'

'Or vocals,' said Aidan. 'You don't need words. You could build up a harmony that way.'

Cath cocked her head and considered him from the corner of her eye.

'I like that idea,' said Jess. 'I like the idea of it having human breath... you know? And you could build a good warm sound.'

Cath hadn't said no.

Aidan asked, 'If we're talking vocals... Are we all OK with this set-up? Or do you want me to bring anything from the car?'

'It'll be different anyway at Mareel. Might as well use my kit for the time being,' said Cath.

'Only I might have a better mic.'

'You're not working with gannets now,' said Cath. She said it with a smile, but Jess winced on Aidan's account, because rule one of Da Boat Shed was never to identify a defect in the venue.

Cath turned to Jess.

'You play. I'll listen. You never know, I might just hear something I haven't heard before.'

There, perhaps she hated it. Jess would just have to stand up for her dad.

There were some pieces which you had to play a thousand times – not just on the violin but in your head, not just practising but imagining a performance – before you could be sure you wouldn't find yourself actually hearing the poison-medicine inside the piece that broke your heart. That would be death to the performance. Jess knew she'd done that part of the work. The de-sensitising. But here and now, with Cath to impress, and Cath's help needed, the stakes were high. She reminded herself: your heart is in this piece, more than anything you've ever written, but you mustn't listen to your heart or you'll falter. You mustn't think about the circumstances in which you wrote it. You must hear as one who listens for the very first time, you must focus on the forward path of that line through the silence, and let the shape of the tune unfold as if you haven't even heard it yet yourself, and you are showing it to the world.

She played with eyes open and unfocused. When the final note had sounded, she let her bow hang loosely by her side and looked across at Cath.

'It *is* a braw tune,' said Cath. 'It's too good to leave out.'

She felt almost sick with relief, but the blank expression on Cath's face told her she couldn't relax yet.

'The question is, where do we go with it?'

'Let's break,' said Aidan.

They went into the house and warmed themselves in the kitchen, and made tea and beans on toast. The last clouds had gone and it was bright and sunny now, and that too lifted the spirits. Aidan took the chair that Archie Mc Nuckert had sat in. Archie with his wild brow, his flashing eyes, his animated, weathered face. Whereas Aidan's eyes were hidden behind those heavy frames. His gaunt features were permanently stuck in neutral. He'd made a great suggestion back there, about the vocals. Why was Jess surprised? There was more to this guy than she'd realised. Things Matt hadn't told her, either because he hadn't noticed or didn't care. This Aidan the sound guy was also Aidan the best man. She could see Annie falling for him, just like Freya had. Without even trying, Jess had put the wedding far from her mind ever since entering the shed, and she loved Cath – who was completely focused on the matter in hand – for not asking about it. Nor had Aidan.

Only yesterday evening, it had seemed urgent to talk to Matt's oldest friend. She'd vaguely intended to do this. Now she watched him take his time chewing like you're meant to, and thought, what was it I wanted to know, exactly? It didn't seem quite so critical, in daylight. Or maybe it was something Auntie Nell had said. She couldn't remember that, either.

All she knew was, her dad's air had been stuck in the mire, and this was the man who'd hauled it out.

Across the table, Cath had taken a couple of mouthfuls and already perked up. She'd needed fuel, that was all. Jess recognised the pattern. Her friend always went at things like a maniac, then suddenly she'd flake out completely, or throw a tantrum. She had the constitution of a five-year-old.

By the time Cath's plate was two-thirds clean, she was back to normal.

'It's going well, isn't it?' she said, and she waved her knife in the air. 'That was a really solid first session.'

Jess could see her eyes greedy for the next. The moment she'd finished eating, she stood up and took her plate to the sink.

'Something borrowed, Jess!' she exclaimed, over her shoulder. 'That's what you need, for luck. And I've got just the thing.'

Jess and Aidan exchanged glances and handed their plates across.

'There's a piece that fits underneath Joe Faber's air. I'm pretty sure. Something I wrote for keyboard. So what I'm thinking is, we can multi-track and turn it into a vocal backing.'

She was out of the door. A few seconds later her crazy red mop head peeked back: 'Come on then!'

Sunny it might be, but the wind still slapped them all the way back to the shed. Aidan wanted to say something, and he had to shout.

'You know, from a technical point of view, that peat shed's a nightmare. I might as well be outdoors with the birds.'

'It's calm next to this,' she shouted back.

They ran inside and he pushed the heavy door behind them. For a couple of seconds, she listened to the difference it made. Cath meanwhile had dragged a set of keyboards out from the wall and was sitting ready for action, leafing vigorously through a folder. Out of the light, she looked grey, with dark rings round her eyes. But her voice was definitely back to bright colours.

'Got it. Right, listen to this.'

It was four-square harmony, one of those simple compositions you could pull in any direction. Major key. She played it slowly, almost like a hymn.

'It doesn't all fit, does it?' said Jess.

'No. But look, I was thinking, pin this chord here...' – she played – 'against the bit where your tune goes like this' – she played a phrase.

Jess picked up her fiddle and they tried that passage together. Cath was right, the one seemed to reflect light back to the other.

They spent the next hour improvising, Cath scribbling down ideas. They agreed where her vocals would start and stop, how they'd fit against the air. It would be a deep, close harmony, not too prominent, not too loud, each line equally weighted and sung by the same voice so that it would be, Cath said, 'like an even bed of sound you can rest comfortably on.' Recording a rough version one line at a time was slow, but there was no shortcut. They all listened critically as it built up, and disagreed what was the point at which you had to say, that was enough, stop now, not one more track, not one more note... Until Aidan said, 'Look, if we go too far, it isn't going to matter. We can decide what to strip back in post-production.'

When at last they took a break, Cath opened the door to reveal daylight as weak as the lamplight in the shed. They still had *Leaving Lerwick Harbour* on the list, and a couple of other traditional tunes, but those were already half worked up from Frenzy week. They'd run through them once, just to say hello, then call it a day.

Jess stood in the doorway. She rolled her shoulders and stretched her head from side to side. There was a world out there. The wind had dropped. She watched Cath's long legs take huge strides over the grass towards the house. You could still see the green of the grass, just about, but a new weather front was coming in and a long flat cloud had drawn itself like a blanket over the barely undulating land, obscuring the sun. That horizontal finger in a different shade of grey out to the western horizon would be the sea, a couple of miles off. She could smell the turf. Also a waft of peat smoke. Another hour or so, and she'd be on her way back down that drive and into the dark. One of them would take her back to Lerwick. She remembered the journey out, the view from the lay-by, the bridges that skimmed the water. Something Auntie Nell had said about her parents: *It's all stuff down a microscope to him.* Tiny stuff, big stuff, who knew the difference? Hundreds of miles across the sea, there was Scotland, England, Matt, his family, her mum and dad, a wedding to arrange. She looked at the sky and wondered if it hurt, to have to carry so many different clouds, all pushed across it, shooed by the wind. It must be so tired.

A low, clear voice behind her said, 'You've nailed it, you know.'

She stepped back inside. Across the room, Aidan sat behind the mixer desk, his face lit from below by his open tablet, like some wizard bent over a fiery cauldron. And God, this place looked like the sorcerer's den, full of shadows, disordered, cluttered with all the paraphernalia that went with their dark arts.

'D'you think so? I don't think I can tell.' She did have a warm feeling, though. The specs glinted but behind them he was holding her in a steady gaze. She wondered how good Aidan's judgement was. Better than Matt's, at least where music was concerned.

'Cath must think so. She did the look.'

'What look?'

'The one where she stares into the distance and sticks out her bottom lip. It means, good, I'm pleased with that.'

Jess knew the look, but hadn't ever given it a meaning. Aidan was observant. Worth consulting then. Obliquely. Subtly.

'So, you and Matt have known each other a long time.'

'Since we were kids, yeah.'

'What do you know about his Life Plan?' To hell with subtlety. They were on their own. This was her chance.

He answered by looking at her. She sat down in a camping chair opposite him. It had arms, which made it easier to sit up straight and appear placid.

'His sister told me about it. He drew up this Life Plan when he was still at uni.'

'Oh, that one. Yeah.' He laughed. 'He was always one for the planning. For as long as I've known him, he's been chasing one goal after another. Ever since year 11 and the Young Enterprise scheme that time expired.'

'D'you think he's delusional, then?'

He tipped backwards on his stool for a moment, hovering like a schoolboy. Then there was a delicate tamping noise as its front two legs came back into contact with the earth floor.

'No. Only we disagree. The way I see it, life tends to win. You can set down whatever fancy targets you like, you can colour-code your life and stick it on a planner. Stuff just happens and you have to roll with it. Fortunately for him, Matt's good at rolling with it. He bounces.'

She snorted.

'He sprained his ankle a while ago and he's been a complete wuss about that.'

'Really? Playing the sympathy card, eh? I can imagine that.' This smile was definitely uncurling and didn't look as sarcastic as he sounded. 'Look, of course he plans, and of course a lot of his plans are over-ambitious. He's an optimist and always will be. It's in his bones. In his DNA. In fact, it's probably a medical condition with him.'

'He's crap when it comes to dealing with pain.'

'Yeah, I suppose comfort is a big thing in his life.'

Hmm. That was one way of looking at it. The smile had turned into an indulgent grin. Affectionate. So much for the big row in the Clickimin bar.

'The main thing is, Jess, Matt knows a good thing when he sees it, and if it interrupts his Life Plan, he'll roll with it. Like he did with you.'

What did he mean by that? She must have frowned, because his reaction was swift, and for some reason he looked really sheepish now.

'He thinks he won the bet, and OK I did cough up a tenner. As a gesture of friendship. But he didn't win really.'

'What bet? What d'you mean?'

'Oh shit…' He closed his eyes. 'I thought that was why you were asking…'

'Let's pretend it was, then. Tell me more.'

'I bet him – years ago – he wouldn't achieve his life goals because real life would get in the way. The day he got engaged to the perfect woman, he claimed his ten quid.'

She felt herself flush, her throat dry.

'But I think *I've* won, because he's forgotten who this perfect woman was. Whereas I distinctly remember her description for the very good reason that she seemed to be modelled on my cousin Mindy, and Mindy wasn't a bit like you. Tall, dark, skinny, big brown eyes, kick-ass heels and matching brief case. An entrepreneuse to the tips of her fingers. Which were seriously manicured and not all stubby-nailed from playing the violin, I have to tell you.'

'So... I'm not his ideal woman after all?'

'Technically, no. But then again, yes. People's ideals are limited by what they know, aren't they? You punched a hole through his limitations and showed him something else. Something on the other side. Something he didn't know he wanted.'

'Aidan, I do believe, you're an old romantic.'

She threw her head back and let the laughter bounce back at her from the curved hull of the roof. Thank God, thank God, she wasn't part of any plan. Matt had started off with his ideal, and she had trumped it.

Dream

Joe had bought them all airline tickets to Zurich. A return for Fran and Jess, a single for himself. He'd booked the clinic, where strangers would administer the lethal injection. There was no panic, just a sense that this was what had to happen, and a solemnity about everything. The sky was blank, there were no shadows; everyone wore pale grey and brown as if in a wartime film, with heavy coats, felt hats and woollen gloves. He felt as one might feel before surgery, sedated, yet aware of an impending action beyond oneself and which could not now be undone. His wife and daughter were impassive, unemotional, accepting of it all. The milky colours suited them and brought out the gold of Jess's hair, the amber of Fran's eyes. Nobody spoke.

He got no further than the runway, because the modest airport had no means of getting him onto the plane.

His eyes opened to a familiar room, and he was glad to be there even though he knew this wasn't a room you were meant to sleep in.

There was beginning to be light from the window. He watched the colour slowly fill from behind the heavy curtains and into the room. Oh, open them, somebody, open these curtains wide and let me see the silver birch across the road, the holly in the garden. It didn't seem to be a sunny day but even a dull sky, even rain or fog, was worth viewing. He had a perfect right to this canvas and he wanted to claim it. Beside his bed there was the linen basket on its plastic legs, which did service for a bedside table, and contained, alongside water bottle, tissues, tablet, phone, a small brass handbell from a junk shop. If he rang it, Fran would come immediately and let the daylight in. But it would give her such a fright, to hear him ring that bell at such an early hour. So instead, he let his dream ripple out to meet the cool dawn, and soothed himself. He wouldn't be going to Switzerland today.

The dream-fog had evaporated by the time Fran came padding downstairs. She drew open the dining room curtains, and the birch tree in the garden opposite bowed a greeting, as if to confirm this was just any ordinary September morning. As usual, she bent to kiss him then perched on the edge of the bed. As usual she wore a smile but her eyes betrayed her, working too hard, scanning, checking.

'You've got a better colour,' she said.

He wanted to smile back. To tell her not to worry. Because *her* colour was dreadful.

He said, 'I feel a bit different today. A bit more… solid. Inside. Like the jelly's setting.'

'That's good.' For a moment, her face lit up, and when that flame died, the smile was a tone warmer than before.

They did ablutions, breakfast. Eventually she went back upstairs and from time to time through the morning he heard her moving about the house.

Although it had been buried in a dream, Joe knew his readiness to end life if ever it became intolerable was genuine. This had come as a surprise. And in its way a comfort.

Now, as the light outside took on that true Michaelmas yellow, and the reds began to glow, Joe took the time to tell himself the true story of what had happened, a story which he'd always obscurely known but never claimed as his own. How one fine day in June, he had woken up an amputee. Only instead of a limb, it was a part of his brain that was missing, and it would not come back.

Every part of him that remained sentient, every available neurone, every waking sinew, had been recruited to deal with this catastrophe. All summer, he had been wholly occupied by the effort to lift the heavy blanket of infirmity and kick it aside. And it was not just physical: those brain cells stretched and strained, groped out towards each other to create synapses not just to help him speak and move, but so that he could think and love and protect himself. Because you had to keep thinking those thoughts which kept you alive.

Not so long ago, the two charming researchers at the hospital had asked the routine question, did he have suicidal thoughts, and he hadn't hesitated to answer no. Because that was the truth. But afterwards, at home, Fran had come close and bent her brow against his and hurt for him. She knew how these questions chafed, how this numbering and naming of the things he'd lost had rubbed his heart red raw.

If he were to tell Fran – say, the next time she launched into one of her 'accentuate the positive' routines – if he were to say out loud, 'But my life is so limited now,' would she hear it as a rebuke? Would she drop her head, and fret, and grow despondent?

He would never be whole again.

He could never have the life he wanted.

It didn't mean he didn't want life.

Once he had grown easy with his Zurich dream, he would tell Fran about it. Give it a few days.

Reality

The flesh of his upper body was peppered with freckles, the shoulders particularly. She always thought there was something puckish about that, as if he hadn't let go of childhood. She drew the towel over them and down his back. The shoulders were no longer even; the right one dropped, and the arm hung awkward and bent. And now there was no doubt, the straight furrow of his spine was growing crooked. It curved out to the left, in a backwards question mark, and the right shoulder blade jabbed out. They needed to stop this, sort it out before it all got worse. It was urgent. He was being physically spoilt. There must be a way of stopping it. They must find one. If his skeleton was twisting, there would be no end of pain. She didn't want to tell him how bad it looked. Find a solution first. She helped dry his arms, one, two, the back of his legs, one, two; and when he shuffled round to face her, he reached for the towel with hands that no longer matched. She noted for the thousandth time how, when the fingers of his right hand opened and closed, the knuckles bent in random order, almost like an infant's. Their grip on the fabric was approximate, and it was the left hand which did the work of guiding the towel up and down. Long, thin, pianist's fingers. Fingers that could sculpt, and fix things. He stared down at them as he used the towel. The look on his face was one she'd seen many times in his previous life, when he'd be at his workbench, gluing something small, perhaps, or painting the dots on a ladybird.

He straightened and looked up, smiled thanks, and stretched the arm out ready for the dressing gown.

'I love you Fran. I love you so much.'

'I love you, Joe.' Oh yes.

He didn't look so peaky today, and the corner of his mouth was settling back to its usual place. He wanted to shower and made it through the kitchen to the bathroom. But even if he might be starting to get over the fall, Joe was a different Joe now. She had to face up to the evidence.

Birds to Roost

When Thursday finally came, and the three of them got into the Mareel recording studio, their music seemed to pick up a sheen from the fair woodwork. The tunes were great, the sound was great, and it was all laid down on schedule. Nobody was more surprised than Jess that it went so smoothly in the end.

Her flight was booked for the next afternoon – Jess couldn't face the red-eye, couldn't afford it either. The last morning was always horrible. So when Aidan offered a lift to

Sumburgh combined with an hour's birding on the way, it was a no-brainer. She'd been cooped up for three days, and fresh air would be her reward. Also, bird watching was something she'd never done before.

It was a fine clear day. They followed the road that snaked gently south of Lerwick. Aidan asked Jess what kind of birds she'd like to see. There were seabirds – guillemots and bonxies – on the cliffs close to the airport. There had been sightings of divers and ruffs at Spiggie Loch, and plovers on the beach; he'd picked that up on his phone. A bluethroat had been seen around Bigton. A bluethroat? She had never heard of this bird but it sounded amazing. He said there were a couple of sheltered spots round there which they could try without straying too far from the main road, and the chances were they'd find other small birds even if the rarity wasn't about. So they took the right fork which peeled them away from the electric blue of the sea and into the brown moorland.

It was a gentle but definite climb, into a drab landscape of peat bog, with flats of water; the patches of heather on the stonier slopes had already gone over, and the purple had leached out in the general muddy wash; but at least today, in the sunshine, the sedges and other grasses brought metallic warmth, with gold, copper, silver all shimmering in the wind, glinting, never still. The plants were mostly ground-huggers, too small to make out from a car. In some places, though, there was cotton grass which nodded pure white. There were outcrops of greenish rock shot through with rust, and narrow clefts where a burn had cut into the peat. Nothing else moving, no birds that Jess could see, though she peered at the moorland trying to register the subtle differences in a tight palette of brown and more brown. A bird with a blue throat would really stand out. When Aidan pulled the car off the road, she was surprised: already? They had reached the highest point and hardly begun to descend. They had a glimpse of the magical landscape which she knew lay to the west around Bigton: lush farmland, sloping in a generous sweep down to the impossibly lacy coastline; the white spit of sand and turquoise water at St Ninian's; the village whose name she never remembered, a sprinkle of white houses rising out of green pasture in the distance.

'Down there,' he said, and seemed to be pointing towards the short sliver of dark blue sea far ahead. 'We're going to follow that burn down. That way we've got the hill behind us and we don't ever break the horizon. That would scatter them. We just walk steadily, quiet as we can. Try to blend in. You've got the right colours today.'

'Dad calls this my army surplus chic.'

'Earth colours,' said Aidan, and got out of the car. The inrush of wind brought that acid smell of the land. Wonderful. He picked his gear up from the back seat, put on a short coat, stuffed something into the pocket and slung binoculars round his neck.

They crossed the road, stepped over the crash barrier and picked their way down to the burn. It hadn't looked a steep incline from the car, but distances were deceptive: it was further away than it seemed and an awkward walk over hummocks of sedge and moss.

'Shouldn't you be out on the cliffs recording the spit of the fulmar or something?'

'Monitoring vagrants,' he said.

'Ah yes.' He'd told her about this, back in August. Non-native birds on their way across the ocean. You had to stick a microphone and a recorder in an iris bed, leave it there, and not go to the pub because there wasn't one. Afterwards he analysed the recordings and identified the species. Warblers, buntings, twites, shrikes. All great names for a band.

'I'm done with the fieldwork now, just writing it up. I'll be back south soon.'

'Seen anything interesting lately?'

'Yup. Last week I got close sighting of a Hornemann's arctic redpoll. He was sitting on a fish box waiting for the Fair Isle ferry.'

They were locked in a low valley now with no real view. Once they reached the burn and started to follow it, they found themselves in the lee of the wind, and it was suddenly quiet.

'We don't want to frighten them. We move slowly. As if we're grazing animals.'

They made their way down the cleft of the hillside. The outline of the stream was blurred by sphagnum moss in a thick, deep carpet of bright green flecked with red, and you couldn't tell whether it was underpinned by peat or puddle. The first she'd know about any little brown job would be if she trod on one.

From time to time they stopped and he trained his binoculars on the route ahead, where the brown of moorland gave way to green. Slender spikes of burnt orange caught her eye: they had dropped down to within sight of an iris bed now, which indicated the path of the burn and spread out as the ground flattened. It felt strange to walk so very slowly and quietly, and she longed to stride out. She hadn't walked properly since that day in Wales when the cloud had come down on Cadair. That was in a different season. Matt borrowed her dad's boots that day, and hadn't used them since. That meant the whole summer had gone by and a pair of trainers had sufficed. Which had been a wicked waste of living daylight.

'Can I ask you something? About the ideal woman thing?'

'Sure.' He was almost whispering, so maybe she should, too.

'When you told me that, I was relieved, in a way. Only... do you think we're suited, me and Matt? Do you think it'll work?'

He stepped forward before answering, 'Don't ask me.'

'Who can I ask?'

He'd drawn the binoculars to his eyes.

'Ask yourself. Do the maths. Work out what he adds, and what he subtracts.'

'Bloody hell, Aidan, you sound worse than him. A formula for everything.'

She immediately had to swallow her irritation, because only a few nights ago, she'd employed that exact method herself. She stared at the burn as if it might have something more useful to suggest.

Aidan remained silent. Was he annoyed? After a while she heard an excited intake of breath, and he passed her the binoculars. There was a commotion down below among the broken blades and dead stems of iris. A flock of tiny birds, like little balls of fluff, with bright orange or yellow on their heads, all moving jerkily about then settling again.

'Goldcrests.'

'They're beautiful. I've never seen so many at once.'

'They're common here. This lot have flown in from Scandinavia. There are plenty in England, only you're more likely to hear them than to see them, where there are trees. We can get closer. They'll be tired, makes them sluggish. We should get a good view. Come on.'

They got to within ten yards and found a green stone to sit on. She watched the birds, wondering how many of these magical little things she'd missed in years gone by. It was the shelter that had funnelled them all here. In a hundred yards, the burn would curve round the hillside and once they set foot there, the wind was going to hit them full on.

'OK, straight question. Do you like him, Aidan?'

'Matt? Yeah. Course I like him.'

'Because?'

'Because he's not like me. He's more positive. Plus, he's good with people, even if he does talk bollocks at times. I know he sounds like he's got this huge ego – I mean you can't squash him, can you? But the bottom line is he'd do anything for anybody.'

All the time they spoke, their eyes were on the birds, little bright bubbles fizzing in the autumn orange of the iris leaves.

'Best quality?'

'Loyalty. If he backs you, he means it.'

There was barely time for this to sink in when her pocket started to buzz. Her phone. She gave the binoculars back.

Spookily, it was Matt. She answered and managed to keep her voice down long enough to enquire whether he had psychic powers. But he was breathless, and speaking in an unfamiliar, strangled voice.

'Oh Jess, thank goodness you picked up.'

Something bad must have happened. She stood up straight and the little birds fled before her eyes.

'What's the matter? What's happened?'

'I don't know how to tell you. I don't believe it myself.'

'Is it Dad? Is he OK?'

'No. It's me.'

'You've had another accident?'

Aidan had risen to his feet too. She turned and mouthed, it's Matt, and suddenly her heart was pounding.

'No, no, but something terrible has happened. It's never happened to me before. In fact... listen to the way I'm talking... It didn't happen to me, I made it happen. I was, like, the subject of this sentence? I did something. Oh God. I just needed to tell you.'

'Well spit it out then.'

'I've had an argument.'

'Jesus, Matt.'

That was one big deal. She swung round to grin at Aidan, who was looking concerned.

'Yeah, I know, me, arguing. How unlikely was that? I still feel weird about it. I mean I'm physically shaking, you know?' She could hear that in his voice. She caught Aidan's eye and enunciated especially clearly, for his benefit.

'Um... You've had an argument? Wow. That's a first. Well done you. Who with?'

'My mother.'

She mouthed, mother, and Aidan pursed his lips to give a nod of approval.

'In fact, it was worse than an argument. I actually lost my temper. I just suddenly came over all big and shouty. I told her off. Like she was the little kid.'

She let her breath whistle out and watched a smirk spread across Aidan's face. 'No shit.'

'I just had to talk to someone. Is it normal, to feel this uncomfortable afterwards? After a big row?'

'Oh yes, of course it is, at first. Just sit with it and tell yourself you've achieved something. One small step for man, a giant leap for Mattkind. Well done you.'

He exhaled and she heard a weight lifting. 'Oh... great. Thank you so much for saying that.'

He seemed to be relaxing into his achievement, because triumph steadied his voice as he went on: 'I told her she was one, patronising, two, offensive and three, just plain wrong.'

'What's she done?'

'Surely your mum's told you? Only I don't want your parents to think it was ever my idea. When she told me to sleep on it – which incidentally I didn't need to do – I never dreamed she'd go ahead and talk to them without coming back to me first. According to her, the opportunity presented itself.'

None of this made sense.

'What are you talking about, Matt? My mum hasn't said anything.'

'She offered to lend them money. To pay the deposit on Higham's Hall.'

'Has somebody got shares in that place?'

Poor Aidan looked totally bewildered. He seemed to be mirroring her every expression, but now he must be well and truly in the dark. She turned away from him and stared back towards the road far above them.

'Oh, it's all Zanna and her wheeler-dealing and her obsession with getting Wonder White effing Weddings off the ground. Mum genuinely thinks she's helping both of us. All of us. She thinks the only reason you're talking about going to the Register Office now is to save your parents money.'

'Well there is that.' It was a consideration, after all.

'Yeah but that's not the main thing, is it? You need space and time for everything else in your life to settle down, for your parents to get back to normal, and the music to sort itself out, and everything, so that you and I have got time to think properly about how we really want to do this thing. At our leisure. You don't care about other people's five-star ratings, do you? You're not even bothered about external appearances. I know you better than that.'

She gulped. So he did, then.

All the same, she had a bone to pick with him.

'OK Matt. One small problem. What if we crash your 28th birthday? What if you're 29, or even 30, by the time we do this thing?'

An exasperated sigh reached her ear. 'Aidan told you about the bet, didn't he?'

'I found out, yeah. Ten quid, though, Matt!'

'Bloody Aidan.'

'He's been very helpful. In a quizzy sort of way. Answered some biggies for me.' She turned back to smile at him, but he'd walked off and placed himself at a discreet distance. He was looking at something on the ground.

'Tell him I'll pay him back. I'm sorry. 28, 48, 60 – who cares? Come home and slow down. Now I'm off the crutches, we can go for a walk in the woods. The trees are turning already, there are loads of red things on them...'

'Haws? Berries?'

'Berries, yeah. Gotta catch it.'

'I know a really good path.'

'You can show me, then.'

All the time in the world

Matt woke from a deep sleep. He didn't need to look at Jess, just to feel her closeness, the warmth of her back, the cool smoothness of her shoulder. In a moment she would stir and he would get up to fix coffee. But not just yet.

Blissed out. That's what Jess called this feeling of being excited and sleepy and happy all at once. They were blissed out, the pair of them. Since last night. All the way back from the airport, from the neon roundabout into the darkened countryside then back to his familiar territory of brick buildings and streetlights. No sensible conversation in the car, just how good it was to be back, how good to have her back, mixed up with a lot of grins and sighs, and from time to time a quiet laugh. A clear run home, and everything back on track. He'd got his flat ready for the perfect homecoming: the heating set just right, a low light in the bedroom, white wine in the fridge. Although as things turned out, he'd forgotten all about that.

The sun was high, so it must be late, gone nine or even ten. He couldn't tell. Through the open doorway, he saw a shadow on the carpet: her suitcase. It was still parked in the living room, because last night that hadn't been the thing that needed unpacking. They'd had so much to say that nothing had been said at all. The tight muscles at the top of her shoulders and in that beautiful, beautiful crook of her neck had needed his attention first, and when he'd helped her to lift off her jumper, she'd slumped against him like a child. She must be so tired; she'd come such a long way. He'd stroked and kneaded, and breathed in the scent of her madcap hair. It had gone absurdly frizzy, like yellow candy floss, and still held the damp of the evening air. Magical. There had been nothing to hurry about, not last night, not this morning. Not ever. When you both knew you really loved each other, you finally understood what it meant to have all the time in the world. Also that all the time in the world would never be enough.

His mobile shuddered on the bedside table. It was easy to ignore it. Barely a minute later it went off again. The second time it was more annoying. He reached out to pick it up and read the caller's name: Zanna. Typical. There would be nothing his little sister had to say to him that couldn't wait, so he put it down. He closed his eyes again and turned back to bury his nose in the nape of Jess's neck. Then sent his arm out behind him, fumbled for the phone and switched it off.

One step at a time

They stood out bright against the blue-green wallpaper of the dining-bedroom: two golden heads, one pale and sleek, the other yellower, fat as a Florentine halo and catching the light like worked gold.

'For God's sake, pull up a chair, you two. You look like a pair of angels hovering at the end of my bed. Makes a man nervous.'

'He's on the mend,' came Fran's voice from the doorway.

She was leaning against the jamb, watching them all, with her arms folded. Joe had overheard her in the hall describing to Jess and Matt his evolving state of unhealth over the last four days. She'd toned down the facts. He'd caught *a little fall, knocked him back a bit*, *nothing serious*, *back in bed for a bit*. Nothing serious? That wasn't how she'd reacted at the time. Wait till he told her about the Zurich dream! She didn't know the half of it. But he understood why she didn't want to tell them the whole truth. Jess didn't look too troubled, and that was good. She came forward to kiss him. She was pink and cheerful.

Matt moved a chair forward pretty nimbly; so, he was off the crutches and back to bouncing around. Lucky boy. Jess refused a chair and sat on the edge of the bed.

319

'Oh, Dad. Poor old thing.'

'How did the recording go?'

'Like a dream, in the end. Magic.'

Joe looked hard at his daughter and her boyfriend. However different they might be in appearance, there was always a look that a happy couple shared. With some people it might be an expression of surprise, with others a lip curled in irony, or the same stretch of the brow when asking a question. Today his eye was drawn to that subtle line where the lips met – that line which every artist knew was the key to drawing a true likeness. Just now, it was a line without tension, ready to part at any moment into a full smile; the same line on both their expressions. There was something going on.

'We've got news,' said Jess.

He knew it. She'd always been a blurter.

'Fantastic news,' said Matt, and the pair exchanged glances which said, *you* tell them… no, *you* tell them…

'The wedding's off,' said Jess.

Her huge smile was matched immediately by Matt's, and he took over the explanation: 'We decided it was better…'

'For the sake of our marriage.' They both giggled like children.

'Better to wait till the boat's stopped wobbling,' Matt spluttered.

Jess laughed.

'Exactly. Because the way things were going, we were heading for a divorce.'

'The timing isn't right.'

The pair of them were swaying about now.

'We knew you'd understand,' she added. 'It's only a postponement. You're not disappointed, are you?'

Joe glanced at Fran, who was still watching them all from the doorway, straight-faced. 'The fact is... I was looking forward to seeing your father in a kilt.'

Joe became aware of something spreading across his lips, a movement he hadn't felt in days. He reached for his daughter's hand. The movement had crept to his eyes and taken over the whole of his face, and was tickling his chest now. It might be a sob, it might be a laugh, or a cough, but it came out with a volume that he thought he'd lost. The sound came from deep in his rib cage, and when it belched forth, it turned out to have words attached.

'It's the best news I've heard for ages.'

Now they were all chortling away as if it was the greatest thing in the world to call a wedding off. Which Joe took as a sure sign Matt was one of the family now.

'Zanna will be disappointed,' he said.

'Zanna? Oh, she's fine,' said Matt.

Jess picked up. 'Nothing's gonna burst her bubble. Because...' Her eyebrows were dancing the way her Auntie Nell's did. Something in those genes.

Matt spoke in a jokey voice: 'Zanna's got her own love interest.' Then he sobered up to add, 'Only this time it's serious. I really believe it is. I feel it in my bones.'

'Yes, Mum, and it's all thanks to you. And Dad, in a way.'

'How's that?' asked Fran.

'You introduced them,' said Matt.

'Harry,' said Jess. 'Good old Harry. Captain Sensible. I tell you, he's gone soft in the head, by the sound of things. Which all means she's well and truly off our backs!'

Her face was full of glee as she watched her parents exchange glances. It looked to Joe as though Fran hadn't seen that coming any more than he had.

Fran opened her eyes wide to think it over. 'Maybe Zanna fits his algorithm.'

'It's the first time I've heard it called that,' said Joe.

After a few seconds sniggering they pulled themselves together and Jess said, soberly, 'Mum, Dad... we're going to take our time. We're going to enjoy planning this wedding. Ourselves. And working the other stuff out first. Like where we live, and how we live.'

'We're going to take it one step at a time,' said Matt. He was sounding quite old-fashioned.

The four of them nodded into a comfortable silence.

Now that the talking had stopped, Joe realised he felt peckish. The sensation was just as new and fresh to him as the strange noise from inside his chest had been a minute ago. If Fran was going to fix lunch for Jess and Matt, maybe she could do him a nice tomato sandwich whilst she was at it.

Allotment

Fran walked past the tall limes on her way to the allotment. The leaves were down, and already mostly swept away. The roads and pavements glistened in that dull, half-hearted way of pewter and gunmetal, unable to dry. This was the first winter sky of the year, ice blue and with so many shredded white-cream clouds tossed in the strong wind, it looked as though there'd been a pillow-fight up there. Down here in the dip, closer to earth, the winds were lighter, and the clockwork chatter of starlings filled the air, chack-a-chack-a-chack.

She hadn't flounced out. This wasn't flouncing. But he'd effectively told her to sod off. So she had – with pleasure. Joe didn't want her company this precious Saturday afternoon. On the step, the cold air caught her lungs but she was warming up now. A good, brisk walk, just as the doctor ordered. A gathering rush of pleasure. She hadn't walked this far this fast in ages. She was always either on a short sprint to and from the car – shops, work – or stuck in the slow lane with Joe. The allotment had suddenly presented itself in a new light: it was simply a place to go. She hadn't even taken tools.

The house was back to normal now that Joe was sleeping in their own bed again, so on the face of it things ought to feel easier. It was a dreadful thing to admit to herself, but now that he was getting stronger and more mobile, it was like having a toddler in the house. He was into everything, clumsy, ham-fisted, unpredictable. She saw danger everywhere, she couldn't help it. And really, this morning's tantrum had been like the terrible twos, and probably born of the same frustration. The same unrealisable ambition to assert the will, and all the bruises that came from fighting against circumstance. But she wasn't his mother and she had to learn to let him thrash.

That was a robin. Where was it? Silhouetted against the sky, on the topmost branch of an apple tree in a garden across the road. Those things would sing all through the night if they felt like it. Charming, on the face of things, but they were territorial, aggressive little birds, when it came down to it. What that song meant was, I won't give an inch. Nothing you can do will shut me up.

She undid the top button of her waterproof.

There was only another week to the deadline. Applying for her own job, or someone else's, or none at all. She had to make it official and tell them, in or out. Mairi was leaving. Harry had told her all those weeks ago that he wasn't after her job. But he might have changed his mind about going for a manager's role now that he was getting married. That whole episode still made her smile. The way his eyes had popped open when she'd asked him was it true about him and Matt's sister, and then he'd said, 'Once you know what you want, why fanny about?' Bashful and crude at the same time, as much as to say, you've caught me out so I might as well be honest. He claimed he'd realised Zanna Harrington was the one the day they met, the day she asked to look under the bonnet of his Mini Cooper. Fran was beginning to see the sense in this. Because whatever else you thought about Zanna, she was well turned out, attractive in her way, and unusually clear about what she wanted in life. And clarity was key, with Harry. So he'd probably be writing his application this weekend. If he hadn't already.

It must be wonderful to know your own mind. To sing like a robin and stand your ground.

She'd tried to talk to Joe about work. But it wasn't really fair because he was part of the conundrum. Maybe she should forget Joe for a bit and get back into the habit of talking to her beans. He didn't need her fussing around him, he'd said. She'd caught him going upstairs, one step at a time, left arm steadying himself against the wall, the weak right arm tensely crooked because the stroke instinct was warning him he might fall over any minute, and with his pockets bulging, so weighed down with things he couldn't carry but wanted to take up to the bedroom – she identified TheraBands, various balls to train his fingers, a flask of coffee – that his jeans were sliding down and a flat diamond of spare denim hung slack between his thighs.

'Stop fussing, woman.'

It had been the tone of his voice that hurt, as much as that awful 'woman'. She never meant to fuss. He was being sensible, after all, going slowly, putting stuff in his pockets so as to leave hands free. He told her he just needed a break from being interrogated on what he was doing all the time.

She was a slow learner when it came to curbing the impulse to do things for him. Just because she was able to carry things upstairs more quickly and easily than he could didn't mean she should.

There was a man called Bob at the stroke gym who lived on his own and swore that his recovery had been the faster for it. He either did things for himself, or they didn't happen. So Bob learnt to do for himself pretty quickly.

She turned into the lane and from habit looked to see how their patch was doing. The lie of the land meant you could always see their beanpoles from here – and she hadn't yet taken them down this year. Odd, that there was no sign of them. The storms must have flattened the lot. Saved her the job.

The last time they'd talked about her situation at the lab, earlier in the week, Joe had been adamant she ought to hang in there. He'd lost his temper that day, too. It started as a rational discussion. Why should they both be invalided out, he argued? She'd end up resenting him. She'd countered: it was so lonely for him on his own all day, he needed company. She really thought he did. But that had made him turn on her.

'Do I though? I know what I *don't* need. I don't need a bloody monitor giving twenty-four-hour feedback on how I'm getting on.'

Harsh.

He'd said it would destroy her, to give up work. What would she do with herself all day?

'They can manage without me. They're cutting back. I won't be missed.'

And he'd thrown in the economic argument – completely out of character, or was his character being cowed by all this? – that to go from two incomes to one, overnight, was tough enough, but to end up with none would be catastrophic.

'We'd have to sell this house. And where would Jess be then?'

She thought he was dramatising. She challenged him: 'Would we really though? We'd find a solution. You're the priority.' From that point it wound up to a full-scale row.

'Listen to me then. How do you think it would make me feel? You can't give up work for me. It would destroy us both. I'd feel guilty for the rest of my life. Besides, I don't need you.'

And Joe had glared at her as if she were his worst enemy.

Sunshine was a mixed blessing at this time of year. It lit some things and obscured others, and when it hit your eyes you were blinded. The tarmac of the road ahead was an unbearable silver now, so she cast her eyes to one side. She was close enough to see in outline that their neighbour's brassicas were looking healthy. Tall, nicely leafy at the top, and pretty straight, just leaning at a 2 o'clock angle from the inevitable wind rock.

But later that same night he had apologised. Like he always did in the end. He had taken her hands in his and said, 'Look Frannie, the thing is this. How can I miss you if you won't go away?'

And she in turn had come to understand that giving up work would be a massive vote of no confidence. It would be like telling him he never would get any better.

Unthinkable.

Realistically, though, there wouldn't be time for the allotment. It was too much work on her own, they'd have to give it up. The metal gate was wet under her hand from the melted frost as it squealed open.

Fran cast her eye down the path. Other people's cabbages, bigger and rounder than footballs, were doing well. Some had been cut already. The dark red ones had that wonderful blue bloom, and the outer leaves – which of course you never saw in the shops – curled generously open, like the petals of a rose. White cabbage, January King well on the way to his coronation. There was a row of the modern, pointed variety, looking very proud and very pale against the black earth. Because the soil was well-cultivated here, dark and in good heart. They could open a veg patch in their garden, but it would take decades to reach this fine texture. Maybe a raised bed over the clay. Import some topsoil. Loads of compost.

She came to the shed and took a deep breath before making the right turn which would reveal their plot, just four spaces down. But it didn't look like their plot. There were no beanpoles ripped down by the wind and strewn on the ground. There were two rows of feeble leeks where she would never put them. And somebody in a greatcoat and a ski hat was stamping his feet, trampling down what looked like an old rug. In their long absence, some chancer had nicked their allotment! A squatter had moved in. What a nerve. She walked straight up, shouting: 'There's a waiting list for these plots. And this one isn't even on it yet!'

The man stopped stomping on the carpet and turned to face her.

Matt?

He smiled his sweetest smile, revealing those perfectly even white teeth – 'Fran! Hi!' – then immediately his face dropped, and he asked, 'Is it all right?'

She stared at the leeks, the rug, the recently cleared ground.

'Did you do all this?'

He started to explain in a faltering, guilty voice, the way a child might explain accidental damage to an heirloom. 'Yeah, I, um, I did. I covered it over, you know. To keep the weeds off. I promised Joe. Did you know, there's no market at all for second hand carpet? But my dad told me it's a pain to dispose of so just ask a carpet place, then I remembered this guy I'd done some work for, and I still had his card, and he actually came here in his van and dropped it off. It's heavy stuff, isn't it?'

All she could do was nod.

'I checked it out and everything, not to get the wrong sort. I didn't realise it was so controversial. I mean gardeners on the internet, right, they're at war over this. So I went for wool, hessian backing, I hope that's OK?'

He opened wide eyes, seeking her approval. She nodded again.

'It'll rot. Only Dad says best get rid soon as, or you'll be picking bits out of your leeks for years.'

'Your dad's right,' she said. 'But desperate times call for desperate measures.'

'So, the guy gave me a choice of pale blue or brown so I said whatever's going to match the soil and he said brown then. It's not the same brown though.'

'It's fine.'

'So, I wasn't sure which way up.'

She stared at the muddy carpet on which he stood. There was something familiar... something in the wrong place... Then she realised.

'Those are Joe's boots.'

'He lent them to me, ages ago. In Wales. For that walk. D'you remember?'

Of course. It had been the last day of their wet Welsh holiday. The walk up Cadair Idris that Joe had done so many times, and now would probably never do again. Matt had come for a week in Wales, and no boots; and Joe had lent him his. She and Joe had walked on Barmouth sands while Matt and Jess had taken the high road.

Muddy boots. Walking through birdsong on a winter's day. The scent of the earth you've dug yourself, the robin at your spade's edge, the fiddly job of tying in the sweet peas. Pulling those leeks. Picking your way through deep wet moss on a steep mountainside. Running along a flat beach. Joys that were open to her and closed to Joe. For months she'd fixed her eyes on the road ahead, and never once allowed herself to look back at what was lost. And now the kindness of this complete and utter idiot had filled her throat with tears. Once they came, she couldn't stop.

Matt stepped forward and easily, gently, brought his arms around her.

New Normal

'D'you know, I've got quite bored with those curtains. They only really work when they're open. Otherwise they're a bit too much.'

Jess considered the stylised fronds, in intense blues and greens. 'But Dad, you told me they were a work of art.'

'Yes well. Maybe they'd be better in a gallery.'

'We can keep the curtains open all the time now,' said her mum, coming in from the hall. 'Seeing as you're not a permanent exhibit any more, Joe.'

Her mum was all smiles today, almost giddy with excitement. After hesitating to authorise this furniture removal – her father had been sleeping in his own bed for weeks not days – she seemed to have embraced the idea of a new start.

Without its bed, the dining room looked strange. And big. Jess definitely didn't remember the carpet being so very blue, although once the dining table was back in place, it would recede again. The piano was the one thing that hadn't moved in all this time. She walked across to it, lifted the lid and played a few chords, then scales up and down to the very limits of the keyboard. It hadn't been played and was better in tune than she'd expected, and sweet, like the welcome voice of a friend after the keyboard she'd been using for lessons. The camping piano, her dad called that, because of the way it folded up. She was pleased on her own account too. No more lessons in the pale spare room.

Her dad stood upright, holding his stick in both hands in front of him, as if he were Fred Astaire about to break into a dance routine, and shot exaggeratedly rhythmic glances from wall to wall.

'I like the dark blue, Dad,' she said. 'It's kind of intense but calming at the same time. My pupils like it. Angela says it's energising.'

'It's not a colour to be sick in. That's all.'

Bumps and the odd grunt came from the staircase in the hall; the frame was already upstairs and they must be lifting the mattress now, because Harry's voice rang out, telling Matt, 'I'll take the bottom end'. A wicked smile of approval crept across her mum's face. Jess had no illusions about Matt's practical abilities, so she winked back.

The dining chairs which they'd brought down earlier stood in a neat row against one wall. For some reason – perhaps part of her fidgeting today? – her mum moved two of them forward into the centre of the room, and sat down facing the window and the street beyond. Her dad's hand felt for the seat next to her and he too lowered himself down without a word. Then, strangely, they both became very still, as if they wanted to savour the moment. So she joined them on a third chair and they were all quiet for a while, in their own little waiting room, listening to the muffled clunks and thuds which meant that upstairs, the spare bed was being re-assembled. Her dad's gaze was drawn to her mother's hands, whilst she seemed focused on the garden outside.

'You came out of hospital with so much kit,' said Jess. This room had been cluttered. 'There was the commode on wheels – that didn't last long – and that funny seat...'

'The perch stool,' her mum said. 'And the wheelchair can probably go back now too. We haven't used it for ages, have we?'

'Surance policy,' said her dad. 'It can stay folded up in the workshop for a bit. Like a brella. Same principle.'

Her mum reached for his hand and she giggled. 'Remember the day they came to pick the Zimmer up? The instructions fell off. There was that piece of paper curved round the strut thing. And we'd never even noticed it.'

'Only an idiot reads the instructions,' said her dad.

Her parents really shouldn't get on.

There was another minute's silent contemplation, of the cornice this time, then her mum became animated again.

'This is the last big moving of furniture. Then everything will be back where it belongs. Back to normal!'

She waggled her head stupidly from side to side, and grinned like a little kid on her birthday.

'New normal,' her dad corrected.

'New normal,' her mum agreed with a theatrical nod, and sucked her bottom lip. 'Unless… Right. I'm going to ask her, Joe. This is as good a time as any.'

'Go ahead,' he said.

'Jess,' said her mum, 'we were wondering. You're always going to need somewhere to give lessons, aren't you? And Matt lives in a very small flat. Also, it's costing him a lot in rent. Whereas this house is big for two people. We could let you have the top floor, the mansard, and you could still see your pupils down here, like you always have. Obviously, it would need some attention. But at least think about it. If it makes things easier for you, it would work for us.'

'Wouldn't we be in your way?'

'We'll burn that bridge when we come to it.'

Two pairs of feet came tramping easily downstairs. Harry stepped into the room, with Matt close behind him.

'All done,' said Harry, with a nod in Fran's direction. He was standing very straight, immaculately groomed as ever, no sign of exertion on his face.

Matt's hair was slightly out of place and needing a cut. He was pink-cheeked, and his eyes were bright and wide open as they sought first Jess's and then her dad's, before finally coming to rest on her mum. That was when he smiled, a broad smile of satisfaction. He was completely in tune with her excitement today.

'All done,' said Matt. 'I'll put the kettle on.' He disappeared again.

Matt and her mum were really good mates now. It had started with his help on the allotment. But they'd talked a lot about work too, and her application. It had shocked Jess more than anything to realise how close her mum had come to giving it all up. Matt argued this was only because the re-structuring had primed her to think that way: I might lose my job, but maybe I don't want it anyway. They'd all stayed up one night, debating whether paid work could turn into an addiction, whether you could wean yourself off it, how you'd re-organise your life if you did. Whether they should sell up and downsize, because it was a big old house; maybe find somewhere with fewer stairs for dad. If he had no stairs to climb, though, he'd lose that chance of daily exercise and with it the ability to climb stairs when he needed to, outside the home. And to pack up the workshop completely was the sticking point. Nobody was ready for that to happen. It was too brutal. Her dad's working life had come to a halt overnight, he'd had no choice. But Matt had argued that as much as income, her mum needed some element of control in her own life, and once she stopped work outside the home – only to be reminded that Joe didn't really need her in his face all the time – it would be a shock to *her* system too. There was a risk her dynamo would run down fast. She'd told them how, in any case, the way Dad felt about all this was enough to persuade her to carry on. The quandary was, how to get the balance right. Matt said, tell the people at the lab exactly what you want. Don't leave them guessing. If you want flexitime, full time, part time, job share – they don't know if you don't tell them. It's all in the melting pot, and you might be doing them a favour. Right, she'd said, I'd like flexible hours, that's what I want. Don't tell me then, tell them in HR, he said. Which she had.

Jess sensed that her parents' suggestion that they move in might be another working out of that conversation; like the musical re-statement of a theme, but in a different key. It didn't sound remote or strange or discordant; it was all part of one music. Matt would recognise it, she was sure.

Harry stood with his hands open at his sides, perfectly still apart from the eyes which slid just once sideways to the dismantled table and back.

'D'you want a hand with that?'

'No thanks,' said her mum. 'We're going to spring clean first.'

Harry looked almost disappointed. If there wasn't anything left to do, there would have to be conversation instead, which meant the wrong guy was making the tea. So as to fill the silence, Jess asked, 'How's the wonder white wedding shaping up then?'

'Sound,' he said, and a smug little honey-pot of a smile puckered his neat beard. 'Rosanna's scheduled around that cancellation you two didn't want. She's quite an operator. Got a great deal on the reception.'

Ooh… Wow… Rather her than me. But it all made a sort of sense.

'Congratulations.'

Jess pondered: was this the language of love? Maybe for Harry and Zanna it was. In a psychic flash, she saw Wonder White Weddings morph into Candy Coloured Christenings, and had a feeling that however different Zanna's tastes were from her own, she would always approach life with total commitment and formidable energy. However blinkered the Harringtons seemed to the Fabers, however clumsy and misguided they could be, at least they didn't sit round waiting for things to happen.

The Mason's Mark

On the second Friday of December the post came before they'd finished breakfast, and Joe found a slew of letters and cards plus two fat padded envelopes all sticking awkwardly through the letterbox. Jammed. When he tugged at them, the bigger parcel fell on his bad foot and sent it jangling. How could something that felt so little hurt so much? This was like an electric shock and must surely be what a snail felt when it came up against copper tape. The parcel contained the orthotic insoles which had been prescribed for him two months previously, together with a checklist of five things the practitioner was meant to do on issue – fit, give instructions for donning and doffing, and so on. Every box on the tick list was blank. Joe wondered about doffing because the only thing he'd thought you doffed was a hat. How quaint. Maybe he was meant to slip the orthosis out and hold it deferentially against his heart if a coffin or a very attractive woman walked by. The other parcel contained a black splint which, the orthotics man had told him, was the sort of thing Andy Murray wore. Ooh. So did Andy Murray have to wait two months for it to be crafted by fairies? Or did he just buy it on Amazon, which Joe now realised he might as well have done? Because it was clearly standard issue, from the packaging. Fran waved her toast at him and said, 'They can't tell you that because the NHS can't assume people can afford fifty quid for a piece of plastic and a yard of Velcro.' And whilst they could and would have found that fifty quid, cash flow was something they were thinking about more often these days.

Joe went back to his exercises and wondered what he could do, now that he couldn't seek commissions. There must be

335

some way of leaving his thumbprint on the surface of each day, some action that changed something for somebody somewhere...

Perhaps he should make a card to congratulate Zanna and Harry. Not on their engagement, though; no, something more along the lines of *Congratulations on cutting that deal!* Or, *Hey, you nailed that discount!* People sent cards for anything these days.

He sat at the computer and looked at all the crafty tat in the on line crafty tat shop, thinking, I can't even do that. I can't even paste a pre-tied baby blue bow on a pre-cut fluffy white cat and centre it on the card provided. Although if I could, I wouldn't.

But there was still one thing he could do. He walked to the hall cupboard where Fran's puffy snow coat was hanging. He didn't think she'd worn it yet this season, so he should still have something up her sleeve. Sure enough, there was the fake flatfish which Matt had placed there on his behalf, the day they played scrabble. It had started life as an impulse buy; it was rubbish as an oven glove, but too splendid to throw away. For years the whole family had been taking turns to hide it from each other, and it might swim anywhere in the house according to the tide of their various fancies. It might fetch up under a pillow, or half way down a pile of towels; it might be sneakily rolled inside a welly boot, or brazenly dangling from the light-pull in the bathroom, that sort of thing. The person who found it was duty bound to hide it, silently, elsewhere. It had often disappeared for months on end. He took it out and admired it, pulling it onto his right hand, which made the fingers feel even spongier. You'd get two portions from a real fish this size. The cotton was beautifully printed, speckled brown, with little orange spots, just like a plaice, and for added verisimilitude it had an indent in the foam along the line where the fins met the body, stitched by machine; his thumb went into a gloved cleft that suggested the opening and closing of gills. It had that lop-sided, squashed flatfish grin which made him feel good about himself. He slipped it inside his wife's briefcase, between the really important lever arch file and the bag which held her sandwiches.

She'd be needing that for her job interview this afternoon.

ACKNOWLEDGEMENTS

This book would never have been written without the unfailing positivity of the NHS in Somerset who kept my husband alive, and then kept him smiling; and were also a tremendous support to me.

Besides being my inspiration, Terry is my first reader and helped this book grow at every step.

I drew encouragement from a broad-based reader panel, who pulled me up usefully at times! Sophie, Jenny, Caroline: a nod from a busy, professional is always precious. Thanks go to Tony Urbainczyk, for checking out the fiddle, and Tim Farr, for help with birding. Mark Chapman told me tales of maquette artists.

Pippa Wainwright is the reader whose reaction to the first scrap of the first draft fuelled my determination to see the project through. I've kept Pippa in my mind right through the process, which meant that writing this novel has never felt like crying into a void.

My Shetland family were in on this from the start. Special thanks to my brilliant sister, Cindy, who drew on vast experience and common sense, and persuaded me not to pull my punches.

Suse Elderkin, the best mentor, helped me lick a first draft into shape.

Juliette Adair, Eloise Bartholomew, and William Davidson: I can't thank you enough for your detailed reading of the manuscript. It was a privilege to have your blow-by-blow reactions. Sue Cameron helped it to the finish line.

Finally, Matt Saunders wrapped the book in an inspired cover. We were moved to learn that it draws on his personal experience of stroke.

ABOUT THE AUTHOR

Gill Oliver was born in Liverpool and grew up with the belief that you could laugh at just about anything, provided you started with yourself. Her earliest attempts at fiction were bedtime stories for her brothers and sister, which carried on long after they'd fallen asleep.

Over a career in education she worked in the Midlands, Essex and Dorset in a variety of roles, publishing teaching materials along the way. A keen choral singer, she now lives in Somerset and concentrates on writing fiction.

Other publications

A Backward Glance (Novel)

Martin's office door was supposed to be shut, because it was a fire door. It was also supposed to be open, because he was a man.

Mr Harper is one of those teachers who hasn't much time for rules; besides, he has other things on his mind. Overwhelming grief for the death of his wife is tainted by guilt and jealousy, and this easy-going, clever guy is, as the kids say, losing it. Enter Wendy Mundy, funny name, funny looks, a feisty seventeen-year-old who knows about loss. This is the one innocent relationship in a world where rumour is easily traded. From estuary Essex to the sunshine of Italy, this is a story told with warmth and humour which gives us all permission to care.

Art My Eye and Other Stories

Are we defined by the things that we imagine, as much as by the things we do? By turns poignant, sinister, hilarious, tragic, these short stories probe that question, dipping into very different private lives and visiting different places.

An eye for beauty and an ear for comedy make this a satisfying and varied read.

www.gilloliverauthor.com
gill@gilloliverauthor.com
twitter@gilloliver__
www.facebook.com/gilloliverbooks

Printed in Great Britain
by Amazon

56624486R00206